Conference with the Dead

Other Books by Terry Lamsley

Under the Crust
Dark Matters

Conference with the Dead

stories by

Terry Lamsley

with an introduction by Ramsey Campbell

Night Shade Books
San Francisco & Portland

Cover & interior layout and design by Jeremy Lassen

First Edition

ISBN
1-597800-00-7 (Hardcover)
1-597800-01-5 (Limited Edition)

Night Shade Books
http://www.nightshadebooks.com

Contents

Introduction by Ramsey Campbell........... 1

Walking the Dog 5

Blade and Bone 39

The Break 55

Someone to Dump On 97

Running in the Family 107

Screens 129

The Toddler 153

The Outer Darkness 173

Inheritance 201

The Extension 215

Introduction

Generosity is its own reward. In my experience that is all too often true when it comes to reading unpublished fiction, an experience from which I flinch these days. At least unpublished work may prove to be worth publishing, however; but we may assume of almost anything self-published that it has done its weary rounds until at last the author, maddened by its latest reappearance as a yet more tattered revenant, decides that astounding the world is worth any cost of publication. Alas, most bookshops avoid such books, and so, unless they promise to be sufficiently comic to reward the outlay, do I. You may therefore imagine my dilemma on being confronted, at the 1993 Ghost Story Society convention in Chester, with a pile of Terry Lamsley and the author in attendance.

I picked up a glossy paperback and gathered that it was published by the author, and illustrated with photographs to boot. Could I have replaced it on top of the heap under the gaze and the genial but, for all I knew, brave smile of its author? Another factor decided the situation for me: Buxton, which I observed was the setting of some of the tales, was where I met Jenny, my wife and one true love, at a convention of the science fiction sort—indeed, in the very crescent that was illustrated. What embarrassment might not have been worth, nostalgia was, and so I stumped up a few pounds and had *Under the Crust* gracefully autographed.

It was probably nostalgia that led me to sit down with the first story soon after my return home, but a much more immediate emotion caused me to ring up Steve Jones, then my collaborator but now sole editor of *Best New Horror*, to tell him in some excitement that I'd discovered a new author who was a must for our annual. Was I responsible for alerting our old friend Karl Edward Wagner too? I should be happy to think so. Karl used a different tale of Terry's in *Year's Best Horror*, at any rate, and our editorial triumvirate must have helped notify the cognoscenti of the emergence of an important author, because the next World Fantasy Awards had Terry Lamsley on the shortlist in no less than three categories, by gum.

I was in New Orleans for the presentation, and happy to be asked to attend the banquet so as to accept on Terry's behalf. In my brief speech I said that Terry was the kind of new talent Karl had been most delighted to support, and so I would like to accept the Best Novella award for "Under the Crust," the title story of Terry's book, in memory of Karl as well. I'm only sorry I couldn't have surprised Terry with his inscribed bust of Lovecraft at the next Chester gathering; I'd gone down south to present Poppy Z. Brite with a British Fantasy Award. Sorry, Terry, but she's prettier than you, and I got a kiss as well. I shake myself and grow sober. Let me restrict myself to saying that while *Under the Crust* was a remarkable debut, *Conference with the Dead* (which I take to have been known as *High Peaks of Fear* and *The Outer Darkness* at different stages of its gestation) is finer still.

Its roots are in the great tradition of the field. "Blade and Bone," for instance, is entirely worthy of M. R. James, not only in its reticence but also in its willingness to horrify, a quality about which some of the antiquary's admirers maintain a silence that seems almost embarrassed. The tale sends the luckless Ogden Minter on the sort of antiquarian quest M. R. James's protagonists pursued. There's an admirably unnerving touch when on learning that Minter has been talking to a character who we gather at this point was spectral, the manageress of a cafe doesn't recoil but laughs uproariously. Minter's enquiries attract a revenant from the days when trespassers were tortured, and the story ends on a grisly turn of phrase.

Like James's spectres, Terry's are memorably inhuman and by no means shy of using the banal devices of modern life to manifest themselves: see "Screens," for example, in which a murderer returns through the medium of a blurry video that hints at where he went just before his death—not, we are led to believe, on an ordinary holiday, given the companions he brings back with him. James himself might have shuddered away from this tale and from "The Toddler," where the results of an episode of sixteenth-century licentiousness manifest themselves today, but the prose as reticent as it is suggestive; even when Lamsley goes as far as this he maintains his taste.

"Someone to Dump On" proves with the great simplicity of utter confidence that the classical ghost story can still work; it triumphantly revives a classic trope of the genre, the ghost that goes unrecognised as one until it's too late. "The Break," set in a seaside resort overrun with confused old people, conveys the nightmarishness of which childhood can seem to consist as powerfully as any piece of fiction I have ever read. "Running in the Family" is also concerned with childhood and its perceptions of an alien world gradually revealed, as the young narrator learns that her father is not a Russian and her mother is not her mother, and becomes psychologically involved with a ghost that can't stop running. I would furthermore count Terry as, along with M. John Harrison and practically nobody else, an inheritor of the influence of Robert Aickman: such tales as this and "The Extension" suggest the affinity to me with their strangeness and the poise with which they are narrated. In the latter story the son of two killers returns to their home, only to discover that they were involved in more than murder and that the past has the power to reclaim him. "Inheritance" is as dark as the book gets, maybe as the genre gets: it would do as an unrelenting study of paranoid schizophrenia, believe me, but it asks us to decide whether that or the supernatural is least reassuring. By contrast, the title story offers the largest helping of the humour and irony which underlie much of the best of the genre, though even this leads to a bleak coda. In "The Outer Darkness" the obsession of two men with the woman they both loved when she was alive leads them to follow her into an afterlife as skewed as at first sight it looks banal. As for "Walking the Dog," it will serve to introduce the reader to Terry's growing originality. It would once have been called science fantasy, presenting as it does the symbiotic relationships between a voracious alien being and the various unfortunates employed to feed it. Despite Terry's fidelity to his genre, he is triumphantly like no other writer.

In this book Lamsley consolidates his reputation as an inheritor of all the qualities of classic English supernatural horror fiction: wit, detachment, an economy of effect bordering on the poetic, a seemingly effortless originality. In 1997 *Conference with the Dead* received an award for best collection from the International Horror Guild. This is a major book by one of the major living talents in the field, and I'm proud to be part of it.

Ramsey Campbell
Wallasey, Merseyside

Walking the Dog

Opening a tin of cat food in the dark can be difficult and dangerous. Steve had cut the big muscle at the base of his thumb on a lid the first time he had tried, eleven days before. Now he was more experienced and knew the moves to make, he had one open in seconds. Nevertheless, he was careful how he went about the task. He'd learned the hard way that preparing an animal's supper could be hazardous work.

He sliced the contents of the tin of "Liver-flavoured Purrfect" with a fork and sprinkled the nauseating mess over the lawn. He still could not believe that hedgehogs could eat such stuff, but each night something did.

The hedgehogs, a whole family of them, were the obsession of an elderly couple who had gone on holiday for a month and who were scared the creatures would desert their garden if they were not regularly fed during their absence. They were paying Steve well to do the job. Easy money, as he had to pass the house at that time anyway, on his way home from his other engagements.

Tonight though, it was not his last task of the day, as he had taken on an extra commitment for which, by his standards, he would be paid fabulously well. The hours were strange, from eleven at night until one thirty in the morning, but he didn't care about that. It was regular, permanent work and, with what he would get from it and his other jobs, he would just about make enough to live on. For the first time since he'd left school almost three years ago, he'd be independent of his parents. He would no longer be a burden. They wouldn't be able to give him such a bad time at home, and make him feel so useless and depressed.

He slipped the tin-opener into his leather jacket, dropped the empty can on a heap of others exactly like it in the wheely-bin by the side of the house, then stood for a few moments watching the vacant lawn.

So far, he had not seen one hedgehog. He had a suspicion they had taken off anyway, perhaps because their admirers were no longer there to make a fuss of them. Still, it wasn't his problem; he was doing what he was paid to do; it wasn't his fault if the ungrateful little buggers had upped and gone.

Something moved in the flower-beds surrounding the lawn, rustling the dry leaves of the dying annuals planted there. He watched and waited. The soft sounds continued, but nothing appeared. It was too dark to see much anyway.

"It's next door's moggy," he thought, "waiting for me to go away."

He dug his hands into his pocket and strode off.

He was due at his new job at Seaton House, on the other side of Buxton. Mr. Stook, his new employer, had asked him to "get there early, to receive instructions." The man spoke like that a lot; like a form from the Social Security. It worried Steve. He liked to get on well with the people he worked for. He hoped Stook wasn't going to be an awkward customer.

Steve had never been to Seaton House before. Mr. Stook had interviewed him at Steve's parents' house for some reason. He had asked a lot of probing questions, mostly about how fit and strong he was, and insisted on references from previous employers. It seemed a lot of fuss to make to hire the services of an animal-minder, which is what Steve called himself in the advertisements he put in the *Buxton Advertiser*.

He walked past the house twice before he found it. It was completely hidden from the road by a five-foot-wall backed by a hedge of tall, black conifers.

It was a huge house. Steve knew nothing about architecture, but it looked old to him; older than most of the others surrounding it. It was enclosed in what amounted to a small woods. Only the silhouette of the roof and a number of chimneys, vaguely showing against the dimly moonlit clouds, made it visible at all. There was no knocker on the door, and Steve had trouble finding the bell. He discovered it by touch in the end; a big, old-fashioned button set in a circle of polished wood about six inches in diameter. He could feel letters cut in it under his fingers and guessed the order "PRESS" was written there. He pressed.

The door opened almost at once, which surprised him, but then he remembered he was expected. A young woman looked down on him from the height of two steps. She clicked her tongue. The way she did it made it sound interrogatory, like a question.

"Steven Cave," Steve explained.

"The pet sitter?"

"Mr. Stook asked me to get here early."

"That's right," the girl agreed. "He did. Come in." As she walked away, he noticed she limped badly. She had trouble getting her right foot flat on the ground.

He stepped into the hallway. The girl preceded him up stairs that were steep and wide. The carpet was in tatters in places and he tripped and almost fell.

The girl said, "Watch your step," which was easier said than done, as the bulbs above him gave nowhere near enough light for him to see his feet. He clung cautiously to the banister rail and thought, "Stook is some kind of miser, in spite of the money he's paying me."

She opened a door on the first floor and walked into a pitch-dark room. He followed her a little way, feeling suddenly uneasy, afraid he might bang his knees against something. The girl became quite invisible, then she must have found a switch, as her face suddenly appeared in a beam of pallid illumination that shone up from the circular aperture at the top of a shaded lamp. She glanced at him (confirming what he had suspected, that she looked odd, but attractive), said, "Wait here, he won't be long," and slipped out, closing the door behind her.

Steve dropped into an armchair and tried to relax. Not easy. The chair was covered in old, bone-dry black leather as hard as wood. There were no cushions. He stretched out his legs, and almost slid off. He pulled himself upright, and looked around. He was in a large, high-ceilinged room, sparsely furnished with big, blunt, graceless furniture. Not antique and interesting, like he'd seen in shops; just old, ugly, and depressing.

He sensed there was something wrong with the room, but it took him a couple of minutes to work out what. Then he noticed there was not a single picture on the walls or ornament on the surface of the tables and cupboards. Acting on a hunch, he went and opened one of the cupboards. It was empty. They all were.

He got down on his knees and peered inside one. As he did so he felt a sensation on the back of his neck, as though something had jumped on it. For a moment, a sharp pain jabbed down his spine. He swore, stood up, and rubbed the affected area. "A crick in the neck," he thought, "whatever one of them is."

The pain quickly receded to almost nothing, but he still felt uncomfortable.

He returned to the leather chair and sat waiting.

Somehow, the ugly furniture had a looming, brooding presence; it too seemed to be anticipating something. Steve glared round at it, but found it was more powerful than he was. Put out of countenance by a lot of dead wood, he looked away, down at his own crossed legs.

There were sounds out in the house somewhere, and footsteps passed by on the corridor.

Once he thought he felt a movement up behind the back of his head as if something was forcing its way between him and the chair. He swatted the area with his hand and jumped up. The chair was empty. He looked behind it. Nothing there.

He shook his head, and immediately felt a slight constriction round his throat, as though his shirt collar had tightened. He took off his jacket and rubbed his neck furiously, wagging his head up and down as he did so. To his relief, after a few seconds, the sensation subsided.

He put his jacket back on and sat down again, feeling worried and slightly foolish.

Five minutes went by.

He remembered he had his Walkman in his pocket. He stuck the plugs in his ear and turned up "Happy in Hell" by The Christians very loud. At once he felt armed and ready to deal with the intimidating atmosphere about him in the room; the furniture shrank back, as well it might, and the place even seemed a bit brighter. He shut his eyes and sank into the music. When he pulled the tape out of the cheap machine to play the other side, he realised he was not alone anymore.

Mr. Stook had joined him.

His employer was sitting at the table near the lamp, reading through a handful of documents. Steve recognised a CV he had put together and guessed the other papers were his references. He pulled out the ear plugs, switched off the hissing Walkman, and pretended to clear his throat. Stook stiffened slightly at the sound, but made no other response. He kept on reading. When he moved his head slightly, as he turned his attention to the next item in his hands, the light glistened and sparked on the silver frame and dark orange-tinted lenses of his spectacles. His face had a fuzzy, unfocussed look. His features seemed to blend into each other with a smoothness that gave them an unfinished appearance, like a clay model awaiting the sculptor's final touches.

At last he finished reading, turned to Steve, and said, "Ah, there you are; the successful applicant." He hissed as he spoke, as though he had someone else's false teeth in. His voice had a querulous edge, suggesting he was not quite sure he had made the right choice. It was soft and barely audible. Steve thought if he were sitting a couple of feet further away, he would not have been able to understand what the man was saying. He found himself leaning forward, twisting slightly in his seat to point an ear towards his employer. He was suddenly alert, like a rabbit that had sniffed the scent of fox.

"Thank you for attending early as requested," Stook continued, "I appreciate your compliance." He stood up, moving carefully, as though he was afraid he might break. He was at least a foot shorter than Steve, who was five eleven. He stooped from a point low down his back, forcing him to hold his head well back to look the boy in the eye. Because of the lack of definition in his features his face looked young; even, in a rather unpleasant way, infantile. In his tinted shades, he resembled a junky baby. His little mouth was cherubic, enhancing this impression. The hands he held clasped together across his chest were thin to the bone. He was dressed in an oddly cut suit with a tight fit that clung to his scrawny body. Steve guessed the man weighed about seven stone at most. He felt he could pick Stook up and throw him in the air, but behind this thought was the conviction that something very nasty would happen to him if he did. Stook looked capable of looking after himself, in spite of his slender corporality. He had a startling, powerful presence.

"Now, if you will accompany me downstairs, I shall introduce you to your colleague," Stook murmured, moving with slow, awkward steps across the room.

As he opened the door, light from the landing outside shone full on his face, and Steve saw Stook's flesh was covered in a fine, silvery, almost invisible down, as fluffy as the feathers of a newly hatched chick. That explained why his features looked blurred. Steve had not noticed it before, when Stook had visited his house, because the man had worn a black trilby hat pulled down almost to the bridge of his nose, and had anyway kept his distance. The sight of the down was so peculiar, Steve found himself staring blatantly at what he could see of Stook's profile.

Stook must have realised this, because he turned, pulled back his lips, and bared his teeth slightly. It wasn't a smile; Steve didn't know what it was; it was not an expression he had seen before on any other face. It startled and confused him. He blushed.

Back on the ground floor, Stook led him through a succession of barely furnished rooms to the back of the house. The final room they went through was a kitchen containing a stone sink with a wooden draining board, a dented zinc washtub, and a large and ancient stove. There was no sign of any plates or food, and no cupboards to store such things. All was spotlessly clean. The air was sharp with disinfectant.

They went out into a large, dark, cobbled yard. In the distance, twenty yards away, a solitary light glowed over a door to an outbuilding.

Stook made towards it, moving slowly and with a peculiar, heavy-footed gait, as though he were wading through water. At times they hardly seemed to be making any progress at all but, if Steve stepped ahead, his employer made an irritable snatching motion in the air with his hand, ordering him back.

When they reached the door Stook rapped on it with his knuckles. The sound was dry, like bone on bone. A bolt was drawn back inside and the door was opened by the girl who had let Steve into the house. They walked into a bare, tiled room containing a long, scrubbed bench built over a drain, a selection of electric saws and knives hanging from hooks on the wall, a hose pipe jubilee-clipped to a tap, and not much else. The atmosphere was cold, as though refrigerated in some way. Steve saw his own breath in front of his face.

The girl was wearing a white apron over her skirt and blouse. Steve noticed there were russet stains on the apron that could have been dried blood. The girl's face was without expression or makeup, but her lips were bright red as were, to a lesser extent, her eyes. She looked as though she had been crying, or peeling a lot of onions. She looked wasted, as if she existed on coffee and cigarettes, or gin and Ecstasy. She was beautiful in a hard, macabre way that Steve found attractive, but the sight of her depressed him. "These people are loonies," he thought, "and they've got a bloody Rottweiler or a panther to exercise. They're going to make me earn my money."

"I know you two met briefly before," Stook whispered, "but it is necessary that you be properly introduced. You will be spending a lot of time in each other's company." He waved a finger in the air between them. "This—is Mr. Steven Cave and this—is Miss Amanda Osmond." Steve nodded, and the girl moistened her lips and blinked.

"Please," Stook insisted, urging them closer together with a gesture, "shake hands."

Steve held his hand out and the girl slipped hers into it. Steve grasped her fingers, waggled them up and down, looked into her face, and smiled hopefully. He felt no response against his palm, but the girl did look him in the eye briefly. She gave no sign she liked what she saw.

"Time, now, for one more introduction," Stook said, with a certain relish. He seemed to like introductions. "I regret *I* must leave you Mr. Cave, but if you would be so good as to follow Miss Osmond. . . ?" He stepped back and gave a farewell wave.

Suddenly, Steve had a hundred questions needing answers. The first was: Could he go away and think if he really wanted the job? He wasn't sure he could handle it.

But the man was going, almost gone.

"Oh, by the way," Stook said, "I want you to realise that Miss Osmond is your senior. I hope you will work in happy partnership, but she will be, at all times, in charge." He stopped, waiting for an answer.

"Yes," Steve said, "of course."

And felt a sudden twinge of pain at the top of his back; a return of the sensation he had experienced when he had opened the cupboard in the house. He rubbed his neck vigorously, giving it the treatment that had proved partly successful before.

"Good," said Stook, "that is *most* satisfactory," and made his exit.

Steve realised Amanda was watching him with a strange expression on her face. He read it as a mixture of pity, distaste, and maybe something else, like fear. She said, "What's wrong?" but sounded incurious, as though she knew the answer.

"What?"

"With your neck?"

"Nothing, just a crick."

"You think that's nothing?" she said. "Well, you just wait and see." She tossed her head, gazed up at the ceiling, and echoed again, "Nothing . . ."

Steve was seriously confused. He seemed to have upset her, but couldn't think how.

Anyway, the pain in his neck had gone again.

Amanda didn't seem in a hurry to get on with the introduction. She stared out of a window into the yard for a minute or so. She looked tired and bored, as though she was waiting for something not very interesting to happen. She made Steve nervous. He wanted to break the silence, to ask some of his questions, to quell his doubts and anxieties, but he sensed small talk would get short shrift from her. Perhaps he ought to keep his mouth shut as much as possible until he knew her better. He wondered if she was a bit. . . disturbed.

Working with Amanda, he decided, was not going to be easy. She was a chilly number.

Even so, he fancied her.

Then, suddenly, as though a bell had rung, the girl became active. She had a bunch of keys in her hand. She set about unlocking a complicated mechanism on a door at the rear of the room.

When it opened, Steve saw it was four inches thick and faced with steel on the inside.

They walked through it into a little closed-up cage. The girl shut the heavy door behind them and, as she did so, a section of the cage, on some automatic mechanism, swung up and out. They entered a room even colder than the last. It was lit by clumps of peculiar shell-shaped lamps along the walls that gave an illumination like none Steve had come across before; a sharp, pearly pink glow that seemed to hover round its source, rather than spread wide. It reminded Steve of dentists' surgeries, or operating theatres, for some reason, though it certainly would not have been suitable for either kind of establishment. The room itself summoned up images of instruments used in such places; scalpels and drills and suchlike.

Before Steve had a chance to take in details of the tidy, clinical, but dingy room something big, an animal, rose up from the floor. It was mostly charcoal grey, with dark green stripes, and had short hair over its head, back, and tail. Its legs and underside were naked greenish flesh. It was almost four feet high. It had a flat face, with eyes that looked forward. It had, Steve saw at once, oddly beautiful, expressive eyes, but expressive of what? He had no idea. The creature stared at him frankly, and seemed to be trying to see into his head.

"It's giving me the once over," he thought. "It's trying to read my mind. It looks as though it could, too. God knows what it is! They can't expect me to walk a thing like that."

"That's not a dog," Steve objected.

"Obviously. Did Mr. Stook mention a dog?"

Steve couldn't remember that he had, during his interview, but somehow he had assumed that was what he was being asked to deal with. He shook his head.

"He's doglike, though, as you can see. Out at night, in the dark, he is easily mistaken for a dog. You don't have to worry about that."

She must have misinterpreted the expression of doubt on his face, because she said, "He's harmless most of the time. He won't hurt you. Touch him; put your hand on his head."

Steve looked from the animal to Amanda. She was watching him very closely, with a slight smile that could have been the start of a sneer.

He stepped towards the thing and scratched between its ears. It had little round ears. It made a gurgling noise in its throat, perhaps indicating contentment.

"What's its name?" he said.

"It hasn't got one." Amanda brushed her hands together briskly, impatiently. "And now we'd better get going," she added decisively.

Something touched the back of Steve's leg. The animal. It was looking up at him with its strange eyes. Its irises were a pattern of tiny black and white diamond shapes, like a harlequin's costume. The outer parts were sea-green, a very deep-sea-green.

It was, on the whole, an ugly bugger, but not unfriendly.

So why didn't it have a name? The anonymity seemed pointless, heartless. People even gave their pet goldfish names!

He decided he would christen it; but what to call it?

He'd have to think about that.

"Okay," he said, "let's go walkies. Show me the ropes, Amanda."

"We go in the van," she said.

"Is this it?" Steve said, looking out at the black night all around.

Amanda lit her third cigarette in half an hour and killed the lights and engine. "It's as far as we go tonight." The windows were shut and the front of the van was full of stale smoke.

Steve opened the side door and stuck his head out. A skeletal moon hung precariously above him, washing the landscape with a pale, sick lumination.

"Are we anywhere in particular?"

"In the middle of the moors north of Leek." She stretched wearily, then clambered out of the van, lowering herself carefully onto her damaged foot.

Steve joined her at the back of the vehicle and helped push the sliding door open. A light in the sealed-off rear compartment came on automatically, revealing the creature sitting on a water bed. Steve had asked about the bed and Amanda told him it was full of cold water. It helped to keep the temperature down. Steve had said "Ah," and thought, "It's a bloody cold night anyway."

Earlier, they had loaded the "dog" on board without any trouble. It had been placid and cooperative. It had made a few noises that had alarmed

Steve at first, but the girl had ignored them.

He was beginning to think that the job might be easy after all.

Amanda pulled a set of steps down out of the back of the van and said something incomprehensible to the animal. It approached them, reversed itself and, to Steve's astonishment, descended backwards. Its coordination was nothing like that of any animal he had ever seen. He noticed it had long, crudely prehensile claws that it used to grip the steps one at a time. It looked clumsy in motion, but seemed sure footed enough. Once on the ground it sniffed eagerly about, like a cartoon pooch tracking game.

Amanda flung her cigarette end away and lit up another.

"You trying to burn your lungs out with those?" Steve asked.

"Perhaps."

"Mr. Stook won't let you smoke in the house?"

She shrugged.

"He probably worries about your health."

For the first time, he heard her laugh. It was a painful, hacking sound that turned into a cough. When it finished she said, "He certainly likes to keep his employees going as long as possible," then coughed again. Steve thought he could hear other sounds in her chest, something glugging and gurgling. He was about to ask her if she was okay, but she gave him a look that shut him up.

The animal croaked softly, as though to draw attention to itself.

"Right," Amanda said, "this is where you do your bit." She clipped an extending lead on a collar round the creature's neck and handed Steve the other end. The lead was slightly luminous, emitting a weird green light. "So you can see where it's gone," she explained. "Okay, beast-master," she said, climbing back into the van, "get walking. Have you got a watch?"

"Yes."

"Time?"

"Almost midnight."

"You give it an hour."

"But where do I take it?"

"Where it wants to go."

She said a mumbo-jumbo word to the animal, and it was off. It jerked the lead, nearly pulling Steve over. As he stumbled after it, he heard her say, "Your eyes soon get used to the dark, and there's plenty of starlight. It's easier if you give it plenty of lead. Just press the button to run it back. Keep it tight or it gets snagged."

And Steve's nightmare began.

The thing trotted off fairly slowly at first. It moved in a peculiar way, pawing the ground like a high-stepping pony with its front legs, but somehow trotting with its back ones. Steve seemed to remember seeing poodles in ballet skirts making similar motions in a circus. Right from the start he had to walk fast to keep up, but the creature soon accelerated, and he found himself running. He let out more lead and tried to slow down but his charge had other ideas. He saw the grey shape ahead of him getting smaller and smaller on the end of its thin strip of green light.

The ground underfoot was uneven and dangerous, riddled with rabbit holes and lumps of sharp rock. He fell after five minutes, without harming himself, then got up and plunged ahead again. The thing had paused when he tripped, but only for seconds.

The rest of the hour was hell. After twenty minutes he called out to the creature to slow down, even though he didn't think it understood orders in English. If it did hear him, it ignored him. It found something to interest it at one point, and began snuffling frantically. As soon as he realised it had stopped, Steve flopped to the ground flat on his back, wound in some of the lead, and gazed up at the stars, gasping for air while his chest heaved almost to bursting point. His heart beat like the bass at a Guns 'n' Roses concert. After just a few minutes a small animal, probably a rabbit, screamed with pain again and again, as though it was being dismembered slowly. Steve looked in the direction of the sounds and saw his charge up on its back legs against the curtain of stars, seemingly dancing. It was hurling some misshapen lump of a living creature into the air, catching it in its jaws, then tugging at it with its paws. Hence the screams. The thing was obviously enjoying itself.

It soon wanted to move on, however. Too soon for Steve, who needed more time to get his breath back. He hauled on the lead, yelled at the creature, and refused to get up. The thing pulled hard, and started jerking at the lead. It was very strong. Steve found himself being dragged along in spite of his considerable weight. He tried to dig his heels into the bracken but failed to get a grip. He slid uncomfortably for a few yards until he came up against a large boulder. He managed to get his end of the lead round the rock in a loop which held. The thing stopped. It made angry, frustrated noises, like the cawing of a giant rook. Steve hung on, feeling triumphant. He had scored a point. It was finding out who was boss.

Then he felt a painful stab in the back of his head. The skin at the sides of his neck was drawn forward, as though something was reaching round towards his chin. Whatever it was grasped the flesh above his breast bone and began to crush his windpipe. At the same time his head was being pulled up and back. It was impossible to breath.

He was holding the lead with both hands but he let go with one of them to feel around his neck for whatever was strangling him. There was nothing there that he could touch. There were indentations in his skin where the pain was greatest, however, as though something invisible was digging in.

He let go of the handle of the lead altogether and jumped to his feet. He saw the glowing green stripe slipping away from him like an electric snake. The animal, realising it was free, became silent.

Steve hung onto his head as though he feared it might be torn off his shoulders. He was in agony, and quite unable to get air into his lungs.

Out of the corner of his eye he saw the creature come prancing swiftly towards him. It stopped a few feet in front of him and stared at him. It reared up on its hind legs and, as it did so, the pain Steve was experiencing became, for a second, much more intense. Then the thing took a leap in the air and sank down onto its belly.

At once, Steve felt himself released. The constriction round his neck was no longer there; the cause of pain had gone. He gasped air, and fell to his knees. He was violently sick. He found himself on all fours. He closed his eyes, and moaned. His whole body was quaking with spasms of nausea.

When he opened his eyes again, he found the creature had moved closer. They were almost nose to nose. The thing's remarkable eyes were inches from his.

It was looking straight into him, or seemed to be. It moved a fraction closer and blinked. For an instant, the pain flashed on and off in the back of Steve's head. Then the animal turned, trotted off a little way, and sat down, obviously waiting.

Steve understood.

Meekly, he went and found his end of the lead.

He looked at his watch. It was almost one, time to get back to the van.

Then he realised he had no idea where he was. He was completely disorientated.

He staggered about lost for three or four minutes, while the creature trotted calmly behind him, almost at heel. Then, not very far away, the van's headlights flashed twice.

When he reached it, the girl was standing at the back with the door open. She slipped the collar and lead off the creature's neck, and it jumped on board.

They got into the van.

"How did it go?" Amanda said.

"A few problems." Steve's neck was so sore, it hurt to speak.

"Yeah, so I heard. You two fell out?"

"That sort of thing."

"You won't do *that* again, will you?"

"I won't have anything to do with it again," he said angrily.

"Oh yes you will." She lit a cigarette, started the engine, and turned to look at him. "It won't let you go."

"We'll see about that."

She started driving cautiously back, with the headlights dipped. "You don't understand, do you? You're hooked. You've got a monkey on your back."

Steve didn't answer.

They drove back in silence.

Steve had too much on his mind to notice how cold it was.

"I don't understand. Why do I have to walk it anyway?"

"I used to take it," Amanda said, "but my legs got broken once too often, and they won't heal properly anymore. Then we got another girl to do it. . ."

"No," Steve insisted, slightly embarrassed at causing her to mention her game legs. "I mean, how come we have to take it out at all?"

"It needs exercise. Can you imagine letting that creature out the back door to roam around for the night? To wander round town on its own?"

"But why do I have to walk *with* it? Why can't we just take it somewhere and leave it to run for an hour?"

"It gets lost. It's got no sense of direction. And it's shortsighted. I don't think it can see more than a few yards."

"Even with those amazing eyes?"

"Perhaps it sees things with them we can't see. Maybe, where he comes from, he can see perfectly."

"And where do you think that is?"

She paused, lit a cigarette from the last half inch of her previous one, and said, "Who knows? Another dimension? Another planet? Hell? Your guess is as good as mine. One thing's certain, it's not part of the indigenous population."

They were driving out for Steve's fourth night on the job. Each time, they went to a different spot, just in case they'd been seen the night before, and someone was waiting for them to return. There had been articles in the local papers about a strange animal in the district during recent weeks, and a couple of eye-witness descriptions had been close to the mark. Mr. Stook had got to hear about them, and had not been pleased with Amanda. She'd been disciplined, she told Steve. She didn't say how, but her "monkey" had played a part in the procedure, so now she was selecting the sites for the creature's exercise with particular care.

On their second trip out, she'd explained that she had a "passenger" on her back, the same as he did. It wasn't really a monkey, but the phrase "a monkey on the back," used by junkies back in the '40s and '50s as a euphemism for addiction, seemed to describe their own predicament exactly.

Even then, in spite of the evidence of his experiences on the first evening, Steve couldn't quite believe her; he thought it was more likely there was something wrong with *him*.

That was what he wanted to believe.

When he'd tried to stay at home on the second night, when it was time to go to work, and the pains had started at the top of his spine, and had only eased when he had left his parents' home and set off in the direction of Seaton House, he had clung to the idea that it might be due to something that was wrong inside his head. He knew nothing about psychology, but was aware that the mind could make you do strange things.

Whatever it was, however, it hurt. It forced him to get to the job on time.

The next evening, at ten, he'd jogged as far and as fast out of Buxton as he could.

His "monkey" had almost throttled him by the time he had gone two miles, and he'd had to turn back. At home again he had run up to his room, stripped off his shirt, and looked in the mirror. At the front of his neck, just above his breastbone, were bruise marks the shape of two little three-fingered hands. The fingers had dug in deep enough to draw blood.

He'd gone to work then—in a hurry.

The fourth night, tonight, he had turned up on time: in fact, he'd been early.

The creature had not given him too many problems after their first trip out together, though walking it was still hard work. Instead of running wild for an hour, and dragging him after it, it had conformed to more doglike ways for some of the time, trotting a few yards ahead of him at a reasonable speed and sticking mostly to sheep tracks and established paths. Steve was glad to find the thing ignored sheep. He had half-expected it to kill and eat one every night for supper.

Amanda had explained when asked (she hardly ever volunteered information) that his first evening on the job had been the creature's first outing for months, so it had had a lot of steam to let off. It never went out between the start of June to the end of September because it didn't like the hot nights.

"It sort of hibernates in reverse in the room we collect it from. It's air-conditioned. It gets as cold as a witch's tit in there sometimes."

As to sheep for supper? "It eats when we get back, after you've gone. Stook sees to that. He's in charge of the pantry."

"What does he feed it?"

"Don't worry about that," she said. "Believe me, you don't want to know."

He mentioned the rabbit it had caught on the first night.

"It must have been a very stupid rabbit," she said, "or a sick or injured one."

"I don't think it ate it; just pulled it apart."

She nodded. "You won't see rabbit on its menu," she said. "It's a big-game gourmet."

They reached some Godforsaken place and stopped. Steve opened the rear door of the van and stood aside as the thing stuck its backside out and reversed down the steps. Not for the first time, he wondered what his monkey would do to him if he gave the creature a kick in the rump. Something very painful, he was sure.

He still thought of the animal as "it." He had dropped the idea of giving it a name. Anonymity seemed to suit it.

So things continued for some months.

Stook told Steve to learn to drive, and paid for lessons.

The money Steve was earning was ridiculous, enough for him to be able to drop most of his other jobs. His standard of living soared. He started buying clothes to spruce up his image.

He had always had trouble with girls. They didn't seem to see him. Steve stared at girls a lot, he couldn't help it, but somehow, for some reason, they never so much as glanced back. It was as if he were invisible. They just looked through him.

He spent a lot of time in front of the mirror, trying to work out why.

He thought he was handsome enough. Okay, he had a slightly pudgy face. But his features, considered in isolation, were good. He looked. . . reasonable. Lots of worse-looking men his age were walking about with delicious girls on their arms, were sleeping with them. Steve's sex life was almost nonexistent, and took place with the few girls who were attracted to him. For some reason, these were never girls he fancied. Something was wrong, he felt; he wasn't getting across to the right women.

So he started buying show-off clothing and having expensive haircuts. He thought girls would be more likely to notice him. He'd be more obvious.

But his new look wasn't having much effect.

Certainly not on Amanda.

She attracted him a lot. But she was an enigma; hard to get on with, and difficult to know. She didn't reveal much about herself.

He dreamed about Amanda.

They were foolish dreams, with him as a sort of white knight, saving her from the evil Stook.

The trouble was, in reality, she didn't seem to realise she needed saving. She put up with what Steve perceived to be an abject, slavish existence.

And she always had her guard up. She had a weary, cynical attitude and way of speaking that somehow put her away at a great distance, out on her own. Steve felt she was beyond him, he couldn't reach her, though sometimes he thought she was beginning to thaw out towards him just a little.

He was not sure how she spent her days, but he suspected she acted the skivvy for Stook and the creature, as the place where it lived was kept ultra-clean, as though scrubbed and scoured by a germ-phobic fanatic. The air around the house always stank of disinfectant, dust never seemed to get to settle on any surface in the outbuilding where the thing was "kennelled," and you could see your face in the gloss paint and polished tiles on the walls. The inside of the house, though furnished with ancient and, in some cases, worn, dilapidated items, was also kept fastidiously neat and clean, and Steve was sure Stook didn't do the work himself.

So it had to be Amanda.

Steve began to think of her as a kind of doomed Cinderella. Cinderella with a monkey on her back.

His own monkey didn't trouble him much. For days, he forgot it was there. Then he'd do something wrong when he was out with the creature, and it would give him a tweak, a jolt of pain that knocked him rigid, and he would remember.

And, often, he felt strangely tired. In recent weeks a lassitude was creeping over him, as though his energy was draining away through the soles of his feet. Things that had once been easy were getting difficult. He'd been a body builder for almost two years, and had got himself very fit. But suddenly it was a strain to lift weights. He kept away from the gym because he was finding it harder and harder to keep up with his friends down there, and his shorts and t-shirts were starting to hang loose on him. People noticed, and made comments.

Also, he'd been sleeping like a dead thing recently, was getting up later and later, and still he wasn't feeling refreshed.

And he was eating like a pig! His appetite was getting out of hand; his mother told him he must have worms.

Steve had a suspicion it was something worse than worms. A couple of times, in the mirror, he had caught an expression on his face that he had seen on Amanda's. A look that he was beginning to understand.

Frequently Amanda seemed to be trying to warn him about something; her conversation, sparse and elliptical as it was, was full of hints and allusions, suggested as much by her tone of voice as the meaning of the words she used. At times, when he thought she was trying to get through to him at some subliminal level, her normally blank, expressionless face would almost come alive. Feelings of frustration, fear, despair, and a terrible isolation would register briefly behind her eyes and in the lines at the corners of her mouth, to be wiped away at once by a grimace of pain, as though she had been whipped.

Reading between the lines of what she said, Steve came to understand that her monkey could somehow read her mind, even control her thoughts to some extent. Only occasionally, perhaps when it was dozing or otherwise occupied, could she communicate obliquely some of what Steve wanted to know. He got the impression she had been its victim for a long time and had almost total mastery over her, and that he would end up in the same condition. His own monkey was growing into him. It was getting to know him, to understand him. It had command of his body; one day it would have his soul. Or so Amanda seemed to be saying. From all this he deduced that he was still, to some extent, free to think and act in ways that she was not. Perhaps there was some way he could get the monkey off his back and then help Amanda deal with hers. Perhaps.

But there was also Stook to contend with. Steve wished he knew more about his employer. He became obsessed with a need to find out just what kind of eyes the man hid behind the impenetrable orange-tinted spectacles that always masked his out-of-focus face. He hardly ever had contact with Stook except at the end of each week, when he went to receive his pay. That, in itself, he found disturbing. And he realised he had never seen the man and his pet (if that was what the creature he took for nocturnal rambles was) together, not even once. Also, Stook never asked about its welfare or showed any concern about it at all, which was not natural. Steve was used to being questioned closely about the animals he cared for by their owners, as though the creatures were their own flesh and blood.

A suspicion evolved in Steve's mind that the dog-thing he exercised was just that, however; Stook's own flesh and blood!

"What does Mr. Stook do all day?" he asked Amanda one evening, as they drove to some remote, chilly location. It was almost Christmas, and a couple of inches of snow had fallen on top of a skim of frozen rain during the day. The girl was driving with greater concentration than usual.

"Goes out," she said from behind the cigarette that waggled at the side of her mouth. "Every day. In the van."

"Are you sure? Where to?"

"Looking for food to feed—it." She jerked a thumb over her shoulder towards the creature in the back compartment.

"And that takes all day?"

"It can do."

"You never did tell me what it eats," he said.

She shook her head and glanced sideways at him. For a few moments she was silent, then said, apparently apropos of nothing, "Every day, you know, people go missing. Particularly kids. It's a sign of the times."

"That's right," Steve agreed, unsure where the conversation was leading. "You read about it in the papers."

"All the time. It's surprising how many of them never do get found."

"Perhaps no one bothers to look for a lot of them."

"Someone does."

Steve grunted encouragingly, thinking he was perhaps beginning to understand. "And when he finds them, they stay missing?"

"Definitely. And sometimes, if he has to, he makes them go missing in the first place," she said, and turned the van off the road along a dark track to nowhere. "If he can't find what he wants, he takes what he can find. He's a good hunter. He knows how to set traps."

The full meaning of Amanda's words skipped over the surface of Steve's mind for a while, refusing to sink in. But what he was hearing, what he thought she was saying, did not come as a total surprise. It was a bit like remembering fragments of an old nightmare. He had formulated wild theories and fantasies about Stook and his "pet" at least as disgusting as the girl's story.

After another short silence, he said, "And the thing eats every day?"

"It has to have very fresh meat four or five times a week at least."

"Very fresh?"

"Lively. Still on the hoof. It likes to do its own slaughtering, though it will take the pre-butchered option if it has to."

For once, she seemed to be able to speak relatively freely, perhaps because her monkey knew if it gave her a jolt, she might loose control of the van on the snow and ice.

Suddenly, extrapolating, Steve understood something more. "So the meal is made to walk into the cage, then out into the room, is that it?" he said, trying to sound casual and inconsequential. "The cage opens automatically. It's a feeding hatch! The metal plating on the inside of the door is to stop dinner, not the creature, escaping?"

She nodded too hard, and set herself off coughing. Her cigarette fell from her lips to the floor. A stink of burning drifted up into the van. Steve bent down to find and extinguish the little fire, prodding around with the heel of his right shoe. Amanda slowed the van's speed to a crawl. As he fumbled he said, "Did you ever see Stook and that thing together in the same place?"

Then his own monkey woke up. He felt pain screw across the back of his eyes. He went blind. It was as though his eyes had been put out; there was that much pain. Black anguish filled his mind for an instant. He jerked back into his seat in one great spasm. He heard Amanda say something like "Drop it," or maybe, "Stop it"; then he passed out.

When he came to he had a searing headache, but he could see again.

The van had stopped. Amanda, looking grey-faced and ill, had got out and opened the door at his side. Fluffy snow was blowing in and settling on his face. The girl was shaking him by the shoulder. He heard a noise behind him, slightly muffled, like the cry of a monster crow trapped in a sack. The thing in the back was getting impatient.

He dragged himself through the door down onto the frozen ground. Amanda gave him the lead and opened the rear door.

The creature was angry. It snarled at him before it reversed out. It charged off as soon as he got its collar on, dragging him behind.

Then it led Steve in a grotesque and terrible dance.

It was a bleak place they had come to. The murky night sky was veiled by drifting nets of wet, swirling snow. He slipped on iced-over puddles a number of times in the dark. Once, he landed awkwardly on his left arm and felt something give in the wrist. His hand went numb, then started to pulse with pain. He couldn't move the fingers of his left hand, and was forced to hang onto the lead with only his right. The creature dragged him along sideways, causing him to stumble and fall a dozen times.

He felt like a sailor, sinking in a storm and sighting a lifeboat when, at last, he saw the van lights flash.

He got Amanda to drop him off at the Cottage Hospital on the way back to Seaton House. She was very reluctant to do so. She would not, or could not, stop the van, and insisted he jump out while she cruised slowly past the drive that led up to the Accident Unit.

He caught a glimpse of her contorted features as she leaned across the passenger seat to slam the door behind him. Her monkey, he guessed, was going to give her hell when she got back.

Steve woke up shortly after noon next day. He opened his eyes and saw his left arm, in plaster up to the elbow, rising and dipping on his chest. He'd spent most of the night in hospital. X-rays had revealed chipped and broken bones in his hand and wrist. The radiographer had told him it could be months before he got full use of the hand again.

When he *had* finally got to bed, he had not been able to get to sleep for thinking about how the accident would affect his prospects with Stook. Strangely, he was anxious he might lose his job. It somehow seemed like a desirable occupation to him, in spite of the fact that most of his working hours were a walking nightmare. Maybe he had become addicted to money or, more sinisterly, perhaps his monkey was influencing his thinking. Either way, like it or not, he was worried.

He dragged himself out of bed. He dressed slowly, like a sleepwalker, then went to the kitchen and chomped through a breakfast of three bowls of Shredded Wheat, a fry-up big enough to hide most of the surface of a dinner plate, half a loaf of toasted bread, and a pint and a half of milk. Then he felt tired again, and was tempted to return to bed for a few more hours, as he often did. But today he had urgent things to do. He had to let Stook know about the condition of his hand. The man was not on the phone, or was ex-directory, so Steve would have to pay him a visit. The idea appealed to him. He had been looking for an excuse to call at Seaton House during daylight hours for weeks.

A lot more snow had fallen. Probably for reasons of economy, the roads had not been salted, and traffic was sparse. Everywhere was eerily quiet; all sound was baffled, trapped in the banks of drifting white flakes. The town had a deserted feel, as though the population had been lured away overnight by the saucer-people.

Steve walked slowly, picking his way with care, not wanting to fall and damage his arm still further.

The first thing he saw when he trudged up Stook's drive was the van, parked where it never was left, at the front of the house. The front end was caved in from some considerable impact. The left tire was in shreds, and the windows were smashed. There were traces of an extra set of wheels nearby in the snow, suggesting the vehicle had been towed home.

He went and rang the doorbell and shouted through the letter box, got no response, and wandered round to the back of the house. The rear courtyard was surrounded by two-storied outbuildings and a wall eight feet high. The one door, bolted on the inside, was impenetrable without the aid of a battering-ram and a rugby team to operate it. On his own, with a duff hand, there was no way Steve could force an entry. He didn't even bother to try. He went among the trees all round the house, aware that he was leaving an obvious trail of prints in the snow, and snooped in the windows. He learned nothing about Stook's way of life, however, as all the rooms he saw were barely furnished and looked unused. He came to the conclusion that Stook chose to live at Seaton House because the building was well hidden, yet close to the centre of town, rather than because he needed a big establishment. It was probably easier to remain incognito, concealed in the community, than it would be if he inhabited some remote place where his activities, or lack of them, would become the object of speculation for farmers and other country dwellers, who commonly possess an insatiable curiosity about their neighbours' doings. Steve had been brought up on such a farm, and the same instinctive nosiness was born in him.

He wandered back into town, called the local hospitals from a telephone box to see if an Amanda Osmond had been admitted anywhere, and got negative replies from all of them. Then he sat in a pub for a couple of hours drinking lager, doing the quizzes on beer-mats, and listening to the barmaid's conversation. She was telling one of the customers (in fact, the only other customer), a sullen, silent man she seemed inordinately fond of, about her various *grand guignol* relationships. She obviously had lots of boyfriends. Steve thought she was beautiful. He fell in love with her. He normally never drank alcohol, but kept on drinking so he could stay and look at her. He thought, if he downed enough quickly, he might pluck up the courage to get talking to her himself. He stared at her shamelessly for minutes on end. She didn't seem to notice him, even when he went to the bar, even though he was dressed in one of his coolest, cost-a-packet outfits.

"I'm invisible," he thought. "I don't register with her. I suffer from negative charisma."

Then, suddenly disgusted with himself, he gulped down the last of his drink and got up to go. On the way out he walked to the bar, set his empty glass down in front of the object of his lust, and almost shouted, "See ya, then!"

"Ta, duck," she said, without turning. The customer in receipt of her monologue glanced askance at him, and raised an eyebrow.

"They think I'm pissed," Steve thought. "Perhaps I am, after five (or was it six?) pints of Special."

When he got outside and found his feet flailing about in the snow, he realised how drunk he was. Not far from the pub he slipped, fell on his backside, and bounced back up. "Ah ha," he thought, "I feel no pain!" and wanted to laugh. He stumbled back to Seaton House, lighter and happier than he had been for weeks.

When he got there he saw a new set of footprints leading up the drive. A woman's; almost certainly Amanda's. They stopped at the front door, and whoever had gone in was still there. There were no prints going back out.

He rang the bell, waited, then hammered with his fist. After a while the door opened slowly about six inches. It was on a chain. Round the edge of the door, thin, dry, scaly fingers appeared, clutching the wood with a crablike pincer movement. Above them, a slice of Stook's furry face, half-hidden behind one lens of his dark orange-tinted spectacles, pressed forward into the gap.

Partly through shock (he had been sure Amanda would answer the door) and partly because he did not want to waft lager-polluted breath towards his employer, Steve stepped backwards. He nearly fell off the step. He regained his balance, but not his composure. He could not think of anything to say. Stook broke the silence.

"Why are you here at this time?" he asked, in a tight, tiny, snarling voice. "What do you want?" His fussy manner of speech and fastidious politeness had deserted him.

"He looks like an insect," Steve thought, "with that fuzzy face and those shades. He even sounds like one. A giant house fly, or a bluebottle. He wants swatting!"

"I had an accident last night. Perhaps Amanda told you." Steve held up his plastered arm. "I fell over when I was walking the—"

"I know all about it," Stook snapped. "It doesn't matter."

"Oh, and I forgot to tell you, I passed my driving test the day before yesterday."

Stook grunted; a sound that may have expressed satisfaction.

Steve suddenly felt stupid with drink. His brain became confused, then blank.

"I don't want you here now," Stook said.

"But what about tonight?"

"Come at the usual time."

"I've broken my arm."

"That doesn't concern me."

"I've got to rest it; take things easy."

"You've got a job to do. You'll be here on time."

"But what about the van?"

"That's my problem." Stook glared at him for a few seconds, during which Steve felt contempt emanating from the man like a powerful smell.

"I want to speak to Amanda," Steve said at last.

"Why?"

"Well. . ." Steve inwardly cursed the lager that seemed to have anaesthetised his tongue.

"She's not here," Stook said, in what could have been a taunting tone.

Then he hissed, "Go away," and shut the door.

Steve stood looking at the varnished wood in front of his nose and became very, very angry. He hardly ever was angry, about once or twice a year, but when he was, it made up for all the times he wasn't, and should have been.

He kicked the door, hurt his toe, and shouted, "You bastard, you know how I broke my wrist last night because *you were there when it happened.* I've got you worked out, you and your bloody 'pet.'"

Then he felt something stirring at the back of his neck. A dull, wavering ache moved out of his spine and across his shoulders. His monkey was trying to push and punish him, and not making a good job of it. He could feel its hands groping to reach round to his throat, but they had no strength, and seemed to fumble. At one point, they lost hold altogether, as though the monkey had fallen backwards.

Gleefully, Steve recognised, in the parasite's powerless confusion, a reflection of his own drunkenness.

"It's more pissed than I am," he thought. "It feeds off me, and somehow it's got alcohol in its system, and it can't take it. It's got a weak head. It's rat-arsed; legless! It can't hurt me."

Finding himself truly free for the first time for months, Steve felt bold.

And he was still angry, deep inside.

And he was still very drunk.

"Time to get things sorted," he mumbled, as he started plodding through the snow to the rear of Seaton House. "Bugger the money. I'll not work for that thing anymore. And I'll find Amanda, and tell her to get her monkey drunk. That's the way to beat it. Then Stook can go and take himself for a walk."

He had noticed, during his prowl through the miniature woods growing round the perimeter of the house earlier in the day, a tree, growing close to the wall, whose branches reached out above the courtyard. Then, it had not occurred to him that he might be able to use it to get over the wall, especially as he only had the use of one arm; now, thanks to alcohol, it looked an easy climb.

Steve rose up the trunk, branch by branch, as though he was ascending a ladder, using the weight of his plastered wrist as a balance. He stepped out along an overhanging branch with all the confidence of a champion tango dancer leading his partner onto a ballroom floor. The branch dipped gracefully lower as Steve moved along it. When, after he had got the wall behind him, it snapped, depositing him in a drift of snow that had formed inside the courtyard, he didn't so much feel he was falling, as flying! He was so relaxed when he hit the ground, he was able to roll over onto his feet in one unbroken movement.

It was dank and dark in the courtyard. The snow, caught in eddies of wind trapped by the surrounding buildings, spun in frantically ascending circles around him. Looking about he saw a vertical strip of light at the edge of the door leading into the outbuilding where the creature had its "kennel." There was a sound, a high, grinding, mechanical whirring, coming from behind the slightly open door, that had been muffled by snow and the wall when he had been in the garden on the other side.

A beam of light stretched across the snow towards him from the slightly open door. He walked along its diminishing width warily, as though he were walking the plank. The noise continued, rising to a shear metallic screech, then sinking back to an even, angry snarl.

When it was at its loudest, Steve gave the door a shove and peered round it into the room.

Then drew back at once in horror.

Stook was in there, naked except for a pair of green Wellington boots and a brick-red rubber apron that almost formed a tube around his body. In it, he looked more than ever like some kind of bug. He had his back to Steve. He held an electric saw in his hands and was using it to cut up a carcass stretched out on the long wooden bench in front of him. The top end of the corpse had been jointed into unidentifiable chunks of meat. It was headless, but something heavy, about the size of a head, hung in a plastic Marks & Spencer bag from a nail driven into the edge of the bench. The lower section of the cadaver, partly concealed under a sheet of thick plastic, was untouched and obviously human. Two feet, lolling apart at the ankles at an angle of forty-five degrees, stuck out from under the sheet and over the end of the bench.

And Steve thought he had seen a hand on the floor by Stook's boots. The hand was moving, sliding down a gutter near the bench, caught in the jet from a hose pipe that was snaking restlessly from side to side under the pressure of water it was ejecting.

The shock of what he had seen, far from sobering Steve up, flung his mind into a debilitating stew of incredulity, revulsion, and blind anger. He wanted to act, to strike against Stook, to *swat him down*, but he didn't do anything of the sort. He stood rooted to the spot, gasping and howling, softly but passionately, along with the sighing of the wind, frozen in an enchantment of disgust and revulsion. He remained like that for a couple of minutes, long enough for the snow to settle as a light crust on his shoulders and head, and for his feet to start to freeze in his sodden canvas trainers.

Then a new sound came from inside the outbuilding. The deeper, harsher grinding of a bigger saw. His employer was getting down to work in earnest, making the final cuts. Presumably, soon, the meal would be ready, and the creature would eat.

The thought was enough to break the icy spell that Steve was under. He walked determinedly into Stook's private abattoir. Stook did not hear him enter; he would not have if Steve had shouted his name, against the noise of the machine.

Wondering if he might need a weapon, or something to defend himself with, Steve looked about for something heavy he could swing. As he did so, his monkey roused itself and tried, ineffectually, to cause him pain. It seemed to be sprawling inside his head, scratching at the back of his eyes with blunted talons, and gnawing his cerebellum with toothless gums. It was desperate, but almost helpless. Steve ignored it.

He got to within a couple of feet of Stook's back when he saw something hanging on the wall that brought him up short.

There was a row of hooks for overalls and waterproofs that he and Amanda took with them when they went out on wet nights. Stook's clothing had been flung over one of these and next to it hung the skirt and blouse that Amanda had worn the previous night, when Steve had broken his wrist in the snow. The girl's clothing was covered in blood stains, and there were streaks of red down the wall below.

Previously, dominated as he was by alcohol-enhanced emotions, Steve had not given a thought to the possible identity of the cadaver Stook was dismembering.

But his main motivation for invading his employer's domain had been to locate Amanda, and somehow to rescue her, as he had many times in his dreams. Now, it seemed he had found her, but too late.

He glanced again at the corpse. It was about the right size, what remained of it. The proportions were Amanda's. The hand, that was now spinning in a whirling current of crimson water outflowing down the drain, was narrow and delicate, like Amanda's. He even thought he could see nicotine stains on the fingers.

Then Stook must have become aware that he was no longer alone. He switched off the screaming saw and turned awkwardly round. He was crouching low, bent forward in his habitual stance, with his chin jutting up almost in line with his breastbone. He looked absurdly sinister and repellent with his wasted, grey downy arms swinging apelike by his sides, and his knotted knees showing in the gap between the tops of his boots and the bottom of his apron. He still held the electric saw in his right hand, and he whipped the tip of the blade back and forth in a tiny arc, in a tense, threatening movement. His eyes, invisible behind his tinted shades, nevertheless drove into Steve's like corkscrews.

Stook said something in a language Steve couldn't understand. It sounded like a question. Stook's tone was demanding, querulous, mystified. As if in answer, Steve felt his monkey stir again; vague waves of discomfort pulsed weakly through his brain.

Stook moved a few inches closer to Steve, and spoke again. Now he sounded angry.

But Steve's monkey seemed to give up. It faded out. Steve thought it might have gone to sleep.

Stook raised his feeble voice and mouthed more incomprehensible words.

"It's no good shouting," Steve said. "Your little mate's passed out. He's sleeping it off."

"You're drunk," Stook observed.

"Right," Steve agreed. "And I'm going to stay drunk."

Stook's lips curled, but he didn't speak.

"That way, we're more or less equal," Steve said, feeling more confident by the second. He had begun to sober up, but now he felt a surge of elation, like a shot of spirit, from the certainty he had disarmed Stook and his minion. "I don't work for you anymore, Stook. I know what you are, and I'm going to do something about you. I'm going to destroy you. Christ knows where you came from, but I'm going to send you to a worse place."

Stook made a buzzing noise with his tongue against his teeth, like an insect at a window. He sounded more impatient and irritable than scared. Hearing him, Steve experienced a moment of self doubt, of anxiety that he had, perhaps, underestimated his employer, and assumed victory too soon.

Stook straightened up a little, and seemed to turn away almost derisively.

Thinking he was going to walk off, Steve was about grab him, by the throat perhaps, when Stook struck. He swung up his right arm, switching on the saw as he did so, and lunged forward at Steve's chest. The little man moved with unexpected agility. The saw blade bit something, and shrieked as it cut.

Steve thought he had been hurt, but felt no pain. He staggered back and, as he did so, Stook moved quickly forward to strike again. Then Steve understood *why* he felt no pain. He had automatically held up his left arm to protect himself, and the saw had hit the plaster close to his elbow and lopped off a slice. He had raised the injured arm defensively, high above his head, out of the way, and it was still there, poised, waiting to be brought down. It felt very heavy.

Perhaps Stook recognised the danger because he snarled, adjusted his position, and sidestepped hurriedly. He lost his balance, and was on one foot when Steve's plaster-of-Paris club landed just above his right ear. The saw, on a dead-man's switch, went off.

There was a crack as Stook's neck broke, and he flew back against the bench sideways, smashing his head on its wooden top as he did so. His skull cracked open like an egg. Inside it, there were things Steve had not expected to see. There was no blood or brain. Instead, Stook's head was stuffed with what looked like dust, ashes, and blackened, shapeless objects that could have been lumps of charcoal, the remains of an ancient fire that had long ago gone out.

Steve stood motionless over his employer's body, staring incredulously as the contents of the man's head crumbled in a miniature landslide onto the surface of water splashing round it from the nearby hose. The ashlike substance floated swiftly away in dark, swirling streaks towards the drain.

Stook's dark glasses had stayed on in the struggle, as though welded to his nose. Steve reached down to remove them.

As he bent forward, someone grasped him by the shoulder and said, "For God's sake, what have you done?"

It was Amanda's voice. Steve jerked upright and turned slowly, dreading what he was about to see. He half-expected to find behind him a dismembered corpse, hastily reconstructed perhaps, and topped by a dead but talking head. Amanda looked battered and bruised. She had a bandage round her head, and a long, stitched-up cut across her forehead. Her face, where it was visible, was dove grey, and her skin had the texture of tightly stretched shiny paper.

"You're alive," Steve said, and looked across at the lumps of flesh on the bench. "I thought that was you. I saw your clothes; the blood stains...?"

"I smashed the van last night, soon after I'd dropped you at the hospital. I got hurt."

"Then who has Stook cut up?"

"The girl who used to do your job. She didn't last long. She fell into a quarry in the fog one night. She died. Stook made me bring her back. He put her in the freezer as emergency rations for the creature. He couldn't get out today so...

"She's still not thawed out, or there would be a lot more blood everywhere. The tools Stook used made a mess of a fresh corpse."

"Anyway, *Stook* is dead," Steve blurted tipsily, as though to reassure himself. "That animal will have died with him. And the monkeys can't hurt you if you get drunk. I've worked it all out. We're free of the lot of them."

"What do you mean, 'the animal will have died with him'?" she said.

"Christ, you must know *that*. You *must* have realised. Stook and that creature were one and the same. Stook was a werewolf, or something of the kind. It's bloody obvious."

The girl gave Steve an agonised look that made his heart sink into his gut. She shook her head. "He was just a man, or what was left of one. As to the creature. . ."

"Oh, *come on*, Amanda. You never saw the two of them together, ever, because they were the same thing in different forms." He gestured towards the sprawling corpse with the toe of a soggy trainer. "And you can't tell me *that* is just a man. His whole body is covered with hair, and see what he's got in his head! It looks like the inside of an oven after somebody burnt the dinner. And lets take a look at his eyes. . .!"

The girl stooped and removed Stook's tinted shades.

To reveal two red but human eyes set in dark tunnels deep behind the man's brow.

"I thought his eyes would be like the creature's," Steve said. "I was sure of it."

"He couldn't stand bright light, that's all. He was a man," Amanda insisted. "An incredibly old one, but that," she pointed into Stook's now half-empty skull, "is what happens to you when you have been preserved, kept alive for a very long time."

"From the look of him, he was in his seventies at most!"

"Stook was over two hundred and fifty years old. He was born in 1741."

"I don't believe it."

She glared angrily at him and snapped, "Tell me then, what age do you think I am?"

"Late twenties. No more."

"I *was* twenty-five, when Stook first employed me."

"When was that?"

"In 1926."

Steve slapped his head with his right palm. "It hurts me to say it, Amanda, but I think you're very confused. I've noticed before. You've got a real problem."

She almost laughed. "I've got plenty of them, and so have you. Even more, now Stook is dead."

"Exactly; so he can't harm us, or make us do anything we don't want to. And like I said, if you get pissed, the monkeys. . ."

"Forget that. You may be drunk now, but you can't stay drunk forever. You will have to sleep, and then, when you've sobered up, your monkey won't repeat the same mistake. Alcohol was something new, something it hadn't come across before. But it won't ever let you near drink again."

"Why should it bother with me, now Stook's gone? There's no one to work for. And I tell you, that creature *will* have disappeared. I *know* it."

Amanda sounded at the edge of her patience. "What makes you think the monkeys worked for Stook? He had his own monkey. It must have got him when he was middle-aged, over two hundred years ago.

"I found out a lot about him. He was famous once, and very rich, born into a family of fabulously successful merchants. He stayed in the business, and twice went exploring in Asia, looking for rare spices, and anything else he could sell. On the first voyage, he did well. On his second trip, an expedition to Tibet and God-knows-where beyond, he must have found more than he bargained for, or it found him, because he came back with that creature and, unknown to anyone but himself, a monkey on his back.

"The animal itself was a seven-day wonder. There were all manner of strange things turning up in England then, in 1783; animate and inanimate items brought back to civilisation from all over the world, and Stook's companion was just another outlandish oddity among many. Nobody knew about its peculiar appetite then, or perhaps someone *did*, as, shortly after his return, Stook faded from the limelight, retired to the country, and became a recluse. He vanished. And there's no record anywhere that he ever died. I'm sure of that; I've looked. So I know what I'm talking about. I know my man."

Steve frowned. The implications of what Amanda was saying were beginning to sink in. She knew what she was talking about. It all sounded true. Suddenly, she didn't seem crazy at all. And he was sobering up fast. And getting scared.

"But I thought Stook was in charge," he said. "You're telling me he was just a slave," he pointed to the bolted door at the end of the room, "to that *thing*?"

"Just like you and me; you've got there at last," said Amanda, bleakly ironic. "The creature runs the monkeys, and the monkeys run us. It's what's known as a symbiotic relationship and, from one point of view, it works almost perfectly."

"The creature's?"

"Not ours." She put a cigarette between her lips and lit it awkwardly, her lighter wavering in an unsteady hand. She smoked it quickly, in silence, while Steve absorbed what she had told him.

Then the creature in the room beyond began to howl, and Amanda's monkey gave her neck a jolt that threatened to tear her head off. She went out of the room and came back immediately, pushing a stainless steel trolley. She rolled up her sleeves and began loading hunks of Steve's predecessor onto the trolley. He watched her limping painfully about round the butcher's bench. She banged against the bag with the head in it, causing it to swing on its nail like the pendulum of some squat, cumbersome clock. He tried to find the courage to go and help her, but his mind was full of horror and a descending, impending monster headache. He was sober now, and feeling very bad. He remembered why he had always avoided drink; because he got terrible hangovers.

"Any moment now," he thought, "my monkey will wake up. It's going to feel sick too, and it will want to make me suffer. It's time to get out of here while I can. I need more drink to keep the monkey quiet while I work out what to do next."

He explained his plan to Amanda, who did not respond. Her face had twisted into a grotesque mask of pain. Blood seeped from the cut across her forehead, and her movements were jerky and uncoordinated. Steve guessed her monkey was giving her a hard time, pushing her faster than she could go in an effort to get the creature fed quickly.

He wondered if there was any way the hungry thing, locked in the room where it lived, could get itself out. He doubted it. How long would it take to starve in there? Amanda had said it had to have fresh meat four times a week. Perhaps, like certain rodents, it consumed energy very quickly! It might burn itself out in a few days.

If he and Amanda could both stay drunk for a week or more, they would have a chance...

"Amanda," he shouted. "We have to get out of here *now*."

She gave no indication she had heard, and seemed to be struggling to work even faster. Most of the joints of human meat were on the trolley. Suddenly, she started to wheel it to the door that let into the creature's room.

Steve ran towards her. "I'm taking you out of here," he yelled, "if I have to carry you. Your monkey will hurt you, but don't try to stop me. Try to relax."

She had her back to him when he reached her. He grabbed her right shoulder with his good arm, and attempted to pull her round. As he touched her, two small, hard hands grasped the top of his jacket, and something invisible jumped from her onto him and began clambering up his chest.

At the same moment, the monkey lodged within him jerked awake. It squawked like a mad macaw inside his head. For the first time, an image of its face—savage, alien, birdlike, with a blunt but serrated-edged beak instead of jaws, and tiny, cold, furious eyes—projected onto the screen of his mind's eye.

It began to thrash and peck and kick. It hit with its fists at the back of his eyes as though it were trying to punch them out. It reached down with its back legs towards his heart to grasp it, to stop it beating.

And the one on his chest had him by the throat. It was digging its taloned fingers into the flesh, forcing his head ever further back, threatening to snap his spine.

Steve could do nothing about the two monkeys that were tearing him apart from within and without, but somehow he got his arm round Amanda's waist and lifted her off her feet. She would not, or could not, cooperate. She squirmed and twisted as he lurched towards the door with her under his right arm. She weighed next to nothing and her struggles were weak, but even so, Steve found he couldn't hold her. The monkey in his head, that seemed to be trying to hack its way out through his eye sockets, was blinding him. Also, it was affecting his balance. It somehow twisted his brain like a steering wheel, so he lost all sense of direction. It got to the point where he was unable to differentiate between up and down. The room seemed like a huge sphere that he was trapped in. Then he realised he no longer had hold of Amanda, and that he was falling. He thought he had walked off the edge of a cliff. The thing in his head gave a scream of triumph.

And something hit him in the belly, like a kick from a vast boot.

And then: Nothing!

Amanda swayed back as the dismembered head in the plastic shopping bag bounced off Steve's stomach. She had snatched the bag off the nail at the end of the bench and swung it at him hard, in desperation. There was no other weapon in the room she could have used except the electric saws, and she might have killed him with them. She wanted to, *had to*, keep him alive.

As Steve doubled forward, clutching his middle, Amanda swung the head again, battering Steve's own face with it. He slumped forward like a shot deer, and landed face down in the drain near the bench. She knelt down and tugged his right shoulder up, to twist his nose and mouth up out of the water. He mustn't drown. She checked that he was still breathing, then sat down next to him in the wet.

The creature in the next room was calling for food with its harsh, crass, rooklike call.

Amanda's monkey, which had jumped back off Steve and onto her when the boy had been trying to carry her away, sent a stab of pain down her spine, to urge her to make one last effort to get up and push the trolley through to its master. But Amanda couldn't even get to her feet. She was breathless, and all her energy was spent. Her monkey, that had known and preserved her for more than sixty years, understood, and allowed her a brief respite to regain some strength.

Amanda fumbled in her pockets, found a battered packet of cigarettes, stuck one in her mouth, and lit up. She drew as much smoke as she could into her diseased, rotten lungs, exulting in the self-damage she was doing, in the knowledge that her ruined, broken body could not take much more abuse. She knew the creature and its servants, the monkeys, would keep her going as long as she was at all useful to them, or until she fell apart.

As it was, she was only just able to get around on her legs, which contained so many badly mended broken bones, souvenirs of the of the years she herself had spent walking the "dog." Now, she was barely able to drive the van. The accident the night before had been her fault. She had been too weak and clumsy to control the vehicle. Anyone else would have been able to avoid the accident. Unfortunately, she had not been killed in the smash.

Anyway, soon, when his wrist had healed, Steve would be able to drive the van.

Then, presumably, she would not be needed. They would let her die.

The creature beyond the door croaked again impatiently.

She got to her feet, pushed Steve's unconscious body over onto its back, and flicked her cigarette end into the drain.

She looked down at the boy for a moment, then said aloud, "Congratulations Steve, you've been promoted. You'll have to advertise to get someone to replace you. You've got Stook's job. You're the hunter now. Tomorrow, the van will be repaired, and I'll have to drive you out to look for game. The creature will need fresh meat, and heaven help you if you don't come back with some."

Briefly it occurred to her that if Steve *was* unsuccessful, she might be on the menu herself.

Then her monkey gave her mind a tweak. She pushed the meat trolley to the door, and started to open the locks.

Blade and Bone

> **WORMHILL.** Within this manor were held the courts for the jurisdiction of the forest laws, within its boundaries were the lairs of those wolves so destructive to the forest animals; but which were the most ferocious, the wolves or the forest laws, is a matter of opinion. Animals sacred to the Norman Monarchs were the hart, hind, boar and wolf. To destroy one of them William I punished with loss of eyesight, Henry II with loss of limb, Rufus had made it a capitol offence, while Richard I devised a torture too barbarous for description.
>
> *Old Halls, Manors, and Families of Derbyshire.*
> J. TURNER. 1892.

With a feeling of release, like a slave casting off his chains, Ogden Minter flung his useless mountain bike against a low dry-stone wall and shrugged his head and arms out of his gaudy, child-size pink and purple backpack. Though there was little weight in this burden, the thin, tight straps had cut notches into the sides of his neck. A pool of sweat had formed under the bag between his shoulder blades, seeped down his spine, amassed in a trench round the line of his belt, and drained away into his shorts. He felt flooded.

He gave the punctured back tire of his hired machine a jaundiced glare. He remembered putting a repair kit into the pocket of his linen jacket before breakfast that morning and, an hour later, deciding a jacket would not be necessary that day after all.

Ogden began to wonder where he was. The countryside around looked particularly lush and succulent. To his left, a line of cottage-like dwellings stretched away at a right angle to the road. A few hundred yards further on he could see a couple of larger buildings, typical, in their austerity of design and structure, of hundreds he had seen in the Peak District during the last week. He pulled the bunch of documents his wife had insisted he take with him out of his backpack, and extracted a tattered yellow-covered O.S. map of the Peak District. Opening it on the ground at his feet, he crouched down to run his finger along the route he had so far covered. It appeared that the long, steep hill up which he had recently pushed his crippled bike had brought him to the edge of an area marked "Wormhill." His wife, he recalled, had suggested that the village may be of interest. He could not recall why exactly, but he thought she had mentioned the Domesday Book.

Carefully, he established his exact position from the map and peered into the landscape towards a quantity of trees (in itself an unusual sight in that particular area of the High Peak) among which the heart of the village supposedly lay concealed. He sorted through the folders of notes his wife had prepared in the months before their holiday until he came to a batch headed "BUXTON + ENVIRONS" from which he extracted some handwritten sheets collected together under the title "WORMHILL (etc.)"

He did this with no great enthusiasm, but with the air of a man doing his duty towards his spouse. Poppy, sadly, was unable to benefit from the painstaking work she had put into compiling the information he had before him. Their tour together had come to an end two days previously when his wife lost control of her bike while descending a steep path down the side of Lathkill Dale. She and her vehicle had tipped twenty feet into an old quarry, and she had broken an ankle in her subsequent collision with the ground.

Instead of ending their holiday early, as Ogden had suggested, Mrs. Minter had preferred to spend the final part of the week at the *Jem Arms*, a Hotel in Tideswell. There, presumably, she now sat, as he had left her, sunning herself on the patio, with her wounded leg propped on a bench in front of her. Meanwhile, Ogden visited the places of interest she had planned they should share together. It was, she had informed him, his mission to view, by proxy, on her behalf, the churches, historic buildings, and prehistoric sites that she herself had been so keen to inspect. It should be understood that Ogden did not find his wife's antiquarian obsessions nearly as fascinating as perhaps he led her to believe. His enthusiasm for the cultures of the past, never more than superficial, had declined noticeably. The ever-mobile pageant of history had marched on, leaving him stranded, but he had no regrets about its passing. He had lost interest in many things in recent years, including Poppy and her several hobbies, and felt none the worse for it. Nevertheless, he had his orders and, to keep the domestic peace, he would obey them. He rifled through the sheets in his hand to determine which local sites he was obliged to find and visit, remembering as he did so that Poppy would require photographic evidence of his pilgrimage, and that he would need to put film in the camera.

At the top of the first page he read:

> *Wyrma's Hill* (Old Eng.)—Wruenele (Domesday Book.): A doubtful tradition says the place was once called Wolfhill, from the many predatory wolves that here had their lair.
>
> *Principal families & individs*: Foljambes, John Le Wolfhunte, and Bagshaws (from 17th Cnt).
>
> *Church*: of St. Margaret of Antioch: built in 1273—little remains except part of tower, as it was rebuilt in 1864.
>
> *St. Margaret*: canonised form of Aphrodite Marina?—daughter of heathen priest, but brought up Christian by nurse against father's wishes. St. M. spurned advances of rich suitor and devoted herself to Christian virginity. Was subject to terrible tortures to make her change her mind. "Her bones were laid bare and the blood poured forth from her body as from a pure stream." Even so, still had the strength to beat the devil who, in the form of a huge dragon ['Aha, I thought there might be one of those involved somewhere," Ogden mused, relishing Poppy's taste for the macabre] swallowed her up, whereupon she caused his body to burst and ventured forth unharmed, except for injuries resulting from her previous torture. After this St. M. was drowned, beheaded, and burned. The most consistent attributes of St. M. are a dragon and a cross.

As he skimmed through his wife's notes Ogden was vaguely aware of a lowering of the temperature of the sunlight on his back and a corresponding decrease in the intensity of the light. He held the papers closer to his face, the better to read Poppy's tiny writing, and immediately three or four large crimson spots appeared on the top sheet with soft, damp puttering sounds.

"Good grief," he said aloud, "it's raining blood!"

He wiped his fingers across the glistening wet places in an exploratory gesture that turned the spots to red smears and, fumbling confusedly, knocked all the notes out of his grasp onto the grass at his feet. As they fell, a stiff crimson card slid out from among them. He realised that raindrops had turned the thin paper sheet he had been studying transparent where they struck, revealing beneath parts of the blood-red card that his wife had thoughtfully included for him to rest on whilst taking notes.

Then it began to rain very hard. Ogden looked upwards. A line of gritstone-grey cloud had sneaked up behind him. It hung above him like a steep, dark cliff, cutting away almost half of the blue summer sky. There was going to be a downpour.

And Poppy's notes were getting very wet. The ink on some of them had already started to run. He scooped them up hastily and looked about for shelter. The cottages he had noticed earlier were close. He might be able to tuck himself into a doorway.

He picked up his bicycle and ran.

He realised the cottages were uninhabited as soon as he reached them. Windows were boarded up, weeds possessed the gardens, and a chimney had toppled down through a roof. The front doors were flush with the walls and offered no protection. He found his way round to the back of the buildings and came upon a stone outbuilding with a door that looked forceable. Then he noticed someone had taken a great deal of trouble to fasten it. It had been sealed shut with a number of large screws. But this had been done a long time ago. The screw-heads were rusty, and the crude planks of wood that formed the door were clearly rotten.

The rain was now a torrent; a monsoon.

Ogden kicked the door at what he judged to be its weakest point and had the satisfaction of seeing the whole thing tear free of the batons that held it in place and swing round into the room beyond. He leapt in after it.

And received a powerful impression, as he entered, that, simultaneously, something made its exit. Something slender, sharp, and oddly-jointed, that burst free in a great hurry. Nothing had passed him through the door, he was sure of that; even so, the little room he found himself in had an air of having been recently, instantly vacated. He was as sure of this as he would have been if he had glimpsed a pair of heels vanishing in front of him, but, in fact, he had detected no actual movement other than that of a swirl of ochre wood-dust in the air around his feet caused by the sudden implosion of the door. He had experienced a vaguely unpleasant sensation, but one that left him more confused than alarmed, since it was over almost before it registered on his consciousness.

A window in the roof gave ample light for him to see that all the evidence indicated he was the first person to enter the place for a long time, however. The walls on three sides were covered with a wide variety of tools for wood and garden work, held in place by hooks, and positioned with scrupulous neatness. Many of their metal parts were edged with a scale of rust, suggesting they had once been infected with damp, though the air was now sharp and dry. All were cowled with ancient spider webs, but it was obvious that they had been kept in prime condition by the craftsman who had employed them, right up to the time of their disuse. They were not so much stored as displayed, and Ogden smiled to think of the obvious pride of their owner. He inspected them casually, brushing some of them free of webbing with his finger tips, as the rain pelted down on the window above him. He wondered about the craftsman who had used them. Dead now, no doubt, he thought; but it occurred to him that it was peculiar they had been left to spoil. Taken together, they could be quite valuable. And some of them looked rather old.

He came up short then, because he suddenly found himself contemplating some very strange tools indeed. If they were tools, in the normal sense! Occupying a space of their own, and isolated in a frame fixed to the wall, were a number of knifelike objects with curving blades and ornately carved handles. They were all quite free of rust. They were obviously part of an incomplete collection, as they had been set out in the form of a tapering cross, and there were three gaps where the missing weapons should have been.

Weapons?

Ogden imagined that was what they could have been, but like none he'd ever seen before. Some of them were very small and delicate. Who would use them? And in what circumstances? Perhaps they were ceremonial; for use in some ritualistic practise? He lifted one off its hook and laid it on his open hand, haft towards him. It was heavier than he expected. Out of balance, it turned on his palm so the blade spun round to point to his heart. It felt strange as it moved against his skin, almost like an animal, alive! And dangerous! The cutting edge was terribly fine and, he was sure, razor sharp.

After hastily replacing it among the others and looking at them all together, it occurred to him that they could be fragments of some quite large object that had somehow come to pieces. He shook his head. It seemed a fanciful notion.

Turning his attention to other items stored in the shed, some piles of old magazines caught his eye: something to read to pass the time until the rain stopped. He took an ancient, flaking periodical from the top of the nearest heap. It was a *Radio Times* from September 1952.

"Has this place been shut up that long?" he wondered. "Almost forty years?"

He found an article about Thomas Beecham, who was to conduct Delius on the Third Programme that week, and started to read.

He didn't notice when the rain stopped, but sunshine suddenly beamed halfheartedly down on him from the window and reached across the floor towards him through the gaping door.

Scrambling up, he retrieved Poppy's notes from a bench where he had dropped them, and sorted through them. They were stuck together with damp. Whole paragraphs were illegible where the ink had run, and the rain had trickled along the creases he had made when he had clumsily grabbed the sheets up after dropping them, obliterating odd words and lines here and there. The page on top, detailing facts about Wormhill Parish Church, looked as though it had been wiped with a sponge. He read:

> [Smudge] . . . "here the rectory garden and churchyard blend. . . [smear]. . . rarely does a modern village church possess that air of repose which often broods over an ancient sanctuary—but Wormhill possesses it. [Three lines missing]. . .oices of rooks calling in the trees surrounding Wormhill Hall." (Frith etc., writing as recently as 1920).

Not much to go on! Obviously Poppy had copied descriptive passages from old books to compare with contemporary reality; something that gave her particular pleasure when visiting new places. Such fragments of her notes as remained were next to useless now however. Ogden stuffed them in his backpack and decided to explore without their guidance.

As, pushing his bike, he descended towards the trees that concealed the church, a handful of farm buildings became visible, including one quite substantial dwelling set behind what could once have been a village green.

A self-important dog ran out and barked at him twice. It seemed disillusioned by the sight of him, and slunk away with a disappointed air. He saw no human inhabitant.

Opposite an old farmhouse a sign indicated that St. Margaret's Church could be found at the end of a wide path to his left. This brought him to a tiny wrought-iron gate that, closed, stood next to an open, and much wider, wooden one. Ogden took the trouble to negotiate the first of these entries, since the other, for some strange reason, looked much less inviting; even, in the slovenly way it gaped, like a hungry maw, sinister. The sun slipped free of the thickening clouds for a few seconds as he stepped into the churchyard, stretching black shadows out from the trees around him. A breeze, the first of the day, troubled the trees and gave them goose-flesh. They shivered, sighed, and then went still.

Ogden closed the gate behind him and, as he did so, saw and heard movement in the undergrowth that grew to the edge of the path ahead of him.

"That damned inquisitive dog," he thought, "come to take a second look."

This time the creature must have gone shy. It didn't show its face, though sunlight glistened in raindrops shaken from leaves as it blundered on through the wild bushes.

He thought the rain had started again: the trees above him were dripping with sullen deliberation. The dampness they deposited had a sticky feel and was slightly malodorous. He imagined caterpillars, eating the leaves overhead and mingling their bodies' outpourings with the rain. An unpleasant notion. He dug out the old, grey-plastic raincoat he used to protect himself from storms while cycling, draped it over him, pulled the hood up, and pressed a couple of the studs at the front to hold it in place. Then, looking suitably monkish, he ventured onto the holy ground. His first sight of the church almost made him laugh. The little Victorian building's squat tower was topped with a steep spirelike roof which, though picturesque, looked highly incongruous. Not at all to Poppy's taste. He could imagine her reaction if she had seen it and was relieved that she was not there to lecture him on the tenets of her religion: Architectural Fundamentalism. Even so, he thought he would take a snap of the building, to prove he'd been there. After ascertaining that the door to the church was locked he strolled out among the tombs, some of them unusual and impressive, in search of a vantage point from which to take his photograph. He had walked backwards almost to the very edge of the little graveyard, inserting film in his camera as he did so, when he heard a noise close behind him. He turned, and fell heavily into an overgrown pit about three-feet deep. He seemed to have been tripped by something emerging from this hollow. His camera arced up and away, out of his hand.

He was fit, active, and supple jointed, so took no harm from his tumble; nevertheless, at his age, it caused quite a shock to his system. He sat still for seconds, then crawled towards his expensive, possibly damaged camera. He'd almost reached it when he thought he saw movement in the tangled weeds ahead of him. The bloody dog again? Had it been that creature that had just tripped him on his back?

Then he realised his camera had landed in nettles that half-concealed what he first took be part of a tomb, the visible section of which had been carved to represent a cluster of human bones: arm bones, leg bones, ribs, vertebrae, all jumbled together.

As he pressed forward for a closer look, the screen of nettles quivered and parted.

Out from behind them the fleshless fragments of three fingers and a thumb, clutching some kind of knife, stretched towards him with the persistence of a hand held out for alms.

And rose up swiftly towards his face.

But they didn't move as fast as Ogden, who rose up very swiftly, and ran like hell. No cripple, cured at last by a miracle, ever flung himself into action so completely as Ogden Minter did then. His mind blanked out briefly, and consciousness only returned when, mere seconds later, he found himself racing out of the path that led from St. Margaret's, and onto the road that led out of Wormhill. Opposite, a man was walking towards him through a garden at the front of a large house. The fellow was watching him with alarm and concern. Suddenly, aware that he was making a spectacle of himself, Ogden stopped running and tried to calm down. He was drenched with sweat in his plastic coat. He pulled the hood back off his head and, as he did so, the clouds above him burst and rain machine-gunned down around him.

The man who had been observing him took fright at the downpour and retreated into the building behind him. As he went he pointed to a sign on the path outside an open door:

Tea, Coffee, Snacks. Homemade Food.

Hardly able to believe his luck, Ogden ran into the house and found himself in a comfortable, well-appointed tearoom. The walls were covered with photographs and other relics of Wormhill's past. The old farmhouse had been partly converted into a cozy museum. A large, smiling woman, who seemed the personification of kindly concern, took his dripping coat and hung it to dry. From the menu she handed him he selected tea, an egg and bacon sandwich (comfort food: he secretly lusted after cholesterol), and cake, which the beaming woman went to fetch.

So sudden had been his transference from a plane of terror to one of deep domestic peace that Ogden sat gaping gawkishly for some time, like a toddler in a toffee shop.

Then someone said, "You gave me a bit of a shock just now."

Ogden turned and saw, sitting in a dark corner, the man who had been in the front garden. "I did? I'm very sorry."

The man shrugged. "Not your fault. Reminded me of something, that's all."

Ogden said, "Ah," not too encouragingly.

"Took me back a few years," the man observed. "Seeing you running towards me in that coat did it."

Ogden felt he had been offered bait, but did not rise to it. He hoped the man wasn't an obsessive chatterbox; people who dwell in tiny villages tend to be.

"Been having a look at the church have you?" the man persisted. "Nice spot. Peaceful. Got a charm of its own."

Unable to concur, Ogden felt obliged to say something.

"Peculiar place; I've never seen anything quite like it."

"It's a one-off, that's for sure. Interested in churches, are you? I could tell you stories about St. Margaret's that never got written down in books, and for very good reasons too."

Ogden took the man to be hinting at local legends, a topic his wife had an insatiable interest in. In spite of a continuing sense of disorientation, he found himself responding to his interlocutor. If nothing else, he could take Poppy back a folk tale as a souvenir of his day in Wormhill. He pursed his lips and raised his brow in an expression of mild curiosity; a strong enough signal to his companion, who continued: "For instance, there's a tale that back in the thirteenth century someone brought a relic of St. Margaret of Antioch here to Wormhill. Some say it was a cross; some say a sword. You know about our Saint, perhaps?"

Ogden nodded. "A little. Had a nasty boyfriend who cut her up because she wouldn't relinquish her religion and her virginity. Eaten by a dragon, wasn't she?"

"By the Devil himself in that form, yes. She got free though, either by the power of a cross she wore, which somehow caused the dragon's breast to burst open, or by flourishing her pagan father's sword and slashing her way free through the creatures belly: opinions vary. Anyway, a sword is very like a cross when held by the blade and, be it ever so sharp, probably wouldn't cut the fingers of a bona fide Saint."

Ogden smiled politely at this conceit and turned his attention to the excellent food the woman was placing before him. When she had gone, the man, who spoke with a local accent, but who Ogden had no trouble understanding, resumed his yarn.

"Whichever it was she used, sword or cross, it somehow turned up here at Wormhill, where it became an object of veneration. It performed miracles by the dozen. Under its influence the community prospered, became influential and, inevitably, corrupt. People abused the power of the relic to such extent that, in the end, on her name day, when the population was gathered on the village green to celebrate (in an inappropriately riotous way), St. Margaret herself stepped down out of the sky onto the street, in full view of everyone. She strode into the church, took up the relic, held it high above her head, and smashed it to pieces on a stone gatepost at the entrance of the graveyard. Then she vanished. She hasn't been back since."

The man fell silent for a while. Leaning back, with his eyes almost shut, he had the air of one recollecting distant events in present tranquillity. Then he stirred himself and continued, "The fragments of the relic were gathered up by one Peter Comfrey, who had served old Sir Godfrey Foljambe, the last in line of the most powerful family in the district at that time. Those fragments had their uses. Whatever the cross (or sword) had been made of, the fragments, sharpened, provided fine blades that did not ever blunt. Peter Comfrey and his son, Howard, earned a reputation locally for chirurgery, and made a poor living plying these tools. But they never throve so well in later years as they had done in the service of the Foljambe family.

"At that time Wormhill was part of the Royal Forest, and governed by harsh laws going back to the time of Richard the First. The preservation of the Royal Game for hunting was paramount. Punishments for poaching or even harming the creatures of the Forest were terrible beyond description. The wolves were culled annually, after their young were born, but were treated as almost sacred for the rest of the year.

"One day a man, a forester himself, was found by his companions standing over the dead body of a male wolf. There was blood on his shirt and the point of his hunting knife was in the beast's heart. He told some tale about coming across an intruder who he suspected was out poaching. When challenged, the felon tried to run off, but the forester, after shouting to his fellows for help, soon caught him . There was a short, hard fight that ended when the King's man drove his knife into the breast of the interloper, who was savagely biting his upper arm. It was then, according to the forester, that he looked down and discovered the corpse of a huge wolf at his feet, with his blade between its ribs. The body of the poacher had vanished.

"Those the forester had summoned to his assistance heard his story, then took him to their master, John Le Wolfhunte, who, after questioning him, had the man's shirt torn off to reveal, on his arm, the unmistakable tooth-marks of a wolf. The forester was declared guilty of the wilful slaughter of the King's Game, and sentenced to death by torture.

"Le Wolfhunte was outraged at his employee's flagrant criminality, and sorely provoked by his stubborn refusal to admit his guilt. He decided to make an example of him. Instead of employing the crude craft of his personal torturer to inflict the proscribed punishment, he summoned Howard Comfrey to him, with his blades and tools, and ordered him to use his chirurgeon's art and knowledge to prolong and intensify the death agony of the accused man. Also, Le Wolfhunte wanted the satisfaction of hearing the man retract the story that had demoralised his simple, superstitious foresters.

"Howard Comfrey was instructed to remove those parts of the accused that were not essential to his existence, slowly, one by one. It was not work he relished, but to decline to undertake it would have meant his death, so he decided to take the opportunity to demonstrate his skills, knowing he would be generously rewarded for a job well done. He managed to stretch the process over three weeks, to the gratification of John Le Wolfhunte, who had the wolf-slayer's jointed limbs and other parts hung above his head for his entertainment and his victim's instruction.

"But the man didn't change his story, up to the time of his death.

"His various parts were buried together in a place a good distance from the churchyard, and without ceremony.

"The fee paid to Howard for the satisfactory completion of his task was the last sizable sum that ever fell into the hands of a Comfrey. Each subsequent generation fell a little lower than that preceding it. Local people were reluctant to go to the descendants of a torturer for help when they were sick. The Comfreys became pariahs and turned from cutting flesh to carving stone and joining wood. That they were able to survive at all was due to the tools they used which, made from parts of the relic of Margaret of Antioch, gave such quality to their work as was hard to find elsewhere. But they were never liked, and often loathed, in the community."

The man paused again, and turned to Ogden, presumably to ensure he still had his attention. Ogden, who had been making a few notes to pass on to Poppy as the tale unravelled, smiled his approval. "Very interesting," he said, "and. . . quaint. The Comfreys died out long since, I suppose?"

The man shook his head. "Somehow, they hung on into this century. The last male, Nev Comfrey, died in the early fifties, and a terrible end he had too."

Ogden poured himself a third cup of tea and sank deeper into his chair. He was feeling pleasantly relaxed now, and was glad the continuation of his companion's narrative gave him an excuse to remain where he was. Outside, the rain had stopped, but he was in no hurry to continue his tour of inspection.

"Nev Comfrey's wife told me some of what happened, a few days before she died," the man continued.

(Ogden took no more notes. This was recent history, not legend, and would have little appeal to Poppy).

"Nev, though a fool, was a fine craftsman, but no good with money. He did wonderful work with stone and wood, but didn't know its worth. People paid him a pittance; in kind, more often than not, and, as a result, he and his wife were slim as scarecrows, and dressed in rags. Nev wore the same old grey gabardine coat, a good few sizes too big for him, for years. In winter, he belted it with string; in summer, it flapped round him like a badly pitched tent. He looked a tramp, and people took advantage of him, but he had their respect, because he was sexton to the parish, kept the churchyard neat, and dug a deep, straight grave. And it was to do with that work that he got in trouble.

"He was digging one day in his own garden when he found bones. A man's bones. He called his wife to see them. Later, she told me they were all mixed up; not laid out end to end, like the remains of the decent dead.

The two of them talked it over, and Nev put the lot in a sack, took them to the graveyard, then, when nobody was about, gave them what he thought was a Christian burial. He spent the rest of the day weeding and cutting grass on graves, and clipping back the ivy on the walls. He worked well into the evening.

"It was a beautiful evening; I know because I was sitting on the wall outside this very building, looking down the path towards the church, and thinking what a grand end we were having to the day.

"Then I saw Nev running out the churchyard gate very fast. Just like you were when I saw you today. You reminded me of him, with your plastic mac swirling round you. You looked the image of Nev, blustering towards me in his old gabardine."

Ogden sat up straight in his chair with a jerk, as though he had been woken from sleep by a shout. His surroundings no longer looked comforting. He didn't want to hear any more of the story, or stay where he was, but felt too weak to get out of his chair.

The man's voice droned inevitably on.

"I shouted to Nev, asking what was the matter; but he didn't stop. I watched him go up the street to his house—"

"Where did he live?" Ogden interrupted urgently.

The man pointed. "Up there. One of a row of cottages. You'll have passed them on your left, if you came in from Tideswell. His family had lived there for generations, though I don't suppose he was aware of it. They got the land cheap two hundred years ago. No one wanted it because of the uses it had been put to, and the things that were supposed to be buried there. But, as I say, Nev new nothing about that."

He shook his head and looked down at his knees. "That was the last I saw of Nev. His wife said they heard something rattling the latch on the back door in the early hours of the next morning. Nev went down to investigate. He was found two days later. Six miles away. In the middle of a field. He'd been cut to pieces; taken apart. The corpse looked like someone who'd fallen into a harvester, they said. As did his wife's body, when they found her. She went missing within a week."

The man put his fingertips together, pressed them against his lips, and peered at Ogden, who snatched up his cup and drained it. He managed to get to his feet. He realised he had not paid for what he had eaten and shouted for his bill.

"Going," the man observed, rather than asked. Then continued, "Those cottages were a bad place to live from then on. Bad things happened to anyone who lived there. One by one, the inhabitants moved out, and nobody else fancied taking them over. And there were... incidents in the village: some quite nasty. I don't know who's idea it was, but one day the local men went to the cottages and boarded them up, after smashing the insides to make them uninhabitable. They took particular care to shut up a stone shed in old Nev's back garden, for some reason.

"Since then, we've had no trouble," the man said. "Not for forty years, we haven't," he added, wistfully.

Ogden could think of nothing to say. He put his hand over his eyes, and shook his head.

The woman returned and Ogden paid her. She looked around the room.

"Are you on your own?" she said. "I thought I heard talking. I thought I had another customer!"

Ogden glanced round and realised the storyteller had gone. "There was a man sitting there," he said, gesturing towards an empty table. "I thought perhaps he was your husband."

"What did he look like?"

Ogden gave a brief description.

"Oh." The woman laughed for some reason. "You've been talking to him have you?

"Hmm. Local chap, is he?"

"Definitely."

"Lived here a long time, I expect?" Ogden said, folding his mac into a tight roll and hurriedly stuffing it into his backpack. "Seems to know a lot about the village."

"Good heavens, yes," the woman confirmed. "He's been around here for... well—ages."

And she laughed again.

Ogden stumbled out of the building and back onto the road. His bike was leaning against a metal rail alongside the path to the church. He hauled the machine upright, and ran with it back the way he had come. When he got to the top of the hill that led out of the village, he slid onto the saddle and free-wheeled down and away, hardly aware of his flat tire. He dropped like a stone out of Wormhill for half a mile, to a bridge across the dried up stream that cut through Monk's Dale, then he hurtled onto the hill that ramped up to the back edge of Tideswell.

He began to find his progress rather slow. The ascent to his destination was, he remembered, long and steep. And the condition of his bike made peddling remarkably difficult. The sun was blazing down again out of a cloudless sky and he felt the heat like an added burden on his back. In spite of his best efforts, the machine almost came to a standstill on a sharp incline, after climbing a couple of hundred yards. Although he had come a long way in a short time, something nagged at his mind, telling him he had not put enough space between himself and Wormhill. He had a sensation that something was reaching out to him from that village; something that was gaining on him.

He jumped off the bike, looked behind him down the empty road, then started to run, pushing the machine along by his side.

Ogden was a healthy man, the fittest sixty-three-year-old he knew, who had run marathons in recent years, but, even so, his energy soon began to flag. He wasn't able to choose his pace to preserve his strength, and felt himself burning up inside. He caught his right ankle against a spinning peddle and fell sideways on top of his machine. That hurt. He decided to ditch the bike, to hide it, and to get someone to come and collect it later. There was a gate in the wall at the side of the road close by. He humped the bike over, clambered after it, and moved it into a position out of sight from the road.

Again, he looked back, this time across Monk's Dale to where he imagined Wormhill lay.

And saw, at the far side of the field he was in, some creature loping towards him. It was a dirty, off-white colour, and moved with a peculiar, disjointed gait. Ogden tried to think it was a dog, but part of his mind insisted on seeing whatever it was as a thin, almost human shape, running on all fours. Though awkward in motion, it was making good progress.

Sunlight flashed on some bright objects it held in its jaws. Ogden blundered backwards and somehow got himself over the gate and onto the road again.

He ran the mile or more up the hill to Tideswell remarkably quickly.

Poppy Minter, out sunning herself again since the rain had stopped, was wearing her reading glasses when Ogden burst through the gate at the rear of the *Jem Arms* and slammed it shut behind him. She closed her book, rested it on her knee, and squinted at her husband. She knew it was him from his shape and the colour of his shirt, but she could not see his expression. Nevertheless, she was immediately aware that something was not quite right with her spouse, if only because he was moving with uncharacteristic speed. He fairly pelted across the lawn towards her.

"Oggy," she said, "I didn't expect you back for hours. Was your expedition a success? Did you bring back anything interesting?" But, to Poppy's surprise, Ogden didn't stop to chat. As he ran across the patio into the hotel, he astonished her by saying, "We're going. At once. No time to pack. We'll have our stuff sent on. I'll settle the bill. Get the car round to the front."

"How rude," thought Poppy.

Very occasionally, Ogden had a liquid lunch. Drink made a beast of him. Poppy decided she would ignore him. She would continue her book.

Moments later, her reading was interrupted by the sound of the gate opening again. Another guest returning! She hoped it was someone who would stop to talk.

She hated to admit it, but it had been a long and lonely day.

Ogden had his wallet open and a wad of notes in his hand, and had almost reached the reception desk when he heard a noise, like the squeal of brakes, that quickly modulated to a more human tone, then became, just recognisably, the voice of his wife. Her sharp, thin scream was suddenly cut short, leaving a silence that seemed much louder.

For a moment Ogden found himself wondering why the hell she had not done as he had told her, and followed him through the hotel to fetch their car. Then he remembered she had a broken ankle, and could not move from where she sat without assistance.

He ran back out onto the patio and saw at once what had been done to her. He did not have long to dwell on this horror, however.

Within seconds, his legs were cut from under him.

The Break

Instead of getting undressed straight away, as Gran had told him to, Danny pulled aside one of the curtains she had drawn together and peered out again at the jetty, on the edge of the harbour to the right of him, to see what the men on the boat were doing. The little craft, a fishing smack, had docked five minutes earlier, and he had watched with admiration as the men aboard had maneuvered it into place as easily as if they were parking a car. The sky was getting darker and the sea was flat, black and shiny, except for the white lace of tiny waves tacked along the edge of the beach. He could no longer make out the shape of the hull of the vessel, but the jetty was built of pale, slightly yellow stone against which he could see, in silhouette, the top of the boat and the activities of the two sailors on board.

They had pulled a cumbersome object, a box of some kind, up from the deck with a winch operated by a third man, above them on the jetty. He had been waiting for them, staring out to sea, for some time before they had arrived. Danny had asked his Gran to open the top window because it was an oppressively warm evening and the hotel room had a flat, earthy smell, like the inside of a greenhouse in winter. Through it he could hear the rattle of the hoist's cranking chain as the box lurched into the air, and the barking shouts of the man operating it. He was a very big man, dressed in heavy, unseasonable garments that made him look like a bear. He moved like a bear as well, Danny thought, with rolling, lunging motions, and seemed to have trouble keeping his balance.

When the box rose to the level of his shoulders the man pulled it round with a rope attached to the top of the hoist, then slowly lowered it onto the jetty. It must have slipped its chains at the last moment because Danny saw it suddenly drop a few inches, and heard it land with a sound that made him think it was very heavy, and made of wood. The bearlike man walked round it quickly, inspecting it, then shouted sharply down to the others on the boat. At once, a light came on in the cabin at the front of the smack. The engine started clunking, the third man cast off the ropes, and the vessel curved away out into the bay beyond, leaving a widening ark of crumpled tinfoil foam in its wake.

"Danny; please; it's so late, and you've not even got into your pyjamas!"

Gran didn't seem at all cross, as his mother would have been, but she sounded strained and disappointed in him. Danny hadn't heard her come in, but she always moved like that; so quietly and carefully, like a phantom. He dropped the edge of the curtain and, feeling slightly ashamed of himself, took the tray bearing a mug of chocolate and some toast she had brought him for supper, and set it down on the table beside his bed.

"I'm not tired, Gran," he lied, then yawned hugely, giving the game away. "I was watching the sea," he explained, somewhat inaccurately.

"You've got all week for that," Gran said, folding a triangle of quilt tidily back away from his pillow to display how temptingly comfortable the bed beneath it looked.

Danny said, "I like the boats. There's hundreds in the harbour. Will we be able to go for a trip on one?"

"I can't take Grandad, and I mustn't leave him behind, but perhaps you could go on your own, if I think it's safe."

"Is Grandad ill?" Danny asked, plugging the sink and twisting the taps to run water for his evening wash. When Gran didn't answer he turned back to her and added, "He looks all right. I can't *see* anything wrong with him."

"He's not exactly ill, like you were last winter, with your chest; it's just that, recently, he's got a bit. . . forgetful."

"Yes," Danny agreed, "I've noticed that," and saw his Gran's face darken. "I mean, sometimes, he looks at me as though he doesn't know who I am. When I met you both at the station, and you left me with him and went to get a magazine, he asked me what my name was."

"Oh dear," said Gran, poking nervously at the grey curl that dangled down over her right eye, "did he really?"

"Then, when I told him, he just shook his head, as though he'd never heard of me."

"I'm sorry."

"It's not your fault," Danny said generously. "He got my name right later." He began to brush his teeth.

Pleased to be presented with this enforced curtailment of the conversation, when she had been thinking how she could change the subject without arousing in Danny an alarming suspicion that her husband was worse than he really was, Gran decided to make an exit.

"Breakfast is at eight thirty," she said, after kissing Danny goodnight on the top of his head.

"Can I go on my own, or must I wait for you?"

"No, you're big enough now to make your own way down, I think."

"Of course I am," Danny agreed. "I was last year, when we went to Brighton, but you wouldn't believe me."

Gran smiled, but she didn't seem to agree with him. "Into bed now, Danny," she insisted. "I'll look in soon to make sure you're asleep."

When she had gone Danny sipped the chocolate and pulled a face. It didn't taste anything like it did at home, when his mother made it. He poured the drink down the sink, ate the toast quickly, got into his pyjamas, then could not resist taking one more peep out the window before getting into bed. The man on the jetty was still there. He was pushing the big heavy box towards the shore with great difficulty. He was bending behind it, almost on all fours, looking more than ever like a fat black bear. Although obviously pushing with all his strength, he was only managing to move it inches at a time. After two or three strenuous efforts he stopped, leaned against the box as though exhausted, then strained to shove it a couple of times more. It made a harsh crunching sound as it moved, as if it was sliding across a surface scattered with broken glass. The box was still only a few feet from where it had landed. At that rate, Danny thought, it would take the man all night to reach the end of the jetty!

He could hear the box sliding and grinding along every now and then as he lay in bed, but it didn't sound as if it was getting any nearer. He felt sorry for the man. Why didn't he get someone to help him? He had looked somehow very lonely out there, and the way he had spoken to the men on the fishing boat, and they to him, had not sounded at all friendly. It occurred to Danny that it was likely that the man was not nice to know, and had no friends.

When Gran peeped in, twenty minutes later, she could tell from his breathing that he was asleep. She was closing the door again when she heard the sound of the huge box being moved outside, and went to the window. By mistake, she had only brought her reading glasses on holiday with her, but was just able to see what Danny had seen and, like him, watched and speculated about the man on the jetty. At that moment he was leaning on the far edge of the box and his white blob of a face was looking up towards the hotel, or seemed to be. He remained in this pose for only a few moments, then suddenly bent down, shuffled his legs back a little, and began to push. His body appeared to compress as he increased his effort; then, though Gran's faulty vision could detect no movement, the box grated on the stone surface of the jetty as it jerked a few inches closer, and the figure behind it elongated. This happened three times; then the man stood up, stretched his back, arced his arms above his head, and glanced up towards hotel again.

Gran stepped away from the window and closed her eyes for a moment as a harsh, cold light shone in on her. She realised it was the headlights of a car turning off the promenade, up into the town. She suddenly felt an unexpected evening breeze from somewhere, that made the edges of the curtains flutter, and caused her to twitch and clench her teeth and shudder.

Because of that, and because she didn't want Danny woken up by any noise, she shut the window before she left the room.

Someone knocked on the door. Danny opened his eyes, registered the dim daylight beyond the curtains, and waited. Gran never needed inviting. When, after a static silence, whoever it was knocked again, Danny sat up and called, "Come in." A young woman in a pale blue overall stepped sideways into the room. Still holding the door handle she showed him a sketch of a smile and said, "G' morning. Tea or coffee?"

Danny had not been expecting this. Hotels he had stayed in in the past had provided equipment for guests to make their own refreshments. He asked for tea and, while the girl was busy at a trolley he could see parked on the corridor outside, hauled himself up out of the last few yards of sleep, feeling obscurely embarrassed and slightly irritated.

The girl placed the tea by his bed and gave it an extra stir. She said, "Sleep well?" in a distant sort of way.

"Mmm; yes; very, thank you."

"Good," the girl acknowledged, and bent down over him and began fussing with his pillow. Danny made some effort to sit up. The girl must have thought he was having difficulty doing so, as she reached behind his head with her right hand and supported the upper part of his back. It was a gentle, helpful movement, but Danny didn't like it. The girl's fingers were thin and hard against his spine and there was something investigative about the way she touched him that made him uneasy, as though she was literally weighing him up, and testing the quality of the flesh beneath his pyjamas. He reared up away from her hand and shook his shoulders. The girls thumb and fingers rested for a moment on the top of his arm, almost squeezing, before she turned away to open the curtains with a flourish, revealing rain-spotted windows and, beyond, the grimy grey sky of the disappointing day outside. "They say it will clear up later," the girl assured him, and the edgy smile shifted briefly across her face again. Danny couldn't understand why he didn't like her. There was nothing about her looks to upset him; she had a sharp, but almost pretty face, and she was obviously trying to be nice. She couldn't help having hard, bony fingers.

After she had gone Danny snuggled down into the bed again until he remembered the man on the jetty the night before. He played a game in his mind, laying bets with himself about how far the man had moved the box. In the end he decided there would be no sign of it. Someone would have been to collect it, and taken it away. He hopped out of bed to check, and saw the box still on the jetty, not far from where he had last seen it. A large sheet of dark green tarpaulin, tied in place with a strand of rope, had been draped over it. A puddle of rain had formed on top of it. There was no sign of the man. The jetty was otherwise empty.

Danny found that if he stood on tiptoe he could just see over the roofs of the hotels on the street below him onto the beach to the left of the jetty. It too was deserted now, except for piles of deckchairs and a solitary dog, jumping and jerking in the foam at the waters edge, tugging savagely at something, probably a strand of black seaweed, that glistened like a hank of wet, soapy human hair. From time to time the dog dropped the weed, held up its head, and snapped its jaws open and shut. Realising his window had been closed, because he couldn't hear the creature barking, Danny climbed onto the sill and opened it. Cold damp air straight off the sea surged into the room. He could hear the sloshing breakers of the turning tide, slightly baffled by the veils of wind-blown rain that were sweeping across the town, and the urgent, worried yapping of the dog, sounding much further off than it really was.

He washed, dressed quickly in a new t-shirt and jeans, and set out to find the dining room. The hotel was full of the smell of breakfast, and he hoped he could find his food by following his nose. He soon took a wrong turning, however, and wandered into a half-lit, grey-painted room full of wheelchairs and pale-blue, uncomfortable looking furniture. There was a large mural on the wall depicting, in faded primary colours, what he thought must be heaven, with naked sexless angels leading stooping elderly humans, in white togas, through an English rural landscape, drawn in such a way as to suggest a vast perspective. At the top of the picture other angels, with tiny golden wings, flew through the sky, pulling strings of smiling old people along behind them. Yet more of the heavenly hosts, playing musical instruments, rested on cotton wool clouds beneath a beneficent, smirking sun, while a multitude of ancient mortals hovered around them, listening to their concert with obvious gratitude and appreciation.

At first Danny thought he was alone in the room, then he noticed, scattered along the walls, a number of elderly people, seemingly asleep in their seats and wheelchairs. They were lolling sideways, backwards, or forward, like inanimate puppets. One old man, his liver-spotted head quite bald on top, with an aura of pearly curls of unbrushed hair stretching up from the back of his neck to above his ears like coral or fungus, lay stretched out face down on the table in front of him.

Danny, chilled by the atmosphere of the room, froze on the spot for a few moments. Nobody moved, or showed in any way they were aware he was there, until a voice to his left called out, "Nurse! Is it you? Can you prop me up? My cushion slipped; I've lost it."

Danny turned towards the sound and saw an incredibly thin old lady leaning at a sharp angle out of a wheelchair. She was resting on one arm, with her elbow in her lap, and stretching so far forward, she seemed to defy gravity. Her other arm dangled, limp as a bell rope, by her side. She had had to lift her head right back to see him, and her toothless mouth hung open wide, as dark inside as a railway tunnel. A pair of red-rimmed glasses rested slightly askew on her nose. Behind them, it seemed, her eyes were shut.

At the sound of her voice some of the other old people began to stir. A man's tremulous voice called out insistently, "I'm hungry." Someone started to cough and spit, another to moan, as though suddenly in pain, and a woman protested tiredly, "Mrs. Grange has wet herself again. When are you going to do something about her?"

Danny stared at the floor below the person closest to the old lady who had spoken last, and saw, under her chair, a dark stain on the carpet. The woman who had complained that she had lost her cushion repeated her plea for help, now sounding cross. Danny moved towards her and must have stepped into her line of vision because she said fiercely, "Who are you? You're just a boy! Are they sending children, now, to look after us?"

Danny snatched up the cushion and thrust it towards the woman, who whined, "That's no good to me, unless you pick me up and pull me back. Can't you see that if it wasn't for the strap, I'd have fallen on my face? You can't leave me like this; I can hardly breath," and her voice died away, as though she were indeed expiring. Danny saw she was held in place by a thick white belt tied tight round her waist and the back of her chair. She was so thin, the belt buckle on her stomach was only a couple of inches from the fabric of the chair against her spine. Danny placed his hand on the top of her chest, which felt like a bird cage under his palms, and tried to push her upright, but he was not tall enough, and must have done something painful, because she gave a shriek and shouted, "What are you doing, child? What are you doing? Let go, for God's sake; your *hurting* me." Some of the other old people started to shout abuse at him then, and he felt his eyes flood and his throat constrict, and knew he was going to cry.

A man's voice, coming from just behind Danny, said, "What's the matter, Betty? You *are* making a fuss. The young gentleman is only trying to help."

The scrawny woman said, "Where have you been, Kelvin? Where's our breakfast? You're ever so late."

"No I'm not," the man said. "I'm just on time."

"You're a bloody liar," the woman suggested peevishly. "What do you mean by sending bits of kids to look after us?"

"He's not on the staff, Betty, he's a guest," the man explained, easily hauling the woman upright and adjusting her limbs so she sat in a comfortable, balanced position.

"Then why is he here? This is no place for kids."

"I don't know." The man, who was dressed in a white jacket, like the Chinese who worked in Danny's local chip shop wore, gave him a curious, slightly angry look that was only partly disguised by the shadow of a smile he managed to force across his face. He had a bony, narrow head, with dark hair brushed back tight against his scalp, and a large nose under which sprouted a walrus moustache. His smile reminded Danny of the girl who had brought him tea half an hour earlier, who had also seemed to find it hard to form her features into a good-humoured expression for more than a second. "I expect he's got lost," the man continued. "Is that right, young man?"

Danny, choking back tears, wiped his fingers under his nose and nodded.

"I expect you were looking for the dining room?"

Danny didn't stop nodding.

"This is the Twilight Lounge. The room you want is on the floor below. You should have kept on walking, down another flight of stairs."

The man clasped Danny's shoulder unnecessarily hard and steered him out of the door. Two or three of the old people shouted, "Nurse, nurse!" in protest at being left alone again. "Back in a tick," the man yelled, with an edge of irritation. His voice was so loud, Danny looked up at him, startled. Noticing this the man explained, in a more moderate tone, "They're deaf, sonny; most of them are deaf," and led Danny to the top of the stairs and pointed the way to the dining room.

Danny, no longer crying, and bursting with curiosity now, said, "Those old people back there; they thought you were a nurse, didn't they?"

"That's what I am."

"But this is a hotel, not a hospital!"

"It's a bit of both," the man said, after a short pause.

"Oh," Danny said, totally confused.

Back in the lounge the old people were cackling and calling for Kelvin, who gave Danny a horrible wink, that briefly distorted the whole of one side of his face, then retreated to join them. A portly woman pushed a heated trolley reeking of bacon out of the lift and across the corridor into the Twilight Lounge. She was greeted with a tiny, ironic ovation from the residents.

Danny ran down to the dining room, which was almost empty. He had left his room at exactly eight thirty, and the incident in the lounge had only lasted two or three minutes. He sat alone at a table close to a rain-flecked window that looked out to sea. He could see the box on the jetty, and, through a gap between two of the buildings below, a slice of the promenade and the beach beyond. The box looked bigger and somehow heavier from the lower level. The wind blew up under the tarpaulin draped across it, causing the hanging sides of the covering to flap mournfully. It looked as though someone inside the box was reaching about through holes in the sides with their hands, trying to find some way out.

When, fifteen minutes later, Gran and Grandad came to join him, Danny had almost finished breakfast. He wondered if he should have waited and eaten with them, but Gran said nothing about that. Perhaps she hadn't noticed; she had a preoccupied, anxious look on her face that Danny was getting used to seeing there. She kept half an eye on Grandad all the time, was aware of every move he made, and turned to give him her full attention whenever he spoke. Something about the way she treated her husband made Danny feel quite grown up, as though he and Grandad had changed places. The room filled up with old people. Danny looked out for anyone his age, but there was only one girl, a couple of years older and four inches taller than him, who pulled a tight face when he smiled at her, and didn't look up from her plate again. When Grandad had finished eating he asked Gran what day it was. She told him Sunday, but a little later he asked the same question and, when she tried to get him to remember the answer she had given him earlier, he said he hadn't asked her before, and if she didn't know what day it was, why didn't she just admit it? Gran put her hand on his arm and, very quietly, said she *had* told him, and not long ago. Grandad insisted she hadn't, in a high, strange voice, and Danny thought he looked worried, even frightened. A waitress came to clear the table and Grandad said to her, "My wife has forgotten what day it is; perhaps you can enlighten her?"

The girl arched her eyebrows, looked from Grandad to Gran and back, and tried to smile.

"Why is it nobody at this place can smile for more than a second?" Danny thought, and for the first time began to wonder if he was going to enjoy the holiday.

The girl looked unsure of how to respond to Grandad's request for such basic information, hoping, but doubting, it was a joke. To avoid her embarrassment, Danny looked out of the window, towards the box on the jetty. A big bird was standing on top of it. As Danny watched the bird started strutting backwards and forwards, half-opening and closing its long, slender wings. It was just some kind of gull, Danny supposed; it was that sort of shape, but he had no idea they could grow so big, and he had never seen one that dark before. Perhaps it had been caught in an oil slick? Suddenly, it launched itself off the edge of the box and soared into the sky.

Danny turned back to the table when the waitress said, "It's Sunday, of course; all day."

Grandad said, "Thank you very much," and gave Gran a silly, mocking shake of his head.

Anger, embarrassment, and some other indefinable pain registered on Gran's face. She got to her feet. As she did so, Grandad automatically rose from his chair, only more slowly, with less agility.

Danny jumped up to help him. "What are we going to do today?" he said. "It's raining. Do we have to stay in?"

"*We* will," Gran said, "for now. But you can go for a walk, to explore, if you want to."

"Definitely," Danny said. "It's *boring* here."

Gran gave him the first real smile he had received all day. "Don't catch cold though, and ruin your holiday."

"No problem; I'll be all right."

As Danny moved round the table to follow his grandparents, something moved out of the grey clouds beyond the window beside him, and descended towards him. The oversized gull he had seen landed on the balcony a yard from the window. It folded its wings with an air of deliberation and craned its neck. It turned sideways on awkward, stumbling feet; cocked its head at an angle; and stared at Danny down one side of its beak. The beak was grimy yellow, like a heavy smoker's teeth. The bird stretched forward and screamed, as though announcing its presence, then stood motionless, watching him. It was at least four times as big as any gull Danny had seen before, and he thought he had been right about the oil slick, because its inky plumage had a glossy sheen, like the wet tarpaulin on the box it had been standing on when he had first noticed it.

"*Danny*!"

Gran's voice. She and Grandad were waiting for him at the door. Everyone in the room turned towards him. "They're all so *old*," he thought.

He knew Todley Bay was popular with elderly people, and owed its reputation to what it had to offer that age group; his mother had told him all that weeks ago, and explained that the holiday was intended as a break for Gran and Grandad, and that he had to be on his best behaviour all the time, and not give them any worries, so he knew the resort would be their sort of place, with probably not much going for kids; but he had not expected to see so *many* old people. Most of them looked really ancient. There was hardly anyone in the room under, what? He wildly guessed—seventy?—eighty?

Except for the waitresses, and the girl he had noticed, he was the only young person present. He looked for the girl again, and saw she was watching him, like the others. She gave him a withering look that actually made him shudder. There was something about her, he decided, that set her among the old people; she looked used up, done in, worn out. Then he realised she was probably very ill, and felt sorry for her at once.

He hurried to the door, but looked back before stepping out. The gull hadn't moved. It was still there, glaring in through the window.

Danny was keen to get spending. He'd been saving up his pocket money for weeks and couldn't wait to drop some of it into slot-machines, or buy sticks of his favourite pineapple rock and things to play with on the beach. But the shops were disappointing. They were dingy and dark, with a lot of old stock that no one would ever buy, and the proprietors watched him all the time, as though they thought he were a thief. In one store down near the beach the rock and other sweets were covered in grey dust, and looked shrivelled-up inside their wrappers. Danny bought a stick, because he had to buy *something*, but it tasted worse than the pencils he was in the habit of chewing at school, so he threw it in a bin. He wandered into the town, that sprawled almost perpendicularly up the hill behind the bay, in search of anything interesting, but soon got bored with endless rows of cream-painted houses advertising Bed & Breakfast or offering themselves as Residential Homes for the Aged. He passed a church that was open, with the bell ringing, but nobody went in or out. A gaunt and gloomy vicar with a lead-grey face was standing at the door, stiff as a waxwork, waiting to shake someone's hand.

It got tiring, climbing up the steep streets, so Danny turned back. His feet wanted to run down the sharp incline towards the beach, so he let them. The soles of his trainers slapped like clapping hands on the wet, empty streets, and he began to feel exhilarated, the way you should feel on holiday. The tide was on its way out and he ran without stopping right down the beach to the water's edge. It was cold down there, and a wind driving off the sea carried a miserable, almost invisible mist with it, but Danny tried not to let that bother him. He threw some pebbles at a jellyfish, played tag with the waves, then trotted along until he was suddenly brought up short by the jetty, half of which still stretched out into the sea. It was about ten feet high, but there were steps up the side, which he climbed without thinking. As he reached the top, and looked across the harbour beyond, something called out to his right, towards the town. It sounded like the voice of a demented woman screeching his name. He turned and saw, five yards away, the box and, hovering above it, with its feet stretching down as it prepared to land, the enormous gull. It called again, almost dancing on the tarpaulin with the tips of its claws as it carved at the air with its wings to keep itself just in flight, then settled and became motionless and silent, like a stuffed bird in a museum. It was staring straight at Danny. There was something threatening about the creature's posture; it looked tense, as though it was ready to burst into furious action any second. Cautiously, Danny took a few paces towards it. It sidestepped once, adjusting its position slightly in a gust of buffeting wind, but showed no fear of him, or any sign that it was about to fly away. Its position on the box put it slightly higher than Danny's head, so its beak was just above his eyes. The beak resembled a scaled-down sword from a fantasy film. It was at least eight inches long, and the upper section curved sharply down in a cruel, hard, hooked point. Danny thought the bird would have no trouble opening up his skull with a weapon like that on its head. When he was a few feet away, and still beyond the gull's reach, he stopped, worried about his eyes, which suddenly seemed very vulnerable. He saw that the bird had a cold and crazy look in its eyes, that reminded him of snakes and alligators. Danny blew air out through his pursed lips, and shook his head. He realised he was afraid, and not just of the gull. There was more to it than that. The air around him felt charged and dangerous. Beyond the jetty, the town itself seemed to be watching him, poised and ready to tumble forward on top of him in a huge avalanche if he did the wrong thing. Something, he sensed, was in the balance.

For the first time he took a close look at the box. It was made of wood, bound with strips of greenish metal that could have been brass, and its unpainted surface was mottled with patches of dank, dark-emerald growth; probably some kind of marine weed. It stood in a puddle of its own making. The wood was waterlogged, which partly explained why the man he had seen pushing it had found the task such heavy going. The lid, if it had a lid, was under the flapping tarpaulin cover, but something about the box gave Danny the impression it was locked up very tight. It looked impenetrable! Briefly he wondered what, if anything, was inside it, then hastily closed his mind to the ugly images that were trying to crawl up out of his imagination.

All at once, Danny wanted to get back into the town. The jetty was narrow, but the box took up less than half its width. He could slip past it easily, but in doing so, he would put himself well within the reach of the gull. If it attacked him, he might fall off the jetty. It was a long way down to the beach, and there were flint rocks sticking out of the sand below. He took another look at the creature's beak. The gull glared back and nodded curtly once, as if to confirm his apprehensions.

"Look," Danny said, without having any idea why, "I don't want anything to do with this. I'm just here on holiday." Then he added, "I'm sorry," in a tone more of confusion than apology, and turned and fled back down the steps.

He didn't stop running when he felt the sand of the beach under his feet, but continued right up to the hotel. When he had almost reached it, just as he was trotting up the drive, the sun slid out from behind the clouds above him, and its light blazed down on all the town like a laser beam.

The rest of the day was showery, so the three of them didn't stray far from the TV in the hotel lounge. When he went to bed Danny thought he could hear the box being pushed along the jetty again, but he was so tired, even though he had done nothing much all day, he fell asleep almost at once.

Next morning, when the girl came into his room, threw back the curtains to reveal a blue, cloudless sky, and came towards him with a cup of tea, he jumped up in bed at once, so she wouldn't have any excuse to touch him. Even so, she put one hand on his head and poked about in his hair while he sipped his drink, as though she was gently feeling for lumps. It seemed to Danny that her fingertips were like cold, hard marbles rolling about on his scalp. He assumed it was a gesture of affection: he couldn't think what else it could be, and resisted the urge to duck away, but, when she sat down next to him, he jumped out of bed, ran to the sink, and started washing.

In the morning he spent an hour in a drab, little seafront café with his grandparents, drinking banana milkshakes. After lunch the three of them went down to the beach. Grandad, in a boyish mood, led the way. He looked as though he was wearing someone else's clothes, because he had lost so much weight in the last year, but Danny recognised the fawn trousers the old man had worn on the last three of their previous holidays together. Gran, Danny noticed, seemed more anxious than ever about Grandad when he was at all boisterous, as though she was scared his behaviour might get out of hand. As soon as Grandad had put his cap on backwards, and his face had taken on the now all-to-familiar clown's witless smile that had come to haunt it recently, Gran's features had responded by setting into a rigid, pained expression. She looked as though she had a bad headache. Grandad had wandered away from her twice, and the second time it had taken her half an hour to locate him. He had been with two men who were leading him away, or seemed to be. They had not spoken to her when she had reclaimed her husband, and she hadn't liked the look of them; they looked like muggers, she said.

Danny, feeling sympathy for both his grandparents, took care to be on his best behaviour when he was with them, but he wished they'd loosen up. He was now definitely beginning to wonder what kind of holiday it was going to be.

Gran decided it was too windy to sit on the beach, so she steered Grandad into a shelter on the promenade from where they could watch Danny doing the things children do on such occasions. He made a cake-like sandcastle without much enthusiasm, because he was beginning to wonder if he was too old for such activities, then stripped down to his trunks and sped towards the sea, now quite a long way out. In places, the surface of the sand had been formed into hard ridges by the action of the out-going tide. They ran along the whole length of the beach. They hurt the soles of his bare feet if he ran, and forced him to slow down and walk carefully. To Danny, it looked as though hundreds of endless fat worms lay paralysed just below the surface.

"Old Man Sand's got wrinkles," he said to himself, and laughed at the thought, though there was something not-very-nice about the idea that he found alarming and he tried to shove it to the back of his mind.

After paddling for a while in the shallow sea, which was starting to warm in the sun, and taking a short, leisurely swim, he noticed he felt constrained and uneasy. Something was missing! Except for the sound of waves breaking on the shore, and the occasional scream of gulls (ordinary sized gulls, that was), the beach was strangely quiet. Conspicuous by its absence, he realised, was hubbub, pandemonium: he missed the voices of children yelling and shouting in excitement to each other, and telling their parents about what they were up to at the tops of their voices. The whole beach, the entire bay even, though now more populated, was muffled; silent, and somehow static, like a painting. Danny looked about him at his fellow bathers.

There were not many. Within twenty yards of him half a dozen elderly people, their trousers and skirts rolled or hitched up, wandered about ankle-deep at the waters edge. A beefy man with bulging eyes and purple skin, looking as though his whole body had been beaten into one huge bruise, occasionally hurled himself into deeper water further out and swam a few stiff, furious strokes. A woman in a lime-green costume, standing in the sea close to Danny, suddenly stooped, lowered herself to her knees, sat on her heels and bowed her head in a praying attitude. Her flesh oozed out around the edges of her costume like viscous liquid when she moved. Her skin was crinkled, like the brain in a bottle in the biology-lab at Danny's school. She seemed uncomfortable in the position she had adopted and wriggled round so she could lay back on the sand. A wave breaking over her created the illusion that she was sliding feet first into the sea. Seconds later, when it withdrew, Danny imagined he saw something in the water, clasped round her ankles, tugging her away from the beach. This impression was so strong he walked closer to get a better look at her. The next wave was bigger, however, and submerged her completely. She did not, as Danny expected, start up when the water covered her face, but her body yawed slightly in the drag of the tide. Her eyes were shut and her mouth was open wide. She could have been shouting, laughing, or even yawning.

Baffled and alarmed, Danny thought he ought to try to help the woman, though she gave no indication that she was at all distressed. He wondered if he should ask one of the other old people for their assessment of the situation, then saw that two of them were now also kneeling down. The red-skinned man who had been swimming had vanished, but Danny was sure he had not passed him on his way back to the beach. The last time he had seen him, the man had been in the act of lunging forward in a clumsy dive. Out in the area where the man had been standing, Danny noticed for the first time what looked like dark shadows under the waves. They appeared to be moving. He thought they must be weed-covered rocks, just visible at the bottom of the grey-green water.

One of the two people who were kneeling lay back in the water.

Danny suddenly looked down at his feet. He thought something had touched his right ankle. The sand next to it was disturbed, as though some fast-moving object had hurriedly dug down into it. He turned and ran a few yards out of the water, stood on the nearly dry sand, and looked back. The tide must be coming in fast, he thought, as there was no sign of the woman in the green costume. He could no longer see some of the other people who had been paddling, but a handful more had stumbled forward off the beach into the sea. He realised that none of them had nodded to him, or given him so much as a glance.

He shrugged, and jogged back to where Gran and Grandad were sitting in the shelter. Gran looked more relaxed, perhaps because Grandad was asleep. She held a finger to her lips to warn Danny to keep his voice down, and asked him if he was enjoying himself. Danny didn't want to upset her by telling the truth about how he did feel at that moment, which in any case would be difficult to explain, so he just nodded. He asked for money for an ice cream. As Gran fumbled in her purse, Danny noticed that a man sitting on the bench on the other side of Grandad was watching him.

He was heavily built, with a bald head and heavy jowls, and was dressed in old, dark, working clothes. He could have been a fisherman. He had one arm along the bench behind Grandad's head. Two fingers of his hand rested on Grandad's shoulder. As Danny looked back at him, he lifted the fingers and curled them back towards his palm. Danny got ice creams for himself and Gran, and hurried back. The bald man had gone, so Danny sat in the vacant place.

"Who was that man, Gran?" he asked.

"Which man?"

"The one who had his arm round Grandad."

"Danny, what do you mean? I'm sure he wasn't doing anything of the kind."

"He was," Danny insisted, and Gran, hearing the conviction in his voice, leaned forward and turned to look at him.

"This is a *funny* place, isn't it?" Danny continued.

"Todley Bay? Don't you like it?"

"Not as much as Brighton."

"I think it's very nice."

"There's no kids."

Gran smiled. "There must be some."

"I can't see any."

Gran pushed her glasses up her nose and looked around. "Not here, at the moment, perhaps," she conceded, "but on the beach . . ."

Danny swallowed the last of his ice cream and wiped his mouth. "No; it's all old people, everywhere."

"You're exaggerating. What about that girl who's staying at our hotel? She's about your age. Why don't you try to get to know her?"

"She's sick. I bet she never leaves the hotel."

"Um," Gran agreed thoughtfully, "she doesn't look well. I expect she's convalescing."

"I think she's dying," Danny said, matter-of-factly.

"Danny!" Gran said loudly, causing Grandad to twitch out of his doze. "I'm sure that's not true. What *has* got into you?"

"What's the trouble?" Grandad demanded. "What's got into who?"

"Danny, Harry: I don't think he's enjoying himself; he's in a very strange mood."

"Danny?" said Grandad, looking at his grandson as though he were a total stranger.

The grim look returned to Gran's face. She glanced at her watch. "Good heavens; look at the time, we'd better start back for the evening meal," she said, rising from her seat. Grandad rose up with her, like a Siamese twin joined to her at the shoulder.

Danny was surprised how easy it was to get lost in the hotel. The corridors and public rooms were decorated uniformly throughout, which made it hard to get your bearings, but even so, it didn't explain why he lost his way quite so often. He kept finding himself on the wrong floor. He'd carefully count the turns in the flights of stairs, so he was sure he knew exactly where he was, only to discover he was one, or even two, floors out. He noticed quite a few of the old people wandering round in even deeper bafflement than usual from time to time, which made him feel better, because it suggested he wasn't the only one experiencing this peculiar disorientation. A couple of times Danny bumped into Kelvin, the nurse with the walrus moustache, who told him how to get to where he wanted to go. He wasn't exactly unfriendly, but he must have been a very busy man, because he hardly stopped long enough to give the necessary directions before he blustered off again.

On the third night of the holiday, after leaving his grandparents in the TV Lounge, Danny searched about down wrong corridors for ten minutes before he found his room. He complimented himself: he was getting better; the night before it had taken twice that long to get his bearings. As he was putting on his pyjamas, he heard the big box being shoved along the jetty. A shining mist, that had crawled up off the sea with the onset of darkness, had vanished when he looked out of the window. The air was clear, and he could see the man had nearly gotten the box to the end of the jetty. Danny was very interested to see what would happen next, because he knew there were two steps up from the jetty to the promenade and the street beyond, and he couldn't see how one man could possibly get the box up them without help. He got into bed and pretended to be asleep when Gran came, so she only stayed a moment. (He felt bad about it, but he had become fed up with her company that evening, because she was wearing herself out fussing over Grandad, who was definitely going gaga. They were both getting visibly worse daily: a lot of the time it was a *pain* being with them.)

When Gran had gone, Danny got up again and looked out the window. The box was about a foot from the steps, and the man had gone. He watched for a while, but nothing happened, so he slid back between the sheets, feeling letdown and disappointed, and fell asleep. Later, something woke him up. Noises, coming from the direction of the jetty. Different noises! He trotted to the window and looked out.

The man was back. He had set a lantern on the edge of the top step, and had placed a long metal tube or roller, four or five inches in diameter, at the base of the box, on the side closest to the steps. He was lifting the box with a jack. When it was the right height he kicked the roller under it on one side, let the box drop, then went round to the far side to repeat the process. When the roller was under the full length of the leading edge of the box, he went behind it and began to push. After a struggle, it moved a short distance towards the steps, and the side of the box above the roller rose a little higher. After giving three huge shoves the man got another, thicker roller from somewhere and laid it in front of the first one he had positioned. Then he went behind the box, and pushed and pushed. The front edge of the thing was soon higher than the bottom step and, in twenty minutes, after the man had put more rollers in place and done a lot more heaving, it was hovering a good distance above and beyond the top of the second. Then the man hit a problem. Because it was inclined at an angle, he was finding it increasingly difficult to move the box. He was having to push it up, as well as forward.

He seemed to give up then, and went and sat on the top step and stared down at the box. Danny watched the slumped figure for a while until he got bored. He thought the man might have gone to sleep. He was just about ready to return to bed when he saw movements on the beach below him. The tide was almost in, and a man was walking off the narrow strip of sand, diagonally out into the sea. The small, thin, stooping figure, dressed in dark clothes, was just visible against the inky water, moving slowly and regularly, as though setting out for a stroll on the ocean bed. When the sea was in up to his waist he stopped, sank back into the water and disappeared from sight. Danny thought—no, he *knew*—the person, whoever he was, had stretched out on the sand, like the woman in the green costume he had seen the day before.

There were a few deckchairs left out on the beach, Danny noticed, spread about near where the now presumably drowning man had been when he'd first sighted him. To his amazement he could see shapes, which could only be people, sprawling in some of the chairs. Danny peered at his watch. It was almost midnight: it had been dark for almost two hours!

"They're moonbathing," he thought, and smiled uneasily in the dark, aware that the people didn't look at all funny.

As he looked back out the window he saw something scuttle up out of the sea, across the beach, in among the parked deckchairs. It moved like a spider. It clung close to the sand, had no definite shape, and at first Danny thought it was dead seaweed, broken loose from its roots, washed ashore, dried in the sun, and blowing in the wind. Until he realised there was no wind to speak of; certainly not enough to set in motion anything more substantial than a scrap of paper. What he could see was moving of its own volition, and soon demonstrated that it had considerable strength! A section of its edge blended with the outline of one of the occupied chairs, which lifted and tumbled over on its side, tipping the person seated on it onto the sand. The figure lay motionless for as long as it took the mobile shape to dart round and attach itself to an outstretched arm, the part of the body closest to the sea. The body twitched once, then slid smoothly to the tide line and into the waves beyond, where it, and the thing pulling it, sank out of sight.

Then, for a time, nothing moved on the beach that Danny could see, though his eyes were alert for the slightest motion. It was a sound from the end of the jetty that grabbed his attention next; a loud grunt of pain or effort, or both. He turned just in time to see the bearlike man heave the box almost into the air and up onto the edge of the promenade. The action seemed to have spent the last of his energy: he flopped around picking up the rollers and tucking them under his arm like a man at the last extreme of exhaustion, then staggered off towards the harbour. Danny watched him shrink away into the darkness, then realised he was stiff with standing still, and crawled into bed. He fell asleep wondering what the man, who was awake most nights, did in the daytime.

It was very hot next day. So much so that Gran and Grandad sat on the beach for the first time. They couldn't walk far in the sand, because of Gran's feet, so Danny put up deckchairs for them at the bottom of the steps that led to the promenade. He sat with them for a while, watching the beach fill with elderly holidaymakers. Then, for something to say, because the old pair was not inclined to talk in the heat, he mentioned that he had seen people on the sands late at night.

"I expect they were workmen tidying up all the litter," Gran said.

"The tide does that," Danny said, "when it goes in and out. No, they were sitting in chairs, like we are, or walking into the sea."

"Danny, you were dreaming. They'd have caught their deaths of cold."

Danny wanted to say he thought they were dead, or looked it, but knew that Gran would say he was talking nonsense and get cross with him. Even so, he couldn't help saying, "I wish we *had* gone to Brighton. This place is *weird*."

"I think it's very pleasant," Gran said, "and restful. There's none of the noise and fuss you get at so many holiday places nowadays. And people are so nice and polite."

"You didn't like those men who walked off with Grandad," Danny observed.

"I was probably wrong about them. I expect they'd realised Grandad was lost, and were taking him to a policeman."

Danny didn't answer, because he had just spotted, not far away along the beach, one of the deckchairs he had seen someone slumped in last night. He knew it was the same one, because it was in exactly the same position in relation to a stack of chairs next to it as it had been when he had seen it from his bedroom window. It was facing away from him but he could tell it was occupied because the canvas seat was bulging down and back. He was about to go and take a look at it and its occupant when something made him change his mind. There was a cloud of flies swarming above the chair, dozens of them, big black ones, he thought he could almost hear them buzzing. No one else had set up their deckchairs for a good distance all round that particular one, Danny noticed.

"Look at all those flies, Gran," he said.

"What?"

"Over there; look." He pointed. "Above that chair."

"I can't see *flies*, Danny, if they land on me. My eyes aren't good enough. I can only just see the chair."

For some reason this remark made Danny rather anxious. He felt suddenly isolated and vulnerable. Looking round he discovered he was, as far as he could see, the only child on the beach. He shut his eyes then, and pretended to sunbathe, but he couldn't settle; his mind was swirling with vague apprehensions. For the first time all week he found he was missing his parents. At first, he had been relieved to get away from them; they had been so grumpy and depressing recently, though they had continued to treat him as kindly as they had always done. Nevertheless, life at home had been different since his father had received the letter telling him his job would no longer exist in ten weeks, and his parents had taken to endless grinding arguments about money. Danny heard them late at night in the room below his, their voices rasping on like two blunt saws taking turns to cut through a particularly thick, hard log. They were worried about Gran and Grandad too, and Danny could understand why now. He realised that the whole family had problems. He had problems! Suddenly he wanted to talk to his parents very badly, but he knew he wouldn't see them until the end of the week.

After half an hour he went and got some drinks. Grandad insisted on coming with him, somewhat to Danny's relief. He tried not to listen to Grandad's talk, because he seemed to think Danny was someone he had worked with years ago in Canada. That was unnerving, but he felt glad he was not walking alone.

The way to the café took them past the huge, brass-bound box parked on the promenade. Even in bright sunlight it looked sinister, Danny thought, though other passersby seemed unawed by it. The wood had dried out a lot, and was beginning to crack, and the mossy weed clinging to it had turned grey and ashlike. A heat-haze shimmered over the tarpaulin. There was no sign of the great gull but, when Danny looked up into the sky, he saw, very high up, a black dot that was growing larger as it descended fast towards the ground. Danny grabbed Grandad's hand to hurry him along. He had a vision of what the bird could do with its beak if it hit someone after descending at that speed from that height.

He made sure, when they returned to Gran with their drinks, they went by a roundabout way along the beach, keeping well clear of the box. The route took them past the deckchair that had been shrouded with flies. It was empty now. Danny got the impression that a small group of youngish men in overalls, moving down the beach towards the sea, were carrying something they had lifted from the chair but, in the confusion of people, it was hard to be sure. He went quite near the chair and saw there were still a few flies on duty there, hovering over a wet, red-brown stain on the canvas seat.

It seemed to be a bad day for insects. Early in the afternoon millions of tiny silver and brown flies with thin bodies and long legs appeared from nowhere on the beach. They hopped rather than flew, and got all over Danny's bare legs and arms. They were strangely dry and weightless, like the congregations of insect corpses that gather on window ledges in empty houses in the summer, and seemed almost without substance. They didn't bite or sting; they were just disgusting. Danny had soon had enough of them. He asked Gran if he could go for a boat trip round the bay.

"You said I could, and if I don't go soon, the holiday will be over," he pleaded.

"There's still three more whole days," Gran said, but she agreed he could do as he had asked. They left their beach-bag and Danny's towels on their chairs because Gran said she was sure there were no thieves about, and the three of them made their way to the harbour.

One of the two boats that did trips was out beyond the headland, just visible in the distance, and the second was almost full and ready to go. It was a big, wide boat that Gran declared quite safe, so she gave Danny some money and told him to get on board. He found a seat at the front and waved at his grandparents with his handkerchief for a joke. Gran waved back, and Grandad copied her movements exactly, a sight that made Danny laugh aloud. A teenage boy in sun-bleached denim jumped onto the boat and began collecting money and handing out tickets, then a man stepped quickly down from the harbour, started the engine, and grasped hold of the wheel.

It was the bearlike man who Danny had seen moving the box. There was no mistaking his rolling movements, and he was wearing the same clothes as he had been the night before; Danny could tell by the shape of him. The only difference was that at night the man wore a cap and now had nothing on his bald head. Danny got a good look at his face, and not for the first time: he was sure the man had been sitting next to Grandad the day before, with his arm round the back of Grandad's chair and his fingers on the old man's shoulder.

Danny jumped up to get off the boat just as, with a grinding growl of the engine that echoed off the hill behind the town, it cut away from the harbour wall. The man glanced sharply at him and the teenager asked him to get back in his seat. Danny did so at once, and tried to make himself small and inconspicuous. The man, at the front of the boat, was facing away from Danny. He made an announcement about safety procedures as he steered the vessel out through the maze of moored pleasure-craft to the harbour mouth, then handed the wheel over to his young mate when they reached the open sea. He turned round, sat down, and lit a little cigar. As he blew out smoke he raised his head and glanced quickly round at his passengers. When he saw Danny, he took another sharp drag at his cigar and seemed to shake his head slightly. The gesture had no clear meaning that Danny could interpret, but it frightened him because he felt he had been singled out, perhaps even recognised. He remembered when he had been watching the man pushing the box along the jetty he had got the impression that the fellow had looked back up at him on a number of occasions, though there was no chance he could really have seen a small boy standing some considerable distance away in the dark, half-hidden behind a curtain. Unless he had remarkable eyesight! He certainly had remarkable eyes, that stared through Danny as though they were focused on a point a million miles behind his head.

Danny thought of the huge, black seagull then, that had been so high in the sky above the box when he had passed close to it with Grandad just a couple of hours earlier. The bird must have good eyesight too; it had dropped down at once when it had seen him approach, or so it had appeared to Danny. Why? Did it think he was going to do some harm to the box, that it seemed to be guarding? Danny couldn't believe that. He hadn't the means or strength to damage it, even if, for some crazy reason, he'd had the inclination to do so. He wasn't bothered about the box; he wanted nothing to do with it, as he had told the bird when he had come close to it on the jetty two days ago. At the time he had felt foolish talking to a seagull; but not so now. He just wished he had said more: he was afraid he had not made himself understood.

When, after a quarter of an hour, the boat turned its prow into the Bay again for the return trip, Danny was glad the ride was half over. He'd been too confused and anxious to enjoy himself and imagined he was seasick, his stomach felt so queasy. He was very glad when the man, whose hard, unfriendly gaze had returned to him every few minutes, got up to take over the wheel again as they approached the harbour.

Gran was waiting for him on the promenade, holding onto a railing at the very edge of the harbour. Danny waved, but he knew she wouldn't see him. He doubted if she could even see the boat, but she knew what time he was due to return, and was just *being there* for him. Grandad sat on a bench a few feet behind her, talking to a man seated next to him. His conversation was animated; he waved his arms and at one point stood up and made a gesture, incomprehensible to Danny, to illustrate some point he was making. Danny guessed he thought his companion was someone from years back in his past, when his life had been exciting, and that they were sharing some adventure together. As Grandad, in his enthusiasm, took a few steps away from the bench, another man, who Danny had not noticed, but who must have been standing nearby, screwed up some paper he had been eating out of and tossed it into a bin. Then he sidled closer to Grandad as though he were on wheels, in a sliding, gliding movement that arrested Danny's attention completely, and totally altered his understanding of the scene he was witnessing. The man on the bench got up, stood next to Grandad, and pointed inland to somewhere in the town. When Grandad turned to look, the man took his arm, and began, with a certain amount of force, Danny thought, to lead him away. The second man, moving as though he were sliding on ice, fell in behind them. Gran, still peering myopically out to sea, was obviously unaware of what was going on behind her. The boat was coming in to dock now, and Danny could see her bland, smiling face staring out at the blur of the world in front of her. He half stood up and shouted at her, and made jerking movements with his hand intended to make her look behind. As he rose to his feet some of the other passengers thought he was getting ready to disembark and also started to get up off their seats. Perceiving this, the man who was steering the boat turned and yelled something to his mate, who jumped onto a chair and called to everyone to be seated. In the confusion of people bobbing up and down Danny lost sight of Gran, but he was careful to keep an eye on Grandad, who was being led slowly uphill into the town. Not a purposeful walker at the best of times, Grandad liked to stop and start when the urge took him, and the two men were plainly having trouble getting him to go where they wanted him to, and were making slow progress.

The boat bumped against the harbour wall and the teenager skipped ashore to fasten the ropes. The bearlike man took his place next to the couple of steps up the side of the vessel and helped his frail, nervous passengers onto dry land by steering them across the short gangplank, whether they wanted him to or not. Danny tried to squeeze forward in the queue, getting a few sharp comments from some old ladies as he did so. When his turn to disembark came he tried to avoid the hands of the man by almost running off the boat, but without success. He felt fingers like tentacles curl round his upper arm to stop him in mid-stride. The man lifted him effortlessly and half turned him so they were face to face. Danny could smell cigar smoke on his breath, and other more strange odours that he had never come across before. There was a scrap of tobacco on the man's lip that must have irritated him, as he flicked it with his tongue, and spat it out over Danny's shoulder with a toss of his head. The action reminded Danny of squirrels he had seen in the park at home, standing on their hind legs and spitting out indigestible fragments of nuts they were eating. Not that there was anything cute or squirrel-like about the man's appearance: his heavily featured face with its sharp, down-curving nose and receding, almost horizontal forehead was set hard in an ambiguous mask of contempt and vague curiosity, as though Danny were a not-very-fine example of something that, had it been of better or different quality, would perhaps have interested him. Either his head was unusually small, or it seemed so in proportion to the bulk of his vast, barrel-like body. His little gimlet eyes bore in on Danny's like nails: in the irises of each of them Danny could see tiny reflections of his own frightened face.

The man loosened his grip on Danny's arms and ran his hands down them to the wrists, pressing with his fingertips, feeling for the bones beneath the flesh. He held the joints of Danny's wrists between his thumbs and fingers and lifted them to the height of his shoulders, so the boy's hands hung in front of him like a half-animated puppet's. Danny squirmed and looked back over his shoulder. Gran was just behind him on the promenade. He could tell from the confusion and apprehension on her face that she was close enough to see what was happening to him. He tried to get away from the man's grasp, and yelled out, "Grandad's gone. They've taken him away again. Get after him. He's gone up into the town."

The man moved then, and held Danny out so he was hanging by his wrists over the side of the boat next to the little gangplank. The vessel was about twelve inches from the harbour wall and rocking slightly, up and down and from side to side, in the wake of other boats passing beyond. Danny thought if the man let go and he fell he might be crushed between the wall and the side of the boat. The water below his feet, the colour of boiled cabbage, and marbled with rainbow tinted whorls of diesel fuel, looked deep, thick, and viscous, like glue. Darker shapes moved below its surface. It somehow looked hungry too: Danny imagined his broken body being sucked down into it, dragged under the keel, and pulled out to sea by swirling undercurrents. He was only suspended thus for a few seconds before the man stretched out over the side of the boat and lowered him slowly onto the edge of the harbour and released him, but they were long seconds, and terrible while they lasted. Some of the elderly people waiting their turn to go ashore thought the man had played an amusing joke on Danny, and squawked with laughter as he ran shouting to his grandmother.

By this time she had discovered her husband's absence and, as soon as Danny's toes touched the ground, went stumbling away on her arthritic feet to look for him.

"Up the hill," Danny screamed, "they've taken him up the hill."

Gran turned to him with a hopeless look, already out of breath and concerned about her hammering heart.

"Don't worry," Danny said as he overtook her. "Wait here. I'll get him back."

The streets were full of old people drifting back and forth from the beach. They reacted too slowly to get out of Danny's way so he had to run a zigzag course around them. He lost sight of Grandad from time to time but knew he must soon catch up with him because the trio had come to a stop halfway up the hill. They seemed to be arguing. They were standing just inside an alleyway between two decrepit-looking red-brick Victorian hotels. The man who had been seated on the bench next to Grandad had hold of his sleeve; he wasn't actually tugging at it, but was making it impossible for the old man to retreat. The other would-be abductor, with the smooth, oily movements, was gliding round the pair of them, talking all the while, and making calming gestures with his outstretched hands. Danny could hear Grandad's voice. He was bellowing at the two men that he'd had enough of their nonsense. He was going to arrest them. Didn't they know he was a member of the Mounted Police? He was back in the past in Canada again. His face looked more worried than he sounded, but brightened when he saw Danny, who assumed he had been recognised for once.

The two men, following the old man's gaze, turned to see Danny running towards them. The one with peculiar movements detached himself from the tableau and slid towards Danny like a skater. He was dressed in a tight black jacket and shiny trousers, like a waiter's. Danny couldn't be sure, but it seemed that the man's feet, encased in narrow patent-leather shoes, hardly moved, and never quite touched the floor; as though he were suspended a fraction of an inch above the pavement. Perhaps because he was, nevertheless, coming at Danny fast, his form seemed slightly blurred, his features indistinct. When they were almost touching they both sidestepped to avoid each other in the same direction, and collided.

Danny expected to get hurt. He heard himself shout to Grandad to get away as he made contact, then automatically shut his eyes to protect them. He felt a sensation as though he had run into a large, soft mattress that gave to the slightest pressure. There was no indication that what he had hit was anything like a human body that contained flesh and bones, and whatever it was gave way on contact and spread out alarmingly, as though it had come apart. Danny thought he had run right through it and somehow come out the other side. He opened his eyes and saw what looked like a two-dimensional drawing of a bloated human figure expanding above and in front of him. It was floating away, and waving its flattened arms and legs slowly, like someone drowning in a dream, and clawing desperately at the air with its hands. Almost at once its fingertips appeared to grasp onto something invisible; a hard thin edge of reality, perhaps; and dug in and held on. Then, with an obviously painful effort, *it pulled itself back together*; it contracted, shrunk into itself, and reformed.

All this happened very quickly and, almost before Danny had time to think, the man was hovering in front of him again, with a mildly expectant look on his bland, undistinguished face, exactly like a waiter lingering at a table in expectation of an order. It was as though he were silently challenging Danny to believe that the astonishing metamorphosis he had just observed had indeed happened, and was trying to suggest, by his unconcerned expression and the shear ordinariness of his appearance, that it could not have done.

But Danny *knew*. He knew what he had seen. He knew a great deal all of a sudden, and what he didn't know he guessed.

He flung himself at Grandad, latched onto his arm, and pulled the old man sideways down the hill with all his strength. They tottered along like the contestants in a three-legged race, barging into a number of ancient holidaymakers who they were not able to brush aside, and stumbling and almost falling on the steep incline. Gran was waiting for them on the promenade. She looked as though she was going to cry when she saw Grandad's face. It was blank and empty, like a paper mask before the features have been painted on it.

Gran said, "Where were they taking him, Danny? What did they want him for?"

Danny couldn't bring himself to say what he thought he knew. He pretended to be more out of breath than he was, and stammered something about muggers. He could see Gran was terribly distraught, but knew this was because of the state her husband was in, and because he had nearly been stolen from her. Thankfully, she could not have seen what occurred when he, Danny, collided with the man in the waiter's outfit, so he wouldn't be called upon to give an explanation of *that.* On the other hand, he realised, if she *had* seen, she would at least be more aware of what they were up against.

He looked back up the hill to see if the men had followed him, but there was no sign of them. Suddenly his stomach lurched, and he felt a surge of dizzying nausea, a return of the seasickness that had started half an hour earlier when he had been on the boat, now exacerbated by his recent experiences.

"Gran," he said, "I'm ill. Let's get away from here. This is a terrible place."

Misunderstanding him—thinking he merely wanted to return to the hotel—Gran nodded emphatically. She put her arm round her husband's shoulder and steered him away. The old man walked like an automaton, staring down at the pavement just in front of his dragging feet and saying nothing. Danny dawdled behind all the way to the hotel, to keep the couple in his sight.

Danny looked even worse than he felt when the three of them got together in the dining room for their evening meal. Gran led Grandad in by the elbow. His walk had developed an aimless, twisting tendency that had to be corrected every few steps, and his eyes looked empty and uncomprehending, like a blind man's, or someone concussed. The old man would eat nothing, and Danny couldn't. Gran stuffed some meat into her mouth and made a show of chewing it to encourage him to do the same, but the smell and appearance of what was on his plate convulsed his stomach and he had to get up and away. Gran's face took on an even more concerned expression when he explained how sick he was. He hated to put this extra burden on her, but he had no alternative. She dug in her bag for some pills, instructed him on the dosage, and told him to get to bed. Danny said "Good night" to Grandad, who made no response at all.

"He's lost his tongue," Gran said, trying to make a half-angry, desperate joke of it, but sounding instead, strangely, much younger than her years, and on the edge of tears again.

Danny dragged himself up the wide blue-carpeted stairs feeling dizzy and disorientated. The spaces around him seemed much wider than he knew they were, as though the hotel had expanded in all directions; a process that appeared to be obscurely continuing out at the edge of his vision. He counted flights from floor to floor grimly, passing hand over hand on the stair rail like a man hauling himself along a rope to safety. It occurred to him to take the lift, but he knew his stomach wouldn't stand for that. On the second-floor corridor he heard a confusion of hushed sounds behind him, and somebody called out sharply for him to step aside. Two men in white jackets were approaching him, pushing a grey painted metal stretcher. On it was a slender human form half wrapped in a loose-knit white blanket. The lower part of the face of this person was encased in a plastic mask attached by a tube to a cylinder slung below the stretcher. A pink tube curled up from the blanket to what looked like a brown bladder on a stick one of the men was holding above his head. Danny realised the figure on the stretcher was the young girl he had seen in the dining room a few times. She was lying on her side with her eyes wide open. The transparent mask had a black rim that underlined and isolated her eyes. They looked like two shiny purple holes drilled into her almost bald head. Her little white ears stuck out like toadstools from the sides of her scalp, which looked as though it was made of scrubbed white wood. Danny realised that normally she must wear some kind of wig. She stared at him hard as she passed, giving him an even worse version of the withering look he was used to seeing on her face, and rose up and turned as she passed to keep him in view. Danny found he was pressing his back against the wall to get away from her. The power of her gaze had a negative force strong enough to repel him physically. It felt like a protracted bomb blast. She struggled to keep her eyes on him, to keep up the pressure, and tried to sit up. As she did so the blanket slid down from her shoulders to her waist and Danny saw what looked like black shadows, just beneath the skin, sliding down over the ribs of her flat white chest to take shelter under the blanket over her belly. It was as though they were afraid of the light. The shapes moved hastily, but with purposeful, controlled caution, like fish seeking the safety of deeper, darker waters. The girl kept her purple-black eyes on Danny until one of the men pressed her back down and pulled the blanket up to her chin. They stopped the stretcher at the service lift and Danny, released from the repulsive attraction of the girl, turned his back on them and staggered away.

He found his room at last, wriggled clumsily out of his clothes, pulled the curtains across the open window to hold back the early evening sunlight, clambered into bed, and fell, sweating and squirming, into feverish sleep.

Suddenly, Danny was staring into the dark. His eyes had clicked open with a snap that was almost audible. His whole body was rigid with tension. His senses were as alert as a hunter's and, when at last he moved, he moved stealthily. He peeled the quilt smoothly back off the bed and stood up. As he did so the sound that had woken him was repeated somewhere out beyond his window. It was a sliding sound similar to the noises he had heard earlier in the week, but not quite the same. It was a lighter, easier sound. The box was moving faster.

Danny crept to the window and edged the curtain to one side just far enough to give him a view of the section of the street visible between two hotels at the lower level. The sound seemed to be coming from down there. Seconds later he heard it again, as a long corner of shadow stretched out to his left along the street below. It was followed by the blunt black end of the box, which slid swiftly into full view and came to rest at a point halfway between the hotels. But only for a moment: the bearlike man behind it hardly paused for rest before pushing it on out of sight. The box was only briefly visible, but Danny noticed that the tarpaulin had been removed from the top, and that an upper section seemed to be slightly askew, as though the lid had been lifted and not properly replaced.

Something has been taken out, or has come out, Danny thought: either that or the box has been opened in preparation for something that was going to be put into it. Or was going to *get* into it. . . For a second Danny had a dim vision of something huge and dark clambering out to make way for something frail and white that was desperate to clamber in. He shut his eyes and shook his head to shatter the fantasy, and went and sat on his bed.

He almost went back to the window to take a look at what, if anything, was happening on the beach, but decided against it. He was still feeling ill. He was weak and cold, though his skin was damp with sweat. The pills Gran had given him had helped, but their effect had worn off. But he knew she had more in her bag.

He went into the corridor, and tapped on the door of his grandparents' room. No answer. He tapped again, louder, then tried the handle. The door wouldn't move when he pushed it. It must be earlier than he thought, he decided, if it's locked. Gran and Grandad always went to bed at ten. They must be somewhere downstairs, probably in the Television Lounge.

He set off at a trot along the corridor and ran down the stairs. It wasn't so easy to get lost going *down* into the hotel because you just kept on going until you reached the bottom, then you stopped. Or so he had assumed: it had worked before. Nevertheless, he misjudged where he was, and found he had wandered into the Twilight Lounge. It was pitch-dark in there, but he knew where he was, because of the sharp, faint smell of urine. He stood for a moment just inside the door and heard a rustling noise, like paper being slowly crumpled, then someone sighed, and he thought he heard liquid dripping. A wheelchair creaked. They're waking up! Danny thought, and hurtled off without bothering to shut the door behind him.

When he found the Television Lounge it was unoccupied. The big set in the corner was still on, filling the room with jumpy silver light and swirls of romantic music from the ancient black and white costume drama that was showing. Danny noticed the clock on the video player below the TV said 01:47. *In the morning*, that was. He'd never been awake at that time before, that he could remember. It wasn't surprising there was nobody about, but why weren't his grandparents in their room? In the past Danny had often had a feeling that grownups did things after their children had gone to bed that they never talked about. It had only ever been a vague suspicion before, but now the idea played on his mind. Where were the adults? What *were* they up to. He would have to find out.

Whenever he had gone in and out of the hotel before there had always been someone at the reception desk, but now even that post was deserted. It seemed that the only people other than himself in the building were the ancient residents in the Twilight Lounge and, young as he was, Danny knew he couldn't expect help or advice from them. They had their own problems. His only hope of finding his Gran and her medication was to contact a member of staff, and ask them to take him to her. Then he remembered he had seen a big sign that said

STAFF QUARTERS
Staff Only Beyond This Point
PLEASE

on a door at the rear of the hotel. Surely, he would find assistance there! He ran down the silent corridor towards the kitchens, found the door, and saw with relief that it was half open. Beyond it, grey-carpeted stairs led down to the basement. He could her music thumping somewhere below, so someone must be awake down there. He glanced again at the off-putting sign on the door, then ventured cautiously onto the stairs. He felt that what he was doing was probably wrong, but guessed that if people were cross with him for venturing where he should not go, they wouldn't do him any harm, and would take him to his grandparents just to get rid of him.

Everything in the staff quarters was smaller and shabbier than on the floors above. The corridors were narrow, illuminated by dim, unshaded yellow bulbs, and the drab carpets were worn and hard. He passed lots of numbered doors, some of them split and cracked, as though the locks had been forced, or they had been punched or kicked. He kept walking, without trying to rouse anyone who might be beyond them, because he could tell, from the increasing volume of the music, he was getting closer to its source. In fact, when he turned the first corner he walked right into it. Two doors, one marked **STAFF** and the other **RECREATION**, stood open wide and he found he had gatecrashed a party in full swing.

There were about two dozen people in the long, low-ceilinged room and most of them were sitting at a couple of trestle tables covered by white paper tablecloths. The air was murky with what at first he thought was smoke, then realised was a thin damp mist, like fog. A couple were dancing, away to one side, and a girl in a black, tight, silky outfit twirled somewhat awkwardly to the music, alone in the centre of the available space. She stopped when she saw Danny, and stared at him as though he were an apparition. He recognised her as the girl who had brought him tea in bed each morning, and at once began to feel uneasy. The girl came and crouched down in front of him, on tiptoes, with her knees bent. She stayed like that for a while, without speaking or moving, weighing him up with her eyes. The calculating quality of her gaze chilled Danny's blood. He wanted to speak, but his lips had gone stiff and his tongue felt like leather. He was aware that other people in the room beyond had become aware of his presence, and were also watching him. Someone with an old man's voice gave a creaky laugh that was echoed by a woman's shrill, mirthless cackle. A man, shouting over the music, said something he didn't catch, then most of them laughed. Danny was just thinking of running off when the girl reached out and took his left elbow in her hand. Then she said sharply, "What *are* you *doing* here?"

As she waited for his answer her thin fingers massaged the bones of his elbow and her thumb pressed painfully into his inner arm. He mumbled something about his grandparents that was inaudible to the girl, who shook her head to indicate she could not hear him. Then, desperately, he shouted, "I've lost my Gran. I want someone to help me find her." As he did so, the rock music tape that had been playing ended abruptly, and he found himself shouting into total silence. His voice sounded like a scream. It frightened him. The girl moved her head back slightly under the impact of it. She rose up again, still holding Danny's arm, and pulled him further into the room towards the tables. A man on a bench moved to one side to make way for him. The girl, by manipulating his arm, forced him to sit in the vacant space. The man next to him gave him a toothy smile. It was Kelvin, the moustachioed nurse who had rescued him from the people in the Twilight Lounge at the start of the holiday. He still looked reasonably friendly.

Danny recognised a few of the faces of the people seated round him. To his horror he saw, opposite him across the table, the man in a waiter's uniform; the one with the strange, sliding locomotion, who had tried to lure his grandfather away, and who Danny had run literally right into.

The man looked very solid now however, and seemed amused to find Danny in his present predicament. Danny licked his dry lips and tried to avoid looking anyone in the eye by looking down at the paper cloth on the table in front of him. It was bare except for dishes of nuts and crisps, a couple of big cut-glass decanters almost full of what looked like tomato juice, and a quantity of glasses containing drinks of this liquid. The people round him lifted these glasses to their mouths from time to time to take a sip, then their eyes would roll and they pursed and smacked their lips with almost ecstatic satisfaction. It was obvious they relished their refreshments. Danny liked tomato juice himself, but he couldn't understand why anyone should make such a fuss about it; it was nothing special. Last Christmas his father had drunk lots of it with vodka, and there had been a row between his parents when his Dad had fallen from his chair when they had guests round, but there was no sign of any vodka on the tables now. Yet the people at the party, if that was what it was, seemed to think tomato juice was the finest drink in the world!

The man opposite him, the one dressed like a waiter, poured a fresh glass of the liquid and handed it to Danny. The drink had a funny smell, not a bit like tomato juice, that Danny detected as soon as he had taken the glass, and he looked at it suspiciously. He raised it to his lips and sniffed. As he did so, the girl, who still had hold of his arm, increased the pressure of her grasp on his elbow. Danny saw, out of the corner of his eye, that the girl's face was flushed and excited and. . . hungry looking. The tip of her tongue appeared briefly against her upper lip, and her brow arched up as her eyes stretched wide. He could tell she wanted him to try the drink. She wanted him to try it very much. And so did all the other people. They were all watching him with sharp, intense anticipation.

Danny held the glass a couple of inches from his mouth. His hand was not quite steady. "What is this?" he asked. "It's not tomato juice, is it?"

"Did we say it was?" someone said. "Did *anyone* say it *was*?"

Everybody shook their heads.

"It's a fine drink," the girl said softly. "A rare old vintage; something you won't have tasted before. But once you've tried it, you'll want more of it; there's no doubt about that."

"I don't like the smell," Danny said nervously.

"Never mind that; it's not the taste or the smell that matters, it's what it does for you," the girl insisted.

Danny said nothing.

"It won't harm you," someone said. "We drink it all the time, and look at us. We're lucky here, we get plenty of it."

"The fine old stuff," the girl repeated, almost singing, as though she was quoting a popular song, "the rare old vintage."

Danny lowered his mouth to the glass and took a sip. The drink was thick and flat and metallic and slightly warm. It was neither good nor bad. He drank some more, and found he was suddenly thirsty. He emptied the glass slowly and put it down.

"Well?" asked the girl.

"It's okay," Danny said, unenthusiastically.

"Would you like some more?"

Danny was a polite boy. "Not at the moment, thank you," he said, and for some reason most of the people seated round him started to laugh. It was relaxed, good-humoured laughter. Danny noticed the girl had released her hold on his arm at last and, when the laughter had subsided, he repeated his request to be taken to his Gran. Someone made a joke that made no sense, about taking Gran to Danny, then Kelvin got up and told Danny it was too late to disturb Gran now, but he would take him back up to his room in the service lift. Danny would have to sort his other problems out in the morning.

To Danny's surprise, the entrance to the lift was at the back of the room they were in. Kelvin went and leaned on the button and, high up in the hotel, the lift lurched and groaned as it began unsteadily to descend. When it arrived Kelvin had trouble pulling the slightly rusty, cagelike bars of the metal outer door open, then cursed as he bent to tug up the inner door that rose and slid back somewhere at the top of the lift. A cloud of the cold, steamy-looking mist Danny had noticed earlier wafted out of the lift shaft, surged across the floor, then floated up towards the ceiling on a cushion of warm air.

Danny saw at once that the lift was not empty. The huge brass-bound box he had seen so many times before was in there, taking up most of the space. It had been pushed up tight against one wall and there was just a narrow gap vacant to one side of it. Kelvin motioned to Danny to get in beside it. Danny shook his head and backed off a little way. He saw that the lid of the box was now in place, but could tell it was loose, unsealed. The dry wooden structure had finger-wide splits in it, and its sides were warped and slightly concave. In places, the wood had sunk away from the brass to reveal sections of the ancient, primitive nails that held it together. The seaweed that had been growing on it had shrunk, withered, and turned colourless, like old wreathes in a graveyard.

Kelvin gave Danny a look that the boy recognised as the expression Todley Bay people sometimes put on their faces when they wanted to smile. It was probably meant to be encouraging, but Danny thought it had an impatient edge to it. Kelvin was in a hurry. Probably he wanted to get back for more of the red juice before the others drank it all.

Kelvin said, "What's the matter? Get in. I'll get you to your room in no time."

Danny pointed to the box. "What's that?"

"This?" Kelvin stepped forward and thumped the lid of the box with his fist. "Nothing for you to worry about. Not for a long time, anyway, I shouldn't think. You needn't trouble yourself about that."

"Is it empty?"

"I expect so." To placate Danny, Kelvin lifted the lid slightly, and peered inside. He took a long, hard look.

"Are you sure?" Danny insisted nervously.

"Well," Kelvin said, lowering the lid, "it's not quite empty, but don't go bothering yourself about that."

"What's in there?"

"If you really want to know, sonny, I'll show you; I'll lift you up so you can take a look, if you think it'll make you happy, but I wouldn't recommend it."

"I don't want to see inside. I don't want to go near it. I don't want anything to do with it."

"You don't have to like it, son," Kelvin said, now definitely irritable, "but if you want me to show you to your room, you're going to have to ride up with it. So get in."

Danny waited for a long moment, and stared at the box. Something could be hiding in there, observing him; staring back at him through the cracks in the sides. But, if there was, he didn't feel it was necessarily out to harm him, it could be that it was just. . . curious about him. If there *was* anything in there, it wasn't him, Danny, it was after—or so, for no clear reason, he began to believe.

He decided to test his theory, since he could see no other option, and stepped quickly into the lift before he could think about his situation anymore. He suddenly wanted to get to bed more than anything else he could think of.

Kelvin followed Danny onto the floor of the lift, shut the outer gates, pulled down the inner door, squeezed in along the side of the box beside the boy, and pushed a button. A stump of fluorescent tube set in the roof flickered and almost died. Something high in the building squealed as it took the strain. The sheet metal panels on the walls creaked all around them, and the lift juddered—hesitated—lurched—then began to rise slowly, swinging slightly from side to side because it was out of balance. Danny kept as far from the box as he could in the yellow-green gloom that was almost darkness, and gulped to relieve his dry throat and mouth, that now seemed to be full of imaginary dust.

Kelvin saw him swallowing air, and said, "What's the trouble?"

"I'm very thirsty," Danny admitted.

"Well, yes, you will be, it's only to be expected. But you'll get used to it. That's the way it is."

"I don't understand," Danny complained.

The lift shuddered to a halt.

"You will," Kelvin said, and stooped to pull up the door. He said something else as he tugged aside the doors of the metal cage, but Danny couldn't hear him over the clanging of the iron bars. Kelvin stepped onto the corridor and pointed to a door a little way away that Danny recognised at once as his own, leading to his room.

"You get to bed now," Kelvin ordered, "and don't go looking for your Gran anymore tonight."

In his room Danny drank at least a pint of water out of the tap at the washbasin. It was warm, and tasted slightly ferric, like the drink he had been given in the basement. He realised then that he hadn't felt at all ill since he had taken that crimson drink. In fact, it had made him feel very good: he was almost glowing with health inside. But he was tired out.

He flung himself into bed and slept at once.

Someone was moving quietly about in his room. Danny knew from the quality of the light it was early morning, so assumed the girl had let herself in to deliver his tea. Good, because he still had a thirst like an ache in the back of his throat. He didn't want to talk to her, however, for obvious reasons, so kept his face under the quilt. Then, whoever was in the room sat down on his bed. Someone big and heavy: he knew this, because the whole bed sank in the middle, whereas it had only dipped slightly when the girl had perched on it on previous occasions. A big person had come into his room, uninvited, and was sitting on his bed! An image of the bearlike man carved into his mind and filled him with fear. He's come for me, or he's come for the box, or he's come for both, Danny thought, and he nearly stopped breathing.

Then the someone cleared his throat and said, "Danny, I know you're awake; it's me, don't worry." It was his father's voice.

Danny sat up with a jerk. "Dad! What are you doing here? What's wrong?"

His father's face was crumpled and tired, and his usually immaculately combed hair stuck up in bristles in a dozen places. His eyes looked sore and the flesh below them was flaky and grey. He was wearing his best suit over a white shirt that looked grimy at the collar, as though he'd worn it one day too many, and his tie was loose and askew.

"Danny, I'm sorry, but the holiday's over. Something's happened; so your mother and I came down here overnight. The car broke down. It's been very difficult, but we're here now, so. . ."

"Has something happened to Grandad?" Danny asked, thinking he could see the light. "Have they got him then? Has he disappeared?" He jumped out of bed, went to the sink, and drank more warm washing water from his tooth-mug.

His father looked confused. "No, he's okay; your mother's with him now. It's Gran, I'm afraid. You're going to have to know. . . I'm sorry Danny, but she passed away during the night."

"Passed away?"

Realising the euphemism was above and beyond Danny, his father explained that Gran was dead.

Three hours later Danny, his parents, and Grandad were waiting in the hotel foyer for a taxi to take them to the station. The manager of the establishment, a razor thin, crop-haired woman in a black-and-white check blouse and grey suit, was commiserating with his mother, who was crying softly all the time that she was speaking. Danny heard part of the conversation, but didn't understand much of what was said. "—terribly sad time—everything done that could be done—first rate staff who are used to dealing with death—see it all the time—we've taken care of the body—leave everything to us—unfortunately, another guest *in extremis*, even now, as I speak—and so young, just a girl—but of course, we prefer to deal with older people—the more mature person—ripe old age is our speciality—you. . . you understand?"

The manageress sounded as though she had been reading from a publicity handout and had suddenly discovered that the last page was missing. She took a dive into sudden silence. Her sympathetic expression, set in stone, seemed only to affect her face below her eyes, which were empty and uninvolved. She and Danny's mother were seated on two gold-painted chairs, facing each other almost knee to knee.

"It was meant to be a break for them both," Danny's mother said, glad of a silence to break. She pushed her nose into her handkerchief and wiped her eyes. "She only had six months to live; that's what they told her, and she was so worried about leaving my father behind. He has Alzheimer's disease, so she was hoping to find somewhere here in Todley Bay where he could spend what time he has left in comfort. He could last years. She wanted to leave him in good hands."

The manageress nodded and clucked her tongue.

"She insisted on bringing the boy, because it would be their last chance of a holiday together, though I didn't think it was right. But you can't argue with someone who's going to die soon, can you? Especially if it's your own mother, so I let him come."

The manageress nodded and looked about her for some excuse to get away. No obvious opportunity presented itself.

"It's so terribly sad, that she should be denied those last few months they promised her," Danny's mother said, and hid her face in her hands.

Danny was keeping an eye on Grandad. The old man was quite oblivious to his wife's death. He had a loopy half-smile on his face, and was rubbing his hands together a lot, as though they were cold, or he were washing them. He kept strolling off, and Danny kept leading him back to his parents. Danny used these opportunities to buy soft drinks from a machine in the bar. He could feel them all sloshing about in his stomach, but he still wanted more. Or perhaps he wanted something else. It was a funny kind of thirst he had, that would not be quenched, and there didn't seem to be anything he could do about it.

He had tried to explain his other worry to his father and mother, about the people who had attempted to lure Grandad away, but his mother had started to get angry with him, and told him that this was no time for him to talk nonsense. It was obvious his father thought he was fantasizing too. He had shaken his head at Danny when the boy had mentioned the man who travelled across the ground without moving his feet, like a skater. So Danny shut up. He realised there was no point in trying to get through to his parents, who were both up to their ears in troubles of their own, so he gave himself the job of protecting Grandad. He was delighted when his father told him the four of them were returning home by train at once, that very morning.

When the taxi came Danny sat in the back with Grandad and his mother, who was now overwhelmed with grief. He held her hand, but got the impression she was unaware that he was there. Strangely, he had no feelings at all about Gran's death. It meant nothing to him yet. He was more concerned with the torrent of weeping beside him, and alarmed at his mother's inconsolable condition. He felt Grandad was safe now.

As the taxi drove along the seafront Danny saw the great bulk of the box ahead of them on the edge of the promenade. Someone had started to push it back towards the jetty, but hadn't got very far. The oily-black, overgrown gull was perched on top of it, standing in perfect balance on one leg. Its head was set at an angle. It seemed to be carefully scrutinising the traffic moving towards it.

The taxi, travelling slowly because a number of elderly people were dawdling and doddering across the road to get to the beach, came almost to a stop less than ten feet from the box. Danny slid down in his seat and turned away, trying to make himself invisible, just as the driver saw a gap ahead and accelerated into it, taking the vehicle some way beyond the box and the bird. Danny, thinking and hoping he had got by unobserved, couldn't resist turning round and sticking his head up over the top of the back seat to take one last look out the rear window at the gull.

The bird was riding the air a few inches above the boot of the taxi. Its beak dipped down towards the glass of the rear window, and it stared with one dead-reptile-eye straight into both of Danny's. It retained this pose for a moment, then broke away from the taxi with a single tug of its wings that took it soaring into the air. Danny expected it to follow the vehicle, but it didn't. It climbed up to a vast height at incredible speed, as though it had seen a hole in the sky it was afraid was due to close. Then it seemed to changed its mind. It plummeted back towards the town and disappeared behind the roofs to the right, ahead of the taxi.

Danny's father, sitting next to the driver, looked at his watch and remarked that they might miss the train. The driver shrugged, indicated towards the clutter of old people crossing the road ahead, and said he was doing his best.

When they got to the station there was no queue at the ticket office. Even so Danny's father had to write a cheque, and seemed to take an age doing so. Danny bought a tin of Coke, gulped it down, then stood with the other two and a little heap of luggage at the ticket barrier, ready to assault the platform to get to the train the instant they were free to do so. When his father emerged running with the tickets Danny grabbed some of the baggage and shot past the ticket inspector right behind him. His father, with one arm round his still distraught wife, scuttled awkwardly alongside the train looking for an empty compartment. They were halfway along the platform before Danny thought to look back to see where Grandad was. There was no sign of him.

Danny stopped and looked all round. Except for himself and his parents, the platform was empty. He shouted to his father, and felt the eyes of dozens of passengers on the train turn to stare at him curiously from behind the dusty carriage windows. His father understood what had happened at once.

"We've got to find him, Danny. Go back. You take the right and I'll go left. He can't be far."

Danny shed his baggage and pelted back through the barrier again. He saw Grandad almost at once, standing by a newspaper kiosk, talking to the man in a waiter's uniform. The man was half-hidden in a doorway. His face was just visible, and only his arms protruded. They undulated in beckoning, luring movements, like the tentacles of an octopus. Grandad, shifting from foot to foot, was rubbing his hands and smacking his forehead in gestures of wild indecision. He also seemed to be laughing anxiously, like a donkey, with his mouth wide open. The man in the doorway slid back a few inches, like a man on roller skates, and Danny could see his feet were definitely *not* touching the ground. His body even seemed to float up a little way as he receded, and Danny remembered that he had no bones, no *substance.*

Danny shouted wordlessly at Grandad, who froze. The man in the doorway glanced at Danny, sneered, and vanished. He went out in an instant, like a fused light. Danny grabbed Grandad's arm and yanked him away, almost pulling the old man off his feet. He seemed to get the idea for once, however, and, to Danny's surprise, started running quite fast. So fast in fact, the boy found it hard to steer him. He urged him in the right direction by pushing and pulling, a procedure that constantly threatened to entangle their legs and trip them both. The man at the barrier, who had watched the whole performance with some amusement, let them through and signalled to the guard at the far end of the station that the train could go. It started moving almost at once, sending Danny into a panic. There was no sign of his parents or the luggage, so he assumed that they had got on board. One of the doors of the nearest carriage was hanging invitingly open. Danny urged Grandad towards it, then trotted alongside as the old man climbed up the step to the corridor. As he did so he glanced back and saw his mother struggling towards him clutching the luggage. Behind her, running desperately through the ticket barrier, was his father, his face purple with unaccustomed effort. Both his parents looked very angry.

For a moment Danny thought he was going to start to scream and cry in protest against the waves of confusion and frustration that were sweeping over him.

He turned to pull Grandad back. It was obvious that his parents would not reach the train in time to get aboard, since the carriage next to him was now moving at running speed. He shouted to Grandad to get down, then realised that it would be very dangerous if he did try to disembark. Nevertheless, the old man turned and appeared to make some confident attempt to get back off the step. As he did so an arm reached out from the carriage door and the big hand at the end of it took firm hold of Grandad's shoulder and started to pull him in. A second hand emerged to take a grip on the other shoulder and Grandad was lifted up off his feet altogether and hauled into the darkness beyond the door. Then a figure leaned out for the handle of the door and quickly pulled it shut. Danny saw the hawklike nose and receding forehead of the bearlike man for just a second, peering out at him from behind the window at the upper part of the door; then the train gathered speed, retreated along the line, and snaked away out of the platform.

Then Danny did begin to scream and cry. He cried even louder when his mother caught up with him and started to blame him for what had occurred. Her face was a damp, white, puffy blotch of grief and anger. His father, when he joined them, tried to calm things down.

"We can phone ahead, down the line, and get someone to go on the train at the next stop and bring him off," he said, but his wife didn't seem to hear him.

"He's senile," she protested. "He doesn't know where he is or what he's doing. He might just open a door and walk out while the train is moving. Anything could happen."

"It's not just that," Danny yelled, now quite beside himself. "One of those men was in the carriage. They've got him now. They've been trying to get him all week."

"What men, Danny?" his father said, trying to conceal his impatience.

"The ones I told you about," Danny said, "but you wouldn't listen."

On the very edge of anger, his father said, "And why would these men want an old man like Grandad, for God's sake?"

"For his blood," said Danny, "and some of them want his bones."

Then his mother dropped all the luggage that she was carrying and stepped very close to Danny. "How could you talk such rubbish," she yelled, "at a time like this? On the day of my mother's death . . ." She spluttered to a halt, overwhelmed with indignation and rage.

A surge of intense and actually painful thirst, a craving for a drink that was not available, a liquid he could not obtain, cut into Danny and made him gag. He put his fingers into his mouth to touch his tongue to see if it was as dry as it seemed. It was. His father, alarmed by the expression on Danny's face, asked him what was wrong.

"I'm drying up inside Dad," Danny said, suddenly afraid to hear his own words. "I've got a terrible. . ." his tongue clicked against his palate, ". . . a terrible, awful *thirst*."

His mother regained her voice then. Her face was wet, wild, and dangerous, like a storm at sea. She howled at Danny wordlessly, and held her shaking hands, half-clenched like claws, in front of her face. "What are you trying to do to me?" she screamed at last. "How *can* you stand there and. . . talk. . . such. . . nonsense? After all that's happened, at a time like this, *you stand there whining about your THIRST*."

Danny, shattered, feeling quite alone, stood grey-faced and devastated by the injustice of it all. Something in his expression must have pushed his mother over the edge of her patience at that moment because, for the first time in her life, she slapped Danny hard across the face. Her ring cut the flesh of his cheek.

Danny broke away and ran. His mouth gaped open in a scream that only he could hear. Warm blood trickled down his cheek and into his mouth. The taste of it was at once familiar. It was like, but not quite the same as, what he was seeking; what he needed to quench his thirst.

Thinking about the dying girl back at the hotel, Danny ran right out of the station into the slowly moving holiday crowds passing back and forth along the front of Todley Bay. He darted through them like a wraith. Nobody seemed to notice him. He moved so fast, he thought he might be invisible.

He hoped the staff back at the hotel would understand, and be kind to him.

When he got there he found they were only too happy to receive him. They took him in, concealed him, and urged him to be patient.

The feast, they told him, though not of the rare old vintage of the night before, was almost ready. It would soon be served.

So, for the present, Danny had to content himself with that.

Someone to Dump On

For days Jean Feltham had been in need of something to aim her anger at. Her frustration at no longer being fully in charge, at having (as she saw it) her role as a mother usurped and her authority in the family questioned, had reached danger point. She needed someone to dump on. Neville provided the perfect target, and she went for him at once.

She did it in a roundabout way, through Robert, her husband.

"How could you have invited him?" she demanded. "You *know* I can't stand him. He may be your cousin, but you admit he gives even you the creeps. What the hell have you asked him down for? God!" She drew her fingertips down the bridge of her nose in an angry gesture peculiar to herself, and stared at him impatiently.

"I didn't," said Robert. "I just mentioned, months ago, that we'd all be here for a week, and I'd get in touch. He must have misunderstood me."

"He's good at that: getting the wrong end of the stick."

"I thought I might go and see him one day, perhaps take the kids, to give you a day off. You know he likes to see them."

"That's just one of the things I hate about him; his obsession with the children. It's not natural. He hangs about and watches them, and tries to join in their games."

"It's only his way. He's terribly lonely. And he's a child himself."

"A clumsy, stupid, middle-aged, sinister one. I don't want him around. I've got enough to put up with. I won't speak to the little sod."

"You're being a bit hard," said Robert. "He's the family albatross, hanging round all our necks. It's only fair to take a turn to look after him every now and then. His mother's an old woman. He's put a terrible strain on her over the years; the suicide attempts, and the trouble with the neighbours. If he's here for a few days it'll give her a break."

"I wish one of his attempts to top himself had been successful," said Jean bitterly. "This is our holiday, for Christ's sake. *My* holiday. And what's it been like so far? A bloody mess. And now *he* turns up! The moment we arrive! In fact, he must have been waiting for us to get here. He was here before we were. I tell you, Rob, I've had it up to here." She held her hand high above her head. "Get rid of him. Either he goes, or I do."

Robert frowned, trying to contain his own anger, aware that there was justice in his wife's complaint. From her point of view, their summer vacation, a three week tour through the south of France, had been worse than no holiday at all. She had hated it. Their mistake had been in going with the other families; four adults and seven children, who they hardly knew, in two big camper-vans. If they had just taken their own three kids, Tina, Nina, and Gavin, and travelled in their own car, there would have been no problem; they would have been under no pressure.

But Jean, a serious, solitary soul, could not function as a member of any group outside her own family. Also, socially and morally, she felt herself to be a thousand miles away from the other two couples and their children. Her ways were not theirs. She was interested in gardens, museums, architecture: culture, which she wanted her children to see and share. The others, who liked to call themselves "The Band of Gypsies," were only interested in good-times, getting drunk, and topless sunbathing. They left their children to do what they liked most of the time, so long as they, the adults, were able to indulge themselves without interruption.

It was not so much the boozing and lounging about that Jean objected to; she and Rob were, of course, free to go their own way while the others got drunk (Rob did not join in the orgies, though she knew he would like to have done; another source of tension and resentment), and the two of them frequently went for walks while the rest of the party caroused. Even so, their conversations during these expeditions were mostly about the slack, irresponsible behaviour of their companions, and were thus repetitive and depressing.

Jean could have coped with that, and with a second-rate compromise of a holiday, if her own children had not been so adversely affected; if they had not, all three of them, sunk in just twenty-two days into a state of anarchy that brought to her mind disturbing scenes from *Lord of the Flies*. The trouble was that all the children chose to wander about together in a rowdy, disorganised, disaffected gang, completely independent of their parents and creating their own kind of small-scale havoc, perhaps in unconscious protest at what they perceived to be parental negligence. Jean was not surprised to find this reaction exhibited by the other children, and even sympathised with them to some extent, but she was aghast to find her own children copying their behaviour so enthusiastically.

Tina, Nina, and Gavin had always been as good as gold. They had kept aloof from the kind of cynical contempt for adults so many young people seemed to affect these days. But recently, all of a sudden, they had succumbed, and had (or so it seemed to Jean) thrown in their lot with the enemy.

She had no idea what to do about it. They were out of her control, and everything she did to attempt to re-establish her authority only made things worse. She felt incompetent as a mother, and feared that she was becoming a figure of fun. She was sure that the rest of the group, with the exception of Rob, were all laughing at her and enjoying her embarrassment.

As for Rob, she was not quite sure about him; he seemed halfhearted in his condemnation of the others, and reluctant to come down completely on her side or discipline his children. But she was used to that from him; he always could see two or more sides to every question, and rarely provided the support she needed when she was really up against it. She could handle that. It was part of the pattern; it was the story of her married life. What she couldn't handle was the realisation that for some reason her own three children found the disruptive, rebellious antics of the other seven attractive, seductive, and exciting.

That was what really rankled: that her children preferred the company of infant outlaws to that of their own parents, and took every opportunity they could to get away and play wild, dangerous, even destructive games with the others. They didn't seem to give a jot about her and Rob anymore. This too sudden rejection was more than Jean could take on board. It stunned her, and she was temporarily overcome, trapped in a mesh of negative, helpless feelings.

And she and Rob were stranded. They had to stand and take it. They had to put up with the situation, at least on the surface, because they were in the minority, and the vehicles they were travelling in belonged to the other two couples, who were having the time of their lives!

But now the three weeks were up at last. They were back in England. They were, all sixteen of them, on a camping site on the side of a dale in deepest Derbyshire, less than two hours' drive from home, and Jean was in a mood to assert herself and get back on top.

The group had originally planned to spend one more week together, and she and Rob had decided to give it a go. It would be easy enough to sneak away from the others if they felt the need to, if things got worse. But she was not prepared to take any bullshit from anyone. Particularly not from a pathetic creepy-crawly like Rob's cousin Neville, the Feltham family curse. If Rob didn't get rid of him pronto—today—she would rent a car and take the kids home in the morning. Rod could stay and piss the week away with the others if he wanted to, and she had a feeling that he probably would. Well, it might be good for him, and for her, if he did!

She waited for him to respond to her challenge.

"Don't paint yourself into a corner over this, Jean," Rob said, with a grim yet reasonable, even reassuring, smile. "After all, we don't know if he intends to stay. I doubt if he does. He's brought nothing with him, as far as I can see, no rucksack or tent, so he can't be expecting to sleep here with us."

"God forbid. Just let him try. I expect his mother got him into a bed and breakfast place somewhere in the village. He's done that before, hasn't he? Dropped in on us out of the blue, and hovered about in the background, like he is doing now. Has he spoken to you yet? Has he even explained what the hell he's here for?"

"No," Robert said lamely, "he hasn't. I don't know what's the matter with him. He's keeping his distance. He seems to be avoiding me."

"He's pally enough with Tina and Gavin. He's got plenty to say to them. Look at him. He's all over them."

"Hm," said Robert, following her gaze towards the trio, who were standing some distance away. "They don't seem to mind. They used to say they couldn't stand him."

"That's because the other kids accepted him as soon as they saw him. He's just the sort of person *they'd* like. He could almost *be* one of them, a member of the gang."

"He looks the part, as though he's been sleeping in a hedge," agreed Rob. "He's really let himself go. I hope he's okay: I don't like the look of him at all."

"Me neither. But that's standard. He looks his shifty, scruffy, nasty little self to me. I expect he's had another of his 'relapses,' as his mother calls them, and got himself in trouble. In which case he'll be on those long-term drugs that turn him into an even more boring little crawler than he normally is. I can't stand it Rob: I mean it. He has to go."

"You're right. I'll speak to him," Robert said, sounding not quite as enthusiastic as she would have liked, and he wandered off towards his cousin.

As he did so, the seven children from the other two families, moving together in a herd, swept out from somewhere and surrounded Neville, Tina, and Gavin in a tumultuous, bickering circle. They started tugging at Neville's jacket and bouncing up and down around him. Even from a distance it was obvious that he was enjoying himself. He was waving his bent arms about, level with his shoulders, as though aping the actions of a bird, dancing on his toes, and giggling in the unguarded, abandoned way that Jean had always found so disgusting. Suddenly the group of children ran away, drawing Neville with them. He stumbled along a few steps behind them, flapping his elbows like a demented, out-of-condition turkey. The whole party vanished through a gate and down the sloping field beyond.

Robert, who had only gone a few steps, stopped.

"I'm not chasing after him now," he said. "I don't think he can come to any harm. I'll talk to him later."

"If you don't, I will," said Jean, using her most dangerous voice.

Robert gave her a bleak look. "No problem," he said, "just leave it to me. I'm going into the village now. You remember we arranged that your sister would send our mail to be collected at the post office. There'll probably be a few things from work that need my signature, and I'll have to get that sorted out. It shouldn't take long, though. I'll take Nina if she's feeling better."

Their eldest daughter had been resting in a tent since they had arrived, hours earlier, and was still recovering from seasickness brought on by a choppy cross-Channel ferry trip.

Jean nodded. "It'll do her good. You can pick up some fresh milk while you're at it."

The evening meal was cooking on the barbecue when Robert and Nina got back. Jean was looking after it, turning the chops and sausages with an absurdly clumsy pair of wooden tongs.

She looked cross.

The other adults were sitting at a rustic table drinking Bulgarian Red out of half-pint glasses. One of them was playing a guitar. They were singing an obscene version (with words of their own composition) of "Don't Cry for Me Argentina," a tune which had, for some inexplicable reason, become the theme song of their holiday. There was no sign of any of the children.

The day had been oppressively hot, but was no longer bright. The sun had turned sullen and moody, and slipped behind a veil of immobile, steamy cloud. Nina, drooping from the effort of even such a short walk, and still not quite well, returned to her tent. Robert stowed the milk in the shade under one of the vans and sat on a plastic chair close to the barbecue.

"I see it's your turn to be chef yet again," he observed.

Jean made a disgusted sound.

"Why?" asked Robert.

"Because I'm bloody hungry," she replied shortly.

Robert opened the big brown envelope he had collected and began sifting through the batch of letters it contained. He sighed heavily from time to time, or clicked his tongue. Twice he laughed sardonically, as though in quiet desperation.

"Anything interesting?" asked Jean.

"It's pretty much what I expected. Leave the staff to run the place for a few weeks, and everything starts to fall apart."

"Nothing serious, though?" she said, smearing taco sauce on chicken drumsticks.

"Nothing I can't handle."

Robert went through all the business letters first, then started opening the private mail.

"Hey, Jean, guess what we've got here?"

"I'm not in a guessing mood. Tell me."

"It's a letter from old Molly Feltham, Neville's mother. First time I've heard from her in years."

"If she wants us to foster him she can piss off. What does she say?"

"It's hard to read. Her arthritis must be really bad." Rob studied the letter for some moments, holding it close to his face. "I think she must have finally gone nuts, or I'm reading this wrong," he said finally. "She seems to be telling us Neville's dead—or 'gone beyond,' as she puts it."

"That's wishful thinking, on either her part or yours," observed Jean.

"It's not, though. I'm right. Look here: she says the funeral was on the seventeenth. That's eight days ago." He handed her the letter, pointing with his finger to the bottom of the first page.

Jean read through the section twice, carefully. "That's the message I get," she said, with a flippancy that sounded slightly false. "What's going on?"

"I have no idea. It can't be a joke; old Molly hasn't laughed at anything since Neville was born, forty-five years ago."

"Then she must be crazy."

"Hm," said Rob, and looked up at her uneasily. Jean busied herself with the drumsticks, spreading them out on the metal grill, concentrating harder than was necessary.

"Well, we know he's not dead, there's no doubt about that," said Rob. "We saw him this afternoon."

"We did. Unfortunately," Jean agreed, avoiding his eyes.

"Where *is* the old bugger?" Rob said, and coughed. "Is he about?"

"I haven't seen him since he went off with the kids, before you went into the village. He's not been back, and neither have they."

"None of them?"

"Not one."

"Christ." Rob got up and began looking around. "I'd better go and find them."

"You had. The meal is almost ready."

Robert noticed that her voice had changed in the last few minutes. It had gone low and lifeless again, as it had been a lot of the time during their holiday.

He was stepping across to the rustic table to enlist the assistance of the other parents when he heard the sound of children's voices. Then he saw small figures running up the hill towards him. He stared at them anxiously. They were the other families' kids: he could see no sign of Tina, Gavin, or Neville among them.

The little gang came tearing up to their parents, then ran across to Jean, the barbecue, and the smell of cooking. They were obviously ravenous. Robert asked one of them where the missing trio was. The little boy seemed not to understand, and Robert took him gently by the shoulders and hunkered down in front of him.

"I'm worried about Tina and Gavin," he said slowly, grimily. "Do you know where they are?"

"They went off with the man," the boy said.

"I know. But when did you last see them?"

"Ages ago."

"How long?"

"When did we last see Tina and Gavin?" the boy shouted to the other children, who were grabbing plate-loads of sausages, chops, and buns.

"*Ages* ago," they chorused.

"See? I told you," said the boy.

Robert let him go. Jean came and stood next to him. "What shall we do?" she asked. He thought she was almost in tears.

The other adults had thrown themselves on the food and were opening more bottles of wine. "We'll get no help from them," said Robert. "We'll just have to search around."

"Yes, but where do we start?"

"Bloody hell, I don't know. Anywhere but here."

They were interrupted by one of the children, who stopped eating long enough to shout, "Here they come, Mr. Feltham." He pointed down the hill to where an evening mist was beginning to form in the bottom of the dale. Three figures, two small and one quite large, were walking towards them out of the haze.

Behind them walked three other people, all men, one of them in a dark uniform. They moved slowly and deliberately, as if they were in no great hurry to reach their destination. The three familiar figures in front seemed to increase their pace, however, drawing away from the unidentified men.

Neville looked, even from a distance, idiotically happy. He seemed to be skipping with delight; or perhaps he was merely tripping on the uneven ground. Jean took hold of her husband's left arm with both hands.

"Oh, Rob, thank God. I was getting really worried, and thinking the most dreadful, silly things."

"Me too," said Rob, and licked his dry lips.

"I'm even glad to see Neville," continued Jean.

"I'm going to give him hell, though, for going off with them like that."

"And I won't stop you,' Jean said. "Look, the old fool's even waving at us. Wave back."

They both waved. Tina and Gavin waved. They all waved at each other. Strangely, for no reason in particular, Robert remembered the last occasion before this present visit that he had seen Neville. Robert had driven him to the railway station, bought him a ticket, and seen him on the train. Neville had hung out of the carriage window until the train pulled out, his big white head bouncing slowly like a balloon in a draught, and had stuck his arm right out as the train left the station, giveng an exaggerated, childish wave of goodbye. Then, abruptly, he had disappeared. Remembering the incident, Robert felt a momentary flutter of panic.

He must have shuddered. Jean felt it, in his arm.

"What's wrong?" she asked.

"Nothing."

"No." She shook her head. "Something's wrong. I don't feel right."

Nevertheless, they both continued to wave. Only Neville was waving back now; Neville and one of the three men at the rear, who was moving a hand about in the air above his head in an uncertain gesture, as though not quite sure what was going on.

"I wonder who they are, the people behind?" asked Jean.

"No idea."

"They seem to be coming our way. I think one of them is a policeman or something like that."

"Christ," Robert groaned, "I hope Neville hasn't done something stupid."

The pair watched in silence as the two small groups drew nearer. At one point the advancing parties dropped down into a hollow and disappeared from view. Moments later, to Jean and Robert's surprise, the heads of the three men reappeared over the crest of the dip. There was no sign of Neville or the children.

They waited as the men, who somehow seemed to be holding back, got slowly nearer. Robert thought that everything had gone very quiet. Behind him, not far away, his fellow holiday-makers were enjoying their wine and half-burnt meal, but he could barely hear them. Their voices were no more intrusive than insects murmuring in the distance. Also, he noticed how huge the landscape around him had suddenly become. The fields seemed to stretch away into infinity.

"I think those men want to talk to us," said Jean.

"You may be right. Let's go and see what they've got to say."

"Where do you think Neville and the children have got to?" Jean whispered, as they walked forward together.

Robert shook his head in obvious distress. "No idea," he managed to say, and gulped for air.

The three men finally reached them. The one in uniform spoke first.

"I'm looking for a Mr. and Mrs. Feltham. We were told at the site office that they're camping out here somewhere."

"That's us," Jean managed to say.

The man's face fell. He suddenly seemed too upset to speak. At last he blurted out, "I'm sorry, I've got some. . ." He fell silent, and looked embarrassed.

Jean nodded, and finished the sentence for him. "Bad news," she said.

Running in the Family

I understood that our house was haunted right from the start, when I was very young. The knowledge didn't trouble me, and I never felt in the least bit threatened by the ghost. Sometimes, perhaps, it did annoy me a little. This was because the ghost was a restless spirit, and was often on the move. For instance, I grew impatient with it when, as frequently happened, it seemed to follow me around the house. I was never sure if it actually was doing this, or if it was just a coincidence that we both wanted to occupy the same rooms at the same time. On these occasions, it got on my nerves. But I could put up with that.

I never saw the ghost then, and I never mentioned it to any other member of the family, not even to Christopher, my younger brother, though I assumed everybody knew it was there. There was nothing much one could say about it really. It was merely an invisible presence, vague and inconstant, like a dull sensation out on the very edge of things, and, as such, was quite unremarkable.

I did wonder, however, if it had free range of the whole of the building. There were certain areas, including most of the second floor, and many isolated rooms and cupboards in odd places throughout the rest of our huge house, that our father kept locked. I assumed he did this to keep the ghost out. There was no reason, that I could see, why he should have taken these precautions to forbid my brother and I entry to these parts of our home. But, as I came to understand, he was not a reasonable man.

And, though I didn't know it then, but learned later, he had his secrets, both real and imaginary: he had things to hide.

Most of all, he had himself to hide.

Father always had half a glass of water on the table next to his coffee cup at breakfast time. The water appeared, courtesy of Mrs. Tangy, our maid-of-all-work, just before the coffee. On the instant of its arrival, its recipient would lift it slowly to eye level for a moment, perhaps to check the cleanliness of the crystal glass, before drawing it to his lips to take a first sip. Then he would smack his lips in exaggerated contentment and give the plate in front of him a tiny half-smile. That was the signal for Mrs. Tangy to serve the boiled or scrambled eggs. Never poached. Father would not permit the poaching of eggs, a process that he thought made them impossible to digest. Fried eggs were, of course, totally out of the question. He was a man with firm but irrational ideas about what was right and wrong. And he knew his eggs. I suspect he had very little education.

My brother and I, if we thought about the presence of the glass of water at all, assumed it was there as an aid to digestion, since father frequently complained of internal troubles of that kind. That may be why, when a piece of toast stuck half way down my throat one morning, my automatic reaction was to reach across the table and grab the water, to attempt to flush out the blockage. I noticed as I did so my mother's face take on a look of alarm, which I attributed to concern over my condition. However, to my surprise, as my fingers closed on the cold glass, her hand took my wrist to restrain me. She turned to my father as if to summon his assistance. He looked indecisive for a second, then shrugged and shook his head, a reaction mother was plainly not expecting because she said, sounding and looking suddenly exasperated, "Are you *sure*, Raymond?"

"Yes," said my father, smiling now. "It doesn't matter."

The efforts I was making to dislodge the toast were causing my eyes to water, and I was beginning to panic. When I felt my mother release my hand, I snatched up the glass and gulped down two or three mouthfuls at once.

The result was quite unexpected, because a bomb exploded under my palate, my mouth seemed to fill up with fire, and I spat most of what I had drunk out in a spray in front of me. Christopher jumped to his feet and howled. He must have thought I had gone mad. He looked from mother to father to see how they were reacting to the situation, and was plainly puzzled by their expressions. Mother, though obviously repressing her anger with difficulty, succeeded in looking nothing worse than slightly annoyed, and was delicately dabbing her face with a handkerchief where my spittle had landed. Father, who avoided the shower by ducking down under the table, had reappeared to laugh at the aftermath of the explosion. I stood gagging and snorting, trying desperately to understand what had happened to me, while the fire bomb that had scorched my mouth sank down into by body and ignited again in my stomach, making me want to retch. After perhaps a minute of total confusion the sensations inside me transformed to a mild and not unpleasant feeling of warmth, but I was so confused and ashamed of the mess I had made that I burst into tears.

Very quietly, and without looking at him, mother said to father, "You shouldn't have done that."

At this, he put his hands, with his fingers outspread, across his chest, as though he thought it might burst or soar up like a balloon, and laughed even louder. Indeed, he seemed hardly able to contain himself.

Christopher, a tender child, and still kindhearted in those days, came round the table to comfort me, though he was obviously still distressed and frightened. He reached out to touch me cautiously, as though afraid I might give him an electric shock, and asked me what was wrong.

I was quaking in my chair. My features were twisted by half a dozen strong but strange emotions, and my nose was running as though I had a cold. When I was able to, I said, "What was that? What did I drink?"

"Vodka," said Father, and laughed again.

The word meant nothing to me. Mother, realising this, said, "It's a spirit; a very strong drink."

"A Russian drink," Father added. "I'm Russian, you see; I was born there. In Russia. In Russia *everyone* has vodka for breakfast."

Mother gave him a strange look then. I saw for the first time that she didn't like him, perhaps even hated him. If he noticed this expression on her face he ignored it, and continued to laugh.

I was unable to eat anything, and was feeling sick and woozy. I got permission to leave the table.

I went up to my room and was slightly aggrieved to discover the ghost there ahead of me. I got the impression it was waiting for me. Because I wanted to be alone with my queasy stomach and wounded sensibilities, I willed it to go away, but it hung around. I thought perhaps it wanted something from me. It seemed a pathetic thing.

I think I must have been slightly drunk, because I soon forgot about the ghost. Instead of feeling sorry for myself, I sat on my bed and started singing. Then I fell asleep.

My brother knocked on my door and woke me up. I let him in. He wanted to discuss the strange new fact that had come into our lives: our father was a Russian. What did that mean exactly? And what did it make us?

Russia was obviously a place. We thought we had heard of it. Was it a town? A county? We couldn't find it on the map of England, so we searched through the index of our ancient Atlas. When we turned at last to the page, we were shocked to see how huge a country it was. It seemed to take up half of the world!

A few days later we went into the school library and found a book all about Russia. It was a terrible place. There had been a revolution in which millions of people had been slaughtered. Modern photographs at the end of the book made it look as though the whole country had been covered by concrete factories. The people who worked in them looked hungry and wild, like the tramps we used sometimes to find sleeping in the outbuildings around our house. According to the writer of the book, they were a heroic generation who were building a model for the future of civilisation. Christopher and I took this to mean that England would soon become like the country depicted in the photographs, and we shuddered. We decided to keep secret the knowledge that father was Russian. We felt sick, guilty, and afraid, and wondered what we could say if anyone outside the family ever found out. For a long time we never mentioned the subject, even to each other, though I'm sure the knowledge weighed heavily upon both our minds.

Our childhood was singularly uneventful. As time went by, what with one dull thing and another, we got through the best part of it. For various reasons we didn't have much contact with our haunted house.

At the age of seven I was sent away to Windhaven, a girls' school run by two ex-nurses, one of whom had been a hospital Matron. They organised the school like a hospital, putting the accent on our "welfare." We were kept slim, fit, and active, but we learned next to nothing. The terms were endless and drab, like wet weekends.

In the summer holidays my brother (who was eventually packed off to a similarly expensive and inadequate seat of learning for boys) and I went away for six weeks to a variety of seaside resorts with mother and a widowed young woman from the village called Becky Kemp. Becky was ostensibly mother's companion, in the absence of our father. However, when we reached our hotel at wherever we happened to be staying, mother absented herself for most of the time, and left us in the charge of Becky.

Sometimes, in the evening, mother would join us for dinner. She never talked about how she spent her days, but more than once we spotted her walking about with a man (but never with the same man twice). At that time, this did not mean much to us, and it was only later that we guessed what she was up to.

Becky was embarrassed by these accidental meetings with her employer, and would grab us and march us off in the opposite direction when we chanced upon mother, even when she was alone.

On the whole, Becky was a decent soul who was kind to us, and did her best to make our holidays enjoyable. But it must have been hard work for her, as we were dismal children. We never really got the hang of having fun, and time and the two of us must have hung heavily around the neck of the youthful, vivacious, and childless widow. Becky, of course, had her own admirers, but she kept them at arm's length, at least when we were around.

We didn't see much of father, who remained at home all year round. He was cared for by Mrs. Tangy while mother was away with us. We did meet up with him four times a year, however, when he took us into Manchester to shop. On those occasions we traipsed from store to store all morning being measured up for every kind of article of clothing, including endless extensions and replacements of our school uniforms. Weeks later, these items would arrive at home or school, or wherever we happened to be at the time, in a number of interesting looking, but ultimately disappointing, parcels.

When our shopping was done father took us to his place of work to meet his staff.

His offices occupied three extensive, high-ceilinged, but almost empty rooms, on the third floor of a huge Victorian building just off Deansgate. I have no idea what work was done there. The staff remained the same for all the years we visited them. Nobody came and nobody went, and they hardly seemed to get any older. They all seemed very old to us anyway, but I suppose most of them were younger than father, who must then have been in his late forties. They always put on quite a show for us, and I now suspect they were under orders to keep us entertained. In winter they formed two teams, under the captaincy of Christopher and myself, and we played football with an old bowler hat round the big desks, using two wastepaper baskets as goals. In summer we improvised a game of cricket, with scrunched-up pages torn from ancient ledgers wrapped round tight with rubber bands for balls, the biggest of the umbrellas that dangled all year round from the hat-stand as a bat, and one of the adaptable wastepaper baskets, inverted, as a wicket.

The victorious team always won a big bag of sweets that they had to share with the losers.

These games never lasted more than an hour, so perhaps the staff was giving up their lunch break. They scattered back to their various "stations" like rabbits when my father, who withdrew to his own private room for the duration of our sports, finally returned to the General Office and loudly shut the door behind him. On re-entry, he always looked red in the face, and glassy-eyed, and he held his chin very high as he walked. He also smelt strongly of spirits.

Then we went for a long meal in Fontaine's, the gilded and deeply carpeted restaurant that was father's favourite eating place. Here we were encouraged to indulge ourselves with the richest and most expensive items on the menu. When we were as bloated and heavy as stuffed pigs, father ostentatiously paid the bill, tipped the lady pianist who entertained the diners with endless Chopin a ten-shilling note, and ushered us out to a waiting taxi. Then we had to go to a cinema to see a film. Often they were dreadful films, because father had no interest in the cinema whatsoever, and simply took us to the nearest "U" certificated programme. He always fell asleep and started snoring after ten minutes. We never had the courage to wake him, but occasionally people in nearby seats were braver, and there were often ugly scenes when he fell asleep and began to snore again, as he always did. He was never asked to leave, but those who objected to him sometimes were. He was able to dominate people, even when he was not quite awake, and the usherettes always took his side.

After the film, a taxi took us to Piccadilly Station. We would arrive early to give father time to refresh himself with two or three "large ones" and us with lemonade, then a train carried us to Buxton where the family car (driven by the multi-talented Mrs. Tangy) would be waiting to drive us smoothly home. Once there, father would vanish at once into his study or one of his locked rooms, having done his paternal duty for another three months.

As the years went by, father spent more and more of his spare time in his secret rooms, where I thought perhaps the ghost could not go. I never gave any thought to the implications of this possibly significant behaviour, because they did not once occur to me. As I said, I was a very dull child.

On the increasingly rare occasions that we all had breakfast together, it was noticeable that the quantity of vodka father consumed was on the increase. By the time Christopher asked the fatal question, father was getting through a glass full before he reached the toast and marmalade stage of the meal.

Over the years, of course, Christopher and I learned a good deal more about Russia. Every snippet of information, gleaned from whatever source, only made things worse.

What we were taught about the subject at school was fairly innocuous, admittedly, but then our teachers' information was out of date and inaccurate in the first place. The staff at Windhaven didn't want to know about the Revolution and the complexities of its aftermath, or the purges and atrocities perpetrated by Stalin and his successors, and what little they discovered by chance they had no intention of inflicting on their physically robust but emotionally delicate pupils. The teachers at Kirkpatrick's Academy for Boys, where my brother struggled to complete his education, had a similarly ostrich-like attitude to the horrors of modern history. Chris had a vague impression that human activity had come to an end shortly after the funeral of Queen Victoria.

Nevertheless, when we were at home we read the copies of the *Mail* and *Telegraph* that were delivered to our door, heard news reports on the radio, and were occasionally allowed to watch instructive documentary programmes on the nine-inch black-and-white television mother had had installed in what she called her "Work Room." Here she practised dressmaking, her hobby. While she ran up strange, gaudy, inappropriate frocks for herself on a fabulously expensive, almost silent sewing machine, in the light from a single lamp slung low above her head, we sat well away from her in the chilly gloom close to the set and stared at the action on the tiny, grainy screen.

Often it showed us depressing scenes from Russia. A handful of pug-featured, scowling men, wearing fur hats and overcoats buttoned to their ears, were shown standing monumentally still on a high balcony. Below them street-wide ranks of marching men, tanks, and other military vehicles bearing guns and rockets passed swiftly and smoothly by, like a wide, grey river that surged along forever, or so it seemed. These were the enemy. There were millions of them. They lived on the other side of an Iron Curtain. The gross, over-padded figures on the balcony were their leaders, evil men who had the Bomb. They were planning to use this weapon soon in a war against the West that would destroy the world. There would be no survivors: everything would go up in smoke.

We tried, when we were alone together, Christopher and I, to make sense of this. We had read, in the book we had found in the library, that the people of the USSR were creating the civilisation of the future, and now we were told they were preparing to bring about "the end of civilisation as we know it," a phrase then frequently on the lips of doom-mongers. This obviously meant that England would not inevitably disappear under a layer of concrete factories, as we had been led to expect, which was a relief. But the alternative, a global conflagration, was in no way preferable. We were very fearful and depressed, and our prospects looked bleak.

It was all the fault of the Reds, the bloody Russians. They were out to get us.

And our father was a Russian!

He did, in fact, look a lot like the cold, rock-faced, emotionless men on the balcony on TV.

"Perhaps the Yanks will save us," Christopher suggested. "They have bigger bombs than the Russkies. They're way ahead in science and technology."

"Let's hope so," I said, and tried to smile. I felt it my duty to try to comfort my younger brother when I could.

Then the Russians started putting up Sputniks. They were beating America in the Space Race. They were going to hang bombs in the sky so they could drop them on our heads. International tension was mounting.

"We've had it," Chris said very quietly one day, as we sat in front of the TV and watched a feature about a Russian scientist who had defected to the West. He was explaining Russian military strategy. His English was quite good, but his unfamiliar accent made it hard for us to understand him. Other English-speaking Russians joined him on the screen for a discussion, and they all had the same funny way of speaking. I lost interest altogether after a few moments, and started counting the minutes to the next programme: my favourite, "Come Dancing."

After a while I noticed that Chris had a peculiar look of consternation on his face. I assumed he was worrying about the bomb.

Next day, at breakfast, father seemed particularly ill. He was having a bad morning. His lips fluttered, and his eyes bulged as though unbearable pressures were building up in his head. He shuddered and twitched a lot. His hand, as he lifted his full-to-the-brim glass of vodka, jerked away from him, causing him to pitch a half inch of spirit into the sugar bowl. Mother motioned to Mrs. Tangy to remove and replace the bowl. She kept her own lips tight shut with obvious effort. She looked as though she wanted to yell at father, who was noisily and ineffectually scraping his knife and fork about among the scrambled eggs on the plate in front of him. Mother's expression of barely veiled dislike reminded me of the occasion, years earlier, when I had snatched up father's "water" to clear my throat of an obstruction and had expectorated a shower of raw spirit over poor Christopher. My brother's memory may have been similarly stirred to the same recollection by the same thought, because he chose that moment to say to father, "If you're a Russian, why don't you have an accent?"

The tradition had established itself down the years, and become accepted as one of the unwritten laws of our family, that at breakfast time my brother and I did not speak unless we were spoken to. Usually this brought a static, nervous silence to our morning meals, as neither of our parents was inclined to promote conversation at any time of day. Father occasionally took the opportunity to issue reprimands or instructions that required nothing more than monosyllabic responses from us, but he was quite unused to being quizzed by anyone about anything at that early hour, when his constitution was inevitably in extreme disarray. It must have come as a particular shock to be addressed impertinently thus by his youngest child. Perhaps he had a cruelly bad hangover that morning, or one of his many malfunctioning organs may have been demonstrating painful symptoms, or more likely it was a combination of both, but his response to the simple query was, to say the least, unexpected.

He jumped as though Christopher had sneaked up on him and shouted in his ear, dropped his cutlery, and dug at his ribs above his heart with his fingertips as though he thought he might be having a coronary attack. He leaned forward with his jaws clamped rigidly open and stared furiously at Christopher for many long seconds, still massaging his chest with both hands. At last his lips moved. He looked as though he was making an effort to speak, but seemed to have lost the use of his tongue. His open mouth looked oddly vacant. I noticed that he had stopped breathing and that his face was turning from red to black. Nevertheless, this didn't disturb me, because I knew he wasn't dying: his eyes told me that. They burned with life and malice.

"What. . .?" he croaked at last, then cleared his throat. "What are you talking about?"

Christopher appeared unawed by gravity of the situation, which must have added to father's confusion and anger. In a clear, rather hurt voice, my brother said, "You told us you were Russian. Years ago. But you don't talk a bit like one." He began to quail slightly under father's gaze. "Why is that? You just sound like an ordinary English person," he ended lamely, and sat blinking, waiting for an answer.

"I said I was a *Russian*?"

"Yes," I insisted, astonished by my audacity in speaking out at all, but wanting to support Christopher, and sensing at least some of the revelations that were to come. "Ages ago. Don't you remember? It was when I drank from your glass that time."

"And you *believed* me?"

"Of course we did," said Christopher.

"You said all Russians had vodka for breakfast," I reminded him, and got a look of stunning contempt from him in return.

Father said nothing for a few moments. The high colour was sinking away from his face, but he wasn't looking any more relaxed. He lifted his glass with a wobbling hand and gulped downed half its contents.

For some reason, Christopher and I both turned to our mother. She was biting her food with calm savagery, as though she was unaware of the recent and fragmented conversation, but the intense energy that crackled across the table from her to us in white-hot, invisible sparks, told us she had heard and was inwardly reacting to every word. We felt a need, that was probably the continuation of a self-destructive urge if we had but known it, to draw her in, to take her place in the family, to get her to speak out.

Again, it was Christopher who made the crucial move.

"*Is* he Russian?" he said, speaking rather louder than before. It was obvious who the question was intended for.

Mother kept chewing, then swallowed and licked her teeth with a flick of her tongue. She wiped her lips with a napkin. "No," she said, without looking up, and immediately took another mouthful of food.

"So he *is* just English?" Christopher said, with a note of exasperation. I knew he was thinking of all the years through which we had suffered the humiliation of having to live with the illusion that our father was an enemy of democracy.

Mother nodded.

"I don't understand," Christopher whined. "Was it some kind of joke?"

"Something like that," Father said, and gave us both a particularly unpleasant smile.

Mother shot him a glance that even he couldn't bare. He saw it, and looked away.

"If he's English, why does he drink vodka for breakfast?" Christopher asked peevishly, and I knew as he spoke he had gone too far. I could see that he knew it too.

"Because he's a drunk," Mother said, and then there was a long silence.

Father looked at her with a muddled expression, an unbalanced combination of sharp resentment, guilty unease, and the smouldering contempt he had shown for me earlier. "*So*, Molly," he said softly at last, but he slurred the two simple words.

"That's what you are," she reiterated, daring him to deny it.

He blew a lot of breath out through a tiny hole he made in the centre of his lips. "Well—it may be true. . ." he conceded. He withdrew into himself. He blinked, gave a shuddering, nasal groan, and tipped his head way back. Then he shocked us by asserting, loudly and pointedly, ". . . but, then, *things are not always what they seem*," apparently changing the subject and referring back to the inquisition Christopher had subjected him to earlier. Or so I thought. But mother seemed to put another interpretation on his words; to detect some different meaning behind them.

"Don't start that," she snapped, pushing her plate away in an unnecessary and uncharacteristically awkward gesture.

Mrs. Tangy, who had been lingering at the edge of the room apparently deaf and oblivious to the charged words and atmosphere around her, swooped down behind mother's chair and stooped to clear her place at the table. Before she could do so mother flicked her away with a gesture, as if she were an insect, and sent her bustling back to the kitchen with her tray of unwanted food and dirty dishes. All four of us had stopped eating now, but no one except mother had eaten much.

Father, reacting to the anger in mother's voice, and her obvious slight but significant loss of self-control, seemed keen to press the small advantage he perceived he had gained. However, he was not quite sure of himself; his expression suggested he was held back from further speech or action by some doubt or irresolution. He suddenly got to his feet and crossed the room to a cupboard that had always, as long as I could remember, been kept locked. He opened it with a key he dug out of his jacket pocket and reached inside. We heard the sharp, painful sound of glass falling against glass as he fumbled about. He returned to the table with a bottle of vodka, holding it by the neck. His grip was so tight, the bones of his knuckles and finger joints showed blue-white through his dry, purple skin. He unscrewed the bottle-top and refilled his glass before resuming his place at the table.

Perhaps the other two felt, as I did, that father had suddenly become dangerous. He looked bent on destruction. He raised his glass deliberately but unsteadily in a mocking gesture towards mother, and drank most of its contents. I glanced towards her in the hope that I might find some clue as to what was going on between the two of them in her expression, but she was inscrutable, at least to my understanding.

So the three of us sat and waited for father to speak again, to finish what he had started. He held us under a spell for more than a minute. At last he ponderously repeated the phrase he had used earlier: "*Things are not always what they seem*," as though it was some kind of incantation. Then he eased himself right back into his chair, pointed at the woman opposite him across the table, checked that he still had the full attention of Christopher and myself, and said, "For instance: that person is not your mother!"

He gave my brother and I a fatuous, hopeful smile, like a comedian encouraging his audience to make the effort to see the point of a lame joke. We didn't react.

"And what's more," he continued, "she's not even my wife."

I don't know what he expected us to say or do, but it soon became obvious that he had not anticipated that we should continue to sit on, dumb and motionless, in our chairs.

Which is what we dull children did.

After some moments father poured more vodka down his throat and glared irritably at us.

And the longer he did so, the less likely it became that we would speak. He shut us right up with that look. For a long time the only sounds in the room were of his breathing and swallowing, and the only movements those of his arm tipping the bottle and the glass.

Soon, I could feel, he was becoming disconcerted. The atmosphere around us changed. For us, it eased; for him it became. . . tighter, and more uncomfortable.

Somehow, we waxed and he waned. We became, my brother and I, by doing and saying absolutely nothing, a powerful, intimidating force of stillness and silence.

After a while it dawned on us that father had not got the will to contend with us anymore. We could see it in his eyes. He'd *had* it, all his life, but now, for reasons we could hardly understand, but had begun to intuit, he'd lost it. He had finally fired off his biggest weapons. They had hit their targets, but they had failed to explode. And opposite him across the table the woman who was not our mother had also escaped, had slipped away beyond his grasp. He tried out of habit to scowl at her, but there was not enough of his former fierceness left for him to make a face of it. She saw his expression and smiled.

Her smile finished him.

He grabbed the edge of the heavy table, pulled himself to his feet, stuck the bottle under his arm, and left the room.

We sat on in silence for a while until the woman sharing the table with us told us that it was true, she was not our mother. That person had died giving birth to Christopher. She had first become ill when I was born, and had been so weak that father had brought a woman from the town in to look after me. That woman was herself. Her real name was Molly Kemp, and she was the older sister of Becky, the merry but sensible widow who came with us on our holidays.

Molly explained that while I was still a baby, father had made his wife pregnant again, though the doctor had told him she was still too ill to bear another child.

With the inevitable result.

So she, Molly, had stayed on with father at his insistence, to help bring us up. She had had no choice because she had no money, and there was no other job available locally for her to do. She had been paid a pittance for the services she had performed. It was work she was not cut out for, and she had not enjoyed it.

Here she stopped and stood up.

"I've not made a very good job of the pair of you," she said, "but it's not been easy for me. I've had to look after myself. Which is exactly what *you* are going to have to do from now on." We waited for her to explain or elaborate upon this last statement, but she didn't. She left the room instead.

One day two weeks later father and Molly, looking very smart in new clothes, went off together in a taxi just before lunch time, leaving us in the charge of Mrs. Tangy. When they came back in the late afternoon father was obviously very drunk. We had to help lead him to his study where Molly said we should leave him. He was stretched out on the floor, so we put a rug over him. Then Molly said, "I made him marry me," and hurried off to a different part of the house before we could say anything.

From then on, we didn't see much of her at all.

Each of us realised that we were *alone*.

I was almost fifteen and Christopher was thirteen and a half.

We were both sent back to school immediately after the marriage, at the end of that Easter holiday. We didn't have much chance to talk, my brother and I, but we began to write to each other regularly then, and tried to help each other understand our lives in long, heartfelt letters. We agreed that we were glad that Molly was not our mother, because we never had liked her, and it was a relief not to have to worry about the possibility that father was an enemy agent, as Christopher had suspected he might be. But that was the full extent of the positive side of our predicament as far as we could see.

Obviously, we were very curious about our *real* mother, and wondered who she had been. We didn't even know her name. I wrote to father about this, and asked him if he had a photograph of her, but he never answered. I didn't try again. Later, we discovered that he had sold his interest in the business he ran so he could spend more time at home drinking, and had taken to disappearing for days on end behind locked doors in what had become *his* part of our home. It's possible that he never got my letter because his new wife intercepted and disposed of most of his mail. She only let him receive bills.

My brother was profoundly upset by the demolition of our illusions about our parents, and began to go off the rails. He wasn't dull anymore. He became delinquent. He set fire to his school and ran off to Liverpool. The conflagration was quickly extinguished before much damage was done, and Christopher was discovered and recovered almost at once. They didn't throw him out of school then or even later, when he caused other serious problems, so probably father paid a lot of extra money to keep him there.

Our family was rich, we realised. Not that this meant much to us, as we hardly ever saw money. Most of the children we were at school with had parents who were well off too, but they always had lots of cash to spend. We didn't. This set us apart from our peers, and made us unpopular. We both became, in our separate schools, very isolated. We became pariahs. This drove Christopher to increasingly desperate behaviour, but had just the opposite effect on me. I wore my dullness like a disguise and practised ways of making myself as inconspicuous as possible. I often dreamed that I had become invisible, and was disappointed on waking to see myself still there. I avoided making friends. That was easy, because there was nothing much in me for anyone to want to make friends with.

The only thing about me I was proud of was my solitude. I liked my own company.

My situation changed somewhat during the next summer holiday when, for some reason never explained, we did *not* go with Molly and Becky to a seaside resort. We stayed at home. It was then that I started seeing the ghost in our house for the first time.

It was mother's ghost. My *real* mother's ghost.

I recognised her because she looked so much like me, only a few years older. She was always a good distance away from me, and she was always running. I could never decide if she was running away from or towards something. There *is* a difference. Someone running *from* something is aware all the time of what is behind them. They're tempted to look back, to see if they're safe. Their movements are wilder and less coordinated. A person running *towards* something has a target. They aim themselves like an archer aims an arrow. Their movements are smoother, more economical, because they know just how much energy they have to expend to achieve their object. They are more in control of their bodies and the situation.

But my mother, poor woman, seemed to be running with no purpose from or towards nothing. She gave the impression she had come from nowhere, for no reason, and with no destination in mind. She was simply... running. Her speed was moderate. Her movements were unenergetic, as though she were slightly weary. But she looked more lost than tired. Her expression was that of a woman who was about to ask a question. To ask for directions, perhaps.

She made no sound.

To begin with, I only saw her for a few seconds at a time, every other day or so. She came at me from all angles, but swerved away as she got nearer. I was never sure if she was able to see me or not, and wondered if she would recognise me if she could. After all, she had only known me as a tiny baby, and, by all accounts, we had not spent much time together then. We had never *known* each other. My hope was that she would see her face in mine, as I saw mine in hers, and that she would understand our relationship. God knows, I needed a mother.

I was not at all afraid of her spectre, but the sight of it aroused any number of other emotions in me that it would be impossible now for me to define or describe. It was a very confusing time for me.

But it is astonishing how quickly one can get used to being haunted. I very soon grew accustomed to having mother near me.

The problem was that I knew she was in some distress; distress caused by the absence rather than the presence of something, I thought, and I wanted to help her, to provide what it was she lacked. But we couldn't even reach each other to make contact. Always she swerved away as she came towards me, and vanished into some other place where I couldn't go. I called to her and shouted, but she gave no sign that she could hear me. I thought, "If only I knew her name! She'd answer to *that*. . ."

However, each time I saw her she seemed to get a little closer.

One day, after I had been seeing her regularly for almost a month, I had an idea. It was a very simple idea, and I don't know why it hadn't occurred to me before. I tried it out as soon as she appeared again. I started running towards her. I knew I should have to run very fast to meet up with her, but I was determined that I would reach her. I'm no athlete, but I put on some speed then. I ran as though I was running for my life.

I was definitely running *towards* something!

And I got to her. Neither of us stopped running. We made contact.

We touched.

She saw me then, when we were very close, and I know that she recognised me.

We didn't stop. We ran on into each other, and she vanished. At least, I think that's what happened.

I never saw her again.

I didn't tell Christopher anything about mother's manifestations while they were happening. I *couldn't* mention the subject, for some reason. I thought if he could see her, then he would understand my silence on the matter, and if he couldn't, then there was nothing I could say that would make him aware of her presence. As I said, I was very confused at that time.

But then, when I had been sent home from school during a flu epidemic, I got a mournful, melancholy letter from him telling me how sad and bitter he felt about father's treatment of us by refusing to tell us anything about our real mother. Out of pity, to comfort him, I wrote back and told him about my recent experiences with her ghost. I explained that the restless and invisible phantom that had haunted our house all our lives had been that of our poor mother. I told him I had seen her and she looked very much like me. I said that her spirit had entered into me and that she was now at rest, and I was sure she would no longer disturb the peace of our home. I tried to make the letter as reassuring as possible because I was worried by the resentful, angry tone of Christopher's letter, and I was afraid he might do something really silly. I was beginning to realise he was capable of anything.

His reply came almost at once, by return of post. He told me I was a sick, delirious, crazy person. What did I mean by raving about ghosts?

Our house had never been haunted! Was I trying to drive him as mad as I obviously was myself? I had always been so sensible, as solid as a rock, as he needed me to be, like a mother, in fact, and now I had deserted him and retreated into lunacy. He had burned my letter, it had distressed him so much, and he begged me to write to him again to reassure him that what I had told him had been nonsense, a silly joke.

Well, I couldn't do that! I knew I had only told him the truth. I could feel my mother, a settled, warm, and quiet presence, inside me all the time, and I wasn't going to deny her reality for anyone, not even my brother.

I wrote to him again. I used all kinds of arguments to try to convince him that what I had told him was true. It was a very long letter, I'm afraid.

He ran away from school when he received my letter and came home to see me. He broke into our house at night and came to my room and started shouting. He said terrible things to me. He'd never spoken to me like that before. I tried to calm him, but he wouldn't listen.

His words didn't hurt me. I had mother curled up inside me, and somehow she protected me. I knew she wanted to help Christopher, as any mother would in those circumstances, but now she had finally come to rest, and she was unable to act on his behalf. I tried to explain this to Christopher, and he hit me. Father came in then. He had heard Christopher's shouts. They had penetrated to the top of the house where father had locked himself away with his bottles. He was, of course, drunk. And *furious*. He and my brother started to fight. Christopher was very big for his age, and because he was unpopular at school was used to fighting. He defended himself well, and managed to hurt father who became even more enraged. Molly came to the door of my room and stood and watched the struggle.

Father finally got the better of Christopher and beat him to the floor. He ordered Molly to phone for a taxi and, to his surprise I think, she went and did so. When it came father dragged my brother out and went off with him all the way back to school. Christopher was crying and howling as he left our house. I think he tried to spit at me as I waved him goodbye. I felt very calm throughout this dreadful scene, and I'm sure my tranquillity was due to my mother's presence, though of course I always have been the placid type. I can take these things in my stride.

I didn't hear from Christopher for about two weeks. In spite of everything, I was expecting him to write because, as far as I was aware, he had nobody else he could share his misery with. In the end I wrote to him, and he must have felt a similar impulse at about the same time as our letters crossed.

Mine had been chatty and cheerful. I avoided saying anything more about our mother. His was hurt and angry, and full of venom directed mostly at father and Molly. He seemed to have forgiven me for whatever he had thought me guilty of in my previous two communications but, as I had surmised, he had to; he had no alternative, no one else to confide in.

From then on we were regularly in touch. He wrote and told me all his fears, dreams, and ambitions; and he had become very ambitious. He was determined to take on the world and win. On his own terms. He wanted revenge, I think.

His dreams were of crime, and his fears were of failure. He began to study hard at school because he wanted to establish himself in a position of power as soon as his education ended. He talked of working in "The City" in the same way that fundamentalist Christian zealots speak of the prospect of spending eternity in Heaven. The world of international commerce attracted him because it provided a vast, soft target for his vengeful lust for plunder. He wanted to be hugely rich, but he had no intention of becoming so honestly: he wanted to hurt and ruin as many people as he could on the way to achieving this aim. He had an outsize score to settle.

Meanwhile, Molly told him she had intercepted angry letters from the head of his school, addressed to father of course, about his disruptive and destructive behaviour and, at the end of each term, reports on his scholastic progress that put him at the head of his class in almost every subject. He had become something of a prodigy. His personality was developing fast; there was an awed, even fearful, note in some of his teachers' written comments about him. He was beginning to burn his mark into the flesh of the world.

I left school and returned to my father's house where I lived very quietly. Father, killing himself with drink, kept to his rooms most of the time. Molly ignored my existence when she could, though I knew she resented my presence. But she was a sensible woman, was Molly, and didn't waste her energy trying to alter circumstances she could not control. She couldn't get rid of me, so she put up with me. And I was no trouble. I kept out of her way.

As I now realise, she was playing a waiting game.

Unlike Christopher, I had achieved nothing at school except

anonymity and self-negation. The only skill I had was that of camouflage, the art of concealment. I was no good to anybody whatsoever. No one would employ me, and I was glad of that, as it was my intention to avoid society of any kind if I could. I was not attractive to men, thank God; my mirror assured me of that.

So I was able to retain my solitude. Of course, this was never quite as total as it had been, because I hosted my mother's spirit, but together we formed a team, and perfectly accommodated each other. I had a strong sense of the truth about all parents and children; that each exists, in some way, within the other.

Perhaps it was my mother's influence and example that made me take up running, or maybe it was just that I grew bored, or decided I needed exercise. Certainly, my inactive life in father's house was unhealthy, and I knew I was going to seed. I never had been very strong and fit, even under the regime of air and exercise enforced by the ex-nurses at school, and I had no wish to be really *well*, but anyway, for some reason or other that I can't now recall, after I had been home less than a year I began to run. Only for short distances to begin with, along the lanes and paths on the edge of town, but I soon found myself going further and further. In the end, I was out for hours at a time. I never knew where I was going; I followed my nose. I ran in a trance, with almost no knowledge or even awareness of my surroundings, and relied on instinct (or it could have been my mother's guidance) to get me back home. Even though I never knew quite where I was, I at no time felt that I was lost. I just ran from somewhere to nowhere and back, and it became a habit. I ran every day.

I never thought of myself as a jogger, or dressed for the activity in special clothes. There was nothing competitive or sporty about my expeditions. Running, for me, was just a way of being out there in the world and retaining a sense of solitude, of not quite being part of my surroundings. Most people looked away for some reason when they saw me coming, as though out of respect for my privacy, and no one ever spoke to me or tried to stop me for any reason. That appealed to me a lot. It gave me an almost cozy sensation, very like what I imagine I would have felt if I had ever achieved my old and still cherished dreams of attaining invisibility.

Meanwhile, Christopher and I continued to correspond. He sent me long, rather frightening letters describing various battles and skirmishes in his war against the world in exchange for my pallid, dull observations of life in our father's house, where the only thing that changed was father's condition as he sank slowly and painfully down. It seemed wise not to mention my running to Christopher. I thought the information might disturb him, and make him angry with me. I was afraid it might remind him of what I had told him about how I had met and mingled with our mother. He had found that so objectionable and hard to take.

But perhaps I was being over-cautious. I began to suspect he no longer bothered to read my letters, since he never commented on anything they contained. And I never had the opportunity to ask him if this were true, if my letters were just a waste of ink and effort. When he finished school, he refused to came home again, and I have not seen him, face to face, since.

Christopher's letters to me were all about himself. He described his progress in detail.

He finally left college in a blaze of glory, with a marvellous degree. He hurtled into the City at once, and set about his task of infiltration and subversion. He was made welcome with open arms. Powerful concerns bid against each other to buy him. He was ushered quickly into the heart of things, where he could do most damage. In a few years he controlled the fortunes and lives of hundreds of thousands of people. He became famously, fabulously rich. He told me that this, in itself, meant nothing to him at all. All the pleasure for him was not in spending his wealth, or counting it and dreaming about it like a miser, but in retaining it, in *holding it back*, in depriving other people of the use of it.

Christopher was stunningly successful. Though we never met again, I often saw him on TV, and he always looked so calm, dependable, and honest. He became a celebrity whose opinions on everything were sought and heeded. His appearances on discussion panels made me laugh a lot. I think I was the only person in the world who knew he was a consummate and dangerous humbug who stood for the opposite of all that he appeared to represent.

When he judged the time was right, he pounced, and disappeared with billions of pounds of other people's money. He shook the world. Thousands of people like father, who had all their wealth invested, woke up one morning to read in the papers that they were ruined. It was the biggest fraud ever.

But father's fortune was untouched. Christopher had taken steps to spare him. He wanted him to be able to afford to continue to drink himself to death. He wouldn't, he told me, see his own father starve. I don't think he gave any thought to my dependent situation, or was even aware of it.

I was, very.

What Christopher could not have known was that father was due to die at that time anyway; the very night, in fact, that his son absconded with a huge portion of the wealth of nations. Father, locked away on the top floor of our house that sweltering summer night, tried to open a window to let in air, or maybe to be sick onto the flower beds below, as was his habit.

He fell out and broke his neck.

I suppose most people would have been shocked to discover they were not even mentioned in their father's will, but it came as no surprise to me. I don't know if he had simply forgotten my existence (he lost most of his memory somewhere in the sea of vodka he drowned himself in), or if his wife had contrived somehow to get him to sign a will totally in her favour, but that's where everything went: into my stepmother's pocket. Empowered by this wealth, she set out to build a new life for herself, one that I knew would not include me.

She gave me absolutely nothing. She presumably thought she had given me enough.

She didn't drive me out immediately; I was able to continue to live on in the house. But I had no money, nor means of obtaining any. Unlike my brother, I was incapable of theft or any other crime and, as I have said, I was unemployable. I could have contested the will; who knows, perhaps I would have done so if Christopher had been there to guide me through the process, but alone I couldn't even begin to face the prospect of involving myself in complex, open-ended litigation. So, although I didn't starve, life became increasingly difficult for me. No one looked after me. Nobody bought clothes for me anymore, and those I possessed began to fall apart on me. I began to look seedy, then decrepit. My stepmother, when she saw me, let me see her contempt for my condition and my helplessness. She sneered at my inability to rise up, like her, out of my misfortune. And I could tell she hated having me around because, I think, I reminded her of who she was, or had been: something she wished, now she was rich and independent, to forget.

I knew that someday, somehow, she would get rid of me.

It took her more than two years to do it.

I continued to run each day, and must, at the end, have looked like a scarecrow come to life. My clothes were so far gone, they were literally falling off me. People who didn't know me stared at me in alarm when they saw me coming. Others, from the looks they gave me, plainly thought I was mad. Some local people tried to stop me to offer me charity, but I wouldn't have that. I suppose, on reflection, I wanted to bring my distant, but crucial, relationship with my stepmother to a conclusion, and did not want to let anything ease my condition, and delay that end.

It came about, quite obviously and easily. One day when I returned home after my run, Molly wouldn't let me in. All the doors were closed against me, and one of the women she employed to do the housework shouted to me from an upstairs window that they had all been instructed to keep me out.

I knew I would never get into my home again. I sat on the front steps of the house and thought about this for perhaps an hour, then I stood up, took off all my rotten clothes, flung them away from me, and started to run again. I ran out of the gate and into the centre of Buxton. People tried to stop me, but I evaded them as long as I could. When, at last, I was almost surrounded, and I saw that I would soon get caught, I flung myself into the road under the wheels of a container wagon, and I died.

But I'm still running. I am the ghost of a naked girl running. It seems I never will stop.

And, even now, I'm not always invisible. Sometimes people who are still alive catch a glimpse of me, and I know they are terrified by what they see. Perhaps they remember the circumstances of my death.

I too am haunted, by thoughts of my brother. I understand that we can never be reunited, but I need to know what happened to him. He didn't write to me after he vanished with thousands of other people's fortunes, and I never learned if he escaped into some kind of freedom. I hope so, but I doubt it somehow. The world is too small a place to hide so much money, and he must have made many enemies.

I never cease to wonder about him. I'm sure he would have written to me if he could have done. Sadly, I think he is either dead, or on the run somewhere.

Or, even worse, perhaps he is both, like me.

Screens

SCREEN. 1. To hide from view as with a screen.
2. To project (a lantern-slide, cinematograph picture, etc.)
O.U.D.

"Of course," said Mrs. Ashe, pausing over the task of wrapping his wedge of Blue Stilton and leering up at him over her spectacles without raising from her customary stoop, "if you've been abroad for the last few weeks, you won't have heard . . ." and she let the last word hang in the air like a baited hook.

Andrew realised he had set himself up. To pass the time while she encased his cheese in layers of plastic and paper, and because something about her always made him slightly nervous, he had asked if anything had happened in the village while he had been away, expecting the usual bland response. Instead, he could tell, she had something juicy for a change, some not-very-good news he in particular was not going to welcome. He wished he had kept quiet. He wanted the conversation to drop, but Mrs. Ashe wasn't going to let it. She stood immobile over her task, demanding a response, as though trapped in an enchantment that only a word from him could break.

"Heard what?" he said flatly, trying to sound disinterested.

Mrs. Ashe slipped the cheese into a bag with his other purchases.

"About your friend," she said slyly, "Mrs. Shaster."

Kate Shaster was his next door neighbour, and his only friend in the village. They occupied two tiny detached but adjacent cottages on the edge of Longton, in a position of comparative isolation. Because they were both single (Kate a widow, he divorced) and recent incomers to the community, and they spent quite a lot of time together, visiting each other's homes, and escorting each other to the local pub, rumours of a romantic attachment between them had naturally grown and flourished. The evidence for this scandal-mongering was all in the looks and innuendoes of local people like Mrs. Ashe. No native of Longton made a plain statement in the presence of an outsider if it could be avoided. All but the most simple communications were, for some reason, elliptical, oblique. Anyway, there was no truth in the rumour: Kate and Andrew were just the "good friends" of the cliché, and sometimes Andrew wondered if they were even that. The joke between them was that she was too ancient and he was too ugly, and they were doomed to stay single for ever. Kate, at forty-one was seven years older than Andrew, whose face had been disfigured slightly in a hang-gliding accident.

"Has something happened to Kate?" he said, noting that Mrs. Ashe's eyes widened slightly at his use of the Christian name.

"Oh, no, duck." She shook her head and showed her dentures behind a cranky smile. "Not as far as we know. But she's not been out; we've not seen her about." She raised the bag of shopping from the counter and moved it slightly towards him. "Young Darrel noticed she hadn't used her milk. The pints he'd delivered for two days hadn't been taken in. He told his dad, and Mr. Lomax called at her house. She wasn't dressed, Mr. Lomax said, when she came to the door at one in the afternoon, so he knew something was wrong."

"What do you mean, 'She wasn't dressed'?"

"She was in her dressing gown. Mr. Lomax said her hair was all over her face, as though she'd just got out of bed." Mrs. Ashe clearly relished this detail.

Kate was fussy about her appearance. Andrew could not imagine her answering the door looking anything but her best. Perhaps she was in trouble.

"Was she sick? Has she seen a doctor?"

"Mr. Lomax offered to get one, but she wouldn't have it. Said she wasn't ill, and there was nothing wrong."

Andrew reached out, removed his groceries from the shopkeeper's weakly grasping hand, and stepped back towards the door.

"I'll call round now," he said. "See how she is."

"You better had, duck," said Mrs. Ashe officiously. "I expect you'll be able to sort her out," and she winked at him, as though they were joined together in some naughty complicity. "She'll listen to you," she added.

As Andrew went out onto the street, and the brass bell above the door jangled, she called, "Are you back for a while now, Mr. Colvin? Shall I tell Darrel to start delivering your milk again?"

"Yes," said Andrew. "Thanks. I won't be going away again for some months."

It was when he came back to it after a spell away that Andrew noticed how deserted the village seemed to be. Except at weekends when, at all seasons, there were booted tourists trudging through on their way from one beauty spot to another, Longton looked an empty, forsaken place. People kept to themselves and their houses to a degree that was downright morbid. Nothing moved for hours on end, and nothing changed except the weather and the gardens, where things sprouted and grew unnoticed for the most part, though they must have been tended by someone, since they were invariably kept in neat order.

It had been a wet afternoon and the darkening effect of the damp on the stone walls of the houses gave them a drab, self-effacing uniformity. The sky beyond the not-so-distant horizon was scarred by columns of sooty clouds that seemed to rise up vertically, and sweep along behind the crests of the hills like a line of megaliths on the march.

Andrew was startled when a girl of about fourteen in a long green coat, her face wedge-shaped in a high, turned-up collar, stepped out of a gate onto the road ahead of him. She had a dog on a lead. She stood and watched without expression as he drove past, leaning back to resist the tug of the big, impatient Alsatian. Andrew saw in the driving mirror that she remained watching his car for some seconds before turning and running off in the opposite direction, and felt obscurely uncomfortable. It was odd how even such a brief and remote encounter with a resident of Longton could make him feel unwelcome.

He parked by his front door, unpacked the luggage from the boot, and dropped it in the tiny hall. He took a brief turn round the house to check it was as he had left it, then looked out of his first-floor window at Kate's house, about twenty yards away from his. All seemed normal. There was no milk on the step by the side door, where Darrel, the delivery boy, always put it. The curtains were drawn back, and a fuzz of smoke drifted out of the chimney.

Probably Old Farmer Lomax was making a lot out of little, Andrew decided. It was the man's way. For all his size and lumpish manner, he was a gossip at heart, quite capable of embroidering a tiny tale into an epic to amuse himself and entertain his friends, especially if it was about the "incomers."

Nevertheless, Andrew felt a need to visit Kate, to put his mind at rest. If she had seen or heard him return, she might think it strange if he went round at once, without pausing to wash or eat, so he did those things quickly, making a meal of the Stilton and fresh bread. Then he remembered he had an excuse to call on his neighbour anyway; he had a present for her.

Moments later, with the gift in its fancy wrapping under his arm, he tapped on the stained-glass sunset on her door. She was a long time answering, and opened the door just as he knocked a second time. He saw at once she had been expecting him; that she was, at the very least, disturbed about something; and that she was going to try to conceal that fact from him. She smiled with her mouth, but her eyes had a different look, suggesting her mind was on whatever it was that troubled her, something serious and mysterious. Her sharp-featured, expressive face always betrayed her thoughts to some extent.

She reached up to kiss his forehead. He pecked her cheek in return, and handed her the present. She pushed him ahead into the comfortable, over-furnished parlour at the back of the cottage, murmuring what he took to be the usual words of gratitude. After handing him a bottle and glass, and instructing him to help himself, she unwrapped the gift. Her movements were uncharacteristically violent. She tugged at the tape round the box without trying to unfasten the simple bow he had tied, and tore at the paper clumsily. She seemed to be trying to regain the self-possession she had unaccountably lost, and to be aware that she was not succeeding.

He pointedly looked away from her toward the television. The screen was mostly dark, but formless, off-white, slithering shapes that he could not identify drifted languorously across it from time to time. He couldn't make out what was going on. He leaned forward and squinted. The volume was low; he was unable to understand a word of the whispered commentary.

When she saw what he was doing Kate pointed the remote control at the set and touched a button. The picture shrank and shrank. There was a whirr and a click, and Andrew realised that he had been watching a video.

He turned back to Kate, expecting some explanation as to why she had abruptly censored his viewing, but did not get one. She glanced at him, and their eyes met. She looked away at once, to the gift on her lap. She praised it hurriedly and overmuch, but without conviction. Words tumbled out of her as though they had been cramped away in some tight place and were glad to be free at last; then she suddenly shut up, and looked annoyed with herself. He beamed pleasure in her apparent satisfaction, and poured a drink for himself. He asked if she wanted one, knowing that she hardly ever drank at home, or at all. After a brief, frozen pause, when her face opened wide like a window, and he could see her thoughts spinning, she nodded emphatically.

Surprised, he went to fetch her a glass.

In the kitchen, he was brought up short. The room was a mess. Empty cans and packages and half-eaten meals were spread about the work-surfaces, and dirty dishes stuck out of greasy water in the sink. A box of cereal had spilt onto the floor and its contents crunched and crackled under foot. The food cupboard doors were open and the shelves inside were almost empty.

After some searching he found and rinsed a glass, half-filled it with Smirnoff, added a drip of lime, and went and handed it to her. He hoped the spirit might loosen her tongue.

As she reached for the drink, she gave him a smile that got strangled at birth, and only increased his rising discomfort.

"How have things been?" he asked. "In Longton, I mean," he added, as she looked at him slightly askance. "Anything interesting happened?"

"It never does," she said, "does it?"

"Not when I'm here. Not so far, anyway."

She shook her head cynically. "Nothing changes."

"You've been keeping okay?"

She sipped her vodka, pursed her lips, and nodded.

"Good," he said.

And thought, "End of conversation! Christ, have I come to the wrong house? Or is this Kate's dozy twin sister that she's never told me about, and always kept hidden?" It was as though she'd fixed a dimmer switch to her personality and turned it to minimum, or taken some numbing narcotic.

"That's it," he thought, "drugs!"

He took a good look at what he could see of her eyes, but they were just dull and lifeless, not high and crazy, or pained and anxious from withdrawal. Something seemed to have been taken out of her, not inhaled or injected in. Something was missing.

He started to tell her about his time away, to give himself time to think. It had been just another dull business trip to Scandinavia, and he was hard pressed to come up with something amusing. She smirked at his attempts at wit, and smiled wanly at his trite tales about a lost luggage crisis and the price of restaurant meals in Stockholm. After a few minutes, he gave up.

"By the way," he ventured, "is your car running again?"

"I had it fixed weeks ago. It's fine."

"Only I noticed you don't have much food in, so I wondered if you were off the road?"

She didn't react. He was still waiting for some comment when he suddenly noticed something else.

"Where's Bruckner?" he said. The dog usually gave him a warm but dignified welcome, being one of the rare ones of its race that was able to exercise self-control when a visitor came through its owner's front door. Now there was no sign of it.

"He's gone." She sounded irritable, almost resentful.

"He's dead?"

"Probably. He just went. I let him out, and he didn't come back."

"That's odd. You looked for him?"

"Of course."

"You must really miss him."

"Yes, well, I did at first." She sounded as though she was finding it hard to remember how she had felt about her pet's disappearance.

Andrew couldn't believe it. Bruckner and Kate had been very close. She had never been silly about him, or treated him like a surrogate child, and they seemed to have developed a relationship based on respect. Bruckner had a steady nature, though he was prepared to look fierce for strangers when Kate required him to. He'd been a good dog. Now he was gone, and she hardly seemed to care.

He noticed her glass was empty. He'd hardly touched his drink. How long had he been holding it? Surely no more than a minute or two?

He drained his glass. "Perhaps it's me," he thought. "Jet lag, stress, something like that." He'd been travelling for almost twenty-four hours. He didn't feel too bad; a bit bleak and hazy, but not over-tired.

Still, he didn't trust himself to wrestle with Kate's problems just then.

He'd sleep on his impressions, he decided, and consider them again in the morning.

When he got up to go, Kate didn't try to detain him, something that, out of affection or politeness, she usually made some small show of doing.

As he passed the front of her house he noticed, behind the net curtains, the glow of her TV set. She must have turned it back on the instant he was out of the room! He remembered the whitish smudges drifting through the cloudy depths of the screen. What had they been? Faces, perhaps, blurred and distorted?

Something, anyway, that she had not wanted him to see.

He spent the next morning unpacking and freshening-up the cottage. Then he drove seven miles into Buxton to pick up supplies from a supermarket.

He thought to ask Kate if she wanted anything, but couldn't bring himself to do so. He had been wondering restlessly about their relationship. He had thought they were, on many levels, quite close, but he had never been sure of Kate friendship. Frequently, what seemed to be affection on her part had an artificial, warmed-over flavour, like fast food. Her amity sometimes had a false edge, but Andrew had not let this bother him. After all, they were neighbours, brought together by chance. On the whole, on the surface, they got on remarkably well.

But he was full of mixed feelings about his visit to her the previous evening. On one hand he had an impression that he may have been treated rather shabbily by her. On the other, he feared that he may have blundered in on Kate when she had been vulnerable and unhappy, and he had not been sensitive enough to appreciate the situation and react accordingly. He shouldn't have rushed round and thrust his gift at her as though it were an invitation to a party at her place. He should have ignored the siren warnings of trouble-stirring Mrs. Ashe and waited for a more appropriate time to visit.

His worst fear was that the loss of Bruckner explained Kate's obviously disturbed state, and he'd been crass enough to go on about the bloody dog, probably the one subject she did not want to think about. Still, there was no way he could have known that the creature was dead, and he tried to shrug off the wisps of guilt that lingered in his conscience.

He had lunch in Buxton and got back to his cottage just before three in the afternoon. He glanced across at Kate's house as he motored up his drive, and saw that her curtains were closed.

He watched part of a football match on TV but, at halftime, couldn't resist going upstairs and looking across at Kate's house. An unclaimed bottle of milk stood by her door.

"I'm getting worse than Mrs. Ashe and the rest of the villagers," he thought. "It's none of my business how Kate spends her days. I'm worrying about nothing. I saw her less than a day ago, and she was okay. Off-colour perhaps, but aren't we all sometimes? So what if she's tired? If she spends a day in bed?"

Then an obvious explanation occurred to him. She had a lover. He was in there with her. She's having a wild affair!

The possibility made him feel worse than ever about his intrusion.

The theory would account for a lot; the disorder in the kitchen which, on reflection, was merely untidy (no time or energy for housework); Kate's distant, slightly nervous demeanour, and her lack of genuine enthusiasm to see him back.

As he half-watched the last half of the match he searched inside himself to see if his speculations engendered any jealousy. They did. Not specifically sexual jealousy, though there was an element of that; more a nagging, resentful envy that was surprisingly painful. He would surely miss Kate's company.

But he felt he had been dumped abruptly, unceremoniously. She should have told him, given him some explanation, and not left him to puzzle things out himself. It was shabby. He was surprised at her for acting so covertly, as though she were ashamed. It was just not like her.

He wondered what sort of man was capable of causing her to behave so uncharacteristically and tried to picture him.

Then he realised that he had made the whole thing up out of almost nothing. There was not a scrap of real evidence to support his fanciful theory! There were a dozen equally plausible explanations.

The football petered out in a draw. The faces of the exhausted, frustrated players as they walked off the field brought the afternoon to a depressing anticlimax. Andrew switched off the TV.

He put on his boots, Gore-Tex jacket and waterproof trousers, and went for a long walk in the pouring rain.

He got back late.

The light was on in Kate's parlour. All looked normal. He peered over the hedge that divided their gardens. The milk had been taken in.

"I'm an idiot," he thought, "and Mrs. Ashe is a bloody witch."

Sunday started well. He was up early. He made a lot of coffee and drank it slowly as he read the papers, filling his mind with national scandals and despairs that he had missed while abroad. This took him to almost midday, when he had arranged to drive to Ashbourne to visit friends. He was running a bath, and pulling the pins out of a new shirt, when there was a knock at the door.

He thought, "Kate!"

He realised that he was unwashed and in his dressing gown, much as Mrs. Ashe had said Kate had been when Farmer Lomax had paid her a call. The thought amused him. He would point it out to her. He should have mentioned to her that Mrs. Ashe had spoken to him about her. It would be easy to make a joke of the whole affair, and perhaps clear the air a bit.

Andrew found a tired, rather aged policeman standing on his step when he opened his front door. The man stepped forward, took off his helmet awkwardly, and pushed a lick of long dark hair back over a bald spot with the palm of his free hand. At the same time he said, "Sorry to disturb you on the day of rest, sir, but we're making enquiries about a child who's been missing from her home in the village for two nights. You might know her: Linda Morris? The family lives at this end of the village."

Andrew shook his head.

"It's got serious," the PC continued. "She took her dog out for exercise Friday evening and didn't come back. The dog turned up at the house last night, badly injured, so we're fearing the worst."

"That's terrible."

"Yes. Have you seen a child, or anyone unusual about?"

Andrew was about to answer in the negative when he remembered the girl with a dog he had seen from his car.

"Perhaps," he said. "How was she dressed. Was she wearing a green coat?"

"She was. You've seen her?"

Andrew described the tiny encounter while the PC took notes. He was aware that the man was taking in his untidy, unwashed state, and watching his face closely.

"You didn't by any chance give her a lift, did you, sir," the policeman asked.

"Of course not. Why should I?"

"It was a raw evening, last Friday."

"She didn't need a lift from me or anyone."

"You asked her then, sir?"

"No." Andrew was beginning to feel the thin edge of anger. "I didn't stop. She looked in no kind of trouble. Anyway, she was with that enormous dog."

"Was that the only reason why you didn't offer her a lift, sir? Because of the dog?"

"I'm not sure what you're getting at. I've told you what happened, what I saw, which was nothing much."

"But you said she was looking at you?"

"She seemed to be, yes."

"That's a bit strange, if you don't know her, isn't it?"

"Not really. She probably recognised me."

"Why would she?"

"I'm an 'incomer.' I've lived here little more than a year; I'm still a stranger."

"And very likely you always will be, sir," the policeman said dourly. "What time would you say you saw the missing girl?"

"About five forty-five."

"And you went next door to see your neighbour about an hour later?"

"That's right."

"So you were on your own during that period," the policeman stated pointedly.

"Correct," Andrew snapped. "And I've been alone since I left my neighbour's house on Friday evening, if its of any interest."

"You stayed in your cottage all that time, did you?"

"I shopped in Buxton yesterday morning, and went for a walk last night."

The policeman looked amazed. "You must be a keen hiker. It was pissing down yesterday evening."

"I like walking in the rain," Andrew said, almost petulantly, perhaps because it was a lie. He had not enjoyed the walk at all, in any normal sense, and had only persevered with it because of some grim, urgent, masochistic need, the memory of which now embarrassed and disturbed him.

The policeman told Andrew he would be required to make a statement.

Andrew explained he was going to see some friends. The policeman looked doubtful at this, thought about it, then smiled and said Andrew had been very helpful. He would be contacted later. Meanwhile, if he remembered anything else however small. . .

The bath-water was chilly when Andrew stepped into it. He poured in more hot. He sat shivering and thinking about what he had said to the policeman. He wished that he had gone straight round to see Kate when he had got home on Friday evening. Because he hadn't done so, and had no alibi for the hour immediately after his return, he knew that the police would look upon him as a suspect. He would be investigated.

"But I'm innocent!" he thought anxiously as, later, he pulled the crisp new shirt down over his cold, damp body.

Then, for some reason, he found himself thinking about Kate's absent dog, Bruckner.

He got back from Ashbourne at about nine thirty, went straight round to Kate's house, and rapped on the door. There was a tradition that they went together to the *Magnus Arms* for the last hour on Sunday night, and he had decided he was going to try to keep her to it. He would do his best to persuade her, if she proved reluctant to go. He had not been able to enjoy his Ashbourne friends' company because his mind had been on Kate, the lost girl, and his interview with the policeman. He had not felt able to discuss anything with his friends, though they heard on TV that a murder hunt was on for a child missing from the village where Andrew lived, and had asked him about it. A feeling of totally unwarranted guilt made him reluctant to relate his slight knowledge of the subject, though his thoughts were of nothing else. Except Kate.

He wondered what the policeman had said to her, and what, if anything, she knew about the absent child. He decided he needed to talk to Kate at once.

The cottage seemed in darkness as he strode up her drive but, when he was close to the parlour window, he saw the cold glow of the TV behind the curtains. He banged the door, waited, then banged harder. He stepped back a few paces and saw that the light from the TV was no longer showing. She'd turned it off. She was in there, knowing he was outside, and she was not going to let him in!

He couldn't believe it.

He felt a surge of rage, picked up a pebble, tapped loudly on her window, and called her name. The house responded with a powerful silence, like an ancient, empty ruin, and he felt like a desecrater, a hooligan bent on mischief. His voice sounded wild and peevish. He called again, deliberately deepening his tone.

No answer.

His anger, with nothing to centre on, seeped away, giving place to confusion and hurt irritation.

"Well, sod you too," he muttered, then was ashamed of himself.

He strode round the side of the house into the chaotic back garden. He was aware, as he passed, of the squat black shape of his own cottage hanging, like a reflection of Kate's, on his right. The night was dark, with only a thin shell of moon to light the autumn sky, but his eyes were adjusting well, and he picked his way through the disorder of untrimmed bushes and collapsing outbuildings without stumbling. He found at one point that he was walking on loose earth, as though Kate had been doing some digging. If so, it was the first heavy gardening he had ever known her do.

Looking round, he could see no sign of life anywhere at the rear of the cottage. Feeling puzzled and letdown, he was about to retreat to his own home when he sensed a movement directly behind him and something pressed hard across his shoulders. Shocked, he leapt forward, turning as he did so. He lost his balance, fell on one knee, but scrambled up quickly, ready to defend himself. Whatever had blundered against him had not been friendly.

Then, out of the silhouette of a collapsed greenhouse that sheltered a dim confusion of moon-bathed broken glass, struts of peeling, white-painted wood, and dark overgrown plant shapes, something rose up and floated towards him.

At first he wondered if he was at the receiving end of an elaborate, foolish joke. He thought someone was waving a shrunken balloon or a partly inflated paper bag at him on the end of a stick. Briefly, the pallid form hovered close in front of him, at a height a little greater than his own. Then he began to get a better idea what confronted him. He realised that the blunt-ended, ash-grey, slightly luminous shape that seemed to be inspecting him, but that had no eyes, was nothing he could account for. It was outside of his experience. It inspired not just fear, but a sensation of awe, of chilling reverence.

The dull, dumb, faceless thing, that still seemed to be somehow solemn, regarded him, then drifted backwards with a silky, dancing motion, swaying like an enchanted snake.

He got the impression that it was hollow, empty, a husk. Its movements had no weight.

As it drew away he saw that the pale blob was a head attached to an impossibly scrawny body dressed in some kind of loose, dark suit. It stepped carefully back on naked, shrivelled, possibly human feet and edged its way silently down into the ruins of the greenhouse, like a crab tucking itself under weed in a rock pool.

When the thing had gone Andrew remained for some moments, paralysed and hardly breathing, in the position into which he had stumbled when he had first caught sight of it. He was overwhelmingly grateful to it for going away. He had been afraid, when it had been close to him, that his heart had stopped beating, and that he had pitched into some afterlife from which there was no escape.

Moments later, when he could think more freely, he realised that, though the thing had retreated into the greenhouse, it had risen out of the freshly dug earth that he had walked over seconds before it had appeared. He had disturbed it. It had come to find out who or what he was.

And now it knew.

He was not aware of returning to his own cottage but, half an hour later, he was in his tiny kitchen when the phone rang. It was the police wanting his statement.

A car with a flashing light came to drive him to Buxton. He thought, "They don't trust me to drive there myself. Why not?"

In a bleak room at the Police Station he was asked a lot more questions. Hard questions. Some of them he couldn't understand. He was confused. The thing he had seen hung in his mind, as earlier it had hovered close to his face, disturbing his thoughts. He had an urge to mention it, but dared not do so.

His hands were trembling when he was asked to sign his statement. The pen shook. Three policemen watched him without pity, their critical faces expressing a mixture of unfriendly emotions.

He was returned home in silence, alone in the back of the car. The driver sniffed from time to time and half turned his head, as though he detected a nasty odour somewhere behind him. He didn't answer when Andrew wished him good night.

Andrew had been awake for hours when his alarm went off at seven next morning. He had decided to go to his office early, to throw himself into the backlog of work he expected to find there.

He felt awful; drained and anxious. He made coffee, and found he had no milk. He couldn't drink coffee black.

Darrel, the milkman, delivered to the cottage at seven twenty-five every morning precisely. A minute after that time Andrew opened his side door and reached down in the dark for his bottle. It wasn't there. Then he remembered he had heard no bottles clinking. Darrel was a punctual boy, but clumsy and noisy. He was late.

As he retreated back through the door Andrew noticed a dim light from Kate's house opposite. He peered over the scruffy hedge that divided their gardens.

The door corresponding to the one he was standing in was open. A figure stood there, with its back to Andrew. Its arms were flung wide, as though it had been crucified against the wall on either side above the door. The two hands remained fixed in place, but the body writhed and reached back, as though it was trying to withdraw from a source of pain. Andrew recognised at once that the figure, dressed in a blue nylon jacket and trousers, was Darrel. Just beyond the boy, inches from him, he could see someone else, facing him. Kate. She was holding her hands up on either side of her face, her fingers outstretched. Her head was tilted back. Her eyes, as far as he could tell, were shut, but her mouth was open wide, as though she were screaming. She was quite silent.

Behind her, in the dark, and obscured by the two closer figures, stood someone else. Andrew could see no details, but he thought whoever it was was male. As he watched, the man seemed to reach round the right side of Kate and stab at Darrel's chest. Andrew thought he saw the glint of glass or a knife. Darrel's back convulsed, and Kate brought her hands together on the boy's face, as though to smother or silence him. Nevertheless, Darrel made a terrible sound. He sank away from Kate, who let go of his head, bent down, and appeared to kiss his chest. It was a long, lover's kiss. It was audible to Andrew. Sickeningly so.

Darrel was handicapped. At eighteen he had a mental age of eight. He had been born badly; his body was unsymmetrical; he walked with a jolting, ungainly stride. His head was huge, and lolled from side to side. Kate had always liked him. She enjoyed his simplicity and his odd, childish sense of fun. She thought his father treated him harshly, and made a fuss of him on his birthdays and at Christmas, giving him generous tips. She had been sisterly and kind towards him. Nothing more. Nothing else.

Now she suddenly drew back from the boy's chest as though the man behind had wrenched her away. She retreated quickly into the cottage, sliding along the wall to allow the other past to take her place. She left a smear of something along the wallpaper.

Briefly, Andrew got a glimpse of the third member of the group. He recognised the long, almost tubular, bare oval of the head and the sharp, yet sinuous movements, as those of the being he had encountered the previous evening. But it had changed. It now had a mouth, and two livid eyes glared out of bluish patches above a sharp, canine nose.

Andrew knew it had seen him. He felt the thing's eyes lock onto his own for one terrible second. The face seemed to sneer at him. It tipped contemptuously back, and remained poised in that position for a moment. Then the wide-stretched jaws lunged down on Darrel's shoulder. The boy jerked, as though he had been kicked, and cried softly, piteously.

Andrew jumped back into his house. He pushed the glass and plywood door away from him into its frame slowly, as though it were huge and heavy; as though by doing so he was protecting and distancing himself from all he had seen. He stumbled round the house in the almost-dark like a thief searching for a way out. He tripped over a coffee table, tipping the things he had prepared for breakfast across the floor, and fell onto the resulting mess. Uncomfortable as he was, he wanted to lie there for the rest of the day, but his curiosity wouldn't let him. It drove him to a window overlooking Kate's house where he stood and gazed across at the open door, fascinated but horrified, and hoping he could not be seen.

As Andrew watched, Darrel broke free, or was released. He seemed to almost bounce away. Unable to run, he seesawed from side to side, wildly trying to make haste on his unequal legs. There were blood stains on his shirt emanating from above his heart where there was a darker patch, like an open wound.

As Darrel disappeared down Kate's front path the lights in her cottage went out and the side door closed. Andrew watched for a while, but nothing more happened. He worried frantically about Darrel, and would have gone out to him, but he was worried even more about Kate. He was also aghast at the scene he had witnessed, and was limp with fear and incredulity. He leaned against the wall by the window with his eyes shut, trying to make sense of it all for perhaps an hour, then sat on the floor hugging his knees for as long again.

Then he called his office and told them he was sick.

Just before midday he had a further visit from the police. It was the constable who had first called, this time with a WPC as company. They explained that the lost child had still not been found and that they were searching all houses and outbuildings in the area. The policeman was even less friendly than before, Andrew thought, realising that yet again he was unshaven and in his dressing-gown and must be creating an odd impression. The WPC was nicer, but unnerving. She kept staring at a point above his nose as she spoke, shaking her head slightly and slowly, as though reading words printed on his forehead.

He told them to search where they liked, and wandered out into his garden. He tried to see over into Kate's, looking for the newly dug patch, but everything was too overgrown; he could see nothing but unpruned roses choking in a jungle of giant, gone-to-seed weeds.

On returning to the house he found his visitors had switched on his television. The screen was a jitter of static fuzz. The WPC was fiddling buttons, trying to get a picture. She explained that they wanted the news as they might be in it. They had been filmed earlier searching local fields. Andrew was gratified to see she was pink with embarrassment as she moved aside to make room for him.

"Something wrong with the set?" she asked.

Andrew shook his head. "You must have pushed the wrong button."

"I don't think so," she insisted. "Mine's the same model."

Andrew made no comment. The set was acting strange. No picture on any channel, and he couldn't get more than a whisper on the sound. Irritated, he pushed buttons at random. The screen went milky, then filled with monochromatic swirling eddies, like simmering oil.

Dim shapes rose out of this slick. One of them reached up and grew big, like a deep-sea creature approaching and peering into a diver's helmet. It almost filled the screen. To Andrew, it resembled a bare bald head, encased in tight opal flesh that looked ready to split and peel. Its mouth was a pale, straight gash. It had sharp eyes like black diamonds that seemed to be searching for something or someone out beyond the screen.

Andrew thought he knew what it was, and who it was looking for.

He swore, and switched off the set with an angry motion.

"You were getting something then!" the policeman said, apparently undisturbed by the images he had seen.

"Not the news," Andrew snapped.

"You should have stayed with it," the WPC protested. "It'll be on in a moment."

"I don't think so." Andrew slipped the remote-control into the pocket of his dressing-gown. The woman looked cross and disappointed. "You're right," Andrew added. "It's not working properly. It needs fixing."

The policeman watched him curiously, as though he suspected he was drunk or crazy and might shortly need restraining. Andrew scratched the scar tissue left by the hang-gliding injury on the side of his face. It itched when he was stressed or nervous, and scratching it was not a pleasant action to watch, as it made one side of his face look like Lon Chaney in profile. The Phantom of the Opera! The WPC stopped reading the lines on his forehead and looked away. Perhaps to change the subject or to distract herself she said, "That was a terrible accident this morning. The boy was badly injured. He may not survive."

Andrew gaped. "What accident? What boy?"

"The delivery boy. He drove his milk-float into a lorry. Head-on. He's in Intensive Care."

Andrew felt himself swaying. "Darrel? The milk-boy?"

"That's him."

Andrew dropped into a chair, his face white, and slapped his brow like a ham actor. He felt the two pairs of eyes watching him closely, and realised the constables must think he was wildly overreacting.

"Friend of yours, was he?" the man asked, with a hint of sympathy.

"No," Andrew said sharply, rejecting the idea. Then, shaking his head confusedly, "Not really. But I knew him, of course."

"Lots of things happening in Longton all of a sudden," the man observed. "Strange, isn't it?"

Satisfied that they had made a thorough search of the cottage, the two constables went into Andrew's long back-garden and began stalking carefully through it. It was not nearly as chaotic as his neighbour's, but weeds had begun to take over during his absence. They spent almost half an hour poking about there when they were suddenly called away. They seemed reluctant to go, and promised to return later that day, with lights if necessary, as it would soon start to get dark.

As soon as they were out of sight Andrew went and banged on Kate's doors. There was no response. He leaned on the side door, then hit it with his knee just below the lock. It gave a bit, but not enough. He went home, found a large screwdriver, and attacked the door with that. He chipped away at the wood, and kicked it viciously. It slammed back against an inner wall.

The first thing Andrew noticed as he stepped inside was the long red smudge along the opposite wall, like the path of a bloody comet, that he had seen Kate make that morning.

He edged into the silent house and called Kate's name. There was no reply, but the beams over his head creaked once, as though something on the first floor had shifted weight.

He went into the parlour and found Kate in the same seat she had occupied when he had last spoken to her, nearly seventy hours ago. The lower half of her body was covered with a blanket that she clutched with both thin hands above her stomach, in a frail old-womanish gesture. She was watching the TV. On screen the pallid, washed-out, floating shapes he was familiar with drifted in and out of a background of metamorphosing grey masses, to an accompaniment of small, almost inaudible sounds.

Kate started to move as he entered the room. She lifted and turned her head slowly, as though it weighed heavily. She nodded blankly at him, accepting rather than greeting him, and watched as he drew a chair closer to hers.

He couldn't help staring at her. She looked terribly frail. Her frizzy blond hair was a mess. She had aged years. Her half-closed eyes were dull, even against the smudges of bruised skin on her upper cheeks. Her face, always thin, was now sharply bony. Her lips were almost invisible, and her nostrils wide and dark. Andrew thought again of drugs, then dismissed the idea, knowing her problems were worse than that.

She said something, probably his name, then coughed to clear her throat. He said hello, his voice faltering.

"You shouldn't be here," she stated wearily. "Be careful. For now, he needs you, but you're next."

Andrew's brow creased uncomprehendingly. "What do you mean, Kate?" he asked gently, and leaned out of his seat towards her.

She shook her head fretfully, said, "It's probably too late; there's nothing you can do," and turned her face back to the TV screen, as though no further explanation was necessary or possible.

Andrew followed her gaze for a while, then said, "What is this that you're watching, Kate?"

"A video. It belonged to my husband. I found it, and others like it, among some of his belongings a few weeks ago.

"I thought I had destroyed everything of his," she added, with a whining note of anger, "but somehow a few things survived. They always do. I should have known."

"What's it about?" Andrew insisted. "What does it represent?"

Kate's razor-thin lips stretched, perhaps in a smile. "It represents my husband," she said. "It's a film that was made just before he died, over three years ago. He went away for a while and returned with this, and other things. You could say they were his holiday snapshots; something like that."

"I don't understand you, Kate," Andrew said uneasily, not sure if she was intending to be humorous.

She turned to him again, her head moving with greater ease now. "Don't you?" she said. "Are you sure? When I first found the videos (he was alive then, and I watched them without telling him), I understood them at once. Mind you, I had some reason to suspect. . ."

Andrew waited for her to continue; then, when she didn't, said, "I'm getting those pictures, or something like them, on my set. I know it's not possible, but I am."

"Then he's got to you," she said. "I was right. It is too late."

"For what? And who's 'he'?"

"Don't pretend," Kate said almost scornfully. "I know you were watching from your door the other morning when there was an. . . incident. So does he. And he won't forget."

She became rigid in her chair, with her eyes half-closed and an intense expression on her face, as though she were reviewing or reliving the grotesque events he had witnessed.

"You never told me much about your husband," Andrew observed, seemingly somewhat obliquely, after a period of strained silence, "just that he was dead."

"Oh yes, he died at last, there's no doubt about that. I know he was dead, I made sure of it."

"How did he die?"

"Violently. Very violently. He was a powerful man. It took a lot to kill him. I learned that lesson a few weeks before his life finally ended. He seemed to have died then, but I was wrong; somehow he survived, and came back for me."

"You mean, 'to' you?"

"I mean what I say," she insisted. "Anyway, I eluded him then; I escaped: he didn't get me. He died, undoubtedly he died, and I thought I was free of him.

"The trouble is," she added bitterly, "I'd locked him up, but I forgot to throw away the key."

She clutched with both hands at the arm of the chair as though to lift herself, but failed to rise up. Andrew wondered if she had the strength to get to her feet. He thought not.

He stood up himself and, without asking, poured two big drinks. Kate took the one he offered without comment. She drank half at once. He drank all of his.

He said, "The police are searching the area for a girl who's gone missing. They're looking everywhere. They've been through my house, and almost finished my garden. They'll come to you next. I wanted to warn you."

She shrugged. "They came before to ask me questions. They could see me through the window. I think they thought that I was dead. I had to let them in or they would have knocked the door in, as you've done. But I had nothing to tell them. I know nothing about a lost girl."

"No, perhaps not," Andrew said uncertainly, "but is there anyone else here with you now?"

Kate's eyes automatically flickered up towards the ceiling. "If the police do come, and insist on searching the house, then they will have to deal with whatever they find in their own way, if they can. It could be interesting."

"Interesting? Christ! I can't believe you can be so indifferent to your situation, Kate," Andrew said impatiently. "The boy who was involved in your 'incident' was in a serious accident immediately after he left here. Our houses are the last on the edge of the village, and yours was the last delivery he made. The police are bound to question you about him, as a matter of course. You can't say you don't know about that."

"You're wrong," Kate replied shortly. "I know nothing about the accident. It's the first I've heard of it."

Andrew noticed she expressed no anxiety about Darrel or his condition, and felt a stab of repugnance that made him wonder if he was beginning to hate her. He remembered her indifference to the loss of Bruckner, her dog. That was bad, but Bruckner was only a pet; Darrel was a friend who was probably going to die, and Kate seemed unmoved. She didn't even seem to find it "interesting."

On the floor above, something stirred. There were heavy footfalls, and a long scraping sound, as though a weighty object was being shoved into place. "Perhaps it's barricading itself in," Andrew thought, with no inclination to go and investigate the truth of his speculation. Kate ignored, or did not notice, the noises.

Andrew was worried that the police would be returning soon. He did not want to be with Kate when they did. He was not sure quite what he thought they would find but, whatever it was, he did not want to be associated with it or with Kate.

She must have detected his anxiety to get away, because she said, "You may as well leave. There's nothing you can do to help."

"But are you sure? What will you do?"

She shook her head slightly, a tiny movement. "Nothing much. I'm very tired; I shall probably sleep."

"I'll call round tomorrow, to see how you are," he said dutifully.

"No you won't," she murmured, sinking deeper into her chair. "Don't bother. I'll come to you, when I'm ready. That may not be for some time, but I will come."

Her voice was so low, it was almost inaudible but, as he left the room, he thought he heard her say, as she tumbled into sleep:

"Don't forget; I told you, you're next."

He didn't like it because he didn't understand it, but it sounded like a threat.

The police returned half an hour later. Lots of them.

Andrew stood at the back of his home in the autumn twilight, and watched as they combed through his garden, finding nothing.

They marched next door to Kate's cottage. They got no answer from the front, then found that the side door had been forced. They got quite excited about this discovery. A small but senior-looking man, an officer in a flat hat, was instantly called up from somewhere. He took charge. He carefully pushed the door open and took half a step inside.

Then there was a vivid flash, bright as lightning, that hurt Andrew's eyes, blinding him for seconds. When he could see again, the air was full of tiny fragments of black ash and the smell of burning.

The officer who had tried to enter the building was screaming. The front of his body looked like burnt toast, his face had turned to cinders that were beginning to ooze blood. Two other men who had been close behind him were writhing on the ground, similarly injured.

Andrew noticed that there was no fire raging, and no smoke. He ran through the hedge into Kate's garden, shouting that she was in the building.

As he got near he could see, through the open door, she could not have survived. The inside of the house looked as though someone had gone through it with a flamethrower. Nothing had moved, but the surface of everything had been charred black by a flash-fire of intense heat.

A policewoman ordered Andrew back into his house. Someone shouted to him to call the fire brigade, which he did, though there was no fire to put out. He spent a confused hour, with people running in and out of his house.

Kate's house was searched, when it was declared safe. Two corpses were found. Kate was dead in her chair. The second was discovered in an upper room. From snatches of half-heard conversation, Andrew got the impression that there was something strange about it, something that disturbed and disgusted those who came across it.

Then the plot of freshly dug earth at the rear of Kate's cottage was spotted, sparking off another round of activity. Men started digging down into it carefully with spades. Something was dug out and taken away. Lights were brought from somewhere, and the site was hidden away behind walls of thick plastic sheeting.

Later, other, bigger finds were made.

Next morning, the press arrived. They pestered Andrew all day. He couldn't even sneak off to work. His house was surrounded. In the end, he gave in, and sold a story to a national paper for a huge sum of money. It was not much of a story; he left out the interesting bits because he knew they would not be believed. He let the reporter think that he and Kate had been lovers, as the man had already been made aware of that rumour by someone in the village. It made a good feature.

At first, the police merely put out the information that Kate had died in a gas explosion. Later, when they revealed what they had discovered in her garden, this explanation was widely questioned, but no more satisfactory cause for the gutting of the cottage was forthcoming, though it was assumed that she and the... other person... had committed suicide.

The contents of the pit, which turned out to have been a grave, eventually became known. First, not far beneath the surface, the remains of part of a large dog, later more or less identified as Bruckner, Kate's quondam pet. It had been there some weeks. Its head and heart were missing, and were never found.

Five feet below Bruckner was the body of the missing girl. She was lying face down and was fully dressed. There were tooth-marks and a deep wound above her left breast. Her green coat and her blouse and sweater were torn above this injury, as though someone (or thing) had bitten right through them. The injury was not the cause of her death. She had suffocated. Her mouth and throat were full of dirt, as though she had somehow died down there, under the earth.

It was what was found under her, however, which totally mystified everyone—with the single exception of Andrew. This was the corpse of a man who had been dead for three or more years. He was lying on his back below the girl and, most strangely, had his arms around her back as though he were hugging her, or so the men who did the digging insisted, though few believed them. But the most singular thing of all was the fact that the male corpse was headless.

The head was found between the man's feet. It had been buried in a crudely constructed wooden box that was a tight fit. Two dozen eight-inch nails had been driven through the box into the skull on all six sides, creating quite a puzzle for the police surgeon whose task it was to sort the whole thing out.

But sort it out he did. He was even able to identify the corpse. It was Kate's husband, a man who, it transpired, the police had been wanting to question about a number of murders and mysterious disappearances at the time of *his* disappearance—at what was now understood to also be the time of his death.

As soon as he was able to do so, Andrew went abroad for six weeks, to get away from the press and police.

His time of absence from Longton did not do him much good. He hated the place when he returned, and decided to move out as soon as he could.

On his first day back he wandered into the *Magnus Arms* in the hope of learning what had occurred while he had been away. People were not particularly friendly towards him, but then they never had been. They were noticeably reluctant to talk to him, even when he bought them drinks. Nevertheless, he realised that the village had quickly settled back into its normal somnolence.

He drank too much in the pub, and tottered home with a couple of tins of lager, intending to watch football on TV. He had not turned the set on since before Kate's death and had forgotten that it had seemed to have something wrong with it.

He opened a tin, slumped into his chair, and thumbed the remote. The screen filled with ugly, oily, swirling shapes. Familiar shapes. They filled him with dread. He swore at them. Feeling his flesh creep, he lurched towards the TV and tried to turn it off.

He hit the off switch, but nothing happened. The pictures wouldn't go away. The shapes seemed to get clearer and more active, if anything.

Kneeling down with his face close to the set, he could clearly hear the soft sounds that it was making. He put his ear close to the speaker and listened, trying to make sense of the nagging noises.

After a while, he thought he could, just. Under the babble and clatter he could hear another sound that recurred from time to time.

It was a human voice; a woman's voice.

It was Kate's voice, and she was repeating the same two words over and over again:

"You're next—you're next—you're next."

He got very frightened then.

He went to the wall and pulled the TV plug out of its socket.

Again, nothing happened. The picture didn't waver. The sounds even got louder.

Then he made a big mistake.

He kicked the screen.

It collapsed into fragments, releasing all that was inside of it, all the things that had come across to him from Kate's house the moment it had burned, and had been impatiently waiting for him to return to free them. They swirled around him triumphantly, terrifyingly.

He saw Kate and her husband among them.

The man smiled.

Kate smiled. She held out her arms to Andrew.

"You're next," she said.

And he believed her.

The Toddler

One

A woman in a torn blue smock much too big for her stood by a long-scrubbed oak table preparing a meal for her master's cousin, Sir Rufford de Quintz. He had been hunting in the Royal Forest for two days and, in the company of a few companions, had returned late, exhausted, and hungry. The woman had been working since first light that morning but, nevertheless, had undertaken to cook for him. She seemed eager to please. She laboured almost in the dark, without a wick burning, but she knew her place of work well, and everything was to hand. She was unclean and hot. Sweat from her brow streamed down her nose and dripped, unnoticed by her, onto the Knight's supper. Her crow-black hair hung forward over her shoulders and she constantly smeared it back past her neck with her long, greasy fingers.

The woman muttered to herself as she worked, but whatever she was saying was inaudible, even to her own ears. Her petulant, complaining voice was drowned in the groans and squeals of trussed and hobbled calves, lambs, and geese awaiting slaughter next morning in the passage outside, and in the roar of the fires under the ovens behind her in the bakehouse. The air was sharp with the smell of the terrified creatures' excrement and the equally powerful aroma of the swelling loaves stacked on iron shelves in the baking ovens.

Not that anyone would have overheard her if she had spoken into perfect silence. She worked alone. The builders who had been working on the inner walls had long since dropped their tools and departed for a nearby inn, and the rest of the kitchen and scullery staff had finally stumbled away to their sleeping quarters to eat and drink themselves into brief, but welcome, oblivion. And they would not have paid any heed to her words had they been there to hear them, as it was the common opinion of them all that she was three-parts mad.

If this were true, and she had lost a portion of her intellect, it was in no way evident from the skilful way she went about preparing the food for de Quintz's meal. She tackled the task of carving the splayed and steaming carcass in front of her on a roasting dish with quick, neat precision. Mad as she might be, she was obviously mistress of her craft. She had to bend forward as she worked, because her belly, swollen in the seventh month of pregnancy, distanced her from the object of her attention, but the knife and two-pronged fork in her darting fingers tweaked the tender meat from bone to the dish at her elbow with a practised confidence that seemed to require no concentration. In fact, she was hardly aware of the complex actions she performed; her mind was all on other things.

If the kitchen, late at night, was a dark, damp, steamy, stinking place, it could stand as a paradigm of the mind of this solitary woman, the tenor of whose thoughts could fancifully, but adequately, be described by the above four adjectives. Events in her recent past had set a black and doleful cast upon her mind, and upon her countenance. From the evidence of her features, an observer, should it occur to him for whatever reason to guess at her age, would deduce her to be a good deal older than she was. The previous three years had transformed a girl of nineteen into a worn and troubled woman, and this over-rapid maturation had soured her face and temper. Whatever beauty she had possessed three seasons previously was now almost all gone. It is an old tale that creaks with age at the telling, but it was her quondam good looks (of course) that had precipitated her downfall. And it was the knowledge that her beauty had vanished, had been stolen away, along with all else precious to her, that had turned her mind and left her, if not quite insane, then tottering on the brink of madness.

The wayward words she uttered were an expression of the chaos of her thoughts; an outlet for the turmoil of her emotions. The latter were a mix of resentment, indignation, outraged powerlessness, and others equally negative; all kept active by a constant, sharp, mind-biting anxiety that drove off any prospect of peace or even hope of rest. She was doing what she had been driven to do by forces and circumstances over which she had no control. Dimly, dumbly, she was asserting herself in the only way she could, and making a gesture that she hoped would hurt the man who had casually destroyed her. But in this she was mistaken. Her faculties were impaired and her judgment wrong. It was not he who was to suffer as a result of her actions that night.

De Quintz, along with a handful of cronies, had arrived at Haddon Hall one bright morning three springs previously. He was a stocky, clump-handed, swaggering man with a loud, high voice and pale blue eyes the colour of frozen milk. His face had been cut in some recent skirmish, and the wounds had not yet become scars. He had also taken the prick of a halberd through the right hip, a wound that had not been well attended. As a result, he leaned slightly forward and to that side as he walked, and his features were set in a constant grimace of pain. He was the cousin of Sir George, then Lord of Haddon who, though he had welcomed de Quintz hospitably enough, was not often seen in his company. It was said by persons close to Sir George that there was some coolness between the two distant relatives; more than would, perhaps, naturally devolve from the great gap in their age and temperament, and the remoteness of their consanguinity. Indeed, it was the opinion of some that the Master was markedly fearful of de Quintz who, in turn, showed little respect for his once notoriously vigorous, but now ancient and enfeebled, relation.

The Knight installed himself in the finest quarter of the Hall almost like a conqueror, and soon made himself the most hated person, not only in the building, but in the countryside around for many miles. He was plainly a man of rapacious habits with no inclination to change his ways to those of mild domesticity. He was, in short, an ogre. There was even some foolish gossip, originating among the few members of the household staff who had survived the rigours of sixteenth-century life long enough to enter the state of superannuated octogenarianism, that there was something unholy about him, something against nature. These old ones, who had been in service at the Hall all their lives, were half-convinced he had visited the house before, when they and their master had been young. De Quintz, then, had not appeared much different to the way he looked now, nor much younger, or so they claimed. If their memories were correct, the old folk said (and smiled uneasily and shook their heads)—which, of course, they could not have been. The younger, and perhaps less superstitious, of the servants spoke of family resemblance, and averred that any such visitor who may have been entertained at the Hall sixty or more years earlier had very likely been an ancestor of their present guest, which surely must have been the case.

De Quintz, once installed in the house, took what he wanted of what he saw around him. One of the first things that caught his eye was a girl who worked in the kitchens. He came upon her when she was collecting herbs in the garden and was as struck by her beauty as she was by his ugliness. He was without a female companion at that time, so he took her to his rooms. He kept her locked up in his apartments for eight weeks. The mother of the imprisoned girl begged him repeatedly to return her, and tried to press Sir George to intercede with his cousin on her behalf, without success. At last, she made the mistake of sending her other daughter, a girl some years younger than her sister, to de Quintz's quarters to plead for the older girl's release. The child obtained her sister's freedom, but at the cost of her own liberty.

The older girl never spoke of her experiences during her incarceration with the Knight, but it was obvious she had been mistreated. When at last she recovered her bodily health, she discovered she was pregnant. She disposed of the baby in her fifth month, only to find herself with child again not long after. The fact that de Quintz had taken her sister to his bed did not mean he had lost interest in the older girl altogether, and he continued to force himself on her against her wishes whenever he could. The two girls were not the only ones to be treated thus by the Knight, who spread his attentions far and wide in the neighbourhood. Once, a group of husbands, whose wives he had outraged, plotted his assassination. He somehow found them out before they could act against him, forced them to confess, and supervised their executions. The men, before they died, swore to the last that he must have used some Black Art against them, since none of them had betrayed the others. They said de Quintz could only have learned of their plans from Satan himself, whose presence they had sought to invoke, in the hope that he would assist their cause and bring down their enemy.

The younger sister must have taken de Quintz's fancy. He kept her imprisoned in his quarters without break. In time she too became pregnant, and he permitted her to bear the child, from some freak of warped affection, it was assumed. When the tot could walk it got in his way, and he would not have it about him. It was, therefore, often left to wander where it chose, stumbling along Haddon's dark passages and in and out of the Hall's bare, inhospitable rooms. When on these peregrinations without destination it would drag behind it, by the arm, a horrid little humanlike figure its father had fashioned for it out of wood and rags. This doll was its only true companion ever.

The child was a pitiful sight. Because of its father's raging temper and thoughtless cruelty, the infant, a puny, nervous, curly haired girl, developed from the start an aversion to the company of men. Women she would cling to if they let her, but all males she avoided like the Pest. However, even the most motherly female members of the household staff rejected and avoided her if they could, because she was the daughter of the man who had darkened all their lives, and was anyway an unappealing, mewling mite, with none of the common charms of infancy. She was in every sense a misfortuned child.

To the elder sister, who, after her brief concubinage, was sent back to her work in the kitchen, the toddler became an object of hatred. The child never ventured into the kitchen, but haunted those rooms that were occupied by the few female servants who were single women. Here the woman came across the infant repeatedly, and loathed it, not least because it had its father's chilling pale blue eyes and sharp, thin nose, rather than her sister's finer features. And it cut her to the quick to think that she was herself related to the solitary, unwanted, ugly child, a creature neglected even by its own mother, who, though she did what she could to protect her offspring, would not risk earning the displeasure of de Quintz by being seen to care for it more than him.

Yet the woman, though she was the poor child's aunt, did not fully understand the girl's position in the house. The Knight had refused to recognise the paternity of any of the other couple of dozen or more children he had sired on various women of the Hall and the district surrounding it; but, by tolerating the birth of her sister's baby in his quarters, he had demonstrated, or so she thought, that he had been proud to father the wretched infant, and that he must therefore, in some sense, love it. Perhaps, she assumed, he cared for the toddler because of its strong resemblance to himself, though this could, of course, only have been a postnatal consideration. However, she was sure he did love, or at least feel some strong attachment to, the child.

But she was quite wrong. He had let his mistress keep her baby because it had amused him to do so. Since that time he had quickly grown tired of the child, and would soon discard its mother. That was the pattern of his life; he kept no one near him long. He was set in his ways, and had been for a very long time. The occupants of the Hall, with the possible exception of Sir George himself, would have been surprised, and even alarmed, to know for just how long.

The woman working in the kitchen was talking to herself about the child. Her thoughts were chaotic. Panic lurked behind them, and, behind the panic, horror; horror at what she had become and done.

"It was fate that threw her in my path," the woman whined. Her tone was of one trying to justify herself to an invisible accuser. "Her fate or mine? I couldn't say. But there she was, in front of me at a moment when my hatred was hottest. The Knight returned starving, and me, of all, they ask to warm his meat! 'Be pleased to I said.' I'll make him a meal to fill his belly to bursting, as he's filled mine, over and again." She pushed the remains of the carcass away across the table, and gazed down at the steaming heap of sliced meat in front of her. "I smiled when I saw the pitiful, foolish child, so lost and alone, and she misread my smile and thought I would be her friend. She dragged her wretched doll towards me and caught hold of my dress and wouldn't let go. I tried to make her, but she would not. Well, I had work to do, so we came, the three of us, down here; me hauling her and she the doll, in a train." She tugged at her hair and held it bunched tight in both sticky hands behind her neck, moaned, then continued: "The ovens were so hot, and I was tired from the day's work. Perhaps I fell in a swoon, or perhaps I slept, and acted in my sleep; I've no recollection of what passed." She released her hair, stretched up, and seemed to draw in strength and resolution with her breath. She shook her head, and said in a louder, firmer voice, "Well, no matter! It's done. Well and truly done."

She lifted the salver bearing the meat, carried it to the door, and woke two of the boys who lay curled up asleep next to the doomed animals in the passage beyond. They took the flesh, and dishes of vegetables she had also prepared, to the dining hall where the Knight and his companions, now hungrier than ever, were waiting. As she watched them go the woman said, "Well, here we are now, Sir de Quintz; your meat is ready. Your little goose is well and truly cooked, so eat your fill."

She ambled back into the kitchen and dragged an ancient wooden cupboard used to store food close to where she had been working. She pushed the cupboard over on its back, opened its slim door wide, and tipped the remains of the carcass she had been carving into it. She stuffed some tiny scraps of clothing in among the bones, and finally, with a flourish, flung a doll on top of it all.

She shut the cupboard and hid it deep in a hole in the wall, that was due to be filled in by the builders first thing in the morning. Then she went to her room to rest.

In the early afternoon of the following day de Quintz's mistress began to fear that her child was lost. Every man and woman in Haddon Hall was set to search for her, but no one found her. She had last been seen wandering along a passage on the ground floor very late the previous evening. Whatever accident could have befallen her, or where she could have gone, remained a mystery. She had vanished.

It was, people said, as if she had been swallowed up by the night!

Two

> Dolls: Possibly such figures were given to female children as talismans or charms, a symbolisation of what was hoped for when they grew up; and possibly, a child's nature being what it is, talisman or charm was converted into a well-loved plaything.
>
> Geoffrey Grigson
> *The Book Of Things*

"Can you get down right away, Mrs. Cooper? The lads have turned up something interesting. Some kind of box, I think, stashed away in the wall."

Myra perched on the edge of her desk and wondered at the foreman's vagueness. Part of his head was always in the clouds, but the men were pleased to work for him, and he got things done.

"Which lads, and where, Ron?"

"Sorry. The team in the kitchen, working on the outer wall."

"The sixteenth-century alterations?"

"Right. Part of the wall's collapsed."

"Is anyone hurt?"

"Just a bit shook up. And excited. They think they may have found treasure."

Myra smiled into the phone and said, "Keep an eye on them until I get there, Ron. Don't let them touch anything."

"I'm calling from home, Mrs. Cooper. They phoned me here. It's my day off."

"I'd forgotten. I'd better get down right away. I'll call you later."

She slid off the desk, grabbed her bag and folder of architectural drawings, and almost ran out of her temporary office down to the Great Hall beyond. There were coach loads of children all over Haddon Hall that day. The rooms and corridors were full of them. Twenty or more were standing close-packed outside her door. They were listening to their teacher, a tall woman with a face like a startled El Greco saint, who was jollying-up history for them at the top of her voice with an enthusiasm close to hysteria. She saw Myra and made way for her through the class with a grand gesture, like God parting the Red Sea for Moses, without interrupting her discourse.

Entering the Great Hall, Myra stepped out into an even more complex disorder of infants who were streaming towards her. Wading in against this powerful current, she was almost turned about by a group of older girls who came at her in a bunch at the door, just as she tried to exit through it. She involuntarily glanced behind her as she was spun half backwards, and saw, at the far end of the Hall, someone who appeared to be in the same predicament as herself. A man, stooping with age, or perhaps in a short-sighted effort to focus on the children milling around him, was also trying to reach the door. His movements were wild and clumsy, violent even, and Myra thought she heard yelps of protest, or perhaps pain, from some of the children nearest to him, but the Great Hall was full of shrill chatter and raised voices calling to distant friends, so she could not be sure. Anyway, there were plenty of teachers about, keeping watch over their flocks, so she was certain no harm could come to any of the assembled young people. But, as she turned away, the man seemed to raise a fist, and he looked up towards her for a second. She glimpsed thin red lips drawn back from clenched teeth and two blank, duck-egg-blue eyes set in a grey face mottled with purple stripes, like war paint. The man stuck his chin out then, and blinked and stared at her. He jerked his whole body forward, as though suddenly even more anxious to make progress, and brought his fist down hard. A child screamed as the log-jam of bodies in front of Myra broke and the pressure of people behind her pushed her sideways through the door like a cork out of a bottle.

Finding herself in the corridor, and comparatively free to move, she hurried towards her destination, feeling somewhat distressed by what she had seen in the Great Hall. Surely the man himself could not have been a teacher attempting to impose discipline over his charges? He looked much too old and, well, downright uncouth, to be active in the profession; and anyway, such aggressive methods of correction had been outlawed years ago! She shook her head to dismiss the incident from her mind, but remained uneasy. The close proximity of so many children had in itself unnerved her. Since the death of her daughter and husband in an accident two years earlier, the company of children oppressed her, and she avoided them when she could. It was a relief when she reached the barriers around the area of the kitchens, where the renovation work was taking place. The waist-high strips of yellow tape were there to keep children, and the public in general, out. She felt more secure with the barriers behind her, and more confident. She was on her own ground.

In the kitchen there were perhaps a dozen men clustered round the area where part of the wall had collapsed. Just three should have been at work on the job. Rumour had spread quickly, and labourers had come from the other sites to see the "treasure." The sight of them standing idly about slightly annoyed Myra, because parts of her project were already behind schedule, but she decided to let them stay while she solved the mystery of what had been discovered. Perhaps they would learn how to deal with any future "finds" they might make. She was concerned that they might do damage from ignorance or excessive enthusiasm. Keen as they were, and glad of the work, they were mostly recruits from the local building trade, used to the methods and materials employed by the likes of Wimpey, and inexperienced in the delicate work of what amounted to archaeological reconstruction. She felt she needed to keep a constant eye on them.

She stepped between the men, peered into the darkness of the recently formed cavity, and was relieved to see that very little damage had been done. A small section of the lower wall had fallen back, and could easily be rebuilt. There was no indication of any major structural fault.

"Can you see it, Mrs. Cooper?" one of the men whispered. "It's dark in there." There was a note of awe in his voice.

The top half of some kind of wooden case was visible, jutting out above the fallen stonework. Myra nodded, took a camera from her bag of tools and instruments, and took three flash photographs of the dusty box from different angles. The men smiled as they watched her at work. They had never met anyone quite like this brisk, yet solemn, detached, work-obsessed woman, who seemed quite unaware that she was attractive. She said, "Can someone clear away the rubble carefully, please?" and stood back to watch while the work was done. Nobody spoke at all. There was a hushed, churchy feeling of reverence in the air as the relic was revealed. At last, when the front and sides of the box were free of the fallen stonework, the man closest to it turned to Myra and raised an eyebrow.

"Shall I lift it out?"

"Is it heavy?" Myra asked cautiously.

The man bent down, placed his hand on top of the box, and rocked it slightly.

"No, not really." He looked disappointed.

Myra nodded. "Very well then."

The box tipped up suddenly as the man tugged at it, and he almost lost his balance. To try to steady himself he stepped back upon a loose rock from the wall and twisted his ankle. He yelped with pain and fell back, hauling the box on top of him. Beyond, inside the wall, something fell away, and a few more stones tumbled into the vacated space. Myra felt a flare of anger at the man's clumsiness that she hastily dampened down because she thought he might be hurt. But he seemed uninjured. He helped two of the others to lift the box off his legs, stood up awkwardly, and smiled in pained apology at Myra. An elderly, tubby man she knew as Greg inspected the box and said, "The bottom's fallen out of it," and placed the object on its back. "What d'you think, Mrs. Cooper?" he added, and sneezed from the dust in the air. "Is it anything special?"

Myra hunkered down next to the find. "It's a 'dole' cupboard. Late medieval, probably," she said. "They were used to store food so the dogs couldn't get at it."

"They kept dogs in the kitchens?" Greg said, sounding oddly prim.

"To catch rats, and other things," Myra explained, and went over to where the cupboard had been discovered. She didn't need to refer to the plans of the walls and floors, which she knew by heart anyway, to deduce what had caused the masonry to fall. An ancient drain ran out of the kitchen at that point, to flush waste into the river Wye, which ran along outside the Hall a short distance from the wall. It must have collapsed. She took a pocket torch from her bag, directed its spindle-thin beam into the vacant space, and saw that her surmise had been correct. There was a black hole in the floor, about eighteen inches across, where the box had been standing. Its base must have been rotten and had fallen away. Perhaps it had been damp at some time. Whatever it had contained, if anything, had vanished down the drain.

The men, looking slightly sheepish, were standing round the excavated box. Myra joined them, and crouched down next to it again.

It was coated in umber dust, and tendrils of what looked like petrified fern or fungus, like thin, grey, bony fingers, clutched at the blackened wood over most of its outer surface. It was about four feet tall, three wide, and one deep, and of very basic design. It had a door in the middle with two dissimilar, quaintly carved holes at top and bottom. The door was flanked by panels on either side that also had small holes, about six inches square, with crudely cut, curlicued edges. The door was held shut by a simple, revolving peg. The cupboard, lying as it was on its back, looked like a coffin for a flattened-out dwarf; a coffin with windows. It was palpably sinister. It looked as shut up and empty as a dead man's face. Myra decided to open it. She reached out to grasp the peg that locked it.

"Might keep out dogs, but it wouldn't keep out the rats," said Greg, who was squatting next to her. To illustrate his point, he put the tip of his finger into one of the holes in the door, and moved it around inside the cupboard.

And suddenly snatched it back with a curse. He jumped to his feet.

"Bloody thing!"

Myra paused with her hand on the peg. "What's wrong?"

"There's something in there." Greg was staring at a bead of blood that was swelling out from the side of his fingernail.

"You've cut yourself," Myra observed, unnecessarily.

"It was more like—it felt like something bit me," Greg insisted.

"Perhaps you were right about the rats," someone said, and a couple of the men laughed uneasily.

Greg smudged the blood off his finger onto his overall. He looked embarrassed. He smirked at Myra and shook his head. "It's nothing," he said. "Just a bit of a shock. I'm sorry." He prodded the cupboard with his foot. "Open it up. Let's have a look inside."

The peg had warped and tightened, and did not give way easily under the pressure of Myra's thumb. When at last it turned, she reached under the bottom edge of the door and lifted it wide open. A cloud of thick, seething dust surged up and out. It swirled up surprisingly high, hung for a moment spinning indecisively in the air, then drifted swiftly towards Myra as though reaching out for her. She was about to move back, to avoid inhaling the dust, when it suddenly dropped, as though whatever current in the air had moved it had abruptly died. The front edge of the cloud settled out, reached as far as her bent knees, and drifted onto her white skirt. At the same moment she experienced a tiny, tactile sensation, as though something more heavy than dust had actually touched her leg. She stretched her hand to brush off her skirt with her fingers, but thought better of it. She didn't want to risk rubbing the ancient, grimy powder into the fabric of one of her most expensive articles of clothing.

"Did you see that?" asked one of the men. "That was very strange."

"I did," said another.

Myra said, "What do you mean?"

Greg answered. "Well, Mrs. Cooper, for a moment then—in the dust—I seemed to see. . ."

"Yes?"

". . . a sort of shape. A little shape."

"I saw it too," said a grumpy voice with an aggressively rational, crushing tone. "It was just the way the light was shining at an angle through where the dust was thickest. It was nothing."

No one seemed to want to argue with this, or comment any further on their own observations. Myra shifted her weight forward and peered down into the ugly little food safe in front of her. It contained a single object that must have been jammed behind one of the doors, because it now lay flat against the back of the cupboard. It took her a few moments to guess that it was perhaps some kind of doll. She reached in and carefully lifted it out. The head, body, and upper arms and legs had been unskilfully fashioned from a single piece of wood. Sections of the lower arms and legs hung loosely down, connected at the elbows and knees with black, shrivelled strips of something, probably leather. The features of the face were two deep holes, that had perhaps been burned in with a red-hot nail, for eyes, a triangular cut for a nose, and two rows of shallow indentations, probably also inflicted with the point of a nail, for a mouth. The mouth curved up slightly in a grin. It had once been dressed, as shreds of faded cloth clung to it in places, but it was naked enough now to reveal its sex. A v-shape had been cut under the belly at the top of its legs. The doll measured about eighteen inches from head to foot. Its surface had not been smoothed, and the chisel marks looked like wounds. Nevertheless, there was nothing sharp protruding from it that could have cut Greg's finger, and she could see no nails jutting out inside the cupboard.

As she studied the doll, she had a sense that she was also being observed, and not just by the men close to her. She looked round and saw, standing at the door through which she had entered the kitchen, a stooping, leering man. He was making some half-completed gesture she did not understand. He held his left hand, with a finger crooked, in front of his face, as though summoning someone to him. The instant their eyes met, the hand moved towards her and the finger straightened. When the arm was fully extended, he was pointing straight at her. He remained like that for a moment, while his expression changed to one of aching, greedy lechery. Myra saw that the marks, the stripes upon his face, were ancient scars. She jumped to her feet, appalled and intimidated by the gross implications of his look.

"That man," she said, grabbing Greg's arm to turn him towards the door, "he shouldn't be here. Who is he?"

Greg said, "I've no idea. . ." as the man slid backwards and away, out of sight down the corridor.

"Go after him, please. Ask him his name, and what he's doing here."

Greg nodded assent, and stumbled off. Myra found she was shaking. She would have been outraged by the mere fact that the intruder was there, at her place of work, on her ground. But the sexual threat expressed on the man's face had been so intense! She was sure he had been the person she had seen earlier, among the children in the Great Hall. Then, he had appeared to be acting violently, and for no reason she could discern. She wondered, for the first time, if he had been pursuing her. If so, why? And she wondered not just who, but what, he was. He had looked, somehow, more or less than human, and so out of place, so alien. This impression was created not merely by his grotesque, mangled face and warped posture. It was something intrinsic to him. Something unknowable; something impenetrable.

She was so shaken, she decided she needed to return to her office to recover. She instructed the men working in the kitchen to remove all the fallen masonry, and fled. She bumped into Greg, returning. He too looked flustered. His face was crimson, engorged with blood.

Myra said, "Did you catch that—person?"

"I couldn't get to him." Greg was anxious; fearful even. "I ran after him, and he was just walking along as if he were out for a stroll, but I kept falling behind. Somehow, he—he kept a distance between us." He rubbed the finger he had pricked, against his overall, as though it itched intolerably. He was gasping for breath. "My heart," he said, in explanation of his condition. "I have to be careful."

"Go home," Myra said. "You're ill. Take the rest of the day off."

She made her way swiftly through the now somewhat thinner crowds of children to her office. She sat for some minutes, composing herself, then remembered the dust that had fallen on her favourite skirt. She was surprised to see that some of it was still there. There were two marks, each of six separate dabs, spread like the palms and fingers of little hands, just above her knees. She moistened her thumb and dabbed one of the stains experimentally, to no effect. The marks seemed indelible. She thought crossly that one of the children in the crowd she had forced her way through when she had set out must have grabbed her skirt and left sticky finger marks that the dust had adhered to. She took off the skirt, put it to soak in the sink, and changed into the jeans she normally wore on-site but which, in her hurry, she had forgotten to put on earlier.

Back at her desk, she discovered the nasty little doll resting on her computer keyboard. She must have brought it with her, and put it there herself, but had no recollection of doing so. She picked it up and took it to the window to give it a closer scrutiny. She turned it face down for the first time and saw marks of some kind scratched into its back. An ornate design? Or numbers, perhaps? Or, more likely, letters? If so, they were unreadable. She put a sheet of paper over the doll's back and carefully made an experimental rubbing with a soft pencil. As she finished this operation, the phone rang. She thrust the doll in a drawer in her desk and picked up the receiver. It was Ron, her foreman, calling from home. He wanted to know what had been found.

"Something and nothing," Myra said. As she explained to Ron that the damage in the kitchen was slight, and what had been found in the wall was of interest but no great value, she twirled slowly round in her revolving chair and surveyed her office to make sure she was alone. She thought she heard some slight movement somewhere quite close to her, and other soft sounds; whimpering whinings, like an animal in pain, or a child pleading. She wondered if one of the young visitors to the Hall had somehow followed her in. But the room seemed empty, apart, of course, from herself. Once, behind her, something scampered a few paces across the floor, or so it seemed. She turned quickly towards the source of the sound and saw—something, and—nothing. A blur, perhaps, that vanished in an instant. I'm tired, she thought, and under a lot of strain. My mind is playing tricks.

She spent the rest of the afternoon working on a drawing for the next stage of the renovations of the Hall. She found it hard to concentrate, because the feeling that she was not alone persisted. In the end, to divert herself, she looked through some old reports and documents from the sixteenth century her researcher had provided to give her background information about the period. It was mostly irrelevant. She read of an insurrection in a local village when the crops failed and the people faced starvation, of a fire that had threatened to burn down the Hall, but that had been put out by a "myrical," and of a legendary warlock who had retired to the Hall as part of a bargain struck between the Devil, himself, and Sir George, Master of the Hall when the latter man was young and foolish. The warlock, who was also a knight, was a "master of Divination and All Subtle Sorcery" who had made the Hall an "eville dwelling playce" by his presence. Evidently he was "a hayter of all womankinde and treated them right cruwly." As an example of his ill nature in this respect, the instance was given of his treatment of a young woman who had been his mistress. He "caused her to be haunted by the Gowst of his dead daughter, to the ende of her days, though people said she was a poore, mad, innocent creture, who had done him no wrong, though he her much." Why he had taken this drastic step was not made clear. Myra soon grew tired of the nonsensical story, and put the papers away.

And still felt she was not alone. She resisted the urge to look round, but became more and more uneasy as the day drew to a close, because she was worried that she could be breaking down when her work was at a crucial stage. The success of the project meant everything to her. It would be the making of her career.

She slept in the Hall during the week, in a tiny room annexed to her office. In bed, she found she could not sleep because her delusions, if that was what they were, continued to manifest themselves, and that in itself engendered deeper anxieties. In the end she took one of the sleeping pills she had been given when her family had been killed, and she dreamed all night of that event. Her daughter, then almost four, had pestered her husband for ice cream for hours one hot summer evening, and, in the end, he had given in to her. He took her with him in the car. On the return journey, they had been hit by a joy rider. When Myra got to the hospital, they were both dead. Myra found, to her horror, that in her own mind she blamed her daughter. If only the child had not insisted that her father, tired from a long day at work, had to take her, there and then! Myra felt guilty about blaming the child, and that guilt provided substance for her nightmares.

When she woke up she remained face down on her pillow for some time without moving, because she was immediately aware that someone was holding her hand; her left hand, which was resting on the side of the bed above the quilt. It was a small hand that held hers. It clutched her fingers tight. It was cold and sticky and damp. When, at last, she slowly turned her head, and looked down along the length of her arm, there was no one there. The sensation that her hand was in someone's grasp weakened and vanished. She looked at her fingers and saw that were indeed moist. Then she realised she was soaked in sweat.

As a rule, after showering, she was used to making her own breakfast of coffee and muesli, but that morning she found she couldn't eat. Instead she went straight through to her office, determined to lose herself in work. When she reached her desk, she found the drawer she had stuffed the wooden doll into on the previous day was open wide. Except for some papers and a calculator, it was empty. She went to the main door of her office and tried to open it, but it was locked, as it should have been. No one could have got in from outside, and taken the wretched little toy.

She spent ten minutes looking frantically for the doll, but found nothing except the piece of paper she'd used to make a rubbing of the marks she had found on the thing's back. She studied it for the first time. There was writing there, crudely etched, but she found it surprisingly easy to read. There were two lines of words:

Thow I comme and go
She remanes with you.

So the doll was some kind of keepsake, she guessed. A gift from someone who had gone away, or was in the habit of doing so. A compensation for their absence. It seemed a rather pleasant sentiment, or so Myra thought at first. Later, when she'd given the words more consideration, and spoken them aloud to herself a number of times, it seemed to her that perhaps there was almost an element of threat in them; they took on a rather uncompromising tone, especially those in the second line. . .

Most days she did a tour of inspection of the various sites of work in the Hall, to make sure all was going well. She decided to stick to her routine, but it proved to be very hard for her. She had the feeling, everywhere she went, that someone was walking with her, someone who found it difficult to go at her pace, who kept falling behind, but who caught up with her whenever she stopped for more than a few minutes. She found it hard to maintain her usual friendly relationships with the men, and in conversations with them she dried-up twice, and totally lost the thread of what she was saying. They were polite, as they always were; there was something about her, a confident professionalism, that had earned their respect right from the start, but she noticed one or two of them reacted to her in an unusual way. They seemed to avoid her gaze, and looked around and behind her while she spoke, and she found their inattentiveness most disconcerting. She was glad when she was able to return to her office, but she wasn't any happier when she got there, because she wasn't alone. She wasn't alone all day.

In the evening, when it was cooler, she walked out along the South Front of the Hall, sat on a bench in the empty Fountain Terrace where she could watch the water playing, and tried to come to terms with the panic growing inside her. She reasoned that, though she was subject to delusions, she was still able to function and do her job. If she sought help, from a psychiatrist say, they would be sure to tell her to stop work, to rest, and that would be calamitous. She couldn't bear to even contemplate the prospect of giving in and giving up. No; she decided to tough it out, to take it easy as much as she could, and hope that her—neurosis, whatever it was, would go away. She closed her eyes and tried to relax in the beautiful, peaceful, already night-scented gardens.

But she was not alone.

The sound, which came to her from a little way along the empty bench beside her, was strange, but familiar. It reminded her of something, but at first she couldn't remember what. It was a soft, wet, slobbering noise, accompanied by a gentle nasal grunting; a sound, all told, of quiet contentment, though it made her flesh creep. What is it? she thought; I know I know, I've heard it before hundreds of times. She was determined to calm her fears by concentrating on unlocking her memory.

She recalled a time, before she was widowed, when, after they had both had their evening meal, she would sit with her daughter and watch tea time children's programmes on TV. Clara would sit beside her, or on her lap, very still and almost silent, hypnotised by the cartoons and puppets frolicking in front of her. The only sound, a tiny sound, that came from her was exactly the sound that Myra was hearing now, the susurrations of a comfortable, slightly sleepy child on the edge of sleep, sucking its thumb.

Something invisible was sitting next to Myra on the bench and sucking its thumb.

And Myra was afraid it might be her daughter.

"She remanes with you."

Myra cried out, got up, and ran to her rooms. That night she took two pills.

For the rest of the week, Myra was never alone. In spite of that, she managed to make a show of continuing with her work.

But on the fourth day, a Friday, Ron called on Myra in her office. He said he wanted to speak to her urgently. He looked as though the last thing he really wanted to do was speak to her, but she told him to sit down. They were both very obviously nervous. Myra's face was pale and drawn with worry, and Ron's was red with embarrassment. Nevertheless, he got right down to business.

"The men have asked me to speak to you, Mrs. Cooper. There's been a lot of complaints, I'm afraid, about you, you see, about the way you're carrying on, and we need to clear things up."

Myra nodded. She was not surprised. The men's attitude towards her had turned right round in the last two or three days, and she felt they almost hated her now.

"What—what am I doing wrong?" she asked.

"It's more what you're not doing," Ron said, almost angrily, then shut up.

Myra urged him to continue with a look.

"All right; it's like this: the boys don't like the way you're treating that child."

"Child! What child?" Myra said, and she could hear fear in her voice.

"The little one, the toddler that goes about with you, the funny-looking little blonde girl."

"Blonde?" Myra's daughter's hair had been dark, like her father's. In spite of everything, she felt some slight relief.

Ron pressed on, determined now to say his piece. "You just ignore it, Mrs. Cooper, and the men can't understand you. The kid's skinny as hell, it's always crying, but it won't take food from them, or let them so much as touch it to comfort it, and cries worse if they try to. It hangs round your feet all the time, and you never so much as look at it or speak to it. To tell you the truth, some of the men are for calling in the police, or social services, to get something done for the poor mite."

"Yes, they could try that," Myra said.

"Now come on, Mrs. Cooper," Ron said impatiently, "I'm trying to be reasonable, to get things sorted out. That's what we've got to do..." and he went on and on and on, but Myra had stopped listening to him. She nodded from time to time, when he seemed to want her to, and managed to appear attentive, but then she must have gone into some kind of trance.

When she came out of it, Ron wasn't there. Myra got up, locked the door, and returned to her swivel seat.

She sat on for a long time, until the room grew dark. Twice someone knocked loudly on her door and called her name, but she ignored them. She was listening to the child as it toddled around her. It had its doll now, to play with. She could see the disgusting little toy moving round the floor as the child dragged it behind her. Once she threw it into the air, dropped it and left it, then came back for it later, and started talking to it. Myra couldn't understand what the little girl was saying: she spoke too softly, and with a peculiarly harsh accent.

Finally, holding the doll in her arms, she came and rested against

Myra's legs. She could feel the weight of the child against her knee. Strangely, in the dark, Myra thought she could almost see her, or at least the shine of her pale yellow hair.

Something changed in the middle of the night. The child suddenly seemed restless, and more solid and real. Her movements, out in the pitch-blackness of the office, were clumsier. She bumped into things; things fell over. Myra didn't stir at the sound of objects falling, because she knew her life was ruined, and that nothing mattered. Nevertheless, she was pleased when the child returned to her, and put its hand upon her leg, because everything went very quiet.

Except for the sound of the little girl sucking her thumb, that was.

The hand on Myra's leg moved caressingly, travelling up away from her knee with an easy, steady determination. Her attention abruptly fixed on the hand, all of her attention, and she began to feel that something was wrong. The hand moved on and up, quite slowly, while Myra sat absolutely still. In the almost silence she could hear her own heart beating, and it was beating very loud. She thought she knew what was coming next, and she was right, because the hand then started doing things a child's hand would not do.

The chair Myra was sitting on was turned sideways and close to her desk. In the dark, she stretched out her right arm and fumbled for the little reading lamp she kept there. She had no trouble finding it. She pressed the switch, and in the wash of light saw the child for the first time. She was sitting on the edge of the desk. She was terribly thin, her face was covered in a rash, she was dirty, her clothes were rags, her nose was running, she was sucking her thumb—and in her other hand she held her doll. So she was not touching Myra's leg, but someone was, and holding it painfully hard.

Myra looked down to her left at the kneeling figure stooping beside her as he turned his scared face up to look at her.

"Though I come and go," he croaked, "she remains with you."

Then he reached out for Myra with his other hand.

The Outer Darkness

Maynard parked some distance from the church because he wanted a walk in the cold air to sharpen him up before he joined the other mourners. He had been driving with the heater on for over two hours, with the usual brain-numbing effects. The dry, fine snow had stopped falling, but the wind, gusting fitfully, tossed hissing clouds of flakes up into his face continuously. This had the required reviving effect on his constitution, but soon became annoying, as snow got into his sleeves and down his neck.

The cemetery rose steeply up the hill behind the church to almost the height of the steeple. The funeral party, a large group, widely spread like chess pieces on a white board, were clearly visible in a far corner at the very top of the rise. Maynard slowed down as he approached, wanting to get to the grave as late as was decently possible. He told himself this was because he had a slight chill, and it would be foolish to stand too long in the cold, but he was aware that he had a phobia about funerals, especially the part of the ceremony where the coffin was actually lowered into the ground.

He timed it wrong and got there just as the long box containing most of Melissa's mortal remains, resting at a slight angle on its supporting ropes, was jerkily descending. Perceiving this, he hung back at the rear of the group round the grave and sought, discretely, to find out where Clive Fletcher was, so he could avoid him, at least until they were due to meet after the funeral.

Clive's abundant, prematurely silvered mane was easy to discover, draped over broad shoulders that, on one side, supported Melissa's weeping mother. He seemed to be holding the portly, teetering woman upright with some difficulty with his left arm only, as his right was in a sling. Also,

Maynard noticed, his old rival had a black eye.

It was inconceivable that Clive could have allowed himself to get into a fight with anyone. So he must have been in an accident!

Somehow, Maynard found the thought slightly shocking. Clive Fletcher falling down stairs or wrecking his car? Never! The man was above such things. The only problems Clive ever encountered in his life had been engendered by his relationship, such as it was, with Melissa, and she would not actually have beaten him up, even if she were alive to do so.

Maynard perked up at the sight of Fletcher's shiner and looked forward keenly to discovering how he had got it. He would make sure to introduce the subject at the first opportunity during the heart-to-heart he anticipated they would have later.

It was an awkward ceremony. The clergyman's words, forced back into his mouth by clouds of windblown snow, were inaudible most of the time. He seemed in a hurry to get the service over and at one point almost ran along the side of the grave.

The other mourners, most of whom were strangers to Maynard, looked even more uncomfortable than people normally do at such occasions; many of their faces expressed irritation as much as sorrow. Only a handful were in tears, and they were Melissa's surviving relatives.

When Maynard stepped to the grave to pay his last respects he gazed briefly at the coffin. Although he knew she was in a very different condition, he imagined Melissa as he had so often seen her, stretched out on her back on his chair, her eyes shut, with her long, fine nose pointing towards him. How he had loved the shape of her nose! How he had loved the rest of her!

But had she loved him? Maynard shook his head.

How she had kept him guessing!

He winked down at her for the last time, then stood well back while the service drew to a swift conclusion.

The clergyman scampered down the hill to the church where, presumably, something warming awaited him, and Maynard followed the others out of the graveyard. Clive Fletcher, he noticed, remained behind with Melissa's mother, who was wailing in an excess of grief. As well she might, Maynard reflected, since her life could well take a very droll turn now she only had Clive to look after her, and her daughter was no longer there to moderate his eccentricities and insensitivity. The poor woman had much to cry about.

Maynard showed his face briefly at the reception, held at the nearby

Church Inn, to savour the atmosphere. It was, as he had anticipated, tense and neurotic.

Most of Melissa's friends did not like each other. They were jealous of the time all the others had spent with her. Melissa had carefully cultivated this emotion amongst those fortunate enough to be accepted into her circle, and had used it mercilessly to manipulate them. It had been just one of the weapons in her armoury, but perhaps the one that, next to her beauty, she had used most ruthlessly.

When Clive finally turned up, alone and looking very miserable, about half an hour later, Maynard ostentatiously left. As he was going out he waved at Clive, held up his left arm, and tapped his watch. Clive caught the gesture, understood, and nodded vigorously, with pathetic eagerness. He would obviously be grateful when, in an hour, the time of his appointment with Maynard, he would have an excuse to get away.

Meanwhile he would not have an easy time of it because almost everyone in the room assumed he had been responsible in some way for Melissa's death.

The *Harun al-Rashid*, a popular but slightly flaky restaurant where Maynard had arranged to meet Clive Fletcher, was a bustling place, even on a Friday afternoon. There were no empty tables, and the waitresses were constantly on the move, like the protagonist in a video game. Maynard had booked a place in the centre of this mêlée, and was very satisfied with the noisy, tense confusion around him. He knew it was the kind of situation that Fletcher found most disconcerting. Clive hated crowds, was self-conscious in public places, and was ultra-conservative in his choice of food. The menu at the *Harun al-Rashid*, though offering a confusion of options, was unrelievedly exotic.

Maynard relished most of the time he spent sipping his wine, watching the waitresses, and waiting. Relieved that the funeral was over, he felt strangely contented with himself and his life. The only thought that troubled his mind slightly was the fact that Melissa's death had hardly touched him at all; so far, he had felt no grief.

In the days before the funeral he had assumed the event would bring home to him the reality that she was gone; that he would never see her again, and was in fact, since he had no close friends of either sex, finally alone. But it hadn't worked out like that. He had not been affected in that way by the ceremony at all, which was perhaps not surprising, bearing in mind the haste with which it had been conducted, but neither had he experienced any sense of loss. He had even been, at the graveside, mildly amused, as though he and Melissa were in complicity in some mordant prank at the expense of the other mourners who would soon discover, to their consternation, that the ceremony was a sham, a joke at their expense.

Then, suddenly, the feeling that Melissa was still alive was for a moment so potent that Maynard would not have been surprised if she had entered the restaurant, woven her way elegantly through the confusion of people and tables, pulled a chair closer with that air she had of only being aware of him when they were together, given him her brief, pervading smile, and started to run her finger swiftly down the menu. The sensation that she had done just that was so strong, Maynard was almost alarmed, as though he had forgotten an appointment with her, and had been taken unawares. Briefly, he seemed to see the glow of her foxy-red hair, and caught a glimpse of her calm, pallid, perfect face.

When, simultaneously, Fletcher appeared at the entrance to the *Harun al-Rashid*, Maynard felt a jolt of vague annoyance. It was as if a tête-à-tête with Melissa, just begun, had been unexpectedly interrupted.

Then, wondering about the power, the conviction of his fantasy, that had almost been like a visitation, Maynard shrugged his shoulders, drank half a glass of wine, and recomposed himself to receive his guest.

The waitress who led Clive Fletcher to the table lost him halfway, and had to wait for him to catch up with her. He was a huge man, wide round the middle, with poor coordination. He flailed circuitously about among the other customers like a soul lost in the labyrinthine outer-chambers of Hell. His piping voice, repeating, "Excuse me; I'm sorry; so sorry, excuse me," gradually got louder as he approached, until, with the same apology, he blundered against Maynard, who, up to that moment, he seemed not to have noticed. To Maynard's astonishment, he found they were shaking hands. He had forgotten Fletcher's awkward formality when under stress.

The waitress positioned a chair behind Fletcher's legs and somehow encouraged him to fold himself down onto it.

"What a nice place, Maynard!" he said, rising again to tug off his jacket. He wore it draped over his injured arm in a way that might have looked debonair on another man. "I'm not late, am I?"

Maynard shook his head and poured two glasses of wine. "I don't think so," he drawled. Then asked, "What did you do with her?"

Fletcher looked shocked, betrayed, as though he had caught Maynard tipping poison in his drink. The effect of the short question was powerful enough to render him speechless. His mouth moved spasmodically; he mumbled senseless sounds.

"Melissa's mother," Maynard explained. "You seemed to be having problems with her."

"Oh, yes, I see!" He sounded very relieved. "I put her in a taxi and sent her home. The whole thing was just too much for her. It's making her ill. I'll get a doctor in to take a look at her later."

"Not many mothers could take the fact that their youngest daughter had thrown herself under the Manchester to London express in their stride," Maynard observed. "Did she *want* to be sent home in a taxi?"

"No. I had to force her. But she was spoiling the funeral reception for everybody else. There was no point in her staying on, was there?"

Maynard made a gesture with his head that could have meant anything.

Fletcher picked up the menu and surveyed it with increasing alarm. "Women!" he said, almost crossly. "What can you make of them? They're quite beyond me."

"I've noticed that, Clive," Maynard interjected, afraid that Fletcher was about to say, "But we can't live without them, can we?" or something of the kind. Then he added, somewhat crassly, "And now, sadly, Melissa is beyond us all."

Fletcher gave Maynard a look that suggested he found the last remark profoundly mysterious. He drew his lower lip back between his teeth, narrowed his eyes, and nodded deeply, involving the whole of the upper part of his body in the movement. "I suppose you're right," he said dubiously.

It was Maynard's turn to look confounded.

"There's no doubt about it. I saw the body myself. As her friend and her dentist, I had to identify her, remember, by her teeth, because she was so disfigured, while you and your... entourage were sailing up the Nile. It was most unpleasant."

"She refused to come with us. I pleaded with her. I told her it was the chance of a lifetime to see the world, and that her mother would soon be too frail to make the journey, but she wouldn't listen. Her family all came along."

"Melissa's mother," Maynard observed, "hates travelling."

Fletcher didn't seem to hear him. "As you know," he continued, "Melissa was so wilful. She had to be off on her own. If she had come, she'd still be alive, of course. She wouldn't have had that dreadful accident."

"Accident?"

"Perhaps she fell, or was pushed," Fletcher suggested hopefully, sounding like a child trying a lame excuse on an angry parent.

"Melissa was as sure footed as a dancer, and she was the only person standing on that stretch of the platform."

"The verdict was 'misadventure'."

"Why do you think she killed herself, Clive?"

Fletcher looked nervously round at the people sitting nearby, then turned his attention back to the menu. "I'm not sure why you asked me here, Maynard," he said.

"For a meal and a chat."

"About Melissa."

"What else?" said Maynard.

Waving the menu, Fletcher said, "There's nothing here I want to eat, and my life with Melissa is none of your concern."

Maynard smiled agreeably. "Why don't you ask them to make you a sandwich?"

"I would, but all the meat in these places has had something done to it. Not that I'm really hungry. And anyway, it's difficult to eat with an injured wrist."

"A sporting accident?" Maynard insinuated, aware that Fletcher had not played any game for twenty-five years, since he had been compelled to do so at school.

Fletcher's good hand went automatically to his black eye. "I tripped and fell crossing a road a couple of days ago. Rather odd, in fact. I felt a sensation as though someone had thrust a stick between my legs. Could have been killed. Someone ran over me on a motorbike."

"You were lucky!"

"He wasn't. He's still in hospital."

"I've always thought of you as a very careful person. Not the kind to allow. . . mishaps into your life."

"Quite right. But recently I've taken a few tumbles."

"Recently?"

"The last few days. Since Melissa died."

"Ah." Maynard shook his head in bogus commiseration, and ordered a meal from a speeding waitress. Fletcher had found something like a salad near the end of the menu and asked for that.

Backtracking to an earlier point in their conversation, Maynard said, "How do you know I've not asked you here to talk about my life with Melissa?" and peered curiously across at Fletcher.

"I know you used to see her occasionally; but then, she had so many friends."

"Nearly all of them male."

"I never concerned myself much about that. I was always confident she would came back to me."

"Like a bad penny! You know, that's strange, Clive, because I felt the same way about her myself; that I was the fixed point to which she returned from her. . . peregrinations."

Fletcher gave Maynard an owlish look that was probably meant to be scornful, and made a sound that was half a laugh. "She had the talent, among many others, to make you feel, when you were with her, that you were the only person of consequence in her life. It was part of her charm. But rest assured, I was her partner; I was the one she lived with."

"You were the one her mother and her family lived with, certainly."

Fletcher's voice showed signs that he was beginning to get angry. "She gave my address as her own. My house was her home."

"A lot of her mail was delivered to my flat." Maynard pulled a bunch of envelopes out of his pocket and waved them in front of Fletcher's face. "Look; see, from all over the place. They're very interesting."

"You've read them?" Fletcher asked contemptuously, though he looked somewhat deflated.

"Couldn't resist it. She left them about: I'm sure she wanted me to."

"Even so. . ."

"They're nearly all from her admirers. Most of them in love with her, of course. You'd be amazed to find who some of them were. Go on, have a look through them."

Fletcher shook his head emphatically.

Maynard shrugged and returned the letters to his pocket. "I get the impression she treated most, if not all, of her would-be lovers like shit. Their letters have a pleading, imploring note, like pariah dogs cast into the outer darkness and whining in the wilderness. They make painful reading. I'm sure they must have been a source of great satisfaction to her."

"I don't understand you," Fletcher objected, and reached out with his bandaged hand to move cutlery about nervously on the table in front of him. Maynard noticed his companion's bloated fingers moved without apparent restriction, and that the action didn't seem to cause him discomfort.

"Oh, come on, Clive, you know exactly what I mean. Even you can't be so insensitive as not to have realised long ago that Melissa had an inordinate appetite for adoration; that she felt a compulsion to test her male friends' admiration to the point of destruction. That's why we survived, so high in her estimation, for so long. We remained interesting to her because we are, in our different ways, robust. You are locked up into yourself, you don't feel or even notice nine-tenths of what's going on in the world around you: you are (or were) always safe, beyond the reach of storms. Melissa used to call you her pet rhino, because your hide was so tough; you had so many thick skins. Your relationship with her was your one indulgence, a single expensive gamble, but one that you, a rich man, could quite easily afford to lose. I, on the other hand, am, in some respects, very similar to Melissa. I enjoy playing with fire, but I'm an escapologist, I don't get caught or burned. Like Melissa, I find it hard to make a commitment to any one person. She recognised that... quality in me, appreciated it, and came to regard the two of us, she and I, as two sides of the same coin. But what it all amounts to, Clive, one way or the other, is that we didn't break, you and I, when she put on the pressure, and all the others did. We bounced back, we always came up for more, so we became her favourite—I almost said—victims!"

"I'm surprised you should even think of casting yourself in that role, after you're previous comments," Fletcher observed, and began to poke at the meal that had been placed in front of him. Momentarily confused, Maynard took refuge in inspecting the contents of his own plate.

After a solemn pause Fletcher added, "You seem to have taken Melissa's death very calmly."

Maynard caught the note of accusation and looked up.

"You almost give the impression," Fletcher continued, "that it has come as something of a relief; you have a slightly irresponsible air, like a man who just got out of prison."

After looking thoughtful, then amused, then laughing aloud, Maynard said, "Or perhaps like someone enjoying his last night of freedom before being locked away. That's very astute of you; that's exactly how I do feel. I can't account for it and, deep down, I find my state of mind slightly alarming and... inappropriate, but, there it is! We can't change our mood at will, to suit our situation, can we? And, come to think of it, Clive, you don't seem exactly inconsolable yourself. You're bearing up very bravely, or so it seems."

Fletcher pushed the fingers of his uninjured hand through his abundant silver hair in an anguished gesture and blinked; then, to

Maynard's astonishment, his face collapsed. His jowls sagged, the bags under his eyes bulged, his chin dropped, and his lower lip quivered. His eyes became red and damp. Reaching for his handkerchief, he made a sound like a desperate, half-suppressed sigh, and began to cry. Tiny tears slipped down the wrinkles round his eyes. His whole body sank and quaked as he sobbed.

Appalled and ashamed, feeling like an RSPCA inspector caught kicking a cat, Maynard leaned over and took his companion by the arm in what he hoped was a consoling gesture. His movement caught the attention of people at nearby tables who began to stare at Fletcher. It was on the tip of Maynard's tongue to say something like "Pull yourself together" when, with an obvious effort, Fletcher did just that. He blew his nose loudly, like a schoolboy, wiped his eyes, and tried to look composed.

"I'm sorry, Clive," Maynard said, unable to keep a note of irritation out of his voice, "I was out of order there, I had no idea you were so. . ."

"The whole thing has been a nightmare, Maynard. You can't imagine. It's not just Melissa's death I've had to cope with, I've had to prop up her entire family. I know they blame me somehow, for everything. They all live with me, because she insisted they should, and moved them in one by one, but now they have nowhere else to go. They're trapped, and they hate being so beholden to me. And what can I do? I can't throw them out. I don't think they'd go if I tried. If they thought I wanted to get rid of them, they'd stay, just to make me miserable. It's all so oppressive. I feel smothered. I nearly broke down. I'm on anti-depressants. I took a double dose this morning, in the hope that it might get me through the day and perhaps it would have done, if I hadn't come here."

"Christ, Clive. . . !"

"I don't understand your attitude. You seem to me to be almost gloating, to revel in the situation, and I can't see that you have anything to gloat about."

Maynard gave a groan of protest that Fletcher ignored. Fletcher was clearly working himself into a state of indignation. He reached his bandaged hand out of the sling, tapped the table angrily with a blue, swollen finger, and said, "For God's sake, Maynard, what are we doing here? We've just buried the woman we both loved. It's not. . . proper to behave like this. It's disrespectful! But I feel you're getting some satisfaction out of the situation. You've invited me here for some particular reason, and I want to know what it is. What are you trying to do to me?" He glanced crossly round, and scowled at the nearby diners who were covertly enjoying the drama being enacted in front of them.

After pouring wine into both their glasses, and sinking right back in his chair, Maynard murmured, "Well, Clive, you seem to have sloughed some of those protective skins at last."

"So that's it?"

"You seem almost human."

"You wanted to see me suffer?"

"I was curious to know if you were capable of suffering. I find that you are."

"And you, it seems, are not."

"I don't miss Melissa, if that's what you mean. Her death hasn't touched me yet. I feel that somehow, somewhere, she's still around."

Fletcher's indignation dropped visibly away. His expression became milder, almost sympathetic. "Even though you saw her dead?"

"It may interest you to know that she seemed to be here with me, in the very chair that you are sitting in now, just before you arrived."

"Really," said Fletcher, sounding slightly jealous, but not surprised.

"As large as life."

"Hm."

"You've felt it too, haven't you, Clive? You've had the same. . . impressions?"

Fletcher said nothing, but, by his silence, seemed to concur.

"Perhaps she's not finished with us," Maynard ventured. "What do you think? She kept us both on tenterhooks when she was alive, and wouldn't or couldn't choose between us. It could be that she's going to resolve the situation now, one way or the other."

Fletcher nodded, obviously deep in thought, then said, "On the other hand, it's possible that she wants to prolong the affair into perpetuity. Has that occurred to you?"

"It has. That's what I wanted to talk about, Clive. I wanted us both to be aware of that."

"Well, now, we are."

"Yes."

"What more is there to say?"

Maynard shook his head slightly. "I don't know."

"You're worried?"

"Aren't you?"

Fletcher suddenly stood up. He pulled a small brown bottle from his pocket, shook a pill out onto his hand, palmed it into his mouth, and washed it down with half an inch of wine. He tried to get into his jacket. Maynard rose to help him.

"I have to get back," Fletcher said. "They're expecting me. I've got to drive them home."

"The sisters?"

"Yes."

"I understand." Maynard sat down again. "Perhaps we can get in touch sometime?"

"If we must."

"We'll see how it goes."

Appearing to agree with this vague arrangement, Fletcher, apologising every few seconds, abruptly wandered out into the crowded restaurant. He was soon lost, lurching about among the tables like a rudderless ship on a choppy sea, until a waitress locked her fingers round his arm and guided him out through the door.

Maynard sat on after he had gone, slowly finishing the bottle of warm Hock. He was wondering what Melissa would have thought about his conversation with Fletcher, had she been there to hear it.

At the back of his mind, he harboured the hope that she might rejoin him.

After an hour, finding himself still alone, he left.

Fletcher saw nothing of Maynard during the next few months but occasionally picked up snippets of information about him from mutual friends. All reported that the man was going through a very bad period. He had had a number of small, unspecified accidents. Never sociable, he had disappeared completely from the one or two pubs he once used infrequently to visit, and no longer attended the ballroom dancing classes that had been his one enthusiasm. (Melissa had never accompanied him to these sessions, though her mother had been dragooned into service from time to time.) There was a rumour that he had sought psychiatric help, and another that he had been visiting a notorious psychic, a glamorous teenage girl with a hysterical temperament and highly unorthodox views on the afterlife, who had been the subject of a recent investigative TV programme from which she had emerged with her reputation enhanced. Maynard dismissed this last suggestion out of hand, and tried to picture Fletcher stretched on a psychiatrist's couch, but fail totally to do so. It was hard to believe that Fletcher, in any circumstances, would realise he needed help, and harder still to believe he would seek it from professional therapists. He was the sort of person who, however ill, refused to consult a doctor. Maynard wondered if he even had one. To his knowledge, Fletcher had never even been ill before.

In spite of the lack of contact between them, Maynard found that Fletcher was often in his thoughts. This may have been due to his old rival's quondam association with Melissa, who was constantly on Maynard's mind; had, indeed, taken up residence there. Dead, she had become even more of an obsession than she ever had been alive. He was uneasily aware of the power of this monomania, and troubled by it, but his feeble efforts to come to terms with it were negated by the strong sensation he had, occasionally, that Melissa was somehow present: sometimes she seemed to be walking along side of him, even in the most public places. He could almost see her.

A number of times he had thought he had seen her. A young woman, walking in front of him in a shopping mall, had given him a cold fright when he saw her face because she wasn't Melissa, but was so like her. Another, seen on a train, at the far end of his carriage, cut his heart with disappointment, almost despair, when she cackled at something her companion said, filling the compartment with a parrot-like noise quite unlike Melissa's controlled, mocking laugh. It was when Maynard glimpsed a girl of Melissa's type, in her late twenties, with the same vivid red hair, sitting behind the reception desk of a firm he had bought some equipment from for his surgery, that the blow finally struck, the axe fell.

She looked up at him as he entered without, for a moment, changing her vague, quizzical expression; perhaps trying to decide if she knew him or not. Maynard was so flabbergasted by her, because she was an exact clone of Melissa, looking, however, as she had ten years earlier, when he had first met her, that he found it hard to walk. He waded towards her as though he were knee-deep in wet cement, staring at her in a way she may have found alarming, and opened his mouth to say... well, not her name, but Melissa's.

He had almost reached the desk when the girl smiled. It was a simple smile, not at all like Melissa's, and it broke the spell, shattering Maynard's obsessive delusion to fragments, because, at that moment, the fact that Melissa was definitely dead hit him for the first time. The truth closed around him like some huge, black, spiny umbrella, or the dank wings of a half-reptilian prehistoric bird. Melissa was dead; she was gone; she was buried. At last, he knew it, and he started to grieve.

Spinning round, he went back through the door, struggled out onto the pavement, and, seeing and hearing nothing of the crowds around him in the city centre, flying blind, on automatic pilot, walked the quarter-mile to the back street where his car was parked. He sat in the driving seat without moving for half an hour, enveloped in the darkness of mourning, then stirred himself awkwardly to start the engine, reaching round the dashboard with his hand as though the action were unfamiliar to him. He nearly hit the car in front of him, that had been parked a reasonable distance away, as he nosed out onto the road, and realised he was so shaken-up that his judgment was impaired.

I'm in shock! he thought, and shook his head in bewilderment. Then, feeling displaced, and unsure of the route, though he travelled it daily, he drove cautiously home.

Three days later he wrote a long letter to Clive Fletcher. When he'd finished it he didn't dare read through it, knowing that, if he did, he would destroy it. It was a chaotic letter, full of the feelings of loss that had suddenly overwhelmed him. It was all about Melissa; he found himself writing her name over and over again. Much of what he wrote was trivial and personal, stuff that he would never, in a million years, have told Fletcher to his face, but he had to express his thoughts, to pass them on to someone, and, he realised, there was nobody else he could write to. He had always kept people at arm's length, and now they all seemed a lot further away: had, in fact, vanished. With the onset of mourning, he had come to understand the extent of his solitude. He off-loaded this knowledge, along with his myriad other anxieties and negativities, into the letter, folded all eleven double-sided pages into an envelope, and flung it into a post-box.

Within an hour of doing so, he was planning to wait for the postman to make his collection so he could try to retrieve the letter; if necessary, to grab it back, but realised he hadn't quite sunk to that depth of foolishness. He let it go.

And spent two weeks of agony and humiliation, anticipating Fletcher's reply. When, at last, it came, addressed from "The Henry Morton Total Therapy Clinic" in Bedfordshire, it was written in a wobbly hand only just identifiable as Fletcher's and was disconcertingly obtuse.

Fletcher started by insisting he was in no fit state to write at all, and that Maynard's letter had made him worse. He assumed Maynard must be unaware of his condition, or he would not have piled such a burden on a sick man's shoulders. There was a deep paragraph down most off the first page full of this sort of thing, that had a tone of mawkish self-pity quite unlike Fletcher's normally lofty, detached, even mandarin style. Maynard skipped contemptuously to the first mention of Melissa, halfway down page two, and tried to grapple with the sentences surrounding her name. He was annoyed to find they made no sense at all; they contained mere ravings. Perhaps Fletcher had become unhinged, even paranoid, because over and again he seemed to be saying he had been "chosen," "selected," "picked"; the words all appeared more than once in a short space, and that Melissa had done the choosing, etc.

Recently, that was! And personally. She had made known her choice to him, Clive Fletcher, in the last few days and she had chosen him.

Chosen for what? Maynard wondered.

The letter got more confused for another couple of pages, then Fletcher must have stopped and taken a rest (or a pill) because the last brief section was written in a neater hand, and contained a message Maynard could understand. Fletcher wanted to meet him, but not until he was feeling better again. His doctor had advised him this could take eight months. Since, at the end of that period, the anniversary of Melissa's death would be imminent, he suggested they meet on that day. Then they would probably both be more composed, could talk things through, and Fletcher would demonstrate the truth to Maynard, that he, Clive, had been—and he used the word again—chosen—by Melissa! They'd meet at the *Church Inn*, where her funeral reception had been held, for lunch. Perhaps they could even visit the grave together! Would Maynard confirm if this was convenient?

Maynard did, by return post.

Fletcher's letter had reminded him of something Melissa had said a long time ago, that had merely seemed amusing at the time, but now echoed with new significance. She had been telling him about Clive's magnificent house and the way he had furnished it. When he had first taken her there he had steered her from room to room, and "explained" each item of furniture contained therein. The furniture was wildly mixed, from all periods, but every single thing was, according to Fletcher, "the best of it's kind," "the finest money could buy," "a perfect example of its type," etc. Nothing, anywhere, was ordinary. At the end of the tour of inspection, Melissa had said, he had turned to her and stood in front of her, with his hands outstretched level with his shoulders, gazing silently at her with a smile of pride and admiration on his great lump of a face, as though he was welcoming her into not just his home, but his collection. She had felt she had been chosen as a perfect specimen.

And, Maynard mused, perhaps that was where Fletcher had made his first error of judgment. Melissa was not a superb example of a type, she was an original, the ultimate one-off, and, if Fletcher thought she fitted into some category—was perhaps the perfect woman of his dreams—he had been dead wrong. She had certainly not become part of the furniture, but right from the start, had instead sat on Fletcher with her full weight. Unexpectedly, he had been strong enough to bear her up, and had not broken when she had tested him out. But, she had explained to Maynard, she was aware all the time that she had been bought. She had been unable to resist Fletcher's sheer wealth, and had become entangled in it, like a lamb in a thicket (her own comparison).

The price she paid had been high. Although outwardly, she had retained and taken full advantage of her freedom, Fletcher had contrived to get value for his money somehow. Melissa had shuddered theatrically when she mentioned this, and refused to be specific as to how Fletcher obtained his part of the bargain, and Maynard had a sense that she was exercising her frequently displayed talent for self-dramatisation and mystification. Nevertheless, she often returned to the nature of her relationship with Fletcher, implying it had a darker side, then abruptly dropped the subject, as though she was scared she might be led into some compromising self-revelation. Maynard knew she had mentioned this to others, as he had found references to her obscure unhappiness with her situation in some of the letters from her besotted admirers that she had left around his apartment for him to read. Many of them had wanted to save her from her plight. One, perhaps more acute than the others, thought he had identified the cause of her troubles and had offered to "dispose of" Fletcher.

Melissa, despite all appearances to the contrary, had a history of depressive illness, and had attempted suicide more than once in her teens, or so she said, and Maynard assumed that her hints suggesting some deep inner despair were symptoms of that condition.

Of course, after her death, because of the way she had died, he was not so sure.

Some time after the exchange of letters Maynard heard gossip about Fletcher, suggesting he had discharged himself from the clinic, and returned home. Opinions about the state of his health ranged from "looking decidedly poorly" to assertions that he was "standing at death's door." The most pessimistic estimate of his condition proved to be accurate as, slightly less than three weeks before the two of them were due to meet,

Maynard read a report of Fletcher's death in the *County Reporter.*

"Millionaire Entrepreneur Dies After Illness" was the front page headline. The article stated that "the 42-year-old inventor of the 'FletcherTex System' and owner of the 'Fletex' highstreet store chain had been found dead in bed the previous evening." After describing how Fletcher had "speedily achieved success in his early twenties," it mentioned his "determination to avoid public scrutiny in recent years" and his "reclusive habits." The item closed by stating that "police were investigating the circumstances of the death," in a way that suggested there was something suspicious about them.

"He's topped himself," Maynard whispered, and felt his face relax into a smile for the first time since he had begun to mourn. Realising he had achieved this emotional breakthrough, he suddenly felt hopeful, even optimistic. Then he began to laugh. It was not a cruel laugh of triumph over the dispatch of an old rival, but of appreciative astonishment at the ironic twists of fate. Maynard was in no way glad Fletcher was dead (though he wasn't sorry either) but, all at once, he felt himself very much alive again; he felt released.

He had wasted a lot of his off-duty hours brooding in his flat during the last months, but he spent the rest of that Saturday strolling happily round the neighbourhood, and even sat contentedly for a while on a park bench, taking advantage of the opportunity to enjoy a brief burst of winter sunshine. As he was sauntering home, he stopped at a florist's and ordered flowers to be delivered to his address on the morning of the anniversary of Melissa's funeral. He would make the pilgrimage to visit the grave alone. Once there, it would be just the two of them, together again, him and Melissa; a much more satisfactory arrangement than the previous one.

Just after the bell sounded and Maynard opened the front door to receive the flowers from the delivery woman, his telephone started to ring. Its troublesome, urgent piping tone continued as he searched for a pen to sign the receipt, took the document to a table to put his name to it, gathered up the bouquet, and ran with it into the kitchen where he had previously half-filled the sink. He shot back to the phone, snatched it up, and stated his number. A faint howling, as of a distant wind, echoed in his ears for some seconds; then a voice, sounding somehow ultra-close, almost inside his head, said, "Hello, Maynard? It's me."

Maynard heard himself say, "Yes."

"You remember we're due to meet later?"

The receiver in Maynard's hand became huge and heavy. He had to strain to keep it to his ear. The arm bearing its weight began to ache. He contemplated dropping it back onto its cradle.

"Don't ring off," the voice ordered anxiously, with a note of pleading and another of threat.

"What—what do you want?"

"I hope you have kept today. . . unengaged. I would like us to go together, you and I, to Melissa."

"To her grave?"

"No, no, of course not. To her. To see her."

"Where are you speaking from?"

"Not far away. Closer than you think."

Maynard looked round the room nervously. "Do I have any alternative?" he asked, hearing how changed his own voice had become, sounding now almost like a child's.

"Not really. But don't worry, I won't harm you. I couldn't, even if I wanted to. I just need you to come with me, so I can make my point."

"What point?"

"About Melissa. That, in the end, she has chosen me."

"Suppose I say you have made it?"

"Not enough! I want you to know."

"It's that important to you?"

"Yes."

"And if I come, later, you'll leave me alone?"

"Oh, yes. Absolutely. You have my word."

"Where can we meet?"

"That's no problem at all. Just get in you car and drive."

"Which way?"

"It doesn't matter. Whichever road you take, I'll be waiting. Stop when you see me."

"You still look. . . the same?"

"You'll recognise me."

"And are you really. . ."

"No more questions; explanations are. . . irrelevant." There was a silence, then the voice repeated, "Get in your car and drive," and the line went dead.

Maynard sat for some time thinking, trying to find some way out of the situation. He didn't for a moment doubt his sanity, or that the conversation had taken place and, though he felt deeply uneasy, he wasn't actually scared of what may lay ahead of him. But he would have done anything to avoid doing what he had been asked to do. Uppermost in his mind was the fact that he might really meet Melissa again. That, under the circumstances, was the hardest part; the prospect he found most difficult to accept. Its implications were alarming. Where was she? How was she? What was she? The questions circled his brain, like infants chasing each other round a Maypole, for almost an hour.

Then, when the phone rang again, he got up and went into the kitchen. He had decided to take the flowers with him.

He took a route that would bring him ultimately to the graveyard where Melissa was buried. He didn't expect to get there, but it seemed the obvious thing to do. He drove slowly, peering out at both sides at the people on the streets. It was a day very different to the one a year ago, when he and Fletcher had last met. It was just as cold, but patches of mist, heavy enough to require the use of the windscreen wipers, had drifted down from somewhere, bringing with them a concomitant gloom, and the day was dull, visibility poor. People walked quickly, eager to get out of it.

Maynard had been driving for ten minutes, and was turning a blind corner, when a man stepped out in front of him from nowhere. Instinct made Maynard spin the wheel away. The rear of the car wobbled, and the vehicle left the road and stopped. Maynard thought he heard a smash and things went dark.

Because, he realised, he had shut his eyes.

He opened them and found he had swerved into a lay-by, that the car looked undamaged, and that he felt okay. The engine was still running, so he turned it off. As he released his seat-belt, someone tapped on the window beside him. He wound it down and Fletcher's big face dropped into the frame. He didn't look too good, but Maynard had not expected that he would.

"You're dead, Clive," he said.

Fletcher nodded almost apologetically and said, "Will you move over please?"

"You want to drive?"

"I have to."

"Can't you direct me?"

"No."

Maynard lifted the flowers on the seat next to him over to the back of the vehicle, opened the door, and eased himself over into the adjacent space. Fletcher, awkward in death as in life, blundered in beside him. "This is a very nice car," he observed.

"It's the best of its kind. The finest money can buy."

Fletcher nodded his approval. "I had one myself, of course."

"So you did."

"I miss it."

"So it's true then?"

"What is?"

"You can't take it with you."

Fletcher gave Maynard a confused look that could have been of hurt or anger, started the engine, jerked the car recklessly back onto the road, and drove away.

Maynard tore his gaze away from the corpse beside him and forced himself to look forward through the windscreen.

Fletcher drove fast, and seemed take no particular notice of the highway ahead. He gave the impression he knew just where he was going, however. He drove with a terrible confidence. He cut ruthlessly in front of the vehicles they overtook, and Maynard got the impression he may have forced some of them off the road. A couple of times he turned in his seat to check on this, but was unable to see anything clearly through the rear windows. He tried to read signposts they passed, to form some idea of where they were heading, but couldn't make sense of them in the poor light. After a while, he was quite disorientated. The landscape they were going through, of featureless, rolling countryside, did not reveal any detail that was familiar to him and he soon sank into that passive, fatalistic mood of boredom, tinged with anxiety, that drivers, compelled by circumstances to become passengers, adopt as a response to their loss of power and control. He asked once where they were going but Fletcher's answer—"I told you, to Melissa."—seemed deliberately obtuse, and designed to discourage further questions.

After about an hour they began to pass extensive, blank-walled structures that Maynard assumed were factories or warehouses, suggesting they were on the outskirts of some more urban area. Fletcher suddenly turned off the main road into a labyrinth of narrow lanes bordered on either side by these tall buildings. Maynard got the impression that the industrial estate, if that was what it was, was empty and unused, as they passed no pedestrians, and there was no traffic to be seen, or any other activity at all. At one point they shot up a steep ramp that took them to the level of the roofs of the tallest of the buildings, then passed between some huge and ancient gateless stone gateposts. Maynard was surprised to find they had entered what he first took to be a cemetery, but then realised was an extensive garden or park, and were travelling along a broad gravel path towards a large, white, modern hotel building, the front of which was illuminated by floodlights. After creeping about for a few minutes looking for a space in the almost full car park, Fletcher stopped, tapped the steering wheel lightly with his fingertips, and said, "Well, this is it; we're here."

He sounded stressed and strange, but it was too dark for Maynard to see his face to read his expression."

"And where is 'here,' Clive?"

"Where Melissa and I are staying."

"You can't be more. . . specific?"

"Leave it alone, Maynard. I won't answer your bloody questions, and it wouldn't help you if I did."

Maynard noticed his companion definitely did not sound nearly so sure of himself as he had at the beginning of their journey, when he had instantly, easily assumed the dominant role. There was now a petulant tone to his voice, and an unconvincing edge of aggression. It was the voice of a man who had reached the end of reason and argument, and was preparing to defend the indefensible. Also, Fletcher seemed even sicker that he looked. He struggled to get out of the car, and leaned motionless across the roof for a while, as though the effort of driving had almost completely exhausted him. Maynard reached back into the rear of the car, took up his flowers, got out, and walked round to stand next to him.

"What now?" he said. "Where is she?"

Reluctantly, Fletcher straightened up and started to move slowly, almost painfully, towards the hotel. Maynard followed a few steps behind, looking about him at his surroundings.

The sky had gone very dark. Maynard looked at his watch. It seemed that the night had come down much too soon, as though they had driven into a different time zone.

They made their way towards the main entrance of the building, the doors of which, from a distance, seemed inconveniently low, as though designed for a race of pygmies. The name of the hotel was displayed in letters of silver on a white background that were, in the sharp glare of the floodlights, indecipherable. The building was designed on a grand scale, and obviously contained hundreds of rooms, most of which appeared to be occupied. To the right of the hotel an area had been taped off with strips of orange plastic. Beyond this barrier various dim lights shone up out of the ground, as though work was going on there, quite deep down. Drains, perhaps, were being laid, or electric cables, or the foundations for new buildings were being set in place, though none of the sounds that accompany this kind of activity could be heard. The whole scene was quiet and still, except for the movements of two men in dark uniforms with luminous patches on their shoulders, who seemed to be patrolling the edge of the area marked out by the tapes.

Maynard saw, as they approached the hotel, what he at first took to be more signs that building or maintenance work was taking place. He noticed a slope of loose rubble, looking as though it had been recently dug up, resting against the base of the walls all along the front of the building as far as he could see. This struck him as peculiar because the building looked too new to require extensive repairs. As he got closer to the front doors, he was astonished to see that they hung a few degrees slightly to the left of vertical. He stopped and, looking up, realised the whole structure was leaning over at an angle. He clambered behind Fletcher over the rampart of rubble and found he had to lower himself down a further slope of broken soil, that had collapsed down onto the front step, to reach the level of the floor of the building beyond. He understood then why the entrance, from a distance, had looked so small. The entire hotel seemed to have tipped over and sunk into the ground to a depth of three feet or more!

Ahead of him, Fletcher was pushing open one of the heavy glass doors that suddenly, to Maynard, looked potentially dangerous. He grabbed his companion's arm and pulled him back.

"What's happened here?" he demanded. "Some terrible subsidence? The building must be unstable, surely; it could collapse at any minute."

Fletcher, his face now visible in the glare of the floodlights, turned listlessly and gave him an anxious little half-smile. "Maynard," he said, "I can assure you this place was built to last. It won't fall down. That's one thing you can be sure of."

Though Fletcher's words were reassuring, his manner wasn't. Maynard released his arm, but held back.

"If Melissa is in there, we should get her out."

"You're a fool, Maynard," Fletcher sneered. "You're speaking without thinking. What possible extra harm can come to her now?" He turned, barged into the foyer of the hotel, and strode away. After a second's pause, during which he felt a wave of panic rise and subside, Maynard followed him.

The foyer was busy. A group of people queued for attention at the reception desk, some stood more or less patiently by piles of luggage, waiting to be shown to their rooms, others strode purposefully about, and, in a corner, a couple of dozen more sat at tables drinking tea and coffee. The place was noisy with loud talk and irritating taped music.

Fletcher stumbled with his customary awkwardness through the crowd, apologising all the time as he careered against people who seemed unable to get out of his way, and pressed a button for the lift. Maynard stood with his back to him a yard away, peering about, fascinated by the activity around him. The hotel had something of the atmosphere of a railway terminus. There was a grim earnestness about the place; the kind of tension generated by people in transit, and not too sure they are waiting for the right train, or have arrived at the correct destination. Maynard noticed that, though a number of people entered through the doors while he watched, no one went out.

He heard the swish of opening doors and followed Fletcher into the lift. They rose in a smooth silence until Maynard said, "I suppose Melissa knows I'm coming? She is expecting me?"

Fletcher shook his head. It could have been in affirmation of the negative, or a gesture of annoyance. Maynard was about to pursue the matter when the lift stopped, the doors opened, and Fletcher lurched, almost fell, into the corridor beyond.

The corridor, painted grey from floor to ceiling, was long, bleak, and empty, but deeply carpeted. A chilly draft, almost a breeze, blew along it from somewhere. Fletcher stopped at the fifth door they came to, knocked softly, and entered. A sharp, cold white light, that was actually painful to Maynard's eyes, shone brazenly out of the room beyond. Instead of going in after Fletcher, he stepped back and shielded his eyes from the glare with the hand that was holding the bunch of flowers. He discovered the transparent paper the bouquet was wrapped in acted as a filter, holding back some of the brilliance of the light. Looking through it while his eyes adjusted, he tried to see into the room. At first he thought the place was, except for Fletcher, who was standing a little way inside, empty, even of furniture. He forced himself across the threshold in spite of the discomfort the light still caused him and, once inside, he saw her, standing against the back wall. He realised that the light, emanating from a point just above and in front of him, was somehow, by its very intensity, obscuring her behind its glare, its blinding brilliance. She was staring at him hard. Her own eyes, open very wide, were as reflective as a cat's, and were apparently unfazed by the light.

She didn't seem at all pleased to see Maynard. She, like Fletcher, looked extremely unwell and ill at ease—or—perhaps, she just looked. . . dead.

Melissa said, "Why have you done this?" Her voice was full of derision and disgust. Maynard realised the question had been addressed to Fletcher, though she was still gazing intently at him.

"I wanted him to see: to know that you had chosen me," Fletcher said, sounding aware of the fatuity of the explanation.

"To share this place with me! You're proud of that?"

Fletcher slumped tiredly against the wall and slid his back down until he was sitting on the floor. Maynard, with his eyes almost screwed shut against the light, went and sat next to him.

"Melissa," he said, "I'm sorry to see you like this."

She bit her lip and looked away.

"Tell me, have you any idea why you're here?" he continued.

She shook her head. "Have you?"

"Why you're here?"

"Why we're all here!"

"Well—" Maynard thought about it. "Yes, I suppose I have got some idea why."

Melissa made a helpless, hopeless gesture. "Anyway," she said, "there's nothing we can do about it."

"No," Maynard agreed. He got up. "I'll have to go. The light is too much for me. I'm sorry." He turned his back on Melissa and walked towards the door. Before going out he stopped and said, "Tell me, Fletcher; I'm interested; how exactly did you die?"

Fletcher, from the floor, said, "Suicide; an overdose."

"I thought so. Any particular reason?"

"Melissa wouldn't give me any peace. She tormented me all the time, to make me join her. And of course," he added, almost as an afterthought, "I wanted to be with her."

"And are you. . . happy with the new arrangement?"

Fletcher made no answer. After a moment Maynard said, "It's odd you should say you killed yourself, because Melissa's mother has been charged with your murder."

Fletcher made a noise, a sharp grunt. "That's nonsense," he said. "I know the circumstances of my own death."

"Maybe. I assume you do. Nevertheless, Melissa's mother is to go on trial. The theory is, she did you in because she thought she'd get your money. Also, they say, you treated her like shit. She had many reasons to want to be rid of you."

"I killed myself," Fletcher insisted, sounding tired and, strangely, uncertain.

"Her fingerprints were on the pill bottle and on the cup you took your last drink from, if the newspapers are to be believed."

"She brought them to me in bed. I asked her to. She unscrewed the top of the pill bottle because, for the first time in my life, I was too weak to do it myself. That was why I decided to finish it then, because I realised I had become helpless. She left the bottle open by my bed. I tipped all the tablets into half of the drink, waited for them to dissolve, and swallowed the lot. She's innocent."

"She had been heard to make threats against your life many times by a number of people. There is more quite strong evidence against her. Things look very bad for her."

"What 'other evidence'?"

"I've no idea. But you should know. Think about it. Anyway, I understand she's decided to admit to it."

"She's what!"

"She's going to plead guilty."

"But that's crazy; absolutely crazy," Fletcher protested, quite lively now. "Why would she do that?"

"Well," Maynard said, "perhaps she's missing Melissa."

He stepped quickly forward out of the room and shut the door behind him. He almost ran to the lift, which, amazingly, was there on his level, open, as though it were waiting for him. As he got in, he heard a door back down the corridor open.

The lift sank down to the foyer. Maynard made his way toward the main entrance feeling self-conscious, scared that somehow he was drawing attention to himself, and that this was not a wise thing to do. A lot of people did turn to watch him as he passed, but did not, as he thought they might, make any attempt to stop him. He was very relieved to get out of the hotel. He scrambled quickly up over the rubble and soil back to ground level.

He had an urge to see just what kind of work was going on in the taped-off area he had noticed earlier, and went across to take a look. He discovered that the hole in the ground beyond the tape was much wider than he had imagined. The rim opposite to where he was standing was at least two hundred yards away. To his left, the breach in the earth reached the side of the hotel; to his right, it curved away out of sight, like a dried up riverbed. After glancing round to make sure the two men patrolling the area were both a good distance away, he ducked under the strip of orange plastic, strode to the edge of the hole, and peered down inside.

And saw what, for an instant, he took to be some kind of maze; then he realised he was looking down into a number of rooms without ceilings. Dozens of them. The rooms were all furnished, and people were living in them. They were cooking food, watching TV, unpacking their baggage, hoovering floors, making love, washing dishes, reading newspapers, going about their lives in a normal way, and seemed unaware that there was nothing but the sky above their heads. All the rooms were bathed in the same vivid light that had shone from some undetectable source in the room Fletcher had taken him to, where he had seen Melissa. Maynard had been staring with fascination down into the hole for a few moments, half a minute at most, when one of the patrolling guards spotted him and ran across to him.

"Get away from the edge," he ordered, "it's dangerous."

Maynard meekly crawled back under the tape.

"Do you mind telling me what you're doing here, sir?" the man inquired, officiously but politely.

"I've been visiting a resident."

The guard pointed to the pit. "Not down there, sir?"

"No, at the hotel."

"Ah, yes." The man seemed mollified. "Well, I must ask you to stand well back. There could be further earth movements at any time."

"You mean more—subsidence?"

The man looked sharply at Maynard, as though he was not quite sure he had caught the meaning of what he had said, and tugged the lobe of his ear in consternation.

"Subsidence," Maynard repeated, clearly and more loudly. "Subsidence. Surely the hotel is sinking into the ground?"

The guard laughed. "You've got it wrong there. It's just the opposite. It's not sinking down, it's rising up!" He shook his head to indicate that Maynard had said something very foolish, and walked away.

Maynard stood still for a moment, gazing up at the hotel, hoping it might move.

Then he realised he was still holding the bunch of flowers he had originally intended to lay on Melissa's grave. The blossoms were in a bad way; petals had fallen off many of them, the stems of some had broken, and the paper round the bunch had come loose. Maynard screwed the bouquet up tight, spun round, and hurled it as high as he could out above the pit. As it descended it began to smoulder; then suddenly it burst into flames. It burned intensely for an instant; then all that remained of it was a tiny cloud of smoke hanging in the air and a few motes of ash that disintegrated quickly as they drifted down.

Maynard went to the car park, sought out his car with difficulty in the dark, drove out through the single exit, and found himself on a different road to the one he had come in on. It was narrow and featureless, with steep grass banks on either side. After ten minutes he had come to neither a sign post or an intersection, and began to worry that he was heading away from where he wanted to be: home. He wished he had asked one of the drivers who had arrived at the car park while he had been searching for his car for directions. He was sure he must have missed a turning.

But there were no turnings. No other traffic passed him in either direction. He drove for what seemed like hours. The grass banks at the sides sank lower and lower until they flattened out to a verge; then even the verges disappeared, and the road stretched out so wide it no longer was a road; it had no definition, no limits. Aware that he had omitted to fill up with petrol before he had set out, and that what remained in the tank would not take him much further, Maynard stopped the car. He looked at the odometer and calculated he had travelled more than eighty miles from the hotel. He turned the headlights on full and drove round in a circle, leaning forward to get the best view he could through the windscreen. The lights showed him nothing except, as he had guessed, that he was on a flat area of tarmac that seemed to go on in all directions without end.

He was nowhere.

It occurred to him to go back the way he had come; it was the obvious thing to do, he should have done it earlier. Then he realised he had no idea which way back was, there was no way of telling; he had lost what little sense of direction he still had when he had circled the car. He switched off his engine and his headlights and found himself in absolute darkness. He clicked on the little in-car light, undid his seat belt, and turned on the radio. Radio Four was not there. Nor was Radio Three. He pressed all the preset buttons, and got nothing. He fiddled around a bit more; then, to preserve his battery (how long would that last?), he turned the dead radio off again.

He sat still for a long time after that, staring ahead of him into the blackness beyond his car. His mind felt still and deep, like an empty swimming pool. He was hardly thinking anything at all, and experiencing no particular emotion. After a while, the realisation of just exactly where he was swam smoothly and slowly into his consciousness.

He opened the glove compartment, which was full of rubbish, and dug about in it until he found a little torch, a pen-light, that had been a free gift from his bank when he had taken out a new account. He pressed the switch to check it was working, then turned it off again and stuck it in his pocket. He got out of his car, leaving the inner light on, and started walking.

After a little while he turned to see how far he had put between himself and his vehicle. He could just about see the dim glow behind the windows; the car itself was invisible. He decided not to look back again.

In front was just. . . nothing: black nothing.

Because he felt he was on the very edge of things, he got the little torch out of his pocket and shone it in front of him. Its beam just reached the ground a yard ahead.

Then he set off again.

Slowly and cautiously, taking his time, finding, to his surprise that the experience was not without interest, he walked on. Away, into the outer darkness.

Inheritance

He entered his silent house cautiously, turning slightly sideways as he passed through the door, edging into the room.

There was a letter at his feet. He glanced down at it, recognised the handwriting of the address, and stepped carefully over it. Then he stood very still, listening, looking hard into every corner, surveying each item of furniture, alert for any small changes that may have occurred to the disorder that lay around him during his absence. There was a cunning expression on his face, a knowing half-smile, that faded slowly as he became satisfied that everything was just as he had left it.

He flung off his overcoat, yanked a tissue from a box on the table, and mopped raindrops off his face. The long hairs he had trained across his bald spot swung down his forehead in a single lock, like a grey rat's tail. He jerked it back with a toss of his head, and massaged it into place with the palm of his hand. He picked up the letter, gasping slightly as he straightened, dropped onto the sofa, untied and removed his sodden shoes, and stretched out lengthwise on his back. He clasped the envelope in both hands on his chest, close to his chin. He remained like that, immobile, for ten minutes. He was still listening for any small noise that might betray the presence of some occupant in the building other than himself. He didn't hear a sound, but he knew that proved nothing. He was sure he was not alone.

The storm outside suddenly intensified, filling the room with a rattling tattoo, as hailstones rapped urgently against the window.

He shivered, but decided not to light the electric fire. He couldn't be bothered to move, and anyway, it was expensive, it burned money.

He watched the ceiling darken as black clouds filled the sky above the town.

Slowly, he nodded off into an uneasy trance-like state, close to sleep, and littered with dream fragments. Scraps and shards of his childhood, the detritus of his earliest memories, flickered tantalisingly on the edge of his consciousness, and danced back into hiding when he reached out with his mind to inspect them. They hurt him with their broken promises of self-discovery. They left him with the sorrowful ache of nostalgic regret.

A spasm of vivid white light pulsed through the room, followed at once by an explosion; a bomb blast in the attic. The thunder jerked him out of his troubled past and back into the room. He started up, glared anxiously out of the window as though someone on the street beyond had threatened him, then flopped back along the sofa. He rediscovered the envelope in his hands, tore it open, and held the letter close to his face. There was just enough light for him to read:

> Dear Eric,
>
> It made me sad to read in your last letter that you are still troubled by an Unholy Spirit. At the Church of the Inner Eye of Christ, we pray for you every day. Holy Mater Edith Butcher had a dream she thinks was meant for you. It was a terrible dream that, in her compassion, she dreamed on your behalf. It contains instructions from one of the All Seeing Elect, a woman who was a friend of your mother when they were both alive, and who has Risen. You used to know her as Mrs. Greenslade. She is concerned about you. She has a great Truth to impart, her words will be as a healing balm.
>
> You should write to the Holy Mater Butcher at once. Please enclose a Sum to help with the continuation of the Work of Clearing the Eye Within. God grant you the comfort of the Sightless Sight.
>
> Your Church Friend,
> Holy Pater Larry Lennox.

He shook his head ruefully, and sucked in air through his clenched teeth. They were good people at the Inner Eye Church, but it had to be said that they were a bit out of touch with reality. It was going to take more than a message from Mrs. Greenslade to solve his problems. Eric remembered her well: a shrill, waxy, ash-flecked little woman dressed in slacks and a sweater. His mother had met her on a coach trip to see Cliff

Richard in Sheffield. They discovered they were neighbours, took to visiting each other frequently, and went to Cliff's concerts together whenever he performed in the North West.

His mother always had reservations about Mavis Greenslade. She said her friend only saw the singer as a sex object, and wasn't interested in his spiritual side, his faith. And she was right; Eric rarely agreed with his mother about anything, but he had to admit that she was spot on in her judgment of Mrs. Greenslade. The woman had been shallow, narrow, tight, and empty. He did not want to know her Truth. She could not possibly have Risen. He would write to Holy Mater Butcher, thank her for her concern, and tell her no thank you. He might enclose a short character sketch of Mrs. Greenslade, to explain why he was rejecting her advances, and point out what a worthless person she had been, to put Church members on their guard against her. He would send them a Sum (he thought he could afford ten pounds) and wish them well, but he didn't think he would trouble them again. He had become interested in the Inner Eye Church because they claimed to have direct contact with the spirit world. Now, he had decided, there was no point in trying to deal with dead people. They couldn't help him, he had been wrong all along to think that. If only that were the answer, and things were that simple!

He realised he was hungry. It was remarkable how a walk to the Job Centre sharpened the appetite. In the kitchen, he opened a cupboard, selected an egg from a batch he had hard boiled some days before, and bashed the shell against the wall. He hated peeling eggs. Anything to do with preparing food exasperated him. Such a waste of time. He chopped the egg into eight slim sections, spread two slices of Mighty White bread with Echo, sprinkled salt, and maneuvered the disparate items together to form a sandwich. Black coffee with a sweetener completed the meal.

He remained in the kitchen, resting and digesting, for almost an hour, while the world outside his window turned slowly black. Twice he heard sounds on the stairs, as though someone was softly brushing the carpet. I know you're there, he thought, and smiled to himself in the dark. He was not alarmed, and did not go to investigate.

He listened to the hissing whisper of the pilot light on his gas cooker. Its tiny flame flickered and danced, agitated by a draught from the door. He detected in the susurration it made an undertone, a voice calling to him, like someone far out at sea shouting over the smash of distantly breaking waves. The meaning of the message was beyond his comprehension, but he could hear words spoken, and knew they were intended for his ears.

At last he got to his feet. He switched on a torch, because half of the light bulbs in the building were blown, went into his back room, and began to root about among his possessions for something that might divert him for the rest of the evening.

He lived in the front of the little house, slept in the smallest of two bedrooms, and used the rest of the space to store his collections, including the archive of his nativity. Since his father's death he had been searching in newspapers, magazines, and books for anything relating to the period between the 6th of October 1937 (which he had calculated to be the day of his conception) and the 6th of June 1938, the day he had been born (one month premature to the 6th of July, the date a doctor had told his mother to expect him).

He had amassed an impressive quantity of material. His knowledge of the period during which he developed from egg to embryo to a tiny boy was immense. At first he had cast his net wide to include events occurring in distant parts of the world, searching, in the cataclysmic upheaval of nations that preceded World War Two, for signs and portents that might illuminate or give meaning to the trauma of his blighted birth. He had been overwhelmed by the sprawling complexity of information, discovered no evidence that led to any conclusion, and had gradually retreated from the outer world to concentrate on the only area he had first hand knowledge of, his hometown. Then, gradually, he had narrowed his focus down to the street he lived on and, finally, to his life in the house his parents had occupied since their marriage, the home he had finally inherited.

He had made a study of his childhood. He investigated his parents' relationships with him and each other with dogged thoroughness. He tried to remember his earliest conversations with his mother and father, and wrote out such scraps as he could recall in cramped, crawling longhand in a series of black notebooks. No domestic event from that time was too insignificant to be recorded. He reread through this material endlessly, trying to make new connections, to find fresh meaning in old words, digging down under the handwritten record for the subtext of his infancy.

Now, blundering about in the back room, he waved the torch beam over the objects gathered there. He appeared to be surrounded by total disorder, but he knew where everything was. He could put his hand on any item in seconds. In places the piles of junk, or relics, as he saw them, reached almost to the ceiling. The sight of so much flotsam and jetsam from his past oppressed him sometimes, but he found it impossible to throw any part of it away. He clung on to everything that came into his possession, by whatever means, and lived uneasily in the museum of his life.

The books that contained his recollections lay in a heap of their own on the floor. He selected a volume more or less at random, after flicking through a couple of them, and took it into the front room.

Back on the sofa he reached up and turned on the wall lamp, put on his reading glasses, and opened the book.

He was conscious of another presence in the room, that came and stood behind him to his right, just out of sight. The figure bent down over his shoulder.

Together, they began to read.

He had first become aware of the presence a few days after his father's funeral, so he had made the obvious assumption that it was his father's ghost. That was why it had not frightened him as much as it might have done if it had manifested itself at any other time; Eric felt none of the terror he might have experienced if he had been visited by some less explicable revenant. After all, it was only as if his father had gone away in body to return in spirit a few days later. His absence had hardly been noticed. Eric's mother, lost in Alzheimer's labyrinth, certainly did not miss her husband, and died herself within months.

Eric, when his father lived, had maintained a policy of avoiding contact with him, a practise he had developed to such perfection that for years they hardly ever set eyes on one another. They were so adept at keeping apart, they were more likely to meet on the street than at home, where, if they did brush against each other, they tended to shout and fight. That made it harder for Eric to understand the reason for the old man's presumed return.

He had never had much to say to his son during his lifetime, except to criticise him as a worthless drone, a jobless, shiftless freak, a family embarrassment; so why, now, when he had all but lost the ability to communicate at all, did he seem to have so much to say? And the spirit spoke to Eric in a voice he could not understand, in a tone that was unfamiliar. It hid its words behind other noises: the tick of a clock, the rustle of a newspaper, the bubbling of a boiling kettle, the beating of rain on the window. To Eric, these innocent sounds were potent with insight, and bursting with hidden meaning that was always just beyond his grasp.

But, try as he might, he could not confront the spirit: it hid away.

Sometimes Eric would become aware of his father's presence behind a picture on the wall, a pile of newspapers on the floor, or marching in line behind him, following like a soldier on parade, but he could never quite see it. It even played tricks on him. It moved things. Bits and pieces of Eric's belongings went missing, and turned up later in places he knew he had searched carefully. It secreted items of food in places where, days later, Eric would find them, maggoty and rotten, their whereabouts revealed by their stink.

Sometimes, rarely, he caught a glimpse of the phantom out of the corner of his eye but always, as it were, by accident, when he did not want or expect to: he could never see it when he made an effort to, when he really tried. But he had seen enough to know that his father had not retained his old form. He no longer had the shape of a man; he was reduced to the merest flicker of a slender shadow that rose and fell like a dark free-floating flame.

In the book, Eric came to a conversation between his parents that obsessed him, that he reread and relived many times. He didn't have to read the words; they were printed in his mind. After a few moments he shut the book, closed his eyes, and remembered. . .

He must have been about five or six. He had done something bad because his father was shouting at him again. His mother was dragging him out towards the stairs, yelling at him to get out of the way, to lock himself in his room. Suddenly his father had grabbed him and pulled him back. He pinned Eric's arms to his sides, lifted him in the air, and shook him.

Eric looked to his mother for help, but she stared through rather than at him, to some distant spot way beyond the walls of their home.

"You've brought misery into this house," his father was shouting. "Your mother and I had peace before we had you. We wanted a child, but why, out of all the kids in the world, are we stuck with you?"

He glared at Eric, as though he expected an explanation.

"You're awkward, unnatural, a curse. Why do you do the things you do? Why do you drive us crazy? Your mother nearly died having you, and now she can never have another baby. And all because of you. You should thank us for being alive, not ruin our lives with your stupid antics."

"Please, Gerry," his mother said weakly, in her worn, creaky, smoker's voice, "don't talk to the boy like that."

"Why not?" His father shook him again. "He doesn't understand. Look at him. Look at his face. It's blank! He's not sorry he's done wrong. Nothing's sinking in. He's not crying. I bet he's even proud of himself, of making us so unhappy, of making me shout and lose my temper."

Eric felt his father's fingers cutting into the muscles of his arms. The man's long nails dug through his shirt sleeves into the flesh.

"I'm not," Eric protested. "It's not true. I'm not."

His father looked at him in astonishment. "Not what?"

"Proud," Eric said. He didn't understand the word; it meant nothing to him.

"I should bloody well think you're not," his father stormed, and thrust him away. Eric sprawled across the arm of a chair and went very still, like a child caught in a photograph of some catastrophe, frozen in the frame of time.

For some reason his mother's anger with him increased. She was glaring at him with a special look that was familiar to him, but that he had never seen her give anyone else. It expressed her particular detestation of him. She took a step towards him, and he thought she was going to hit him.

"Your father's right," she said, "you always were bad. You're not like other kids. You don't learn. I wish you'd never been born. You're ruining our lives."

"All right then," said Eric, "I'll die, if you don't want me. I'll die right now."

His father gave a scornful grunt. "Don't talk to me about dying, you don't know what it means. You don't understand."

"I do," Eric insisted. "It means you stop, you go quiet, you don't move."

Perhaps the defiant tone of Eric's voice enraged his father, because he grabbed his son's head between his hands and jerked him to his feet. "You think that's it, do you? You think death's that easy? You think you know all about it?"

Eric looked up at the contorted face above him, and saw something embedded there, deep in his father's head, lurking in his skull, way back beyond his eyes. It was a dark thing that had possession of his father and was looking for new territory, new worlds to conquer. Eric understood that.

"You don't know what death is," his father said, his voice bubbling and slobbering and strange. "But I'll show you. This is death." And he put the palm of one hand over Eric's mouth and grasped his nose with the other, forcing Eric's nostrils shut.

Eric thrust the book away from him.

He hadn't, he realised, remembered the thing that had looked at him through his father's eyes before. It was a new detail; something that had emerged at last from the dense jungle of his memory. How had he come to forget something so strange and important and terrible? Even now, fifty years later, the incident was painful to recall, but this new element made it much worse. He shut his eyes and rubbed his temples with his wrists.

Perhaps his father had been haunted then as he, Eric, was now! If so, it was by something far more alarming than the man's own lingering spirit.

Or so Eric assumed. He realised that he had never looked his father's phantom in the face.

Then, for the first time, he began to have doubts about the identity of that which had returned to the house after his father's death. He began to wonder if perhaps it was something... other. His mind shrank away from the thought. He shook his head vigorously and said "No, no..."

He sat hugging his chest in his arms, rocking backwards and forwards, trying to give himself comfort.

Then, reluctantly, he returned to his childhood.

And felt his father pressing down on him with his whole body, forcing him to the floor.

A voice was coming from his father, but it wasn't his father's voice.

The man's mouth was moving, shaping words: he was yelping like an ape; he was screaming to Eric that this was death.

Eric kept his eyes open and watched his father's face. Whatever was behind his father's eyes looked back at him.

It seemed to like what it saw.

It bestirred itself. It uncurled and unfurled. It reached down towards him with arms like tendrils of smoke, as though eager to embrace him. Eric wondered if it was going to save him.

Then he could see nothing at all. Deep red shadows swooped down on him from all sides. His head filled with a tide of blood that rose up all around him, turned black, and drowned him.

He thought he must have died.

Later, somewhere, his mother was sobbing.

He opened his eyes and was amazed to see his father and mother standing over him, both in tears. His father was saying, "I'm sorry, I'm sorry," but to his mother, not to him. They were holding and comforting each other as though it was they who were hurt.

He got to his feet unnoticed, slipped out of the door, went up to his room, and shut himself in. He sat on his bed and stared out of his window at the slate-grey November sky.

He didn't cry; he felt no pain; he felt nothing.

He thought: I was dead. Perhaps I still am.

Eric woke up on the sofa at two in the morning. A car, parking on the street outside, disturbed him when its headlights blazed briefly through his uncurtained windows.

He felt sleepy, but an urge to get to work on the character assassination of Mrs. Greenslade was too strong to resist. He found a ballpoint, turned to the back of the black notebook, where there were some blank pages, and began to write:

> Dear Holy Pater Lennox,
>
> Thank you for the kind thoughts in your last letter. *However*, I think I ought to warn you *at once* about the being known as *Mavis Greenslade*, who is probably acting as my *mother's agent* in the spirit world. *Do not* trust a *word* she says. It is *impossible* that she has Risen and joined the All Seeing Elect, she *must* be claiming Powers that she does *not* have...

It was a long letter that took him most of the night to write. When it was finished, as dawn was breaking, he sealed it in an envelope, with two five-pound notes, slipped out to post it, then went straight back home to bed.

Lying there, unable to sleep, he heard a voice in the room below.

It's talking to itself, he thought, and buried his head in the silence under his pillows.

Next day he woke up a little after noon. For some reason, he was very reluctant to open his eyes. He held them tight shut until they began to ache, then he put his hands over them, and slowly allowed his lids to part. He stared into the blackness of his palms for a long time, then gradually slid his hands down his cheeks.

He was facing a window. Beyond it, above a strip of ancient, shrivelled net-curtain, he could see the scaly, fish-grey roofs of the houses across the street, overhung by a great slab of grimy, weeping sky. What light there was in the room was shadowy, heavy, almost misty. It bleached the colour out of things.

He slid out of bed into a monochromatic world as still and flat as a picture in an old newspaper. The shirt and underpants he had slept in were adhesive with sweat. Even so, he was shuddering with cold. He jerked a blanket off the bed, folded himself into it, and almost ran across the landing to the toilet.

While he sat there he heard a door open somewhere in the house.

Something was moving from room to room.

When he unfurled toilet paper from the roll, the wooden spool chattered at him; a sound that seemed to contain a brief snatch of urgent speech that almost made sense. He tugged out more paper, trying to get the simple mechanism to speak again, but the message was not repeated. When he pressed the flush handle, there were more voices in the air as the tank emptied and refilled itself.

He wrapped part of the blanket round his head, scurried down to his kitchen, got together a hasty egg sandwich, then went back to bed to eat it.

He lived like that for the next two days, until he ran out of food.

On the third day, his Social Security cheque came in the post. He put more clothes on over those he had been sleeping in, washed his hands and face, and went to the post office to get his money.

The girl in the corner shop at the end of his street, where Eric always bought his provisions, was very wary of him. She didn't like the way he looked at her. In the past, he had asked her a lot of strange questions: Why she wore her hair the way she did? What she did on Tuesday evenings? Would she accept a gift from someone she hardly knew?

Once, when they had been alone in the shop, he had slipped a letter across the counter to her. It had her name on the front, and that frightened her, because she didn't see how he had got to know it. He must have been finding things out about her, investigating her in some way. She had burned the letter unopened, in spite of her curiosity about its contents, and the gesture had given her some satisfaction. He had never mentioned it when he returned to the shop, but he had looked uneasy, shifty.

The man was thirty years older than her at least, and there was something menacing in his obvious, oppressive loneliness. She wished she had a boyfriend she could set on this awkward customer, to sort him out, but she was lonely too; she had no protector.

That day, when Eric burst into the shop, the girl thought she might refuse to serve him; his appearance was so wild and—dangerous! She noticed his jacket was buttoned up wrong, and she could see he had two shirts on. Normally, he was at least tidy and clean. Now, he looked as though he was wearing someone else's cast-off clothes and, when he got near her, she detected an odour like the smell that hangs round waste bins on a hot summer day. She quickly got what he wanted (he bought more or less the same food, week after week) and loaded it into a box. As she was giving him his change a ventilator fan at the back of the shop came on automatically, making a combination of rattling and sighing sounds.

Perhaps because the atmosphere in the shop was strained and tense, the noise was startling. It made Eric jump. He stared open-mouthed at the machine, his ear cocked, listening intently.

His face took on what could have been a tight smile, but was in fact a grimace of terror. The fan was speaking to him, and this time he thought he could understand the words. After a few seconds he turned to a man standing behind him, one of two people who had come into the shop after him and formed a tiny queue.

The man was also looking at the fan, or so it seemed to Eric. He took a step backwards when Eric grabbed him by the shoulder and said, "You can hear it too?"

Thinking Eric was referring to the sound of the electric motor that drove the fan, the man nodded.

"Ah," Eric breathed, almost triumphantly. "But does it make sense to you? Do you know what it's saying?"

The man looked into Eric's eyes, and saw something there that chilled his blood and lifted the hair on his head. He realised that Eric was speaking to him from a different reality, one he was glad he could not enter. He shook his head emphatically and moved further away, stepping on the toes of the woman behind him.

There were a few seconds of embarrassed apologies and shifting of positions that Eric ignored, or was oblivious to.

Then the fan switched itself off.

In the ensuing silence Eric gazed at it for some seconds, still with the twisted, knowing, anxious smile on his face. Then he thrust his change into a pocket, picked up his box of provisions, and said to the astonished shop assistant, "I heard it clearly that time: I understood what it said!" The tone of his voice, the look of him, made the girl want to hide, to scream.

"Did you?" she said, retreating along the counter.

"Yesss," Eric said, extending the sibilant so it sounded like a whistle. "Shall I tell you what it said?"

The girl shrugged.

"It said, 'You don't know what death is, but I'll show you'; I heard it clearly."

"Well. . ." said the girl, appealing with her eyes to the other customers for support. Neither seemed inclined to give it.

Then something happened that did make the girl scream, though her voice was drowned in another sound.

Eric held back his head, opened his mouth, and howled something—a forlorn, wordless, barking shout.

Then he turned, went to the door, and walked off slowly down the street towards his home.

He shouted out again twice as he went. The sounds that he made were bleak, inhuman, awful to hear. People pottering about in their houses heard the cries, and froze over whatever they were doing. It took a little while before one or two of them plucked up enough courage to go to look out of their front doors to see who or what was howling. By the time they did, Eric was back in his front room again. The street was empty.

There was a fat envelope waiting on his doormat. He recognised the Holy Mater Edith Butcher's prim, tiny handwriting on the cover. He grabbed the letter and stuffed in into one of his shirts. He dumped his box of provisions on the arm of the nearest chair and sat down next to it.

The terrible sounds he had made still echoed around him.

And blood was pounding somewhere in his skull, making a squelching noise, as though it were seeping into his brain. His heart was lurching out of its usual rhythm. He was short of breath and very tired, though he had made no great physical effort and the box he had been carrying only weighed a few pounds.

He shut his eyes and became lost in his body's confusion. His mind seemed to sink into itself, to shrink down to a tiny focus point; then his thoughts vanished altogether, leaving him blank, empty, without memory or identity.

He must have slept then.

He was startled awake when the box by his side fell to the floor, spilling tins and bags of food around his feet. He gazed down at the mess he had made, but made no attempt to pick anything up, to restore order.

At last he got out of the chair and slowly climbed the stairs to the first floor. When he was near the top, he heard steps behind him, following him up. He didn't bother to look round to see who was pursuing him: he knew.

In his bedroom, he opened the doors of a huge old wardrobe he had inherited from his parents. It was half-full of cracked and dirty shoes, unwashed, unwanted clothing stuffed into plastic bags, and other, less easily identifiable items. He leaned forward into this mass and started scooping the rubbish out onto the floor behind him. When he finished that task, he pulled the blankets off his bed and began lining the wardrobe with them. He worked carefully, making sure everything was positioned just right.

He was making a nest.

As soon as it was ready, he got into the wardrobe and snuggled down into the blankets. He draped one over his head, like a hood, and closed it round his face, leaving a gap in front of his eyes so he could just see out.

Later, he remembered the envelope he had tucked into his shirt. He searched about for it, moving for the first time since he had climbed into the cupboard. He was surprised to find that his limbs were stiff and painful. He wondered vaguely how long he had been sitting there. Probably for quite a long time.

When he had found what he was looking for, he slid his hands out of the blankets and held the envelope in front of his face. He read his name and address on the cover two or three times.

He tore the letter open slowly, with a reluctant air, then cast his eyes over what it contained.

The Holy Mater thanked him for contributing a Sum. Then, after a brief introduction, which he skipped through, explaining how the letter's contents had come to her in a disturbing dream, she gave, presumably verbatim, the message that Mrs. Greenslade wanted Eric to hear.

The words he then read were extraordinarily vivid: it was as though he were hearing them spoken. The voice coming up to him off the page was so clearly that of Mavis Greenslade he could hear her very tone and accent and see the shape of her mouth as she spoke. It was as if she was standing in front of him, personally delivering the message. He could have no doubts about its authenticity.

Unfortunately, it only told him what he had recently discovered. His father had not returned to haunt him when he had died, as he had assumed. What had come to Eric after the old man's funeral was something that had been handed down to him, that was part of his inheritance. It would stay with him now until the end, then it would show him what death was.

After that? Who knows?

Eric had no one to pass anything on to. He had no brothers or sisters or children of his own. He was the end of his line. And thankful for that.

He had read about half of the letter when he became impatient with the voice of Mrs. Greenslade. He screwed the remaining pages up and flung them away from him.

He dug himself down deeper into his nest and pulled blankets right up over him.

Night came.

Something walked across the room to the wardrobe and closed the door. Inside, Eric heard a key turn in the lock. He was in total darkness, and knew he would remain in the dark for ever.

Cramp caused him agony for days, then his body went numb. His bowels and bladder burst and emptied, leaving him without hunger.

Over the weeks he became small and thin. The only time he moved was when gravity tugged him down. His senses ceased to function; he could not see, hear, taste, touch, or smell anything.

He could not even smell the stench of his own corruption.

Nine months to the day after Eric had climbed into the wardrobe, the key turned again.

The door opened.

Eric slowly collapsed forward, onto the floor.

That which had closed and opened the door bent down and tenderly picked him up. It held him in its arms and spoke to him, telling him all the things it had whispered to him from behind the sound of the gas flame in his kitchen, the ticking of his clock, the rustle of a breeze turning the pages of a book; a thousand other meaningless sounds. It repeated all the things that it had wanted Eric to know during his lifetime, but that Eric had never been able quite to grasp, to understand.

It was happy.

It had waited a long time for Eric, and it was pleased now that it had him. Finally, at last, Eric was a wanted child.

The Extension

Except for the point, the still point,
There would be no dance, and there is only the
dance.

Burnt Norton
T. S. Eliot

Oliver's walk round the lake was almost over when he caught sight of the hotel for the first time. It was situated about three hundred yards from the water's edge, between the bases of two low gorse-covered hills, and was invisible from Cramby, the tiny village half a mile beyond it that had been, four hours ago, his point of departure, and was now his destination. He was struck by the ugliness of the building, which at first he thought might be some kind of factory or perhaps an oversized, flat-topped barn. As he drew nearer he realised that the edifice had been constructed in a style that would have been considered "modern" sixty years ago, in the early thirties, but the architect, or whoever had designed it, seemed not to have fully understood the principles of form then in fashion, and had produced an ill-proportioned parody of those ideals. There was far too much creamy wall, and not enough window visible. The place looked like some huge Second World War gun emplacement set there to defend the shore against attack from the lake; a ludicrous idea, of course. Nevertheless, there was something serious and threatening about the stark right angles of the building that set it at odds with the endless green curves of the countryside surrounding it; a benign landscape that it seemed to stare at with insolent contempt through the tight slit-eyes of its windows.

When the footpath he had been following neared the road that passed in front of the building, Oliver, taking a short cut, found himself stepping over a fallen sign hidden in tall grass, that informed him that he was approaching *The. . . Edge Hotel.* The paint under part of *The* and all of the second word had peeled off, but Oliver guessed, from the size of the space, that the missing word was almost certainly *Lake;* an obvious deduction. Above the name of the hotel were the words WELCOME TO. In the lower half of the advertisement there was much information about the facilities the establishment had to offer, an excess of facts written in letters that were surely too small to have been deciphered by a pedestrian standing on the road, let alone read by the driver of a passing car, suggesting that the proprietor of the hotel had been, at the time of the sign's erection, desperate to attract custom.

Oliver saw, as he eased himself through a squeeze-stile in the wall on the edge of the road, that the area was in a state of general dilapidation. The metalling of the road was gouged and deeply pitted. Marks like tank tracks crisscrossed the surface and wound away into the grass verge on either side, leaving gashes inches deep in places. It looked almost as though a battle had taken place there, but not recently, as opportunistic weeds sprouted thickly from the rubble to which the road had been partly reduced. There was no evidence that any vehicle had been that way for months at least, as none of the thriving plants was flattened or damaged, except along the side close to the wall, where a single track, a narrow, barely visible and obviously rarely used footpath, meandered on towards Cramby.

Oliver, hot, bothered, and over dressed in his jeans and heavy sweat-shirt, sauntered along this track towards the hotel. As he approached, its bulk expanded, loomed up, and seemed to stretch towards him, as though it were coming to meet him halfway. Its creamy mat walls didn't so much shine in the sunlight as glower. As he got closer, thousands of tiny crystal or glass fragments embedded in the outer surface became visible, flashing and glittering in complex constellations against the prevailing flat whiteness. The walls were blotched with areas of lichen, like liver spots on an old hand, and the windows, what he could see of them, were grey and blank, absorbing rather than reflecting the light around them. They were set in painted metal frames. Good and bad weather had split and perished their coating of enamel gloss; rain had got in and rust had seeped out of these wounds, and dull orange stains sprouted like bloated tentacles down the walls below the sills. At first Oliver was sure the building was deserted, but he noticed the windows had curtains hanging behind them, and that some of them were open. The curtains stretched apart and fell together again fitfully in the barely perceptible breeze. Also, tire marks on the road in front of the hotel and the drive that led up to it indicated that the place had been visited recently, though not often, from the Cramby side, suggesting it was perhaps not completely uninhabited. There were no "For Sale" boards to be seen.

Oliver slowed down as he reached the hotel, compelled to do so by curiosity and something else he couldn't account for; an uncomfortable feeling of *déjà vu* that affected his mood and put him on his guard. He knew the building was quite unfamiliar to him. Indeed, he had previously been totally unaware of its existence and was sure it was not marked on the newly purchased map he had glanced at before setting out. This reflection brought him to a standstill and he stood for a while, giving the place a thoughtful scrutiny.

The hotel had a locked up, out-of-season look, though it was mid-June, and was the most uninviting building of its kind he had ever come across. To add to its unprepossessing appearance, a squat, red brick, flat-topped, single-storey structure had been added to it at one end. A huge crack ran diagonally down the front wall of this extension, from the outer edge of the roof down to the bottom of the door. The crack had been filled in clumsily with cement, and a window, which had probably been damaged when the flaw had occurred, had been bricked-up with blocks of sandstone. A sign over the door invited people into "The Other Place": a bar open to non-residents. Oliver hardly ever touched alcohol, and he had an aversion to pubs and the society of the kind of people who frequented them, but he had been walking a long time in a hot wind along a dusty path, and his throat was dry. The thought of entering somewhere cool where he could rest and refresh himself for ten minutes was appealing. He went through the open gate, strode up the drive to the centre of the hotel building, and tried the main door. It was locked. He peered past his own youthful, healthy reflection, and the menus and fly-blown notices hanging on plastic suction-cups fixed inside the glass panel, into the dimness of the foyer beyond. Nothing moved in there. The place looked orderly enough, but drab, and gone-to-seed. The sea-green carpet was faded, and the white woodwork could have done with a wash or fresh paint. The interior had a sad, seedy look that told a tale of the long, slow decline of a failing business that had ended, most probably, in bankruptcy. Oliver shuddered at the thought, and walked on to inspect The Other Place. He confidently expected it too would be closed, and he was right.

He wiped his dry lips, and decided to continue on to Cramby to quench his thirst. As he turned to go he sensed a movement and heard a sound, a dry scuffling, up above him on the roof of the extension. He had been so confident he was alone that he jumped, as he had done earlier when a rabbit had sprung out of the grass almost from under his feet. He turned, put his hand to his brow to make a shade and, with the light of the afternoon sun in his eyes, squinted up. He saw, in a confusion of slats of sharp light and long, shifting wedges of shadow, the outline of two figures, apparently looking down towards him from the roof. The nearest and smallest of the two, a child, he thought, seemed to want to jump down onto him. He or she was perched on the very edge of the roof, and was crouching like a diver about to leave his plank. The impression that the child was going to leap on him was so strong and alarming in its implications, since he could not see clearly enough what was going on to hope to catch it, that Oliver shouted in protest. At this, the child held back for a further moment, just long enough for the adult figure behind to grab it by the upper arm and pull it back out of sight. The incident, over in seconds, left Oliver confused and upset. There had been an unnecessary violence, even brutality in the way the taller person had jerked the child back from the edge of the roof, and he thought he had heard it give a yelp of pain.

He ran a few paces away from the extension and turned to look back. The drive descended towards the road, so was in no better position to see up onto the roof. Anyway, there was no sign of anybody there, so he assumed the pair had retreated through a trapdoor into the bar below. Or perhaps there was an entrance up there through the end of the hotel into the main building? A few steps sideways put him in a position to ascertain that the latter was not the case. So they must have gone down into The Other Place!

Well, so be it. Whatever had happened, it was none of his business. A family affair, probably; a concerned parent and a naughty child playing dangerously near the edge of the roof. What *had* he got so hot and excited about? His heart was still rapping against his ribs, and his throat had gone as dry as the inside of a talc tin. The incident had taken him by surprise, and shaken him up, but it was over now. He was uninvolved. He was free to leave.

But didn't. He pulled a black baseball cap out the back pocket of his jeans and crammed it, visorlike, low on his brow to shade his eyes, and stared back at The Other Place. It looked dwarfed and weak in comparison to the size and brutal strength of the concrete structure beside it. The wall with the bricked-up window facing him was darkly shadowed and seemed frail and insubstantial. He noticed the diagonal crack had other, lesser faults spreading from it like cartoon lightning, suggesting the building was unsafe. After a moment Oliver thought he heard furtive movements inside, and it occurred to him that perhaps the bar was about to open. It seemed unlikely, at two-thirty in the afternoon, in this remote spot, but the proprietor of such an establishment, if he or she was in residence, would almost certainly be desperate for business at any time of day. As if to confirm this, after the muffled slide of a bolt being eased and the snick of a latch, the edge of the door withdrew inwards about six inches, revealing a slice of the cool gloom beyond.

After the briefest hesitation Oliver stepped up to the door and pushed it open wide. Simultaneously, a strip-light above the bar fizzled and snapped on, illuminating the far end of the room with lemon-tinted light. The bulb was old, its glow palsied. It cast tiny, teetering shadows at the edge of things. The back of the room seemed to vibrate slightly under its pale glare. Oliver strode to the bar. There was nobody behind it to serve him. Looking hurriedly round, he discovered the place was empty. Whoever had opened up must have made a hasty exit through to the rear of the building. The room was bland and characterless, and scantly furnished. The bare walls were painted, or nicotine stained, pale ochre, and the only ornaments were beer mats and dusty ashtrays. He stood by the bar for some minutes, leaning on one elbow, then took a coin from his pocket and rapped it sharply on a pump-head. He coughed loudly. He discovered that a lump of brass, cast in the shape of a girl in a hooped dress, was a bell. He rang it a couple of times. Nobody responded to any of these signals. Oliver saw himself in the mirror behind the shelves of bottles of wine and spirit at the back of the bar. He looked like a hooligan, he realised, wild-eyed, hot, and angry. He took off his cap and forced his short hair upright with his fingers. He wiped the glistening sweat from his forehead with the cap, then stuffed it into his pocket. Above him the fluorescent tube buzzed like a bee in a tantrum. Otherwise, there was total silence.

He began to suspect someone was playing some kind of inane trick on him, taunting him with refreshments he couldn't have. There were dozens of cans and bottles of soft drink and beer within reach behind the bar. He could have leaned across and helped himself, but he had a feeling that, if he was foolish enough to do so, someone would step out of concealment and accuse him of theft. It was a dismal situation to be in.

He considered leaving, but lingered on.

A door next to the bar led through to the toilets. Oliver stuck his head round it and found he was looking down a passage past two doors marked "Guys" and "Dolls" to a steep flight of uncarpeted stairs leading to a third door at the top. He was mildly surprised that it wasn't a trapdoor but didn't give the matter any further thought. He shouted "Hello!" at the top of his voice, to no effect, and slunk back to the bar. Then he thought of a solution to his problem. The shelves were marked with the prices of the drinks stored on them. Oliver had plenty of change in his pocket. He selected exactly the right amount for a "Sunset Surprise," a mix of mango and orange juice, placed the money on the bar, grabbed a bottle, and snapped the top off on an opener next to the lager pump. He sloshed the drink into a glass and drank it quickly, feeling he had stolen a march on someone invisible. The drink was excellent. He bought another, and sipped it more leisurely. He bought himself some nuts from a card on the wall and began to munch. There were now a lot of coins on the bar in front of him, but he still had plenty to spare in his pocket.

He took a closer look at his surroundings. He realised the room had been dark when he entered because curtains at a long window down the side had been pulled shut. He opened them, and stood for some time gazing out at the view across a stretch of the glistening lake to a cluster of foothills at the base of a range of dark mountains in the county beyond. Feeling the need for yet another "Sunset Surprise" (the drink came in tiny, toylike bottles), he turned and mooched back to the bar. As he did so, he noticed something odd about a large alcove, almost another small room, that projected out of the back end of the extension. The perspective bothered him. It didn't change as it should have done as he approached. He stepped across towards it and, in an instant of shock, realised that he was looking at a flat wall that had been skillfully painted with a *trompe l'oeil* that was so effective, it was impossible at first to establish where reality ended and illusion began. He was looking into what seemed to be a space filled with tables and chairs just like the ones around him, set against walls decorated in the same way as those of the actual Other Place. The source of light that gave depth and contrast to the picture appeared to come from behind him, creating an odd effect, and its artificiality was only betrayed by the absence of his own shadow, which should have stretched into the "alcove" ahead of him. To add to the contrived confusion, sections of chairs and tables had been sawn off, fitted to the painted surface, and projected back into the design, so that, from one particular point, the illusion was complete and uncanny. As Oliver adjusted his position to find this precise, he became aware that there was a single figure depicted in the painting, seated at an angle on a chair, half-hidden by a trailing curtain, and looking away from him, into the back of the picture. The slightly stooping figure occupied the darkest, most obscure section of the non-existent room. It seemed to have an unusually large head and was dressed in a tight black outfit; perhaps some kind of uniform. Oliver, having established the whereabouts of the ideal viewpoint, stood there and held his breath in wonder as he gazed at what he was sure was a considerable work of art. He had no special knowledge about such things, and despised most of what he had seen of modern painting, but could respect the skill and cunning of the artist who had created such a convincing depiction of "reality."

He was moving closer, to try to get a better look at the seated figure, when he heard footsteps passing across the ceiling above him. He looked up, as though he expected to see the soles of feet making tracks across the ceiling, and stayed in that position, alert, listening hard. He hoped to hear whoever was up there come through the door he had seen, and down the stairs into the bar. All that happened, however, was that, after a short silence a rhythmic sound, like music on a distant radio, with a heavy bass beat and accompanied by wordless singing or chanting, began to filter down into the bar. It sounded vaguely Eastern, like the soundtrack of a film about Turkey, or a tape played in an exotic restaurant. After a while someone stepped into the middle of the floor above and began to dance. There was no doubt about it; a person none too light on his, or her, feet was leaping about up there on the roof in time to the music, and clapping their hands now and then, in castanet-like bursts. This continued for what seemed like five minutes, and was becoming monotonous, even irksome, to Oliver's ears, when suddenly someone shrieked and at once what must have been at least a dozen pairs of feet joined in the dance. Oliver crossed to the bar, fumbled more change from his pocket, reached for the drink he had promised himself, and wondered what was going on.

The people up above were not barefoot. They must have been wearing hard-soled shoes and the noise, reverberating in the little bar below, was deafening; savage and alarming. The light in The Other Place flickered violently as the ceiling vibrated. Wisps of dust tumbled from the light fitting, out of cracks in the ceiling, and drifted down onto the tables below. Oliver slid off the bar stool he had perched on, feeling slightly claustrophobic and panicky in that restricted position, and knocked some of the loose change he had absentmindedly stacked in a line of little towers along the bar onto the floor with his wrist as he did so. He stooped to recover the coins and was on his knees when the din above stopped as abruptly as it had started. A solitary, deep, probably female voice was then just audible, intoning words that could have been a weather report or some other long, solemn announcement, until an object fell with a clatter to the floor overhead. Total silence reigned for a few seconds, then there was a scampering of feet, and a door above opened slowly, then slammed shut again almost immediately. Oliver guessed the door had to be the one he had seen at the top of the backstairs, and stepped into the corridor behind the bar to make himself known to whoever had come through it. He could hear unsteady descending movements on the stairs.

He saw a large thing, an animal, stumbling down the stairs towards him. It was an oversized bird, like an elongated chicken, and, if it had had a head, would have been over two feet high.

It had been decapitated at the base of its neck. Its scraggy body was almost bald, with only a few patches of ruffled rusty feathers here and there. When it reached ground level it strutted a few steps toward him, then pitched forward and collapsed. Blood seeped from its neck onto the carpet. It flapped its wings once, and Oliver thought it was going to get up and try to run again, but it didn't. It seemed to shrink slightly, to sink into itself; then, with a final jerk, it went rigid and still.

Oliver blundered away, back through the bar and out the front door. He looked back up at the roof again. There was nobody there. He ran past the side of the extension to the rear of the hotel, jumped on top of a waste bin, and climbed onto a wall. He could see over the top of The Other Place. The roof *was* deserted; there was no sign of anybody there, or anywhere, in any direction, as far as he could see. He returned to the entrance to the bar and looked inside. It was still unoccupied. At first he thought nothing had changed in there, then he noticed something peculiar about the "alcove," the *trompe l'oeil* painting at the far end. The seated figure he had been about to inspect when the activity above the roof had interrupted him had vanished, or so it seemed. Anyway, it was no longer visible from where he was standing. For some reason Oliver was reluctant to re-enter the bar to establish what was causing this rather peculiar illusion, for illusion it must have been.

He had decided to go, to get away from the place quickly, when, somewhere quite nearby, an engine came to life with a crack and a roar. Oliver spun round automatically to face the sound. A red and black motorbike came into sight round the side of the hotel at the far end. It was moving fast. It accelerated down the drive and slipped and skidded sideways out onto the road, sending a diagonal hail of rubble against the wall beyond. Oliver, who had owned a few bikes in his time, recognised it as an old Triumph Tiger, a vintage model that appeared to be in almost mint condition. The helmeted driver, encased in midnight-blue leathers, seemed to be only just in charge of the machine, and flopped slightly from side to side, like a dummy nailed to the seat and tied to the handlebars by the wrists. Oliver expected whoever it was to fall off at any second, and for the bike to crash, but it didn't. It veered round towards Cramby and drove away quite upright, with the driver obviously now in full control, and disappeared in a few seconds round a bend in the road.

As the sound of its engine died in the distance, Oliver realised he was shaking. His heart was thwacking inside his chest as it had done earlier when the child had appeared on the edge of the roof above him. He had become as nervous as wren during the last half hour or so, since he had first caught sight of the dismal, desolate hotel. Now the unexpected appearance of something as mundane as a motorcycle was enough to put his nerves through the shredder, to shake him up completely.

Feeling rather pathetic, he made a conscious effort to steady himself. He walked determinedly down the drive and headed off in the direction the bike had gone, towards the village. Behind him he was aware of the bulk of the hotel crouching between the two small hills that surrounded it. His sense of the presence of the building didn't seem to recede, to dwindle away as it should have done, as the distance between him and it increased. He had a feeling that, if he turned round, it would be just behind him, following at his heels.

So strong was this sensation that he didn't look back until he came to the gate of his mother's cottage, at the edge of Cramby. Then, after glancing once down the empty, overgrown lane that had brought him out of the village, he hurriedly let himself into the property he had so recently and inconveniently inherited.

Inside the house the air smelt of decaying vegetation, like a hidden place deep in a wood in autumn. Oliver had found fungi growing on the walls and in the corners of cupboards in various rooms on both floors. Some of his mother's clothing in the wardrobe in her bedroom was blotched with green moss that crumbled at the slightest touch, but left an indelible stain on the fabric of her dresses. All the windows in the building had been screwed shut long ago and the only heating had been provided by three portable Calor gas fires, which had caused condensation that had made the place start to rot. The atmosphere everywhere was stale and lavatorial.

Oliver went into the cramped little kitchen, filled a plastic bowl in the sink with cold water, took a deep breath, and immersed his face. He scooped water up over the back of his head, then stood up and shook himself. There was no towel, so he dried himself with a tablecloth. He felt very alert then, and alive and aware. He felt determined to do some of the things he had come to do; to finally get round to making a start on sorting through his mother's possessions in preparation for having the cottage cleared and sold. He had known, even before he had seen the place, that he would never want to live there. His main preoccupation, since he had heard it had become his, had been to get rid of it. At first, he had not even wanted to visit it, and had considered employing a house-clearer to strip the building in anticipation of placing it in the hands of a local estate agent, but his curiosity, long dormant, about who and what his mother had been, had suddenly roused itself and got the better of him. He had not been able to resist the urge to confront her and her past, through whatever of her life she had left behind, feeling that now she was dead, it must be safe to do so.

Rita, his wife, had not liked that idea. It was the busiest part of the tourist season for the seafront restaurant they ran together, and she had not relished the prospect of having to deal with staff problems that had begun to plague them recently. That, they agreed, was his department. Rita was good at managing *things*, he was good at managing *people*, because he didn't get involved with them as she did; he was needed on site until their troubles died down. But, after a day of unresolved argument, he had left her to it, telling her that anyway they were not as busy as they had hoped and anticipated they would be, and that he would only be gone for a very short time. He had led her to believe, and believed himself, that he would be absent a night or two at most; she would hardly miss him. But they had parted in anger, and he had not driven fifty miles before he had begun to feel the sharp edge of guilt cutting into what little peace of mind remained to him.

That had been almost three days ago, and he had still not started what he had come to do. The first day he had arrived late, tired from the drive, and had crawled into the only bed he could find in the cottage and tried to sleep. Before he had been able to do so, it had occurred to him that he was almost certainly lying in the bed his mother had died in, not many weeks before. The thought rattled him, and banished sleep. In the end he got up and turned on all the lights. He then spent hours creeping from room to room, opening and shutting draws and doors, lifting ornaments and papers and replacing them carefully after a brief, uncomprehending inspection, and standing stock-still for minutes on end, listening to the silence in the rooms around him. In retrospect, he seemed to have spent the night in a trance. He'd got no sleep at all.

The following morning he had furtively explored the village, gone to the local shop for provisions, made himself a meal, then fallen into a nightmarish doze until late afternoon. He had had vague, but deeply troubling dreams, the details of which he could not remember. He knew they were about his mother's funeral, a ceremony he had deliberately not attended. Nor, he had been told, had anyone else (and this was probably why thoughts of the event were unsettling his mind), except the local vicar, and he had performed his part with great reluctance and considerable distress. So much Oliver had learned from Mrs. Tench, a neighbour who had been entrusted with the key to his mother's house, and who had spoken to him at some length when he had first arrived. She was a compulsive gossip who would not let him go, but who at the same time seemed resentful, even hostile, towards him, and looked at him with an expression of queasy, fearful contempt.

The second evening Oliver had forced himself to look round the cottage. It was full of evidence that his mother had lived a fairly normal life. The rooms were untidy, the furniture was old and worn, and redecoration was long overdue, but old people tended to let such things slide, especially if they lived alone, and she had certainly been very much alone. Downstairs there were cabinets and drawers stuffed with tinned food and a mishmash of other junk he did not feel inclined to investigate. In a cupboard under the stairs he discovered bin-bags full of unopened mail going back ten years or more. He wondered if his mother had been indifferent to, or frightened of, what these communications might contain, and formed a vague plan to sort through them later, but for various reasons the thought of doing so made him uneasy, and he doubted that he would get round to the task. He didn't look too closely at anything.

Upstairs, on the tiny landing, there were shelves of tatty old volumes that seemed interesting, even sinister in the dusky gloom, but which were merely cheap book-club editions of popular novels from twenty years ago. He leafed through a couple and felt their pages clinging together with damp, as though they were reluctant or ashamed to reveal the fact that they had no secrets to hide. On the bare floorboards below them was an untidy pile of thicker books with plastic covers: photograph albums. Oliver stooped down and flicked the top one open halfway through. It was full of snaps of small groups of people taken mostly outdoors. From the clothes they wore he judged the period to be the early sixties, not long after he had been born, when the Beatles were beginning to make their mark on fashion.

Oliver studied the photos to see if he could recognise his mother. He had avoided even so distant a contact with her in the past, and had not read the sensational books and articles about her and her husband that had appeared from time to time. He had not more than glanced at a portrait of her since his fifteenth birthday, when his foster parents had given him a scrapbook of newspaper cuttings they had unwisely kept so that they could show him who he was, where he'd come from. He had burned it as soon as he realised what it contained, but the memory of the crude, ugly mug-shots of his parents' faces had never gone away, and never would. The pictures had been chosen by newspaper editors to show the couple in their worst light, and they had been successful in that. Those were the images that Oliver and the papers' readers had retained down the years. His father and mother were embedded in his and the nation's consciousness as famous monsters. They were the "Spare Part Killers;" the "Frankenstein's Sister Murderers." They had set the standard of evil and madness for their time. They were a pair of ghouls.

"Mum and Dad," he whispered to himself, without irony, when he held the album up to the light and was able, finally, to identify the pair from memories of the old press cuttings.

His father, then in his late teens, looked little more than a boy in the photograph. He could have been his wife's other son, an elder brother to the infant Oliver she was holding in her arms. She was almost twenty years older than her husband, and looked it. Though her body was trim and straight, her face showed the full count of her years, and her expression indicated that she did not wear them lightly. The creased skin above the muscles that held her eyes almost shut (she looked as though she was staring into a bright light) folded back into a network of lines that ran down her cheeks to join others clustered round her nose and mouth. Her lips were slightly compressed into a smile that was gnostic, strange, tired, and irritable. Oliver wondered if his arrival as her first child so late in her life had caused her a lot of pain. Her face bore the marks of the memory of recent suffering; she had a martyred look. She was no beauty, and probably never had been. Oliver was relieved to find no resemblance between himself and her; a sensation that had nothing to do with the gratification of his vanity.

And he was nothing like his father either, who, at the time the picture had been taken, had started to imitate the pop stars who were then his contemporaries. He looked like a rustic, gormless version of Brian Jones, the Rolling Stone who died of drugs and drowning. His longish fair hair hung down his brow to partly conceal eyes that were dark and anxious, stirring memories in Oliver's mind of a Disney deer peeping out of a thicket. He wore a tight, collarless jacket buttoned almost to his neck that was obviously uncomfortable, and a dark tie about an inch wide. The vapid grin on the lower part of his face made him look like someone trying to appear cheerful in a straight-jacket. There was not, however, anything blatantly evil about him. Oliver could imagine his farm-boy father slaughtering a chicken, or even a pig, for food, but nothing in his face suggested he was capable of committing the acts the law found him guilty of two or three years later.

There were other people in the photograph, clustered behind his parents, whose faces meant nothing to Oliver. One figure, who seemed to be stepping forward between them, was featureless. He or she must have moved as the shot had been taken: the head was a large spherical blur, like a glass bowl filled with smoke. This person had one hand on Oliver's mother's arm, and she was twisting slightly away, as though whoever it was, was pulling her forward or back against her will. Baby Oliver, held tight in his mother's embrace, was staring up in some consternation at this person, as though he were about to burst in tears.

Oliver had no memory of this time. He turned a few pages. The photographs were dull, unimaginative. His mother or father, or both, with their baby son, reappeared again and again, along with various representatives of the same group of about a dozen or more people. The figure with the fudged face was in a few of them, always indistinct. He or she must have been camera shy, and deliberately moved as the pictures had been taken.

When it got too dark to see, Oliver dropped the album and stood up. He felt dizzy, and almost too enervated to move. But there were things he wanted to do. There was one door on the first floor he had not been able to open. Mrs. Tench had omitted to give him the key, or he had lost it. He thought it must be a bedroom door, and had intended forcing it in the hope of finding a comfortable bed beyond that hadn't been his mother's, but he'd left it too late. He lacked the strength to make the effort.

He crawled downstairs and spent the dark hours half-awake in a creaking armchair. He thought a lot about his father that second night, wondered if the man was still alive. If so, he was in some psychiatric prison and was probably much madder than he had been when they had first locked him up. And he'd been very mad then. Or so the newspapers said after his trial. Three years earlier Oliver had heard by chance, on a radio programme he had hastily switched off, that his father, then very ill, had become an enthusiastic convert to Christianity. This morsel of unwanted, unwelcome information had disturbed him for weeks. To Oliver, it seemed that memories of his father, which he had succeeded almost in smothering to death, had come alive again. Hopelessly, pathetically alive.

Next morning, feeling like hell, Oliver had gone for a walk round the lake to try to sort through his thoughts. Unsuccessfully. Instead of clearing out the chaos in his mind he had discovered *The. . . Edge Hotel* and The Other Place, and as a result had fallen somehow into deeper confusion.

The effect of the cold-water dunking he had given his head did not last long. His resolve to complete a methodical investigation of his mother's things soon burned out. He emptied some drawers onto a table and began rummaging through the resulting heap of bric-à-brac, but was immediately overwhelmed by a feeling of depression tinged with a sensation almost of nausea. He hated to touch the old woman's junk: it wasn't so much that it felt unclean, it felt alien and unnatural, like dead parts of some life-form that had fallen into reality from some worse and other world. The everyday objects he picked up and put down, though in one sense quite ordinary, seemed at the same time mysterious and portentous; fragmentary clues that suggested a vast problem that was beyond solving because its totality was beyond his comprehension.

He gave up after just a few minutes, and returned to the armchair that he had occupied during the previous night.

Looking round the room, he realised that nothing there gave any impression of the individuality of the person who had lived there. The place lacked authenticity. It was like a stage backdrop built to comply with the direction, "The scene is set in the country cottage of a reclusive old lady in the early 1990s." The resulting design, though generally convincing, and full of well-observed detail, lacked atmosphere, and said nothing about the personality of the woman who had, except for the short time she had spent in prison, lived there for more than fifty years. It was just an old person's house. Anonymous. His mother had left no mark on the place that he could identify and understand. He had come there in the hope that he would find the essence of her in the relics of her life, but she was not there. She had died, and left him nothing, except useless rubbish and bricks and mortar. His wife had been right; he should have stayed at his place of business and supported her; his journey had been a waste of time.

Then it occurred to him that he had not contacted his wife for nearly three days, since he had set out. At first, he had not anticipated he would be away long enough for it to be necessary; then he had felt it would be difficult to explain why he had decided to stay longer, because he couldn't really justify lingering on in aimless inactivity even to himself. His desire to confront his mother's ghost, as it were, was an abstraction he would find hard or impossible to convey through the medium of the telephone. And his wife would probably not be in the mood to want to understand.

Nevertheless, he felt a compulsion to talk to her. Some good might come of it. There was no phone in his mother's house, so he decided to call on Mrs. Tench to ask if he could use hers. This would kill two birds with one stone, as he wanted to talk to *her* as well. Or, rather, he wanted her to talk to him. He wanted to hear what she might have to say about his mother.

The phone rang once before it was snatched up. Anne's voice said, "*Barnacle's Restaurant.*"

Oliver got the picture. She must be taking a smoke break. She sat in his wife's office, perched on the desk near the phone, for ten minutes or so every couple of hours, while the two of them slagged off their more awkward customers. It seemed to do them both good.

"It's me," Oliver said. "Is Rita there?"

"Is that you, Mr. Standish?" the waitress asked, speaking louder.

"Of course," Oliver shouted. Mrs. Tench, standing with her back to him by the window, stiffened at the sound.

"I'm sorry; I *thought* it was. It's a bad line."

"It's okay at my end," Oliver bellowed. "Will you put Rita on please?"

A second later Rita said, "Oliver?" as though there was still some doubt about his identity.

"Rita, how are you? How are things going?"

"Fine," she said, very quietly, "things are fine."

"Good. No more problems then?" Oliver forgot to shout.

"I can't hear you," Rita objected. "What did you say?"

"The staff," he yelled, making Mrs. Tench jump. "You've managed to sort things out?" He hoped his voice wouldn't reach Anne, who was no doubt standing close to Rita, doing her best to listen in. She had been one of the problems.

Rita didn't understand him, or wanted to change the subject. She said, "Have you finished up there yet?"

"Well, not quite. It's more complicated than I thought."

"What is?"

"The whole situation."

"What situation?"

"Everything. The place is a mess. There's a lot to sort out."

"I don't get it. What are you talking about? Are you telling me you still have things to do up there? That you're not coming back?"

"Of course I'm coming back! But not now; not today. There are a few loose ends to clear up."

"Loose ends?" Rita was beginning to sound impatient.

"Christ, Rita. My mother's just died. It's all taken me by surprise. I didn't know things would be so... complicated..."

Oliver's voice died on him. For the moment, he was lost for words. Mrs. Tench turned and gave him a wide-eyed, measured look, and kept her gaze fixed on him. He tried to will her to go away, to leave him alone with the phone, but she wouldn't budge. Perhaps she didn't trust him with her collection of ghastly china ornaments that cluttered every horizontal surface in her dingy little parlour. Oliver squirmed uncomfortably. The house was hot and steamy. The air was thick with the tart, disconcerting aroma of the marmalade Mrs. Tench was boiling-off in a huge black pan on the range in the kitchen. Sweat dripped from Oliver's nose onto the telephone receiver. He dabbed it dry with his sleeve.

"Your mother died six weeks ago." Rita said, after an awkward pause. "She meant nothing to you. You told me so a hundred times. What are you doing there? What are you up to?"

"I'm not *up to* anything," Oliver protested indignantly.

"Then come home. I need your help. We're getting busy again."

"That's good news. I'll be there as soon as I can."

"What's holding you back?"

For some reason, Oliver didn't like that expression. "Rita—really—it's hard to explain. I just want to... round things off."

"Oliver," Rita said heavily, with a note of finality, "you're not making any sense at all."

Suddenly angry and frustrated with himself, because he knew his wife had just told him more of the truth than she knew, Oliver said, "And you're not being very helpful, Rita."

"I'm sorry, Oliver. I didn't get that. Speak up. What did you say?"

"I'll get back to you later," he yelled, "from a call box. This line is just too bad." He put the phone down.

Mrs. Tench began moving about, as though by doing so she might make it look as though she had not been hanging on to every word of his end of the conversation.

"Bad line," Oliver said unnecessarily.

Mrs. Tench clucked her tongue in commiseration. Her earlier attitude of guarded suspicion had abated, and she seemed more openly friendly, even sympathetic, towards him.

"Thanks for the use of the phone." He handed her a pound coin, which she accepted without demur and dropped into a brass dish on a side table.

"Left a mess has she?" asked Mrs. Tench.

Still thinking about is wife, Oliver gave her a quizzical look.

"Your mother. I couldn't help hearing you say you've got problems up at the cottage."

"Oh, well; in a way I suppose, yes."

"She never let me in, you know, in all the time I knew her. Even at the end, when she was very ill, dying. Not at *all* hospitable. She had no sociability. And very abrupt. Not the sort to stop for a chat. An awkward cuss, if you don't mind me saying so?"

Oliver shrugged, in some confusion over the sudden venom in her voice, then shook his head, as though to lure Mrs. Tench into further indiscretion.

"Not that I ever held anything against her," the woman continued more sweetly, peering keenly at Oliver to judge his expression. "Not like the others in the village. After all, she paid her debt to society, for what she'd done, hadn't she?" Mrs. Tench's tone suggested she had strong doubts about the truth of her last interrogative statement.

"I assume so; I'm not sure," Oliver said. "I mean, I don't know much about what happened. I was a baby at the time, and I never have felt. . . concerned enough in the affair to want to know more about it. I preferred to remain ignorant about the details of exactly what did occur, to tell the truth, though now—well—I'm beginning to wonder."

"Yes," Mrs. Tench said blankly. "To wonder. I see."

"You were saying. . . ?" he urged.

"That a lot of them round here never forgave her for what happened. When she came back after she was set free, they wanted to get rid of her, to drive her out, and they tried a few times to do so, but she was too much for them. Some of them got hurt and, in the end, they all got scared. They left her alone."

"But surely it was my father who committed the crimes. As I understand it, she was just drawn into it by him. That was why she was given such a short sentence."

Mrs. Tench pursed her lips and made her head quiver. Her eyes darted from Oliver's to the floor and back again indecisively, as though she were bursting with things to say, could hardly contain her knowledge, but was not quite sure how much she should let out, or how much he wanted or was prepared to hear. In the end she said cautiously, "That was what she told them in court, and the law believed her; she was very convincing, and *he* admitted everything. But people here knew better. They'd known *her* for years, and that fool she took for a husband was born and brought up in the village, so people knew what both of them were made of. She was made of iron, and he of water, or something wetter. There was no question about that. She was hard, and he was as soft as—"

"I'm not sure I understand you," Oliver interrupted. "Do you mean you think my father was innocent?"

"That's the word exactly. That's why she married him. She took him and used him. She wanted to have a child, you see."

"That sounds like a reasonable excuse for getting married."

"Well, yes, but she *couldn't* have a child. She had a disease when she was a girl. She had all her insides taken out when she was still very young. She was barren."

"That can't be true," Oliver protested. "I'm here to prove it."

"Hmm." Mrs. Tench gave him an uncomfortable smirky smile. She adjusted the collar of the ancient floral dress she was wearing and fell silent for a while, perhaps contemplating some scruple, then said, "I'm making tea. Will you have a cup?"

Oliver thanked her. He had the impression she wanted to give herself time to decide about something, to put her thoughts in order. She left the room and he sank into an armchair to reflect on what he had just heard. He wondered if Mrs. Tench was slightly unhinged, or if perhaps he had misunderstood her. When she returned with the drinks she looked sane enough, however, and seemed to have made up her mind about whatever had been troubling her. She gave Oliver a confiding smile as he sipped his tea, and said, "I remember you as a baby. How long ago would that have been. . . ?"

"I'm thirty-three."

"That long?" She shook her head, screwed up her eyes. "I can understand why you didn't want to know about your parents and what they did, but I *can* tell you what really happened, if you want me to. Or what I and the rest of the village think happened. And that's not what was written up in the papers, which was bad enough."

"The truth is worse?"

She nodded.

"Go on," said Oliver.

Still somewhat tentative, she said, "Perhaps that woman who died up at the cottage *was*, in some sense, your mother, but him she took for a husband was definitely not your father. She wouldn't let him near her. She just wanted him as a front, so that when she *did* produce a child, people wouldn't ask questions."

"How do you—produce—a child, if you're barren?"

"She sought aid elsewhere."

"Elsewhere?"

"Don't ask me for details. I'm not one that knows such things. But she and her friends had contacts. They called on someone for help, and that—that *person*—came."

She fell silent and shut her eyes. Then she said, "Later, when she had you, and she wanted a sister for you, they called the person back. . ." She gave a tiny shudder, like someone caught in a sudden draft, and fell silent again.

Oliver wanted to ask who this "person" might be, but sensed Mrs. Tench had said all she was prepared to say on that subject. Instead he observed, "My mother *had* friends then, at that time."

"Yes. Eleven, to be exact. They used to come to visit the pair of them at weekends and they all went off together at night."

"Wild parties, eh?" he observed, thinking of the Swinging Sixties.

Mrs. Tench grunted. "So we thought," she said. "Some of us followed them once, just to make sure. We didn't want any of that drug hanky-panky going on in our village. We'd got kids of our own we didn't want exposed to that kind of influence."

"And was that it? Orgies?"

"Not exactly, no," muttered Mrs. Tench.

"Were you there? Did you go after them?"

"Henry, my late husband went. He saw—what they all saw."

Beginning to feel like someone humouring a lunatic, Oliver said, "Whatever it was, it was obviously unpleasant, I take it?"

"I can remember Henry's face when he got back. He'd been running, and had fallen a number of times. He was bleeding from a cut above his eye. Even so, he went round the house and shut all the doors and windows before he'd let me clean him up. Then he wouldn't go to bed. He insisted on peering out round the curtain down the lane, the way he'd been. Someone had followed him back, he said."

"One of my mother's friends, angry at being spied on, I suppose."

"No. They *weren't* spied on. They had set. . . guards of some sort, among the trees by the roadside, to make sure they weren't followed."

"But surely—a team of men from the village were not so easily discouraged? They must have been very big guards, or there must have been a lot of them?"

"You'd have thought so. Henry and the others were fit and strong enough. But he said not. He said there were only one or two of them out there, and they were quite small and there was not much to them, from what he could see. It was just that they were very—"

"Persuasive?" Oliver suggested.

Mrs. Tench looked slightly cross at this interruption. "That wasn't the word I was going to use," she said.

Her story seemed to be getting out of hand, Oliver thought. It was dotty, leading nowhere. "So you never did find out where my mother and her friends went?" he said.

"We did. Next day. They left tracks the local gamekeeper could follow. They'd gone out to a place beyond the village: *The Lake Edge Hotel*, as it was called. She used to work there, your mother. She as good as ran the place for the owner, who lived abroad at that time."

"I was there this morning. A depressing place."

"It's a ruin. It's been closed for years. A long time ago someone drove an excavator down there, and dug the road up so no one could get to it from outside the village. Not that they needed to have bothered. People always kept away. It always had a bad reputation. That was *her* fault of course."

Either Mrs. Tench was exaggerating the decrepitude of the hotel, or she was confused, and they were talking about two different but similar places. Oliver almost made some comment about this, but didn't. He said,

"So they'd just gone out for after-hours drinks, I suppose?"

"There was more to it than *that*, because of the guards, whoever they were. They'd been up to *something*, your mother and her pals. Something they had to hide."

"I was forgetting the guards," said Oliver. Mrs. Tench's first mention of these characters had convinced him she was batty. Living alone had got to her, he assumed. This impression was reinforced by her behaviour during the next few moments. In the distance a motor bike engine could be heard, getting nearer fast. At the sound of it, Mrs. Tench's eyes went haywire, almost jumping out of their sockets, and she raised her fingers to her face and began nervously stroking her swollen purple cheeks. Oliver thought she might be suffering some kind of fit. He rose to assist her just as the bike snarled past the front of the cottage. He caught a glimpse of it through the net-curtained window as it flashed by the gateless gap in the hedge at the end of the front path, and thought he recognised the machine. It was the old Triumph Tiger he had seen earlier in the day!

The unmistakable engine sound continued for a few seconds, then cut out. Oliver realised that whoever was driving had reached his mother's cottage at the end of the lane and stopped. He or she must have come to call: there was no other reason to make the journey down what was in effect a cul-de-sac. He (or his mother) had a visitor.

After establishing that Mrs. Tench, though apparently in a state of speechless panic, was not in the grip of some sudden illness, Oliver, glad of the excuse to get away from her, strode out of the cottage onto the lane. He expected to see the bike parked outside his mother's house, but there was no sign of it; the lane was empty except for his own car, parked on the grass verge. Mystified, curious now about the possible identity of the driver, he almost ran to the cottage and searched round the outside of the building for the machine. It wasn't there. He went round again, peering over hedges into the fields beyond, knowing that no one could have pushed the heavy machine more than a few yards in the short time since the engine had cut out. There was no sign of the bike anywhere. In the end he even went to the wooden garage at the side of the cottage, which he had not yet investigated, and peered in the dusty windows, though nobody could possibly have opened and shut the doors and vanished inside so quickly. He could not see in much detail what was inside the garage, but something metallic gleamed red in the darkness there. He identified the padlock key among the collection Mrs. Tench had given him and, with difficulty, turned the rusty lock. The heavy door, its top hinge loose, was awkward to open.

He had to lift it as he tugged it back.

The garage was lined with shelves piled high with ancient tins of dried-out paint and other useless junk. Car and motorcycle parts were strewn about the grease-stained cement floor. The only complete vehicle there was a red and black Triumph Tiger parked against the wall at the far end. It appeared to be in perfect condition, but was covered with dust and cobwebs, as though it had not been used for months or even years. Oliver was nevertheless sure he had seen it drive past Mrs. Tench's front garden minutes earlier. He gave the machine a long, hard, incredulous look, and shook his head at it. He went and touched the engine. It was warm, but the day was hot; perhaps the sun had got through the grimy window to shine on it earlier.

Oliver hastily dusted the bike down with a rag and dragged it out of the garage. Sunlight flashed on the unpainted metal sections as it emerged, hurting his eyes. He rested it on its stand and cautiously sat astride the saddle. The ignition key was in place. He turned it and kicked the starter. The engine fired at once, as he had intuited it would. It sounded sweet. He listened to it for half a minute, then switched off, went into the cottage, and dunked his head in the sink again. He drank a beaker of lead-flavoured water from the tap and sat in one of his mother's broken chairs breathing stale, static, smelly indoor air, and dozed for an hour or more. Then he went back into the garage for a ladder he had noticed there. He took the ladder out and set it up against the wall below the window of the room he had no key for, and which he had not been able to enter. He climbed up and looked through the window.

The sun glared over his shoulder into a room that was almost empty. It looked spotlessly clean. The floorboards were bare, the walls were painted bright red, the ceiling black. By twisting round Oliver could see sections of three of the walls. Set against each of them were three chairs. He guessed there were another three placed along the other side of the wall his ladder was up against, making twelve in all. There were no pictures or drawings on the walls, and no marks of any kind on the floor. The door he had not been able to open was painted red on the inside, exactly like the walls.

He returned to ground level, re-entered the cottage, and hacked two thick slices off a loaf he had left in the kitchen. He made a sandwich of tinned tuna and lettuce, wandered back into the garden, sat at the bottom of the ladder, and stared at the Triumph Tiger parked ten feet away from him. He was feeling weak and his nerves were frazzled again. He took a bite from the sandwich but forgot to chew it.

The sun was going down behind the encircling hills, and the evening light was going soft. The bike's paintwork didn't shine as aggressively as it had when he had pushed it into the open, but the machine still looked impossibly hard and bright and new. In spite of his trepidations, Oliver had a strong inclination, a wild desire even, to climb on the saddle and go for a drive to God-knows-where. That was what was supposed to happen, what was expected of him, he was sure of that: the invitation was obvious, but he couldn't quite bring himself to accept it.

He sat so still for so long in contemplation that the garden filled with birds. They hopped about in the space between him and the Tiger to get at berries that had fallen there from nearby bushes. Oliver was hardly aware of their squabbling but, when a hedgehog nosed out of one of the overgrown flowerbeds and began to snuffle up slugs by his feet, he suddenly realised night had fallen. Darkness had crept up on him, bringing with it dull, ominous thoughts, and the realisation came upon him that he could not possibly spend another night in the cottage. It was out of the question.

He found he was still holding the dried up remains of the sandwich he had made. He broke it up and threw the crumbs at the birds too hard, scaring them off. Then he got stiffly to his feet and pushed the motorbike out of his mother's garden onto the lane.

He was feeling somnolent, even stupefied, but the shout of the engine, when it started, woke him up. He realised then he had been half-asleep for a long time, for what seemed like most of the day.

The headlights, when he switched them on, didn't give much light. He drove slowly off towards what little illumination they provided. At the end of the lane he turned left into the road that led towards the deserted hotel, and tried a little speed.

Or perhaps it was the bike that wanted to go faster. Riding it, Oliver had the sensation he was being driven somewhere. He couldn't remember starting the engine, and had not been aware of making the decision to take the left turn, though he was not averse to going that way. He gave the bike its head. It didn't take him very far, however. When it topped a hill at the edge of Cramby, at a point from which a traveller leaving the village would get his first glimpse of the hotel, the engine gave up the ghost and died under him. He didn't bother trying to start it again, sure that to do so would be useless. He pushed the machine off the road into scrubby woodland and dumped it. Then he walked a short way down the hill towards the hotel to a position from which he had a distant but uninterrupted view of the building. He sat down then, on a lump of stone, and watched its great white bulk as a miser watches his treasure; anxiously, with unblinking eyes, and with his heart gnawed by the certainty of ultimate, inevitable loss.

The cloudy, floating moon was as flat and blank as a disc of cartridge paper, and gave a fragile, dusty light to the landscape. The night air was sultry, but the surface of the lake looked cold and hard, and had a dull shine, like old pewter. He was aware of tiny sounds in the trees around him that must have been caused by drowsy, restless birds perching in their branches, as there was no breeze.

Oliver was no longer tired. Though outwardly calm, his body burned with hectic, undirected energy. His mind seethed with thoughts he had striven successfully to damp-down and suppress for half of his life. His memory seemed to have fragmented suddenly and violently, like a sheet of shattered glass, and shards of the past were flying dangerously all around him. Images and sentences from newspaper cuttings pasted in the scrapbook he had been given to read by his well-meaning foster-parents clambered up from the depths at last, and cluttered his conscious mind, clamouring for attention. They shouted and swore at him, and would not be quiet. He had to give an audience to them all. He saw again the blurred newspaper photographs of tiny coffins sprawling empty by the side of desecrated graves, the muddy tools that had been used to dig them up, and the tiny ice-encrusted body parts that had been found wrapped in plastic sheets in the freezer in the cellar of his mother's house. He saw the sharp-edged, fat black headlines that screamed about the "Kill For Life Lovers"; the crazed couple who "plundered the bodies of children living and dead for spare parts to custom build a sister for their lonely son," and described his father as the "Village Frankenstein," the "Rustic Resurrectionist." He saw the dark, grainy, and distorted faces of his parents smeared across the front pages of a dozen tabloids, the artists' impressions of their features on posters for hysterical films that claimed to "reconstruct" their crimes, and the more glossy, focused portraits of the pair on the dust jackets of the string of books that had each told its own version of the truth about the terrible events they described. At last, the closed book of his own past had burst open in front of him, and he was forced to try to make sense of what it contained.

But he knew he had left it too late.

What he had been was not as powerful as what he had become, which was an obsessively anxious creature with tunnel vision, like a mole who was afraid of the dark. He had trained himself with care over the years to become just such an animal. A lifetime of holding back and looking forward, of staring too hard into the bright light of an imaginary future, to avoid looking over his shoulder into the miasmata of his origins, had almost blinded him, and damaged him in other ways. He realised he was unable to confront any part of himself alone.

He felt he desperately needed help, and he thought he knew where he might find it. He stood up slowly and began to walk down the hill towards the hotel by the lake.

He sensed that he was being followed. He had been vaguely aware of some presence, or presences, moving up behind him when he had been sitting staring at the desolate white building, quite literally lost in his thoughts. There had been more than just birds moving among the trees around him! This knowledge hadn't disturbed him much; he guessed that whoever or whatever might be tracking him had come to stop him turning back towards Cramby, and he had no intention of doing that. Nevertheless the company, such as it was, was not welcome, and was not the company he was seeking. Characteristically, he didn't turn to check his impression that he was not alone.

There seemed to be a pale light glowing in the main body of the hotel but, when he reached the glass door, he discovered it was merely the reflection of the moon trapped in the huge mirror at the rear of the foyer. He made his way past the main entrance and past the far end of the building to the extension. There was a light on in The Other Place, and the door was open. As he entered he heard a scuffling noise on the floor above him, as though someone who had been looking out for him, satisfied that he had indeed arrived, had hastily retreated to the rear of the building.

The quivering strip-light burned so dimly now it was almost extinguished, but it shed enough light for Oliver to see the place was in ruins. The chairs and tables had been battered to pieces, their arms and legs lay scattered everywhere, and the bar itself had been ripped from its position close to the rear wall and upended. The mirror at the back of the now-empty shelves had been shattered, and fragments of glass lay in a great arc across the floor, as though something had burst violently through from behind it into the room. The walls were deeply scared with long scratches, and the stained wallpaper had peeled back in places and now hung in ragged tatters from the gouged plaster. The ceiling was badly cracked, and sections of it had fallen. There was a smell of burning in the air; not the usual barroom stink of tobacco smoke, but of singed hair and burnt meat, and the floor and upper surface of every broken object was covered in grey dust as fine as wood-ash. The window, like the mirror, also appeared to have imploded, and had been boarded up from the outside. As Oliver, cautiously picking his way through the heaps of wrecked furniture, stumbled past the *trompe l'oeil* on the wall, he noticed it too had changed, and now depicted something like the chaos around him. But he didn't stop to inspect it closely because he sensed rather than saw that there were a number of figures there now that definitely had not been there before. They were clustered together at the edges of the painting, as though they were waiting to press forward out into the room. He passed them quickly.

The door leading to the stairs at the back of the extension had been torn off its hinges. Oliver rolled aside the remains of a table that had tumbled through it and stepped into the passage beyond. Here there was no source of light except that which came through the door behind him. It only penetrated a little way past his short shadow. He could vaguely see the lower steps of the stairs that rose up into the darkness above and beyond.

A stiff, shrunken object lay on the floor at the base of the stairs. Oliver remembered the animal, the bird, that had died there. He bent down and picked it up. It was a bird-shaped thing, but made of stitched leather and stuffed with straw. A few feathers had been stuck to its surface with glue that had perished. Tiny black insects had made themselves at home in the straw, and a dozen or more of them tumbled out at he turned the thing in his hands. The dry, dusty feathers became detached, and adhered to his sweating palms. He hurled the object from him in disgust, and began to climb the stairs. As he did so he became aware of sounds, the beat of basic, repetitive music, somewhere above him. And someone—a woman?—started chanting.

When he reached the top of the stairs Oliver passed through another open door into a room above the extension. As he did so, the chanting stopped, but the music continued.

He found himself in a bleak place, with bare floorboards, red-painted walls, and a black ceiling. The little room was full of light and people: People who all had tightly knotted ropes round their necks. The ends of the ropes were attached somehow to the ceiling. Some of the people wore the remnants of disintegrating clothing, but most of them were naked. Their bodies looked old, and were variously swollen or shrunken. They all turned to look at Oliver when he entered the room, but none of them spoke. He recognised their faces. He had seen them before in the photographs in his mother's album. They had been her friends. There were eleven of them; not so many as he had thought when he first entered the room, but the space around them seemed to be closing in, as though the room was shrinking.

He realised that it was getting smaller; he saw the walls take a lurch towards him.

Oliver looked desperately round. He noticed one important member of the cast of people in the photographs was missing. His father was not present in the room, and Oliver was sure then that this was because he was the only member of the group who was still alive. However, at the centre of the crowd, he saw his mother. She was twitching on the end of her rope. She had been hauled up a little way so her feet only just touched the ground. Her face was purple and black. Her head was twisted back at an angle, and she was spinning slowly. She stared at him with one bulging eye. Her mouth moved as she tried to speak. Oliver couldn't hear what, if anything, she was saying for the din of the music, which seemed to come out of the very air.

Then someone he had not noticed before stepped forward from behind the crowd and reached for him with both hands. It was the individual he had seen in just a few of the photographs in his mother's album, the one who seemed to have moved as each shot was taken, to conceal, so Oliver had imagined, his or her identity. As the figure got close to him, he realised his assumption had been wrong; whoever it was didn't have a face. It was, moreover, unmistakably a female. She too was naked.

She spoke to him. Her voice was very low but he could hear her because she whispered the words almost into his ear. "I want you," she said. "I made you. I let you go; I gave you to her; but she couldn't keep her side of the bargain, so now I claim you back."

She came closer to him, and he understood where the smell of burning originated. Where her face should have been was an oval of tightly swirling smoke. Behind this insubstantial mask, just discernible, were crude features carved into a substance that was not flesh and blood. Her lipless mouth hung slightly open. Her raw eyes glowed and smouldered. A fire burned inside her. Oliver could feel the heat of it scorching his cheeks. Her hard fingers, pulling him towards her, coiled in on his shoulder, and threatened to cut through his skin to the bone. He wrenched himself away and turned to get out of the room; but when he pushed against the door he had so recently come through, it wouldn't budge.

Behind him, he thought he heard the female thing laugh. He pressed harder with both hands, and felt his palms slither on some oily film. He looked at his hands and realised they were streaked with blood-red paint. He had been trying to pass through a painting of a door. The paint (or was it blood?) was still wet. He turned again, ran back into the room, and darted past the female figure, who made no effort to stop his progress, but turned slowly to follow him.

Oliver forced his way through the tangle of dangling bodies. The walls were shifting, pressing steadily forwards. The people in the room were being forced closer together all the time, yet the ropes round there necks, instead of slackening off, were being pulled tighter. Oliver glanced at the ceiling and saw that it was slowly moving upwards. He noticed his mother had been lifted inches off the ground. She was jerking in her harness with wild, spastic movements. The other tethered occupants of the room were stretched up on their toes, like ballet dancers, though the movements they were making were anything but balletic.

It occurred to Oliver to try to throw himself out of the nearby window, the room's only remaining exit. He leapt towards it. He was surprised to see bright sunlight shining on the landscape beyond the glass panes. He looked out and down as he crouched to make his jump, and became aware that someone was standing below him, near the door of The Other Place. It was a man who was turning slowly, awkwardly, towards him. He was shading his eyes with his hand. He seemed confused and alarmed, and half-blinded by the blazing sunlight. For a moment the pair of them were perfectly still; then the man stumbled back a step as Oliver started to fall towards him.

Then the man below looked up and saw the little figure poised above him—and Oliver came face to face with himself, but only for a second, and much too late.

He was grasped from behind and snatched back into the arms of the female form behind him. He yelled with pain from the sudden heat. Their heads were so close, his hair had begun to burn.

She held a noose in her hand. "You're mine, and I'm taking you back, as was always understood between us," she said, as she put the halter round his neck.

For an instant Oliver wondered if in fact he was a child who had merely *dreamed* he had been a man. He was not sure he had really ever had a life.

The thought made him furiously angry, and the prospect that he might have to go through the illusion of existence all over again occurred to him.

And terrified him.

He screamed and cried and struggled and kicked and punched, but his feet and hands hit against nothing now but a yielding softness that gradually enclosed him.

"And anyway," the faceless thing added, as the room finally folded in upon itself and the ceiling flew away, "it's time for you to join the dance."